The FORBIDDEN REALMS
Pronunciation Guide

Broken Order Brotherhood
Nerana (Neer) – NEER-ahna
Y'ven – YEV-in
Druindarvenia (Dru) – DROO
Reiman – RIY-man

Evae
Aélla – AYLA
Reiman – RIY-man
Thallon - TALON
Nasir – Nah-SEER
Ithronél – EE-thro-nell

Vaxros
Y'ven – YEV-in
Vrogrün – VRO-groon
Torvüg – TOR-voog

Races
Evae – EE-vay; elves
Vaxros – VAX-ross; brutish desert natives
Faeth – faith; elemental pixies
Klaet'il – klee-uh-TIL; evaesh forest clan
Rhyl – RILL; evaesh forest clan

— *The* —
FORBIDDEN
REALMS

H. C. NEWELL

The

FORBIDDEN REALMS

Book two in the Fallen Light series
To be read *after* Curse of the Fallen

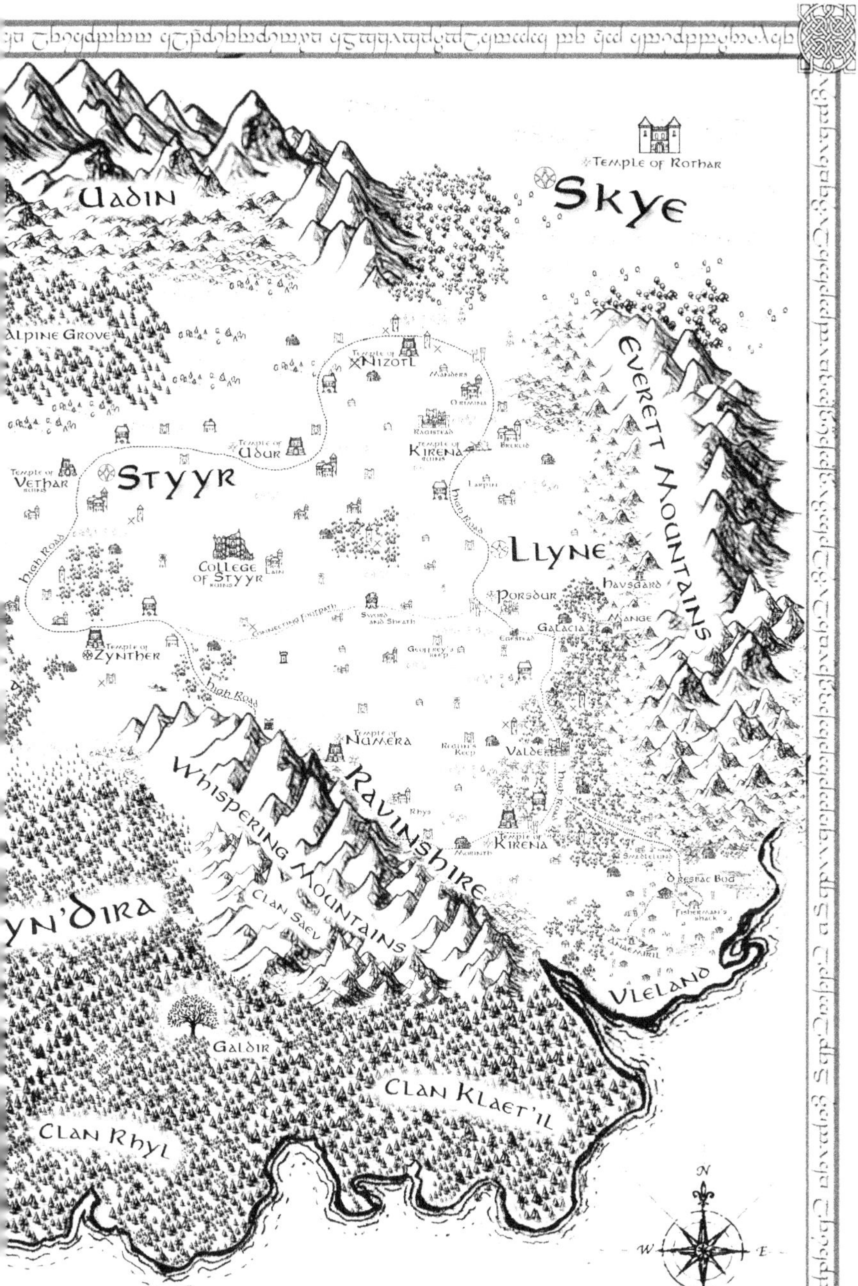
Uadin
Temple of Rothar
Skye
Alpine Grove
Temple of Nizotl
Everett Mountains
Temple of Udur
Temple of Kirena
Styyr
Temple of Vethar
ruins
High Road
Llyne
College of Styyr
ruins
Havsgard
Porsdur
Connecting Footpath
Sword and Sheath
Galacia
Mange
Temple of Zynther
Geoffrey's Keep
High Road
Temple of Numera
Valde
Ravinshire
Whispering Mountains
Rhys
Temple of Kirena
Fisherman's shack
Clan Saev
yn'Dira
Vleland
Galdir
Clan Klaet'il
Clan Rhyl
N
W
E
S

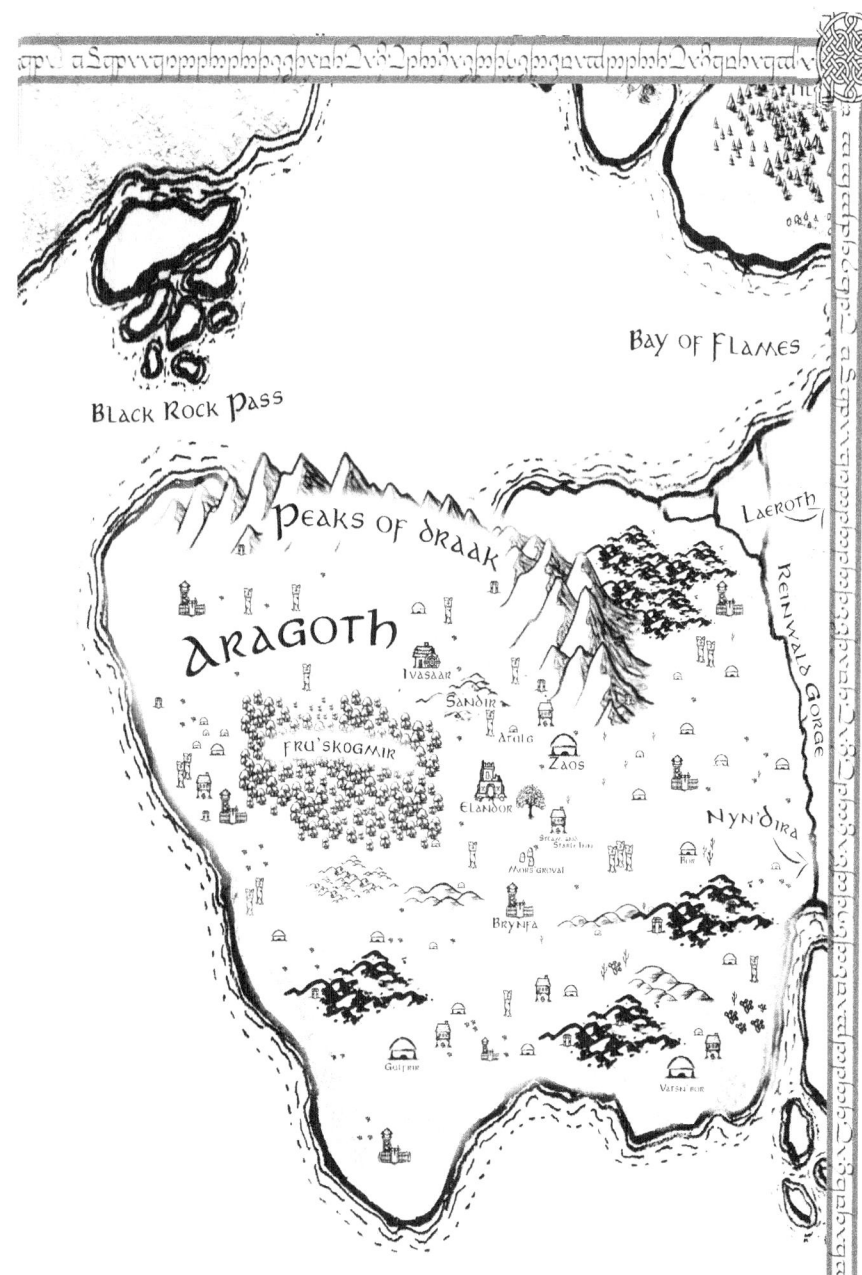

BAY OF FLAMES

BLACK ROCK PASS

PEAKS OF DRAAK

LAEROTH

ARAGOTH

IVASAAR

SANDIR

REINWALD GORGE

FRU'SKOGMIR

ARULG

ZAOS

ELANDOR

NYN'DIRA

MONS URNVAL

BRYNFA

GULJMIR

VATSH'NOE

To Camila, Elias, Arlen, Benjamin, and Elijah.
There are too many bad words in this book, but you can read it
when you're older.

Much *much* older.

CONTENTS

The FORBIDDEN REALMS
Pronunciation Guide

Human Territories
Laeroth – LAYR-oth; country
Llyne – Lin; region in Laeroth – home to the Broken Order
Brotherhood
Porsdur – POHRS-durr; Neer's hometown

Non-Human Territories
Laeroth – LAYR-oth; continent
Aragoth – AIR-AH-GOTH; desert region
Anaemiril – ANN-iy-MEER-ill; ancient cave system
Nyn'Dira – NIN-DEER-ah; dense forest region

<u>Important references</u>

Order of Saro – Religious faction that oversees the human-led territories of Laeroth
Circle of Six – Six Divines worshipped by the Order of Saro
Shadow Blades – Band of mercenaries hired to track and find the Child of Skye
Trials of Blood – Magical trial that saw Nerana to Nhamashel
Nhamashel – Cave where Nerana lifted her curse

SUMMARY OF BOOK ONE

During the events of book one, Nerana embarked upon a long and harrowing journey to find the arun and release the curse that bound her to the Order of Saro. This curse was given to her at a young age, during a time she doesn't fully remember, and allowed the Order to track her whereabouts with the use of a stone that would glow when magical energy was used nearby.

Neer, along with her best friend, Loryk, traversed the forbidden and dangerous land of Vleland to reach their destination of the Trials of Blood which would see them to the cave of Nhamashel. This cave was located deep within the ruins of Anaemiril, a cave system built by the long extinct Ahn'Clave, or First Blood. The waters of the cave were said to be magically enhanced and would lift even the most dangerous of curses.

Along the way to the Trials, whose entrance was located along the border of Vleland and Llyne, Neer and Loryk were attacked by spindra, fierce creatures of darkness in the form of arachnids. These creatures (along with wispers, ravenous canines, and other monstrous beings) would fade to ash upon their demise. It was later revealed that creatures of darkness spawned from the disturbed and manipulated energy of the deceased.

Neer and Loryk fought the spindra and were saved by a magically gifted elf named Klaud, who revealed that he was also on a mission to find the Trials of Blood. In his letter from Azae'l, whose identity is never fully explored, we learn that she had been cursed by a man called the Nasir. The Nasir was the leader of the Klaet'il, an evaesh clan of Nyn'Dira, who sought power and dominion above all else.

Throughout their journey to the trials, they learn the klaet'il had invaded the human territories, and an evaesh assassin, Avelloch, was located in a village far north of the border. He had been interrogating the Nasir's followers when he was discovered by Klaud and ultimately joined the group in an effort to help them through the Trials.

During their journey, the group was separated when the High Priest attacked and abducted Nerana and Loryk. In an effort to save him, Neer fought back, and plunged her sword through the High Priest's heart. While fleeing, she turned back to find the High Priest had risen and was watching with angry eyes as she fled into the night

Afterward, Avelloch, Neer, and Loryk found their way to a village called Mange where they were healed of their injuries from the fight with the Order. During their stay, Neer touched a Tree and was approached by who she believed was a Divine of the Circle of Six, Numera. Numera gifted her with a prophecy that led her to believe she was meant to travel to the realms of magic.

After Mange, the group moved on to the hidden entrance of the Trials, and it was there that Neer came into contact with a creature of darkness known as a *fench*. While Loryk and Avelloch heard only chiseled grunting and growls, Nerana was able to understand and speak to it.

From there, the trio entered the Trials of Blood and made their way to Nhamashel, where Neer was able to lift her curse after Klaud snatched the arun and left her with his potion.

I AM NOW A WARRIOR OF FLAME.

ANCESTORS GIFT ME YOUR STRENGTH.

BLOOD OF MY BROTHERS HONOR MY VALOR.

HEAT OF THE FLAME FUEL MY RAGE.

I GIVE MY LIFE TO THE PEOPLE'S DEFENSE.

I AM THE SHIELD IN THE SUN. THE AXE IN THE NIGHT.

I WILL NOT COWER IN DEFEAT.

VICTORY IS MY HONOR AND BLOOD MY SACRIFICE.

I SHALL BEAR NO CHILDREN. I SHALL TAKE NO MATE.

I GIVE MY LIFE, AND MY DEATH, TO THE AL'YAVAN.

UNTIL THE SUN FADES TO ASH SHALL MY OATH REMAIN.

VOW OF THE AL'YAVAN WARRIOR

CHAPTER ONE

BLOOD AND STEEL
Nerana

*"Give me your blessings, O God of Death, and grant me peace
in the life hereafter."*
— Prayer to Zynther, Divine of mortality

HER LIFE ENDED THAT DAY.

Six months past, when she embarked upon the dangerous
and forbidden Trials of Blood. Now, she walked alone, tired
and hungry, as she made her way to the village of Rhys deep
within the heart of Ravinshire. Clutched tightly in her arms
was a worn leather notebook, the pages filled with scribbled
stories and songs written by the friend she'd never see again.

Wolves howled in the distance, and the moons illuminated
the dark sky. Neer wrapped her arms tighter around the notebook, vowing to protect it before herself should trouble find
her. Dried blood, blackened with age, stained the edges of the
crinkled pages.

After Loryk's death, she spent weeks in the crypts beneath
Porsdur. The old sconces were hardly enough to keep the
moist hollows illuminated, but still she sat, speaking to his
grave, and reading every word of his lengthy journal. Now,
she walked through his home of Ravinshire, where she
planned to gift his family, though undeserving, with his final
thoughts and poems.

Neer didn't do this for them. She needed closure, a way to move past such a deep and dreadful end to what was once the most valuable friendship she ever had. She couldn't carry his writings forever, and she knew, despite their differences and beliefs, Loryk loved his family. For that, they should know the truth of his fate.

Dirt shuffled beneath her boots as she carried on down the desolate High Road. Tall yellow grass covered the empty fields surrounding the road in every direction. Heavy trails from wagons and carts rutted the packed dirt, though the sprawling road of Ravinshire didn't see much use. Each village was at least a day's walk from another, and since her entry into the region two weeks ago, she'd only passed by a handful of merchants, couriers, and bandits—none of which noticed the teal of her eyes as they walked by with pleasant smiles or attempted to steal her coin. She was lucky, for the Child of Skye was forbidden in all of Laeroth, and in a place such as Ravinshire, the Order would've been contacted immediately upon her recognition. So, she kept her eyes on the dust and pebbles at her feet as she walked through the night.

Hours passed before orange light slithered through the peaks of the Whispering Mountains and broke the heavy darkness. The endless wheat fields and creaking windmills faded into dense woods as Neer moved closer to the logging district.

She passed by a faded signpost, and the faint whine of rusted hinges caught her attention. Sun and rain had washed most of the chiseled letters away, but she could make them out enough to read Morinth. With a heavy, relieved sigh, she headed toward the small village.

Each step took her closer to civilization, and she breathed in the scent of fresh cut pine. A river, flowing through the foothills of the Whispering Mountains, carved through the thinning trees, its water lapping against the banks.

Tanning racks were set out along the streets, quickly changing the scent from fresh pine to hot leather. Doors creaked as residents ventured out of their homes. Their red hair and round waistlines were typical of Ravinshire natives. Deep wrinkles laid cracks across the faces of men far too young for such aging, their tired eyes and calloused hands proof of the hard labor they daily provided.

Neer focused on the road and wandered through the street as the villagers whispered of a stranger's arrival. Morinth was three weeks from the border of Llyne, far enough into Ravinshire territory that the possibility of a straggler walking through was near impossible. Whoever would come this far into the southern hold had reason, and the villagers weren't eager to welcome strangers.

"Six blessin's!*" a man greeted Neer with reserved disposition. Being from the South, where a man's hide is as thick as it is strong, it was clear he wasn't looking to extend an invitation. "Where's yer pa, girl?"

"He's ill," she lied. It was known that in Ravinshire women were lesser than men, and the residents had no trouble enforcing such beliefs. Had Neer explained she was traveling alone of her own volition, she would have been accused of sacrilege and publicly lashed. Even her clothes, which were tight trousers and a long-sleeve top, were considered too masculine of attire for the women of Ravinshire. Luckily, they didn't invoke such strict rules upon travelers, but she kept herself guarded all the same. "I'm to bring him wares from Dorthe.†"

"Dorthe, aye? Let's see what ya got there."

She sighed and turned to the sky. With a wince, she slung the bag from her shoulder and opened it for the man to see. He peered nosily into the white canvas, finding clothing, a small coin purse, and medicine. The man eyed her for a quick

---

* A common greeting among the devout, though to Neer it's more a warning than welcome. The phrase refers to the six divines of the Order of Saro. Anyone faithful enough to speak such a harmless phrase is viewed as an enemy to our heroine, as they'd see nothing more than to put her head on a spike.

† A village in Ravinshire. Neer chose one at random. She had never been, and hoped it was still a working civilization to better suit her lie.

second and then backed away. His attention moved quickly to the weapon on her side, and he tensed.

"Women shouldn't be carryin' weapons. That an elvish blade you got? You know them're forbidden in Laeroth."

She stepped back, keeping her eyes on the ground to avoid him recognizing their color. "Yes. My father bought it off a merchant during first winter when he fell ill. Spent most of our coin on it, but he said it'd do me better than a human weapon if I'm to find myself in trouble on the road."

He eyed her suspiciously. "Well, you don't look like much trouble. Keep that thing hidden, 'less ya want to be findin' yourself in the temple dungeons."

She nodded. "I'll keep that in mind."

The man grumbled while crossing his arms. "Well, the Mansker Inn is just up the road an' to the left. Be sure to ask Mariah for a bath. You could use one."

"Thank you." Her voice was unenthused. It had become her natural tone since she returned from Nhamashel. She performed the usual bow with her hands cupped together in front of her chest.* The man returned the gesture and then stepped aside.

The village had come to life within the minutes Neer had spoken to him. Chickens squawked and cows lowed while farmers tended to their daily chores. She kept her head down and made her way past the residents that walked the streets.

Upon entering the inn, she was greeted with the smell of freshly baked bread and strong mead. Her eyes averted to a man sitting by the hearth. The soft melodies of his drum mixed with the quiet conversations of the patrons. Mist filled her eyes, and she quickly wiped it away.

A young girl swept nearby, paying no mind to Neer as she carried out her duties.

---

* A common gesture of prayer, thanks, greeting, or goodbye used among the richly devout, though it seemed reserved for those of Ravinshire or anyone in the presence of a Priest. Neer never found herself using such a gesture as it was forbidden in her rebel hold of Llyne.

The tinkling of chimes brightened the dull noises of the inn as a woman dressed in nothing but a thin skirt adorned with tiny silver bells sat across a man's lap. The innkeeper, with fiery hair and a red face to match, angrily swatted their table.

"Knock that off! This 'ere's a family place!" She nodded to the girl sweeping across the room.

The patron slowly stood and slipped into her top.

The innkeeper eyed Neer suspiciously while scrubbing a tankard with her dirty apron. "Need a room?"

Neer nodded silently, purposefully averting her eyes to better hide her identity. "And a bath."

The innkeeper turned to the sweeping girl. "Enid! Show our guest to the downstairs rooms."

The young girl went happily to Neer's side and took her hand, leading her down a narrow staircase behind the bar. They entered a small basement where deep wooden tubs sat behind long curtains. Barrels along the left wall dripped with liquid that left the place reeking of southern ale.

"You can stay 'ere." The girl opened the door to a small room. Inside was nothing but a bed and dresser. "Why're you so filthy?"

Neer glanced at her dirty garments. With a huff, she stepped into the room and sat on the flat feather mattress. "I like dirt," she said while removing her worn boots.

The girl stepped closer and touched the hilt of Neer's sword. Its glowing veins, which were hidden within the scabbard, had become dull and translucent since its time with Avelloch. "Where'd you get this?" Enid asked. "Looks real different."

"A friend."

"Women aren't supposed to be carryin' such weapons. You can get in big trouble, should the Order find out!"

Neer scoffed in offense, and then watched as the girl inspected the frayed hilt. "What's your name?"

"Enid."

"I used to be a kitchen wench too. When I was about your age."

"Really? Did you like it?"

"No. Not really."

Enid shook her head. "Me either. I want to be an adventurer, like you. I'll bet you've seen all kinds of stuff." She sat on the bed and twirled her fingers. "Ma says I'm not meant for such things. Said I'd best get used to cleanin' the inn."

Neer was silent as she fell into her memories—the long nights waiting tables and cleaning the grimy, sweat-stained sheets at the Sword and Sheath. How she wished she could go back and tell herself to take another path. To find a home and never let go of those she loved.

Her thoughts broke when Enid slowly stepped to the door, and Neer, though desperate to help her, was at a loss for words.

"I'll fetch you some hot water for that bath, Miss. For three bronze, we can clean your clothes."

"No thanks," Neer said.

The girl stood silently for a moment and then skipped away.

Neer closed the door and leaned onto the mattress. The road would've been comfier, and it was free, but she couldn't complain. At least the inn was safe, so long as no one suspected her of being the sorceress she was.

She sat atop the bed and pulled a weathered note from her boot, where she'd safely hidden it. It had been enchanted to withstand the elements and time, never to be destroyed or lost. Lying back, she unfolded the page. It was from Loryk's full adventure book. Of all the stories, poems, and ballads, this was the only journal entry. One she couldn't part with.

We're still in this bloody cave. Neer's unconscious from the rune, and I'm stuck in this house with ~~Avlock Evalork Avvahl~~ the blond one. He's okay enough. Seems to really care about Neer. He won't stop looking at her and making sure she's okay. I hope she's all right. Never been to no place like this…We may not make it out. If anyone's holding them back, it's me. I should've just stayed back home. I'm no fighter. I'm nothing, really. This place has been hell.

I don't know why I'm writing this. Feels foolish. But I guess I can feel it coming. The end, that is. We aren't all going to make it out of here, and if it's me that falls, I just hope that my stories can live on. I never had much in life, but I did have a family. The Brotherhood was always good to me, and I'll always be grateful.

Neer, if you're reading this and I'm gone, just know that I love you. Always have. You're my best friend. My family. You can do this, and you aren't alone. That evae over there cares about you. I can see it in his eyes. He's good, Neer. Plenty of people are. Don't go getting all cynical and crazy like before. Whatever happens, we'll always be together. You'll never be alone.

Go send the High Priest and all those blasted people of the Order to the farthest reaches of the deepest hell. I'll be waiting for them.

Guess this is it. I'm getting sleepy anyhow. Not sure how to end this thing right.

Farewell.

She wiped away her tears and scanned the page multiple times, though she didn't need to. The words were engraved in her mind. She had spent days in Nhamashel, waiting for her energy to strengthen enough for her to teleport back home with his body. After a reunion with Reiman and Gil, and a beautiful ceremony for Loryk where he was laid to rest in the crypts beneath the Tree of Porsdur, she set off on her journey to Ravinshire.

Her thoughts lifted when Enid lightly tapped the door with her knuckle and announced, "Your bath's ready, Miss."

Neer placed the folded note into her boot, undressed, and stepped out of the room. Chills covered her cold, aching body as she stepped into the tub, turning the water murky from her filth. She exhaled a deep breath, and her muscles relaxed.

Her eye quickly reopened when hard footsteps raced across the ceiling.

"Mariah!" a man exclaimed. "Have you heard?"

"What is it?" the innkeeper asked, seemingly unenthused by his outburst.

"Priest Ealdir° is here!"

"Truly?" She was more alert. "What could he want with a place like Morinth? We're naught but a logging village."

"Word has it, they've found a sorcerer nearby."

Neer's stomach dropped. She lifted from the water to listen closer.

"Sorcerer?" Mariah asked. "There ain't no sorcerer here."

"They got word of one living around here. Said a neighbor saw them creepin' around in the night, using their magic."

"That's enough, Roger. Fetch some water and clean the glasses. There'll be no more speak of such blasphemy."

Footsteps echoed away and then disappeared behind the creak of a heavy door. Neer slipped quickly into her clothes and gathered her things. Upstairs, she handed the innkeeper a silver coin.

The woman raised her brow. "You ain't stayin'?"

"Change of plans."

The innkeeper shoved the coin in her pocket, which Neer then apported back into her palm. She pulled up her hood and headed to the door. Outside, hundreds of soldiers sat atop their horses. They slowly stopped as residents gathered along the streets.

The innkeeper stepped outside with a mug still in hand. When the horses parted, a priest rode through the crowd. His silver cloak and golden robes revealed his position as a Priest of the Order.

Dark hair hung across his shoulders, and tan skin revealed his nationality of Llyne, where years ago he was forced out of his home when the Brotherhood took siege of the land. The people of Ravinshire, hearing of the treachery inflicted by the

---

° Not to be mistaken for the High Priest, who is Neer's most formidable foe. Priest Ealdir is one of many Priests that reign over Laeroth..

rebels, came together to construct him a new temple in their territory, where he now resided.

Neer watched him with a careful eye while everyone bowed on their knees. Dust swirled beneath his robes when he leapt from his steed. He walked down the street, and two knights, wearing thick plated armor with golden scapulars, followed close behind.

"Simon," the priest said in a smooth accent.

The smith stood and bowed. "Your Grace."

"I've received word that your village is harboring a sorcerer."

"I'm sorry, Priest Ealdir, but if there was such a person here, we would never—"

"I understand." Ealdir placed a hand on Simon's shoulder. The smith's large stature shifted under the priest's touch, and Ealdir turned with a subtle nod.

The knights unsheathed their weapons, and harsh light reflected off the newly-forged steel. It glinted in Neer's face, and she covered her eyes.

The smith faltered. "These're good people. We follow the teachin's and do naught a thing out of line!"

"Simon, friend, we aren't looking to shed the blood of the innocent. A demon walks among you. Do you want your children to be influenced by a sorcerer? One with a soul so twisted and foul that only the Divine Nizotl* himself could have created it?"

---

* Nizotl, the Divine of trickery and deceit, is one of the six Divines of the Circle of Six: a collective name given to the six divines of the Order of Saro.

Since the reign of High Priest Karlo, the predecessor of the current High Priest, Beinon, the Divine Nizotl has been viewed as the giver of magic and darkness. Any human born of magical blood is considered a demon of his creation and is therefore sentenced immediately to death.

There are many beliefs as to why Nizotl would gift a human with magical blood, the most widely accepted being his own desire for power and chaos.

Simon shook his head. Ealdir nodded in approval while his men scoured the town. Neer stepped back as they walked into the inn. The stillness of morning was quickly broken by the throwing of furniture and frightened screams.

"That's 'er!" a patron shouted. "It's the innkeeper!"

Knights rushed to the porch with their weapons drawn.

"What? No! You're mistaken!" she cried.

The butcher and smith rushed to her aid, but three knights quickly blocked their path.

"Please!" the smith begged. Tears carved clean trails down his red cheeks. "It isn't true! You've got the wrong person!"

"Simon!" the innkeeper called to the smith.

"This demon is your wife!" Ealdir said. "You know the penalty for such treason!"

Enid whimpered as she was dragged to their sides. The family cried and begged while the villagers stood by mutely. Some wept and covered their faces, while others wore satisfied expressions.

Ealdir stood before the smith and his family. "Six Divines of unity and peace," the priest started, "protect these souls as they're transferred into your realm from this life. Clean their spirits so they may once again be free."

Ealdir bowed to the family, who sniffled and begged at his feet. He drew back his weapon and struck at the smith's chest.

Neer ripped her sword from its scabbard and transported instantly behind the priest, sinking her weapon deep into his back and through his chest. Blood spurted from the wound and painted the family in red. The priest gasped as she twisted the sword, feeling the rip of his organs.

Neer pulled his head back. Solid black overtook the prominent teal of her eyes. An angry, satisfied whisper left her lips as she warned, "Send the Divines my regards."

She pulled her sword from his body, and the knights charged. Her gaze moved to the family, who stared at her in horror and rage. She was crushed by their anger. The heavy clank of metal armor filled the silence as the knights drew nearer.

Neer took one last look at the family who cast hateful glares at her, and then she closed her eyes and disappeared.

CHAPTER TWO

THE RAVEN
Nerana

"Stay away from the wastelands, for the devils of red will feast on your bones and flesh."
— Human warning of the vaxros

SUNLIGHT CAST ACROSS AN EMPTY desert, sending waves of heat rippling above its rocky surface. Not a soul would dare trek such a dangerous and unforgiving place. The place men came to die — or so the saying goes — their secrets kept forever hidden beneath the scorch of an unrelenting sun.

What was meant to be a quick escape led Neer, untrained in long-range teleportation, over one thousand miles away into the forbidden land of Aragoth. No one ever stepped foot into the desert who saw their home again, their footprints were all that remained of their journey into the land of fire and fiends.

Into the land of vengeance and rage.

The land of the lost and forgotten.

A raven's caw sounded across the plains, drifting through the open air. Its wide shadow circled far below, a void scanning the empty ground. Dark eyes focused on the world as a shimmering rift rippled into existence.

Neer rolled across the coarse wild brush as the rift collapsed into itself. Sunlight reflected against the sword that had fallen from her grasp. Its once dormant veins glowed softly beneath the priest's still-wet blood.

With a light groan, she struggled to her knees and then collapsed to the ground. The exertion of such energy relieved her of strength, and her body ached with depletion. Darkness pulled the corner of her eyes, and her focus wavered on the fading world.

The raven landed nearby, and the beating of its black wings gifted Neer with a soft breeze. It tilted its head and hopped closer, inspecting her. Neer anticipated the scratch of its talons or the stab of its beak as she lay motionless, waiting. The bird made no such advance. Instead, it watched her for a moment longer and then took flight. Its shadow distorted over the many rocks and cracks as it disappeared from sight.

With a deep breath, she allowed the darkness to pull her into a deep, unending sleep. Unable to fight its temptation, she closed her eyes and lay beneath the ruthless desert sun. Unmoving, she laid beneath its heat as it slowly drifted through the sky, until an aggressive voice jolted her from her sleep.

The stranger marched closer, but Neer's falling eyes couldn't focus. The light faded when a large shadow crept over, and she relished in the relief it gave her burned and blistered skin.

A muscular figure stood above her. His warrior's braid hung to his mid-back and was filthy with dust. He wore nothing more than a war skirt and leather straps to secure his weapons and shield. Yellow scars along his arms, back, and chest laid a map across his thick red skin.

He was a vaxros, brutish desert natives who revered honor and battle above all else. The vaxros man kicked Neer over, and she toppled aside. Shrouded with delirium, she opened her dreary eyes and found it wasn't a stranger kneeling above her. Instead, it was another. Someone she never expected to see again.

"Come on, Neery."

His voice was clear and strong. His brown eyes sparkled, and light peeked through his curly auburn hair. She reached up to touch his face, unable to believe what she was seeing.

"Loryk?" Her tired voice was barely a whisper.

"Shh," he started and leaned closer. "Just rest now, Neery."

She closed her eyes and fell unconscious. The stranger lifted her from the ground and tossed her into his cart atop animals fresh from the hunt. The desert native hopped onto the saddle of his large, two-legged reptile and rode off, with Neer in tow.

Wagon wheels creaked and moaned beneath the weight of such cargo. Four rams, with twisted horns and slack jaws, lay dead beneath Neer. Thick blood and notched ribs were evidence of the fate they endured.

The vaxros man sat on the bench. His thick red skin, exposed to the sunlight, absorbed its heat, slowly healing the razor-thin lacerations across his forearms. Sunlight gleamed against the shaven sides of his head where three intentional bright yellow scars extended across his scalp on either side. His glowing orange eyes scanned the desert as he rode alone, moving closer toward a small village in the distance.

Large homes made of stretched leather were collected within the confines of a ragged fence made entirely of bone. Skulls, femurs, and ribs were stacked together and solidified with hard clay. Full-length spines twisted through the discolored fragments like angry serpents.

The hunter rode through the barrier's wide opening at the head of the village. Two red-skinned children, devoid of any yellow scars, guided the hunter's mount to a nearby stable.

Objects rattled, and the cart shifted when the hunter climbed to the ground. He moved to the back of the cart, eyeing the still unmoving human. Her eyes were closed, the slight rise of her chest the only indication of the life coursing through her.

"What is this?" a woman said with a hiss. She spoke their native language and stormed to the cart. "We can't feed the village with such little game!"

The hunter growled through parted lips. "Then *you* go out and hunt. The *shadosalaan*° feast at night. There is nothing left."

The rams' horns clacked together as he pulled one by its foot and lifted it from the cart. The woman turned, and her fury faded. Glowing orange eyes set to the human lying with the animals.

"What is this?" she asked. "Is it…a human?"

He grunted in response, passing the ram to a stableboy and reaching for the next.

She retched with disgust. "She smells like death. This meat is no good to us."

He ignored her furious scowl and passed the fourth ram to the boy, who handed them off one by one to the butcher's apprentice. As the woman stormed off, the hunter grabbed Neer's foot, and she twitched beneath his touch. He grabbed his spear, preparing to strike her chest and end whatever life remained, when the sudden chaos of a fight broke out nearby.

Six vaxros warriors painted in yellow scars marched into the village. Their skin was deep red, and their large, muscular bodies towered over the evae they pulled through the village with ropes on their wrists and necks.

The prisoners wore dark cloaks and fought against the restraints. But one captive remained calm against the fury of his captors. He paid them no mind as he walked alongside his unruly comrades.

They were led to a cave near the center of the village, where a heavy wooden door was opened, and the evae were forced inside. The wood creaked as the door was slammed shut and then locked with a thick iron bar.

"Morök," a vaxros man called.

The hunter turned to face his leader, who bore a waist-length warrior's braid and thick war skirt made of layered

---

° Pronunciation: Shad-oh-sah-lahn
In the language of the humans, Shadosalaan are referred to as creatures of darkness.

15

leather and furs. "We found these evae in the desert. Have you come across others?"

Morök glanced at Neer.

His leader pushed him aside with a snarl and leaned over Neer. He pulled back her hair to inspect her ears. "*Human*," he sneered. A scar peeked from beneath a tear in her sleeve, and he ripped her shirt further, revealing the traitorous mark upon her skin.

Furious, the leader turned to Morök, and with deadly command, he said, "Lock her with the others."

CHAPTER THREE

THE KEY
Aélla

"There is no one else... it has to be me."

— Aélla Líadrinel

PLATINUM HAIR WAVED IN THE soft breeze. A woman, with fair skin and dark blue eyes, stood by the riverbed. She was alone, staring with contempt at the water flowing quickly through the canyon.

Rock and stone surrounded her at every turn. High above, across the wide cavern, was a city made of red bridges. The suspended pathways led to various shops and homes supported by tall rock columns. Crimson canopies stretched over the largest areas, allowing shade to protect their goods and wares.

Gruff voices echoed through the chasm as villagers carried on with their day, paying no mind to the woman standing beneath them.

Her hands fidgeted, and she chewed her lip. She turned to the sky with a deep exhale. Sunlight radiated from the heavens, casting a warmth that stung her skin.

"Come on...," she begged in her native evaesh language. "Where are you?"

Her gaze averted to Dru—a small pixie-like creature who landed atop her shoulder. The tiny creature, though not who she expected, smiled at her. With large round eyes and a bright red glow around her orange, leafy skin, she stood at just ten inches tall and held two beautiful translucent wings that extended high above her head. Two others reached just beneath her knees.

"*Drimil!*°"

Y'ven approached from behind, his heavy footsteps thudding against stone. He was a large vaxros man, standing at the typical seven-foot height, with large muscles and short black hair that hung across his shoulders. Yellow scars were bright against his deep red skin, displaying his valor with a mix of intentional and battle-worn marks.

While many would be intimidated by such beasts, who were often regarded as the most brutal and courageous in battle, Aélla was unafraid of their reproach. Her lineage gave her amnesty, and with it, she chose a path which led her through their homeland and into the forsaken realms of her ancestors.

"What is it, Y'ven?" she asked.

Y'ven straightened with purpose. Glowing yellow eyes peered to the companion refusing to meet his gaze. "You are all right?" His evaesh was broken and hard to understand. "Why do you come here alone?"

With another glance to the sky, she admitted, "He hasn't returned. It's been days."

"He will return." His shadow engulfed her smaller frame when he stepped closer, and he placed a large hand on her shoulder with an ugly, sympathetic grin. "Show faith, Master Drimil."

Her sorrow faded into a breathless laugh at his attempt to console her. It wasn't typical of the vaxros to show kindness

---

° Pronunciation: Drem-ell
In the language of the humans, Drimil directly translates to Magic User and refers to those that possess any magical energy or abilities, limited or otherwise, of the Realms.
In addition to this title, those who possess magic from all seven realms of magic are also considered full sorcerers.

or empathy toward others, but Y'ven was different. In their weeks together, she came to learn there was more to some of the brutish desert beasts than meets the eye. Speaking a foreign language, for instance, was such a rarity, she believed Y'ven may have been the only vaxros to have ever learned.

They stepped away from the water, moving closer to the suspended village, and the coolness of the river's wind was overtaken by dry heat.

"Enough with the formalities," she said with a smile. "Call me Aélla."

"I cannot."

Her lips scrunched into a playful grin. Y'ven paid her no mind, leading her up a spiral incline to the base of a tall pillar. They stepped to the edge of the city and walked across the taut canvas bridges.

The scent of tanning leather and charred meat filled the air. Aélla's stomach growled and ached at the mouthwatering aroma. Baskets of leather clothes, armor straps, and the occasional half-eaten vegetable were stacked messily across the platforms. Where some open areas held clothes and wares, another had racks of weapons thrown together.

She plucked a green, spotted vegetable from a basket. Sour juice dripped down her chin, and she enjoyed her late morning meal. The residents, each with deep red skin and bright yellow scars, sneered as they walked past the evae. The vaxros were not a welcoming or forgiving people. Known for their brutality and strength, they honored themselves with valor. While Aélla had done nothing to warrant such disfavor, she was an outsider, and the natives, in all their resentment and distrust, did not accept her arrival.

Aélla kept her chin high and looked into the eyes of each passerby. Though they heavily outmatched her height and size, she wasn't afraid. It was her right to be there. Should they put up a fight, she wouldn't back down.

And more importantly…she wouldn't lose.

Aélla walked alongside Y'ven with firm demeanor. "Were you able to summon a meeting with the dül?°" she asked.

"Yes," he said, with no further explanation.

They slipped through a thick crowd and onto a large, blood-stained platform. Unlit torches created a barrier around the platform, and a wide circle was drawn close to the edge, creating a perimeter not to be overstepped.

"This is a *gaelrog*?" she asked.

Y'ven nodded in quiet response. As they stepped across the blood-soaked ring, Aélla became lost in her wonderings of the brutish and fight-ready race. She had heard tale of the gaelrog, or *fighting rings*, which were used in ritualistic acts of strength between two warriors. No weapons were allowed, and only once a combatant could no longer fight was a victor announced. There was no submitting or abandoning the dual once it had started, lest the defeated sought to lose all their honor and respect as a warrior.

She peeled her gaze from the overlapping blood stains and followed Y'ven through the dense village. The wide bridge eventually broke off into smaller sections attached to door-ways carved into the canyon wall. Each of the doorways were stacked in rows of three as far as she could see. Voices seeped from the homes and shadows overlapped in the windows as families gathered inside.

At the edge of the suspended village, they came to a large rock platform. Their journey came to an unexpected end, and they stared out into the open canyon. The doorways glowing with firelight were far behind, and the many overlapping bridges had turned into one narrow path.

° A dül, in simple terms, is equivalent to a shaman. Typically, the dül lives in seclusion within their shelarr, or tribe. They are regarded as the most valued member of their shelarr, as they've earned the right to their title through blood, loss, and sacrifice.

A dül can be either male or female, as both sexes are considered equal in all regards among the vaxros. The dül is the oldest member of their shelarr. Dül'Muirin of the Grenghat'shelarr is the youngest ever at 319 years.

A single torch stood across a rock platform, its flames waving endlessly beneath the beating sun. Beautiful, swirled patterns were etched into the stone beneath their feet, and the blackened crevices extended along the outer reaches of the platform, coming together in the center.

Y'ven stepped to the torch and cupped his hands around the flames. The glowing heat transferred from the torch into his palms, and he stepped to the platform's center, taking care to keep the flame alive. He knelt atop the stone and pushed the flame into the ground.

Aélla jumped back when the flames erupted throughout the blackened design. Bright orange light flickered atop the ground, sending embers through the air.

Rocks shifted along the canyon walls, and a deep grinding reverberated through the canyon. The bridges shook, and the world rattled. Aélla steadied her balance as large boulders extracted themselves from the canyon walls. They floated slowly toward the platform and aligned themselves into a floating bridge. The fiery platform slowly snuffed out, leaving behind the blackened remnants of the shallow designs.

"Come," Y'ven said, stepping across the newly formed bridge. Aélla stared timidly at the new formation, and her wide eyes fixed on the vaxros striding across without hesitation.

She followed behind, taking care not to slip or fall beyond its untethered edges. Relief washed over her when they came to a hidden alcove within the canyon. A large archway surrounded beautifully detailed doors carved into the wall. A battle axe rested within the stone above them. Broken skulls, blood-stained pelts, jewelry, and incense were laid outside the entry.

Y'ven knelt in front of the door, whispering a sacred chant, and orange light brightened the creases of the doorway. Aélla stepped back when the doors shifted and the light faded.

He heaved, pushing the doors open, and together, they stepped inside.

21

A deep rumble shook the air when the door closed. Small fires burned brightly within goblets that stood in arched hollows along the walls, keeping the large cavern alight. The dome-shaped ceiling glowed with red designs leading to an enormous chandelier. A bright flame flickered within the metal constraints of the beautiful fixture.

Standing in the center of the room was an enormous statue of a scaled beast. Its long tail curled around the pedestal, while its winged arms stretched out to the sides. Fire glowed from its open mouth and wide nostrils.

Four large horns extended back along the length of its head, and spiked scales lined the edges of its spine. Sharp fangs rested within its wide-open mouth. Aélla had never seen a creature so fierce or intimidating. Even in the presence of its statue, she was frightened. The serpent-like creature stood atop a ten-foot pedestal. Its body rose to the ceiling, where its open mouth hovered beside the glowing chandelier.

"What is this?" she asked, gazing upon the creature whose smoothed stone scales glistened in the firelight.

"Draak.° Born of fire and power. First rulers of Erolith."

"The rulers?" Her face twisted as she turned to Y'ven.

"Vicious. Bloodthirsty. First magic users. Men learned to harness magic. Used it against them."

Her gaze returned to the statue, and she touched its tail. Cold, glistening stone lay beneath her fingers. Fear trickled through her as its glowing eyes bore into her own. With a half-step back, she put space between them. "I've heard of the draak from First Blood text, but there are so many stories and legends that it's hard to tell truth from fantasy." She paused.

° Roughly translated: dragon, though the ancient word has become lost as the myths and legends of such a race have been wiped from Erolith. The evae, with all their knowledge and wisdom, were mostly ignorant to such magnificent and deadly creatures, only finding mention of such a powerful race in ancient texts.

Only the rët'grugnah, or sun-blood, still tell the stories of the ancient and powerful draak.

"My old friend, Thallon, used to say they were just the imaginings of parents who wished to keep their unruly children from sneaking out at night."

A deep thud echoed through the quiet chamber. Aélla gripped her chest with a gasp, while Y'ven turned sharply to the east. A vaxros dressed in dark, layered robes and a headdress of bones stood atop a large stairway. Her bare scalp showcased beautiful yellow scars trailing across her forehead and cheeks.

Aélla followed Y'ven and Dru, who knelt at the base of the stairs. While they focused on the dül standing above, Aélla's eyes moved back to the statue, which was just as fierce from behind as it was in front.

A rumbled voice came from the stranger. Heavy footsteps echoed down the stone steps, getting heavier as they approached. Aélla stiffened when dül'Atyana stood before them and spoke in her native language. Y'ven responded, and she placed the end of her staff to his chin. He slowly met her gaze. The dül nodded subtly, and Y'ven's broad shoulders relaxed.

"Blood of evae, faeth, and vaxros," dül'Atyana said in her native language, "why have you entered these sacred chambers?"

Y'ven's focus remained intently on the stairs as he spoke in vax. "Dül'Atyana. I bring Aélla, blood of the First. Drimil of light. She wishes to speak with you about her journey."

"Drimil'Rothar…" The woman stepped to Aélla, and the evae bowed. "Your arrival comes at the brink of war. Shadosalaan have risen. Naik'avel is near."

"Dül'Atyana," Aélla began in the vax native language, which she learned beforehand through use of her magic. "It is an honor to be in your presence. I have come to the desert to enter *tre'lan Aenwyn*."

"The tre'lan° are forbidden, Master Drimil. The doors have been sealed for many centuries."

"I must find the key." Her intense gaze met with the dül's. "And you know where it lies."

Dül'Atyana stepped back, her jaw agape and eyes wide. She stammered over her words. "For you to come to this sacred place. To demand such atrocities — !"

"This is not a request, dül'Atyana. Without my magic, this world will fall into chaos. You know as well as I the strength of naik'avel." Aélla brought herself closer to the woman thrice her size. "But you do not know the strength of a true drimil."

The dül hardened as their gaze lingered. Her muscular arms were stiff at her sides.

Aélla hadn't the patience to wait for her dispute, so she explained, "Once I've found the staff that can unlock the tre'lan, I must collect each of the four elements. I need your guidance in finding them." She carefully took the dül's hand. "Please, dül'Atyana. I will not disrespect your customs. I will *not* desecrate the ruins."

The dül's eyes met with Aélla's. "You will find the staff within the ruins of Koehevar." She straightened her back and gripped her staff tightly. "*Rema'üklahg*. Good luck, Master Drimil. May the spirits guide you." Her lip twitched as she glared at the evae and spoke with anger.

Aélla bowed respectfully and swiftly exited the temple.

Outside, she closed her eyes and breathed in the fresh air. The weight of misguidance was lifted as she now understood her path. Her journey into the desert wasn't made without preparation, yet she hadn't the tools needed to achieve her goals. With no help from the natives, her last hope was dül'Atyana.

° Tre'lan are gateways to the magical realms. Hidden within the continent of Laeroth, their origins are unknown, though it is believed they were constructed by powerful Ahn'Clave, or First Blood, scholars.
Tre'lan Aenwyn is the Realm of Elements. Anyone born of elemental magical energy may enter its doors and obtain the power inside.

"Where is Koehevar?" she asked.

Y'ven rubbed his face with a heavy sigh. "Two cycles° north."

Aélla nodded, looking at the ground. Two days until they'd reach their destination, and he still hadn't returned. She glanced at the sky, searching.

"Drimil," Y'ven started, his voice timid yet firm, "dül are great warriors. Esteemed. Admired. Do not make them your enemy."

With a gentle nod, Aélla silently agreed to do better. She understood that her actions in the temple were dishonorable, but the vaxros didn't respect her kind. Had she not shown her strength, dül'Atyana would have never given her what she needed.

The silence was broken when the caw of a raven echoed from above. Aélla turned toward the noise, staring anxiously at the heavens, awaiting his arrival. As his shadow moved across the sky, Aélla's heart raced with excitement. The raven swooped down, landing softly on her extended arm.

"Altvára." She greeted the bird while rubbing its neck with her finger. "I was so worried about you!"

The raven ruffled its feathers and shook its head. But when their eyes met, Aélla's smile faded. Altvára spread his wings and lifted into the air.

"Master Drimil," Y'ven started. His eyes focused on the raven circling high above. "What is wrong?"

She watched Altvára flying above, giving his warning. He had found what he was looking for, and the time had come to retrieve it.

"Follow Altvára," Aélla said, still watching the raven. "He will guide you. Make haste, Y'ven, before it's too late."

"Drimil…I do not understand."

° A cycle, or sun cycle, is a vax term meaning day. Each cycle is one day on Erolith

She watched Altvára soar through the air. Her lips were dry, and her face was pale. With a subtle nod, she explained, "She's here."

Chapter Four

Awakening
Nerana

*"This land of fire is not for the weak. We will stain the dirt with
their blood and cast their shadows away with the sun."*
— Sayings of the vaxros

NEER LAY ASLEEP ATOP THE cold desert floor. She twitched
and whined as nightmares of darkness and pain flashed
through her mind—visions of Loryk lying beneath the Tree,
the emptiness of the cave, the betrayal of Avelloch's disappearance. Deep, thunderous growls and the vicious shrieking
of monsters clawed at her sanity. They tore into her skin, ripping and shredding as she lay helpless on the ground, watching from above as her life was taken.

A flash of light broke through the darkness, and she
jumped from her slumber with a frightened gasp, gripping her
forehead with an exhausted groan.

Cold air kissed her skin, and the smell of damp rock lingered in the air. As her vision focused, she found herself
within a dark, empty cave. A single torch flickered across the
chamber, casting waves of light against the jagged walls and
uneven floor. Shadows the size of men shifted her delirium
into panic.

Neer scurried back, her boots sliding across the smooth
ground. Pressing against the wall, she watched as five figures
emerged from the darkness. They stared down at her, and
their long faces held deep scowls. Black markings covered
their skin with intense, sharp designs.

They were evae who spoke a variation of evaesh Neer didn't understand, and their eyes bore into hers with unrelenting oppression.

A man with dark hair and a long marking across his temple strode across the room. Neer pressed herself further into the wall and stared at his face, crushed beneath the weight of his power. Cold fingers gripped her chin, and he leaned closer, peering intently into her frightened eyes.

Unable to muster even the weakest energy, Neer was powerless in his grasp. The effect of her teleportation still lingered, leaving her depleted and weak. She pushed his hand away with a feeble swipe of her wrist.

"*Nizotl vek'Drimil,*" he whispered.

Her eyes widened at the mention of the deceitful and cunning divine. The stranger turned away, staring into the distance as if in deep thought.

A harsh voice cut through the silence when a woman pushed forward. Her arms were bound behind her back, and Neer wondered if the man was her captor. But the evae and vaxros didn't coexist, and he bore the same markings and attire as the others here. He must be a prisoner. The man tensed, and his eyes hardened as the woman drew nearer. Her angered voice sawed through the air as she spoke in quick, growling outbursts.

When she stepped closer, bringing herself within view, the man grabbed a rock and smashed her head. Neer jumped with a loud gasp, reeling from the sudden attack. Blood sprayed through the air, landing on Neer's tongue and filling her mouth with the taste of copper. The woman fell to the ground with a hard crash. Thick blood leaked from her broken skull, and the life faded from her angry eyes.

Neer shuddered when the man turned back to her. Her throat was tight, and breaths were quick. Not a shred of remorse or shame was present in his calm eyes. Something far worse stared back at her, something she feared more than the man himself.

28

Confidence.

Confidence born of pride and strength.

The cave fell silent as the man focused on Neer. She pushed him back when he pulled up her sleeve. He paid no mind to her frail attempts of freedom as his fingers slid up her shoulder, revealing her branding. His eyes glistened. Chills covered her skin when his cold fingers stroked the marking.

She pulled away and spit at him. He turned sharply, and a haunting gaze overtook his expression. The hard crack of his hand smacked against her cheek, and Neer fell aside. Her head collided with a rock, and blood trickled through her dirty hair. Specks of white flickered in her vision.

Hurried footsteps paraded through the cave, drawing nearer with every step. The man hissed sharply, and the cave fell instantly silent as his companions came to a halt. He took one final glance at Neer and then turned to the entrance. A light rumble shook the stone before a heavy door creaked open. Streams of dancing firelight illuminated the cave from the entry.

A vaxros warrior stepped inside, enveloping the bright doorway in shadow. He stood nearly seven feet tall and wore thin leather armor. His black hair was pulled back into a waist-length warrior's braid. Thick red skin pulled tight across his muscular arms and chest, and yellow scars etched his body in beautiful designs.

Neer stared at him, awestruck. The legends of the vaxros— a dangerous and fight-ready race—were true. No one who had ever visited the desert returned, but their stories survived. Tales of enormous brutes with deep red skin standing tall as the sun were more myth than truth to the people of Laeroth.

Being in his presence, Neer couldn't decide if she was more afraid or impressed.

The evae curled their fists and snarled as the vaxros warrior approached. His orange glowing eyes landed on Neer, and with a deep inhale, he broadened his wide shoulders. A low growl emanated from his throat. He looked back at the evae and pointed to the door.

The man with the facial markings held a calm, relaxed expression, standing against the intimidating guard. He held his hands behind his back, giving the illusion of his wrists being bound. Without the slightest hesitation, he calmly stepped from the cave, and the others quickly followed.

Thunderous footsteps thudded to Neer.

"Oölak mēgrove," the guard growled in a raspy voice.

Neer leaned back, unable to escape as the sharp blade of his enormous battle axe touched her throat. He leaned closer, bringing his face inches from her own. The bitter smell of his breath filled her nose, and his fiery yellow eyes pierced into hers. A menacing growl left his throat.

With a hard snatch, he gripped her hair and pulled her forward. She yelped and slid her fingers across his hand, never able to free herself from his hold. Her feet fumbled across the dirt as he dragged her to the village center. Half a dozen leather-wrapped tents surrounded a large fire. Embers sprayed into the air, drifting through the darkness as the flames roared below.

Several dozen villagers gathered around as she was thrown to the ground. The men, women, and children all bore yellow scars across their thick-skinned bodies and wore thin loin cloths around their waists.

Neer was shoved forward and forced to her knees, completing the short line of evaesh prisoners taken from the cave. In the firelight, she could see them clearer. Their tan skin was covered in dark tattoos, and their deep scowls reminded her of the fighters who massacred the villages of Vleland and Llyne long ago.

The vaxros captor lifted his arms and spoke to his people, breaking Neer's thoughts. His voice was assertive and rough. The villagers' confused expressions faded to anger as they stared at Neer. She glanced between them, uncaring of what may happen. Not a twitch or snarl interrupted her permanent sullen expression.

Even in the face of death, she was hollow. Broken. Sitting amidst the evae who resembled those she fought long ago brought memories of her time in Vleland with Loryk and Klaud. The sadness of her loss outweighed the anger she felt when she thought of the man who betrayed her. Klaud wasn't one she thought of often—her grief kept her consumed in thoughts of sorrow and despair—but when she did think of him, there was nothing but rage and hatred.

The villagers chanted and cheered as Neer's captor lifted his axe above his head. He turned to the first evae with a menacing snarl and swung his weapon. The evae sneered and cut a harsh phrase before the axe sank deep into his chest. Blood sprayed across the ground, and the crowd cheered with satisfaction. The vaxros kicked him away and retrieved the weapon from his body. He lifted the axe above his head and let out a roar that echoed far throughout the empty desert.

Blood shimmered in the purple moonlight. It dripped from the edge of the blade, rolling down his arm. The crowd cheered as he stepped to his next victim, moving closer toward Neer.

CHAPTER FIVE

SIN'LOHAI
Aélla

*"The token of peace, a blood of the First, shall be retained a
hero and savior. Do not seek harm upon them or the wrath of
this council will see you to your tomb."*

— Sin'Lohai excerpt

AÉLLA STOOD AT THE TOP of the cliff overlooking the
suspended village below. Altvára, the raven, stood on her
shoulder. His head twitched as he looked through the
darkness. Dusk had crept over the land, leaving them in the
stillness of night.

"Drimil," Y'ven started. "What shall we do?"

Aélla gulped through a dry throat and became lost in
thought. In all of her imaginings and visions, she never
thought this one to be true. Another sorcereress walked
among them. Another soul cursed with power and responsibility.

"You must find her," Aélla said. "Follow Altvára. He will
guide you to her. I will go to the ruins and wait for you there."

"You cannot go alone! The others —"

"I will be fine, Y'ven." She smiled at him. "Who are we to
oppose what is already fated?"

"But Drimil —"

"Please" — she touched his arm — "do this, Y'ven. Find this
sorceress. We cannot do this alone."

With a silent nod, his shoulders slumped. "As you wish,
Master Drimil. We will return."

As Y'ven stepped away, Aélla quickly pulled him back. She carefully retrieved a woven trinket from her pocket and placed it firmly into his hand, wrapping his fingers around the old, fragile object. She looked deep into his eyes. "Give this to her. She will understand its meaning."

Y'ven bowed. He tucked the trinket safely into a pouch on his waist. Dru, the small fiery faeth, was perched atop his head. Her tiny fingers curled as she sadly waved goodbye to Aélla, and they followed Altvára into the desert.

Aélla smiled and returned the gesture. As they disappeared, she was left alone, staring into the void where the horizon and rock met. Traveling during the night was dangerous. *Kanavin,* or creatures of darkness, lurked in the shadows, becoming ever present after the sun hid itself beyond the reaches of the sky. But the creatures she could handle. The sun, with its blazing, incurable heat, was far worse than any monster she would face in the darkness.

The first step was hardest as she trekked alone. With nothing but her wooden staff and an old indecipherable map, she wandered the forbidden desert plains and worried about losing her way.

Beautiful streams of light danced across the clear sky. Colors of green and blue illuminated the tall rocky mountains in the distance.

She walked until the sun crept over the peaks, bringing with it a gentle warmth that soothed her chilled and aching skin. Empty plains surrounded her in every direction. No trees, flowers or green gave a sign of life to the dirt and rocks. It was an unfamiliar sight, and while beautiful, she found herself feeling sick. Since the start of her journey long ago, she had traveled to the northern reaches of Uadin and across the sea to the Isles of Erasin. But nothing made her as homesick as the desert, as it was the complete opposite of her forested home of Nyn'Dira, and even with its striking mountainous backdrops and glowing night skies, there was no comfort of home.

Though Aragoth and Nyn'Dira shared a border, Aélla had never felt so far from home. So far from her family and the people she loved. For the first time, she was entirely alone, and it filled her with a sense of despair she couldn't quell.

Through the long day, her legs grew weak and tired, and her boots dragged against the dirt as the sun dipped beyond the horizon.

In the darkness, she stood alone, staring into the emptiness of a cold and lonesome desert. Aélla glanced from north to south, east to west, searching for anything that could be hiding nearby.

As the darkness around her grew, so too did the threat of danger. She needed to find shelter, but there was none nearby. The closest settlement was over a day away, and unlike Nyn'Dira, Aragoth was absent of any abandoned shacks, hunter's cabins, or small settlements sprinkled throughout its territory.

With a final glance at her surroundings, she decided to make camp where she stood. She placed her pack and weapon on the ground at her feet and then knelt with her eyes closed. Magic swelled inside her, and she formed it into an iridescent barrier that climbed above her in a wide dome. The shimmering energy met above her head where it solidified into an invisible shelter.

Aélla retrieved an enchanted flint from her pack, struck it, and created bright flames atop the ground that produced no smoke. With a deep breath, she leaned against the barrier and closed her eyes, drifting in and out of an uneasy sleep.

The next morning, golden rays filled the sky in a kaleidoscope of orange and pink as the sun overtook the night. Aélla extinguished the enchanted flames, collected her belongings, and then disintegrated the barrier with a touch of her hand.

Staring up at the brightening sky, she prepared herself for the long day, and then trekked alone through the grueling heat.

Nearing mid-day, she stopped beneath a tall rock formation and basked in the coolness of its shadow. She wiped the sweat from her brow before gently cupping her fingers around her left forearm and healing herself of her painful sunburn. Once the sting of her skin had faded, she pulled her map from her cloak and concluded the village she sought must be nearby. With no roads, villages, or signposts to guide her, the trip was long and unbearable.

Suddenly, the mundane silence of an empty world was lifted when an angry, violent shriek came from above. Shadows passed, and two dozen glynfir—large, winged beasts with leathered skin and razor-sharp teeth—flew overhead with klaet'il riders saddled to their backs.

Aélla watched them with a careful eye before ducking behind a large rock as the riders shouted war cries. They headed north, in the direction of the ruins.

To the place she was meant to be.

The creatures swooped down and out of sight, and Aélla ran after them. Not many would subject themselves to the grueling task of riding such temperamental and aggressive beasts. None but the klaet'il, who were strictly forbidden from the desert at all costs.

To know they were here, that they were seeking out the ruins, struck her with pain. Their presence could propel the vaxros and evae into another vicious and bloody war.

And she feared this might be their goal.

She came closer to the ruins, and the shattering sounds of desperate cries filled the air. The clash of swords and iron axes echoed above the screams as the klaet'il attacked the village.

A vaxros warrior growled as an arrow landed deep in his shoulder. He looked at the sky, where an evaesh warrior nocked his bow from above. The vaxros hurled his spear.

The evae pulled the reins of his glynfir and they spun aside, dodging the attack by mere inches. A deep snarl pulled the vaxros's scarred face, and he grabbed another spear. His attacker drew back an arrow.

From behind, an evae leapt over a broken wall and aimed his daggers for the vaxros's neck. The vaxros hurled his spear and then turned around, grabbed the evae, and used him as a shield from the man above. His victim gasped when an arrow impaled his chest.

The spear pierced the glynfir's side, and it squealed. Leathered wings flailed, and its blood rained over the warriors below as it crashed to the ground.

As the vaxros was pulled into another battle, Aélla approached the village and noticed an evae fighting with the natives. He wasn't klaet'il, that she knew for sure, as not a mark covered his pale skin.

He wore dark robes that were stained with dust and blood. His hood had fallen to reveal his filthy blond hair and full beard. He was an older man, with faint wrinkles creasing his light blue eyes.

A loud roar disrupted her trance. She leapt over crumbled debris and drew her staff. With an upward spin, she caught the face of a klaet'il charging at a child. As the fighter tumbled aside, Aélla struck his back with her weapon, and he fell into the dirt.

She turned back, spinning the staff quickly in her hand, and her weapon quivered when it struck against a blade. The klaet'il pulled his weapon back and slashed at her head.

Ducking beneath his swing, and feeling the air against her scalp, Aélla struck forward with her palm open. A powerful blast of energy rumbled through the village, and the klaet'il fighter was thrust into a building. His skull cracked as it met with the stone wall.

Blood and brain splattered against the wall as his body slid to the ground.

An injured vaxros lay on the ground nearby. Dark blood dripped from his abdomen, leaving him powerless against the approaching klaet'il. The evaesh warrior licked the blood from her lips, drawing closer with dual swords.

Aélla reached out to the vaxros, prepared to heal him from afar with her magic, when a voice disrupted her concentration.

"Don't!"

In her distraction, she turned, curious to find the voice that had interrupted her. Her gaze fell to the older evae as he raced closer. He dodged an arrow and swiped his sword through the gut of a passing klaet'il. Blood sprayed across his robes, and he continued onward, paying no mind to the dying man he'd left behind.

Aélla turned back to the vaxros when a light wheeze came from his throat. The klaet'il leaned over him, watching the light leave his eye. His body slumped further into the ground, and the evae pressed her boot against his chest before pulling her sword from his body. Aélla stumbled back, unable to believe what she allowed to happen.

What she could have prevented had she been able to heal him.

"Do not heal them," the evae warned, coming to her side. "To give them aid would dishonor their valor."

"He was defenseless!" Her voice was sharp as glass.

"He was a vaxros warrior. Now, grab a sword or fall behind, but do not give them aid."

The evae ran back to the battlefield. Aélla was stricken by her morality and fell into anger. She watched their blood stain the ground, her heart thumping loudly in her ears. Overwhelmed by her desire to help, she was forced to step aside. Fighting now would only lead to the consumption of her rage, and with that power, she could shift her fate, transforming it from one of purity and peace into chaos and fury.

Unable to quell the anger and confusion, she left the battle and knelt to the ground. Shimmering magic formed a circle around her. Its iridescence climbed upward into a dome, sealing just above her head. With her fists together and eyes closed, she meditated.

She felt foolish for focusing on her energy at such a dire time, but any loss of focus could be perilous to the world she sought to save. This was the only way to ward the anger and chaos rising from the energy that surrounded her. Energy that festered and sizzled deep in her soul, fighting for control.

Focused breathing allowed her the strength to eliminate the sounds of the battle. Heat rose within her, though not from anger, but magic. The calming waves of energy soothed her into a tranquil state. The madness once flurrying deep within became hollow and empty.

Sadness filled the void, but sadness was acceptable. Perspiration slid down her face and dripped from her chin. Slowly, her eyes opened, and she watched from the confines of her enclosure as the battle came to a grueling end.

The village was left with less than half its inhabitants. Bodies of men, women, and children lay sliced and bleeding. As a dying woman took her last breath, Aélla slumped forward in sorrowful defeat. She scanned the village, spotting the older evae lying in a pool of blood.

A klaet'il warrior stood over him, speaking with vengeance and reproach.

The klaet'il lifted his sword, ready to end the evae's life, and Aélla created a half-dome barrier, shielding him from the deadly attack. She fell to the ground with a gasp when her magic was struck. White cracks formed in the air where the sword met her invisible shield. The evae turned to her with wide eyes and watched as she crawled to her knees. With a pained cry, she created another quick barrier.

As his assailant swiped downward, the evae lifted his sword to block the hit. A shockwave of pain coursed through Aélla when her magic was struck a second time before it shattered.

The evae slashed his blade through the klaet'il's throat. He kicked the man away and rolled to his side. Bruises and cuts littered his face and arms.

Aélla clutched her aching chest and rushed through the village to his side. She placed her hands on his back, and energy pricked her skin, moving from her chest into her arms.

Deep pain coursed through their entwined energies. His pain cut through her like a razor's edge as the shallow cuts marking his arms and face slowly vanished.

The evae struggled beneath the weight of Aélla's magic. Beads of sweat formed across his brow as her hot, stinging magic coursed through him. The injuries faded, and Aélla backed away. Feeling weaker now that she'd exerted such energy, she slumped forward. Wiping the sweat from her forehead, she eyed the village. The injured and lifeless lay in pools of blood. Vaxros healed one another with small flames, while the klaet'il remained motionless on the ground.

Clutching his wrist, where a deep wound once marked his skin, the stranger asked, "You are Drimil? One of the *eólin*˚?"

"I am *Drimil'Rothar*," she explained, to his surprise. It was a highly respected title known by all non-humans. "I'm here under protection of the *sin'lohai*.† You, however, are not."

He rubbed his face, hesitant to explain. "I'm here of my own accord. Word has spread that klaet'il warriors have invaded. I want to know why."

Aélla turned when firelight brightened in the center of the village. Two vaxros warriors lifted the deceased by their wrists and ankles and tossed them into the flames. Embers and smoke sprayed into the air, and burnt flesh filled the area with the stench of death.

Surrounding the warriors were the ruins of an ancient First Blood village. Two dozen large tents, made of varying

---

˚ Those not born with inherent magical energy, yet still hold its power, are considered eólin, or unknown.

It's unclear how these individuals came to possess the energy of the realms, which is only attainable to those born to the First Blood, though many have their own theories and suspicions.

† A treaty made by all non-humans that grants amnesty and voyage to those who partake in matters which affect the lives of the many.

colors of stretched leather, stood along the outer rim of the settlement. The vaxros who protected this ancient village would never desecrate it by setting up home within its borders.

On a nearby structure, Aélla spotted a familiar symbol painted on the stone. The blood, used to depict such a traitorous word, dripped slowly from the edges of each mark, cascading down the uneven surface of a crumbled wall.

It was the mark of the *nesiat*…the lost. Such a design was used only for those who were considered without purpose or a soul. She knew of one person who carried such a burden, and to see it marked on the homes of her ancestors filled her with terror and rage.

Her fixation on the symbol lifted as the stranger stood and brushed himself clean. Aélla stared at him, wondering where he was from. Though they'd never met, she knew he was of her clan as his evaesh features were unmistakable.

"We cannot stay," he said, watching the villagers. "These vaxros are not like the others. They are more accepting of our kind, but we should not linger. If we overstay our welcome, they will attack."

Aélla watched them with the sting of guilt and sorrow. A vaxros man carried a woman to the large firepit. Her arms hung aside while her lifeless eyes gazed to the heavens. Tears streamed down his face as he knelt into the flames and gently placed her with the others.

The older evae climbed over the ruin. "We will make camp near the cave entrance."

A curious tug pulled Aélla's brow. She watched him slip over the debris and crumbled walls before anxiously following in his path. They approached a large cave entrance nestled just beyond the reaches of the village. Even beneath direct sunlight, inside the hollow was dark as night.

Aélla perched within a natural rock barrier, while the stranger sat opposite her, leaning beside the entrance of the cave.

They rested beneath the tall rocks and basked in the coolness of dark shadows. Aélla hadn't realized the intensity of the sun's heat until it was shaded. Touching her arms, she relieved herself of the shallow cuts and burns. Her color faded from dark pink to its regular light ivory, and she leaned back with a soft sigh.

The ache in her back absolved as she sank into the smooth stone. She peered at the evae when he cleared his throat and offered her a sack of berries.

"What has brought you to the ruins?" he asked.

She accepted his offering and explained, "I am to find the *rástalfür*. It's a magical staff that holds elemental energy."

His eyes widened with intrigue. "You plan to enter the tre'lan?" There were equal parts amusement and puzzlement to his stale voice.

She was surprised by his quick conclusion. Not many knew of the staff or its purpose. "Who are you?"

He picked the edge of his fingernail and smiled. "Just a man."

"You are very knowledgeable for being *just a man*."

With a knowing look, his face twisted inward, expressing his agreement. "I believed the rumors to be untrue. That someone of your inherent power lived among us." He paused with intent. "Is that why you refused to fight? Why you meditated in the midst of battle?"

She respectfully nodded. "I am Drimil'Rothar."

"I see. You must remain pure with your intentions, even if they are justified."

"I cannot taint my soul with chaos or darkness. I must remain in the ways of the Light."

He scoffed with a smile, took a drink from his canteen, and leaned back. The wrinkles of his forehead deepened as his eyebrows raised. "Following the philosophies of the ancients will only lead you down their path, and they vanished millennia ago."

"Are you suggesting that I forego the ways of my ancestors?"

"Your destiny is your own, Master Drimil. Whether you choose to follow in the beliefs of those long past or carve a new way for yourself—the choice is yours. Do what you *think* is right, not what you're *told*."

She crossed her arms to quell the tightness in her chest. Never had she been advised against the teachings of those before her. The First Blood were among the most esteemed and respected scholars in history. To disregard the path built by the blood of those far greater than she could ever hope to be was foolish.

Still, she respected the man for speaking so candidly, even if he was a stranger. Even if his words were said with ignorance and disgrace.

"And what if I'm wrong?" she asked, humoring him. "What if the path that I choose leads to naik'avel? What if it leads to the deaths of so many that could have been saved?"

His answer surprised her, as she'd never met such confidence and pride. "What if you aren't?"

Her shoulders slumped, and she turned away. She stared into the cave entrance, questioning her beliefs and those of her ancestors. To be the last living descendant of a long-forgotten race was a privilege and an honor. Could she forsake the long existing prophecies of her predecessors and go against all she'd ever known in hopes of creating a new future? One that saw the end of the cycle of Naik'avel?

One that saw an end to her power and destiny...

"For centuries, the world lived in peace," she said, her eyes still fixated on the dark cave. "It wasn't until my people disappeared that chaos returned." Her gaze shifted to his. "There is no one left but me. If I refuse the prophecies and guidance of those before me, the world will fall."

"I heard there is another. A *human*."

A chill ran down her spine. She knew of this human—the sorceress with bright teal eyes and fully capable energy. Yes, she knew, but she'd never dare tell a stranger. This human sorceress was meant to accompany her on this quest. This sorceress, who by her own people was considered a demon, was being tracked by Y'ven, seeking to ally her with Aélla.

"A human?" she asked, portraying the act of ignorance.

The man narrowed his eyes ever so softly and then leaned back with his hands folded over his lap.

"Yes," he explained. "A *sorceress*. I've heard she has incredible power. If left unchecked, it can surely be disastrous."

"Magic is nothing more than a retention of balance. Our actions guide us, not the energy we hold inside."

"Very well said, Master Drimil. I couldn't agree with you more."

This time, her eyes narrowed. "You don't believe her to be a threat?"

"If you give the sightless a dagger, their attacks are dangerous but non-threatening. Teach them to anticipate, and they become unpredictable. Teach them to fight, and they become powerful. Teach them to see"—their eyes met—"and they become unstoppable."

Aélla was perplexed by his proverb. She wondered if he was suggesting she guide this human and teach her to properly control her energy. Without direction she would be blinded and uncontrolled. Surely, there were no humans willing to teach her the dangers and techniques of magic, and Aélla wondered if she was meant for such a feat.

The visions Aélla received of the sorceresses' teal eyes made her believe they were meant to travel together but teaching her to contain her energy was a matter Aélla wasn't sure she was equipped for.

Her deep thoughts were broken as the evae patted his hands clean. Pulling a cloak over his head, he prepared to revisit the unforgiving terrain in search of answers he might never find.

"You're leaving?" she asked.

"My path leads me elsewhere." He tipped his head with a respectful bow. "The world is watching, Master Drimil. Do not forsake us in our time of need."

He gifted her a pleasant smile before climbing through the rocks and wandering into the desert alone.

CHAPTER SIX

BROTHERHOOD
Nerana

"All living beings are born of equality."
— Tenet of the Broken Order

FIRELIGHT DANCED IN WAVES ACROSS the faces of the prisoners. The first victim lay in the dirt. Blood drained from his body like a quick moving river. The crunch of steel smashing into bone filled the air when his skull was smashed. Neer closed her eyes when a roar of cheers erupted from the vaxros.

The evae beside her stood firm in their places. Darkness stained their eyes as they glared at their captors. Hissing and sneering, they tugged against the ropes binding their wrists.

While most of them fought and provoked the vaxros, the man who attacked Neer was silent. He stood next to her with absolute resolve, staring up at the sky as if the world around didn't exist at all. His dark hair fell just over his shoulders, and his sharp evaesh features reminded Neer of Avelloch. So much, in fact, that she started to wonder if he *was* the man she knew. Their faces were nearly identical. If not for this man's sickly pale skin, black hair, and facial marking, Neer may have been convinced.

Still, she watched him, mystified by his relaxation. He wasn't afraid, but eager. Her eyes shifted to his hands, which were still unbound and held together behind his back.

The squelch of an axe sinking deep into flesh tore her concentration. A male evae at the opposite end of the line screamed as his intestines slid from his body. They slithered through his fingers as he struggled to hold them in place. Blood gushed from his body, creating thick puddles around his feet.

A sneer came from the calm evae beside Neer. His eyes veered from the sky to his screaming comrade, and he watched with disdain as the man collapsed to his knees. With a disgruntled shake of his head, he returned his gaze to the sky.

The vaxros laughed and sank his axe through the neck of his victim, then moved to the next person in line—a woman with bright emerald eyes and short dark hair. Neer was stricken by her appearance. Her white skin, long face, and narrow eyes were identical to Klaud's. Their only difference was the color of their eyes. Markings covered her from the left side of her neck down to her exposed naval. The vaxros leaned closer, bringing his large head inches from hers.

With a sly smirk, the woman unclenched her fists, which were held behind her back, also unbound. Her fingers curled in slow waves. Neer watched curiously, recognizing these movements to be that of a magic user. Dust began to swirl, forming into a shallow vortex leading from the ground to her hands.

The captor exhaled a vicious growl. With half a step back, he lifted his axe and struck at her head.

Neer held her breath, waiting for the woman's execution. But the klaet'il clenched her fists, and the vortex strengthened. With a backward flip, she pulled the swirling air beneath her and catapulted the vaxros. He was flung through the air before crashing far into the desert.

She knelt to the ground, staring at the warriors now clutching their weapons. As they charged, she leapt into the air, soaring high above the others. With a somersault, she pulled her arms forward and landed softly behind the relaxed man. He slipped a dagger hidden in his armor, and together, they faced their enemies.

When two vaxros lunged forward, the male evae struck a warrior through the eye and ducked beneath the second vaxros's battle axe. The woman swung her fist and a large rock hurled through the air, smashing into the warrior attacking her companion. Bones crunched and snapped as he crashed to the ground. The stone rose from his twisted body and flew through the air, trailing the woman's arm and striking a warrior coming from behind her.

She grabbed her comrade and swooped her arm outward to create a funnel that lifted them into the air. After they landed safely in the distance, she raised her arms and looked up at the sky. The villagers rushed forward, and the ground trembled. Their war cries and shouts echoed far into the empty desert, overlapping and disappearing into the void.

The woman's eyes glowed a vibrant green. She turned to the charging vaxros, struck her fists to the ground, and produced a shockwave that rippled across its surface. The warriors fell back, their weapons crashing and bodies colliding hard against the dirt.

The ground quaked, and homes shifted. Neer stumbled back and fell as the receding wave moved through the village. Her arm was sliced when she crashed into a cart of weapons.

The green-eyed evae gazed upon the destruction she caused. Her companion smiled with a twisted grin as a winged beast soared through the open air. The large, leathered animal landed softly atop the ground behind them. With one last glance to the village, they leapt onto the saddle and fled into the night, leaving their remaining comrade behind.

In the village, Neer stood amidst several angry vaxros. Despite her fragility and pain, her eyes glowed with vengeance and rage. With most of the warriors still in the desert, where the evae fled, Neer was left to defend herself against the half-dozen vaxros who stayed behind.

She glared and waited, watching as they growled. With no chance of escape, she grabbed a pickaxe from the cart and struck it through the chest of the nearest vaxros.

Turning aside, she evaded the powerful swing of a war axe. The sharp weapon swiped a hair's breadth from her nose. Teleporting back, she put distance between them and thrust her attacker back with a pulse of energy.

The vaxros crashed into a home, and its thick stone walls crumbled beneath her weight. Two warriors rushed to Neer, lifting their weapons. They struck at her, but in mid-stride she vanished from their presence.

Appearing behind them, Neer apported a short sword into her grasp and plunged it blade to hilt through one of her attacker's backs. She tugged hard, attempting to yank it from her victim, but the weapon resisted.

Vanishing to evade a blow to the head, she came up above the second warrior and grappled his back. She wrapped around him from behind and placed her hand over his mouth, forcing a surge of energy deep into his body.

He collapsed to the ground, blood foaming from his mouth, ears, and nose as he seized and tremored. He rolled aside, the glow of his eyes fading, and she stepped back.

"*Nizotl vek'drimil.*"

Neer turned when the last prisoner, a boy no older than fifteen, spoke. His arms were bound, and his face had been slashed. The others abandoned him—a child. She wanted to free him, but her wit told her otherwise. For now, at least, he'd stay a prisoner.

"Who are you?" she asked.

A sinister smile pulled his lips, and she was suddenly afraid. The deep contours of his brow mixed with the laughter choking from his throat gave him a menacing appearance. He was a klaet'il warrior, through and through, and of all things she knew, it was to never trust the prideful and deceptive evae of the east.*

When his eyes shifted slightly to the left, Neer realized she was being attacked from behind and quickly disappeared. The vaxros man charging at her stumbled forward with a hard swing of his battle axe. His weapon sliced through the neck of the evae, partially severing his head.

Neer stood behind the vaxros, watching him search for her. Her anger intensified when she realized he was the executioner who killed the prisoners. He wore leather war skirts and thick chest straps that held his iron shoulder pads in place. A long warrior braid flowed past his waist.

Fury ignited within Neer. Energy rippled like waves of heat from her palms. She cast her magic into a surge that hit his back. The impact created a bright explosion that hurled him into the firepit.

Burning logs crumbled beneath his weight, and embers sprayed through the air.

His heavy battle axe appeared in her grasp as she turned to the others. She slumped forward, appearing more like a sickly child than a warrior. Dark circles formed beneath her eyes. Blistered, sunburnt skin covered her face and arms with a deep shade of red, stinging with every movement.

She was weak and tired. So damned tired. But the vaxros were ruthless and strong. If she gave in to her exhaustion now she'd find herself face down in a pool of her own blood. She had to keep fighting.

---

* A term used by the evae in reference to the klaet'il, who hail from the eastern reaches of the dense and mysterious forest of Nyn'Dira.

Her attention moved to the fire when a powerful war cry rose from the flames. Neer was stricken with fear, watching as the executioner stepped from the fire. He marched forward with glowing, blood-thirsty eyes set on Neer. Not a burn or blister marked his thick skin.

Several warriors marched closer. They gripped their weapons tightly, preparing to strike, until the executioner lifted his hand, and they halted their attacks. The executioner snatched a spear from one of his allies and sliced it toward Neer.

She spun aside. Slashing outward, she drew a thin red line across his shoulder. He shook with fury and lunged forward, but she ducked beneath his heavy swing. He followed her movement and struck downward.

As she vanished, the blade clipped her arm. She rolled across the ground several yards away. A deep laceration opened the skin just below her shoulder, and her rib ached when a thick boot sank into her side. She inhaled shallow, wheezed breaths. The executioner leaned over, shrouding her with his shadow. Fiery eyes met her gaze, and he lifted his spear.

His face twisted as he struck the weapon downward.

Neer lifted her hands, and white cracks fragmented the air when his axe struck hard against her weak barrier. Every muscle and bone burned as her magic shattered.

He drew back his weapon, ready to strike again. Neer lay weak and immobile, her vision fading to darkness and her eyes rolling back. She closed her eyes, accepting her defeat. She couldn't fight. Could hardly breathe from the agony pulsing through her veins. Tears flooded her eyes as she awaited his final attack, one that would end her life.

Her parent's faces appeared in her mind. They opened their arms with wide smiles, welcoming her into a warm embrace. She stepped closer, imagining the reunion she longed for. Relishing in the peace that death would bring.

The spear came down, inches from her face, ready to sink into her skull. But its iron handle sparked against the shaft of another. The executioner roared as he turned, looking into the eyes of the vaxros holding him off.

"*Y'ven vorlök muireēn,*" he said with a vicious growl.

Neer never opened her eyes. She savored the moment with her parents, willing them back into existence.

Above, her savior stood firm, matching his opponents' deadly glare. The executioner shoved him back and slashed at his chest. The savior spun aside and pressed the knife-end of his war hammer to the executioner's stomach. A trickle of blood slid down his skin where the blade's end struck.

Their thick, angry voices cut through the air as they fell into a fierce glare. Neer opened her eyes, astonished to find the war hammer was pointed in her direction. The executioner's eyes shifted away from his opponent's to meet with hers. His lip twitched and eyes were full of rage as he marched away.

Neer eyed the vaxros who saved her. His frayed and torn cloak waved elegantly against the soft winds of the flames.

He placed the war hammer onto his back and calmly approached Neer. "Human." He spoke the evaesh language, though it was broken and hard to understand. "Your name?"

Her head fell aside, and her eyes rolled as she struggled to stay alert. With a deep breath, she forced herself to focus. She examined the man before her and noticed the sigil of the Broken Order Brotherhood carved into his chest. The yellow scars reflected with firelight.

"Who are you?" she asked. Her voice slurred with fatigue.

"Your name, *ürok.*"

"Neer. Are you…with the Brotherhood?"

His brow raised curiously. "Yes."

Feeling more alert, she blinked her vision into focus. Thoughts filtered through her mind too quickly for her to comprehend. She stammered for a moment, trying desperately to piece together the words escaping her.

"How?" She closed her eyes. "Why?"

"Humans threaten all. We fight. Protect."

She gave a suspicious glare through tired eyes. "Why did you save me? Did you know I'd be here?"

"I am with another. Foresaw your arrival. Came to find you."

"I'm here by accident. How could they—"

"She is drimil. Magic. Like you," he interrupted.

Her gaze fell away, and she was perplexed at the possibility of another sorceress searching for her. Before she could speak, to ask more about this sorceress, the vaxros passed her a small item.

She hesitated before accepting his gift. It was a circle of woven sticks with overlapping twigs and twine in its center. Tracing the designs, she came to a sudden realization— only one person would have gifted her with something so meaningful and unique. Something meant to bring peace to those who are lost.

"Avelloch," she whispered.

He had taken an interest in the trinket hanging on the wall of her childhood room. They shared stories of how they believed it would bring them peace, and their disappointment when that wish was never fulfilled.

Sorrow weighed her chest when she thought of him. After Nhamashel, she awoke alone in the cave. He and Klaud had taken the arun and fled, leaving her with Loryk's body. Too weak to escape, Neer spent days alone with him, forced to watch as he turned bloated and blue. The stench of his rotting flesh still burned her nose.

She never understood why he left her. Why they had taken the arun and allowed Loryk to die. She didn't understand much of what happened that night, as many of the events were erased from her memory. They had approached the water of Nhamashel, and then she awoke to find the cave crumbled and destroyed.

Klaud and Avelloch were gone. His potion vial was empty, and a deep, hollow pit had filled Neer's chest where magic once festered.

She clutched the trinket tight in her grasp, desperate to find him. Desperate for answers she may never have. "Where is he?" she asked. "Why did he send you to find me?"

"Only one. Aélla."

Filled with grief and rage, she turned away. Wiping her tears before they could fall, she asked, "Is he alive? Is he okay?"

"Do not know."

Neer's attention diverted to a small humanoid creature that flew nearby and landed atop her savior's shoulder. The tiny creature spoke to the savior in a soft, high-pitched voice. He responded in his native language, and the creature crept closer, examining Neer.

"What is that?" Neer asked, her eyes once again starting to close.

"Druindarvenia," he said, introducing the creature on his shoulder. Overlooking the empty desert, he explained, "Must leave. Journey is long."

Neer huffed, tired of talking. Tired of wandering and fighting and being in such physical agony. "Why can't this drimil retrieve me herself?"

"She fights. No time to waste."

He turned and left the village without another word.

Neer groaned as she crawled to her feet and hunched over, gripping her slashed shoulder. Following behind, she suddenly stopped herself. Her eyes darted through the village before she spotted the hilt of her sword lying within the weapons in the crashed cart.

She hobbled over and retrieved it. Her sunburnt fingers grazed the filthy metal as she carefully inspected the blade for any damage. Placing it securely into the scabbard on her belt, she followed after her savior, and left the village without a backward glance.

CHAPTER SEVEN

THE EVAE
Nerana

"Let go of your grief and seek comfort in the Light, for the soul knows no peace like an eternity in Arcae."
— Zynthary, Book of Mortality

NEER TRAILED BEHIND AS THE vaxros marched across the pathless desert. Not a road sign, village, or trace of civilization was in sight, nor had they seen an animal or source of water. Despite its emptiness, he seemed to know exactly where he was going. His every step was taken with precision and thought. Neer, however, would find herself lost should they become separated, and being without direction this deep in the desert could only lead to a very slow and painful death.

Her raw skin blistered and peeled, making the journey insufferable and long. She licked her lips, hoping to absolve the dryness that left them cracked and bleeding, and bundled into a thin cloak, though the chill of night never lifted from her bones.

Moonlight cast deep shadows from tall rock formations. She kept her eyes on the darkness, wary of what might be watching from the shadows. In the silence, her mind drifted, and she came to the revelation she was one of the only humans to step foot in Aragoth.

The vaxros were keen on keeping outsiders from entering their land. During childhood, she heard of the beasts of the desert, with deep red skin so thick it couldn't be penetrated, and orange eyes capable of seeing through even the darkest of nights. These were tales told by the Order, ones she was reluctant to believe. In the hours she had spent with her savior, whose name she learned was Y'ven, he had proven them wrong. But as she learned throughout her lifetime, there was no trust to be given to even the kindest of strangers.

Despite all the tales and horrors of Aragoth, Neer was still determined to meet this sorceress, though she wondered who she might be and why she had summoned a stranger. She dug through her pockets and collected Avelloch's gift, admiring its beautiful woven patterns. Whoever this sorceress was, Avelloch wanted Neer to trust her.

But her thoughts were still heavy with grief and anger as she battled over her trust in him.

Neer swallowed the dryness of her throat and forced the thoughts aside. Her hardened eyes scanned the desert, and she began to question her reasons for being there. Another jump could take her back to Laeroth, where she could continue on her mission to the colleges and Skye.

But it wasn't truly the vaxros or sorceress that convinced her to stay in such a wretched, dangerous place. Neer knew this but was reluctant to admit it, even to herself. She was there because it was fated. With a sour sneer, she cursed the divine Numera, who had prophesied that she would need to survive 'four trials' in order to defeat the High Priest.[°]

Although she was hesitant to believe it, Reiman, much like Avelloch, believed the divine spoke of the realms of magic.

"Come," Y'ven said.

[°] "A heart of gold turned to stone. A familiar embrace in arms unknown. Four trials you must take if energy you seek. Many years shall pass, but few will you need... Shadows fall upon a sleeping land. Stay close to the light. Aerón'dok'fan."
Numera is the divine of nature and elements. Neer believes she was approached by Numera during her stay in the town of Mange on her way to Nhamashel.

Realizing she had absently slowed her pace, Neer hobbled forward on weak legs to catch up to his stride. Her body ached, and her feet were blistered.

"*Binderis* nearby. Food. Shelter."

Neer hadn't the care to ask for a translation. Food and shelter were good enough explanations. Clutching her blood-coated shoulder, she closed her eyes and shuffled her feet across the dirt.

Rock pillars, glowing cacti, and spotted lizards scattered the empty plains. A large mesquite tree stood alone beneath the glow of the moonlight. White lilies blossomed in the night. Their glowing petals broke away with every light breeze and floated beautifully through the air.

Light chatter filled the silence as Neer was led to three lonesome buildings. Tall and narrow, they sat together in the midst of rock and dust. Firelight flickered brightly from every open window, giving life to the arid wasteland.

Shadows moved across the openings, giving brief shade to the luminescence stretching into the desert. At the door, Y'ven exhaled a gruff sigh and then calmly entered.

Gruff voices filled the air when they stepped inside. Two dozen vaxros sat around a long table bordering a roaring fire. Smoke rose past the second and third story balconies, exiting through the flue in the roof.

The musky scent of ale surrounded the dirty, unkempt patrons. Their fiery eyes darted to Neer, but she focused on the floor, not caring about their angry sneers or remarks.

She stepped to the bar with Y'ven and leaned against its sticky surface. Old ale rings and blood stained the wooden grain. Several bent nails held the cracked, uneven surface together.

An owl sat in the rafters, flittering its wings and moving its head from one place to another. Its gaze settled on the vaxros and human at the bar, and with a quiet *hoo,* it took flight.

It swooped down to the bar and transformed into a rush of hot, white magic. Standing in the haze where the bird landed was a dreled. She slipped into trousers and a loose tunic before climbing a wobbly step stool.

With a beaming smile, she greeted the travelers. Not a wrinkle creased her face, as was true of most dreleds, though Neer could tell the woman was in her youth. She pulled her wiry blond hair into a bun and said, "Bless the makers…first an evae, and now a human. Times are surely changin'.'"

"You speak the common tongue," Neer said, much to the surprise of the other patrons, who grew quiet at the sound of her foreign words. She glanced back at them before eying the dreled.

"Aye. You've come to the wrong place, lass. Aragoth's not for your kind."

"I wouldn't expect it's for yours either."

The woman shook her head with a cackle. "Oh, you humans and your pesky jests."

Neer's bland expression never faded. "I'm not jesting."

"Aye…o'course you ain't." With a deep exhale, she regained her composure. "All right, lass, I can give you two a room, but I can't guarantee protection. This place's meant for all, but these warriors're good-paying customers. I won't be tellin' 'em who they can and can't rustle with."

"We aren't looking for trouble. Just need a place to sleep and food to eat."

"Aye. You do look pretty sickly, there."

"I am." Her voice was as dry as the desert. Tired eyes, devoid of emotion or purpose, peered at the barkeep.

The dreled tilted her head aside with cautious approach. "I'll give you a room. Free of charge for the night. Food's double."

Neer placed her hand into her cloak. Six cogs° vanished from various places across the floor, appearing in her grasp,

---

° Cogs are the currency of the civilized peoples of Aragoth. While the vaxros don't barter with currency between themselves, the many other inhabitants do.

and she handed them to the barkeep. The dreled snatched the cogs and stiffly nodded.

"Right then. Second floor, Room 11."

Neer accepted the brass room key.

"Food'll be ready in a bit. Make yourselves comfortable, and for the love of all, don't go tearin' this place down. I just patched up the bar. If you break anything in a fight, you'll be answerin' to me." She climbed down the ladder and, with a flash of hot light, transformed back into the owl.

Neer slid the key into her pocket and turned to view the room. Her eyes settled on an evae sitting in the corner, alone. His wooden chair was pressed against the wall as he sipped his tea and observed the patrons. For a moment, she was frozen, staring at a face she never expected to see again.

His hair was straight and dark, but his body was the same. Small arms, callused fingers, and a face nearly identical to the one she knew so well. If not for his heavy evaesh features, she'd mistake him for a human.

She'd mistake him for a bard.

"Come," Y'ven stated, jolting Neer from her trance.

As he bounded to the stairs, Neer took another glance at the evae across the room. His short hair was swept back, revealing his slender face and focused eyes. Dark green robes faded to brown where dust had collected across the bottom hem.

"Ürok," Y'ven called.

Neer's sad, desperate eyes fell away from the evae. As she and Y'ven climbed the thick wooden steps, a vaxros man below roared with anger. Neer turned, watching as he dug into his pockets, before tossing two cogs onto the table.

"What's happening?" Neer asked, her hand already on her weapon.

"Thief. Stole from him."

All cogs are made of copper. They hold no value anywhere else in the world.

Neer glanced at the bar, where she had handed off this stranger's money in exchange for food.

A chair flung across the room as the vaxros stood and leaned against the table, staring at each of the patrons. His teeth were exposed through a blood-curdling snarl. His eyes set on the evae, and Neer stiffened. She stepped closer, clutching the hilt of her sword, waiting for the vaxros to make the foolish mistake of attacking an innocent man.

The vaxros marched closer, and the evae jumped to his feet, raising his hands in defense. He spoke calmly to the angry warrior.

"He's speaking your language?" Neer asked of the evae.

Y'ven listened with a mixture of disgust and surprise. "Yes. Says he is innocent."

The vaxros below struck his fist at the evae, who quickly ducked to evade the hit. Wooden splinters fell as he smashed his fist and forearm through the wall where the evae's head would've been. A large hole was made, and the owl dove from the rafters, landing hard atop the vaxros's shoulder. She sank her talons deep into his skin.

The warrior roared with anger before turning to the barkeep, who was still in the form of a bird. Their gazes met, and she released her grip, flying back into the ceiling to watch from above. With a growl, the vaxros returned to the table. Ale spilled from the patrons' large tankards as they roared with laughter and shoved him aside.

The evae dusted himself off and shook his head while looking around the room. His eyes met with Neer's, and a confused half-smile pulled his lip. She found herself entranced by his familiarity, wishing more than anything for him to be the friend she longed for.

"Ürok!" Y'ven called as Neer moved downstairs.

Ignoring his pleas, she walked through the tavern. The angry-eyed vaxros sneered when she marched past, but she hardly noticed. Her eyes were set on the evae as she strode hastily to his side, eager to know who he was. Praying to the Divines that Loryk had returned.

But when she stood before him, close enough to touch, she was at a loss for words. His smile was different. It wasn't as wide or jovial. Not as genuine or kind. Dark blue replaced the brown of his eyes, and his hair was without its famous curls.

"Who are you?" she asked, her voice caught between anguish and strength. This must be an illusion. A test of fate or cruel jest of the Divines.

His smile widened, and her heart shattered at the sound of his unaccented voice. "I'm Thallon."

She blinked away her tears and attempted to release the sorrow building up inside with a deep exhale.

"You speak evaesh?" he asked.

"Yes." She avoided his eyes, which were wide with interest and wonder.

"Fascinating. I had no idea your kind had the capacity to learn such an intricate, complicated language." He paused as she glanced around the room. "Why don't I buy you a drink? You look like you could use one."

Before she could answer, Thallon stepped across the room to the bar.

Y'ven came to her side, but she stared at the floor. He glanced between the evae and human. "Friends?"

"No," she said quickly.

Thallon returned with a full tankard. "Hope you don't mind, but it's just water. Figured ale would just dehydrate you further."

"Thanks." She winced as her shriveled skin pulled and ached.

Thallon led her to a small table with several scrolls and notebooks. Y'ven stepped closer and crossed his arms. Thallon glanced at him with a sly smile. "This your bodyguard?" he quipped.

"No," she said flatly.

Thallon followed as Neer sat at the table. "So, what's a la-nathess doing way out in the desert?"

"What's an evae doing?"

He chuckled. "I'm on an important top-secret mission. It's real hush-hush." He smiled, waiting for a reaction, but her bleak expression never faltered, and with a scoffed laugh, he turned away. "Guess you really aren't the kind for conversation. Are all lanathess this...stiff?"

She remained silent, staring at him with sorrow and pain.

"All right...well, so long as you aren't trying to kill me, I guess we're okay. Can't say I've met a lanathess that isn't out for blood, though."

She turned away. "That makes two of us."

"So, that's why you're way out here in the sun-dried country of the dead. You're running."

"Don't mistake me for some common fool, *elf*. If I want you to know why I'm here, I'll tell you."

Licking his lips, he smiled wider. "Don't worry. Of all the theories and possibilities I've gathered on you in this conversation, being a fool was never one of them."

They were silent, and her gaze fell away. Not wanting the conversation to end, yet not knowing where it should lead, she asked a more obvious, important question. "Are you with the others?"

"The others?" He asked, his brow raised.

"The other evae. They were held in a vaxros camp and executed. One of them was magic. She could—"

"What?" The color washed from his face. Wide eyes burned into hers as he leaned forward, his posture full of tension. "She was drimil? Was she manipulating the elements?"

With a glance at Y'ven, who held the same bewilderment as herself, Neer returned her gaze to Thallon. "Yes."

"And she was with others?"

"Yes..."

"Oh no…oh no, no, no." Parchment crinkled, and leather notebooks bent as he hurriedly collected his things from the table.

"What is it?" Neer asked.

He came to a sudden stop and turned to her. "Was she executed?"

Unable to think under the pressure of his panic, she stumbled over her words. Coming to her senses, she recalled the fight, and explained, "No. She escaped with another. A man."

"*Kila…*" He shoved his things into a large satchel and slung it over his shoulder. "Whatever you do, *stay away from them.*"

"What?"

In his hysteria, he glanced around the room, as if searching for someone. "The vaxros aren't the only ones who want our kind dead. If you see those evae again…you run."

With another glance around the room, Thallon rushed to the door and fled into the night.

Chapter Eight

Hunted
Nerana

"The Hunters are ruthless, vicious, and vain. Knowing no mercy, they stand upon a mountain of corpses, a bag of gold replacing their soul."
— Tales of the hunters

THE NIGHT FADED INTO A grueling and painful dawn as Neer and Y'ven left the inn, setting off through the sweltering desert. She tucked beneath a thin cloak that provided minimal protection. A bright glow masked the world in a hue of orange as the sun nestled along the horizon.

Neer couldn't keep her thoughts from Thallon. His warning, in particular, repeated in her mind like a boisterous song that couldn't be silenced. Her eyes shifted to the sky, and she imagined the evae soaring through the air. She thought of the evaesh sorceress, or *drimil*, who cast rock and wind in her defense. Neer had never seen such power or magic. It was frightening, and exciting, to see the potential of such energy.

But the man, the one who remained calm and confident, unsettled her. Chills ran down her spine at the thought of his dark eyes peering into hers. His ice cold fingers and listless gaze correlated more with the dead than living. She pictured his face, hovering close to hers, and the captivation he expressed at the sight of her teal eyes.

They passed beneath an arched rock formation, and her view of the sky was obscured. Lifted from her thoughts, she closed her eyes and relished in the shade. With a deep breath, she came to a slow stop. Y'ven didn't seem to notice and carried on. Though she knew they shouldn't separate, she needed a moment's rest.

She found herself standing alone and glancing over her shoulder, searching for anyone who could be lingering in the distance. Every soaring vulture and swirl of dust caused her heart to race. She questioned if Y'ven was leading her to a village at all, or if there was truly another sorceress to be found.

Each time she doubted his sincerity, she reminded herself that he knew Avelloch, so she needed to trust him. Even if he abandoned her in the cave, which she struggled to believe, she knew he wouldn't put her in harm's way. He couldn't. Not after all they had been through. Not after sending this reminder of his affection and trust.

She had to put her faith in him. It was the only form of hope she had left — to know there was someone out there who understood her pain. To know there was someone who cared.

"Ürok!" Y'ven called. His yellow scars illuminated in the harsh sunlight, creating glowing patterns across his chest and arms.

She leered at the vaxros staring at her from yards away and cursed under her breath. "My name is Nerana."

"Apologies," he said as she approached him. "Ürok names not easily remembered."

She winced, stepping from the shadow and into the heat. "It's okay. Just call me Neer."

"Neer," he repeated.

"Yeah. It's the opposite of far."

She smiled at her bad humor and ignored Y'ven's disapproving headshake. Dru, who sat atop Y'ven's shoulder for the majority of the day, flew into the air, her wings moving quickly. She pulled a lock of his hair and pointed to the east. Neer and Y'ven followed her gaze.

Standing tall within the large rock formations were enormous marble monoliths. The large structures were beautifully arched along the tops, and deep cracks ran along the sun-bleached stone.

"What are they?" Neer asked.

"Statues. Ancient."

"But they were built out here in the desert…with white stone?" She stepped closer. "What are they for?"

Y'ven came to her side. "History. Many secrets. Best not to seek answers."

"You don't want to know how they got here or what they're for?"

"Is not the vaxros way."

Dru perched herself onto his shoulder as he continued toward his destination. Her large eyes were focused on the pillars in the distance. Neer, still mesmerized, was forced to push away her curiosity and follow after Y'ven and Dru.

The waning sunlight faded into darkness, and the glow of two bright moons filled the night. Neer was happy to be relieved of the constant sting gripping her burned and blistered skin. Y'ven slowed as the sun faded, walking at a pace better matching Neer's.

Together, they found a secluded place amidst a dense field of glowing flowered shrubs.

"We rest here," Y'ven said, gathering dried brush into a small pile. "Dru," he called, and she came instantly to his side.

Without speaking, his fiery companion created a ball of flames in her hands and set the tinder ablaze.

Neer stood by the fire, while Dru hovered within its heat, cross-legged with her eyes closed. Each night, Dru performed this strange behavior. In the time that passed since they set off toward Koehevar, where they were to meet this mysterious sorcereress, Neer had spoken hardly a word to her companions. The intense sunburn on her arms and sweltering heat left her too exhausted for conversation. Y'ven and Dru didn't seem to mind the silence, but to Neer, it was unbearable. Her loneliness was bitter, but the silence was deafening.

"What's she doing?" Neer asked about Dru.

"Absorbs energy from flame," he explained.

"What is she? Some sort of butterfly?" She leaned close to examine her.

Dru opened an eye and then closed it tightly in frustration. With a great huff, her face curled angrily. Neer, oblivious to Dru's anger, leaned closer, looking at her beautiful wings and fiery skin. One of her four wings was bent and broken. Dru puffed her chest and snapped her teeth at Neer, and she quickly backed away.

Y'ven chuckled while shaking his head. "Fire faeth," he explained. "Native to Aragoth and Iziazan.°"

He plucked a purple fruit from a nearby bush, tossed it to Neer, and then took another for himself. Neer bit into the fuzzy fruit, and her face twisted at the bitter juice. There wasn't much fresh food in the desert, and what little they came across always made her retch with its foul taste.

"How did you two meet?" She forced herself to take another bite.

"Dru was tortured. Lost two wings. Pulled from her back. Insolent children. Her home…her family, destroyed."

Dru fell from her meditations. Her eyes slowly opened in despair.

"Saved her. Was a child myself."

Neer looked at the faeth. Two wings raised high above her head, one of which was bent and crazed with white markings. "I'm sorry that happened to you."

° Pronunciation: Is-ee-ah-zan
Known as the land of fire, Iziazan is the ancestral home of the vaxros. When the volcano erupted five hundred years ago it left the continent heavily destroyed and forced the surviving natives to flee into the wastelands of Aragoth.

The faeth turned to the ground, and with a deep sigh, her eyes closed.

"I lost my family too," Neer said. "Insolent men raided my village. I was also taken and tortured. Seems we've come out strong."

Large eyes glanced at Neer. Dru turned to Y'ven, and he smiled sadly at his friend. Neer was puzzled when Dru suddenly took flight and fled into the darkness, leaving a fading trail of red light in her wake.

"I didn't mean to upset her," Neer said.

"Is all right. She will return. When ready."

Neer turned to the flames. Her mind shifted from the faeth to her own grief. She retrieved her sword and absently twisted it between her fingers. Her brows pulled together at its purple glow, and she wondered why it had regained its luminance after all this time.

Turning away, she exhaled a deep breath. Not wanting to fall into a state of despair, she changed the subject, asking, "Do all vaxros speak evaesh?"

"No," he remarked. "Do not allow their kind here. Do not allow *your* kind."

Their eyes met for a brief second before he turned and tossed the core of his meal into the flames. They popped and whirled as the fruit burned. "You are lucky," he said, "Drimil'Rothar is great ally. Much respect and admiration."

"Drimil'Rothar?"

She understood drimil meant magic user, but Rothar was the most powerful of the Divines. The overseer of the immortal planes. To use the words together in such a way caught her attention.

Surely, Rothar wouldn't subject himself to such things as mortal magic. And surely, the evae and vaxros didn't believe so much in the divines to name a respected sorceress after them.

Y'ven explained, "Drimil of Light. Most rare and powerful magic."

"Really? What can she do?"

He lightly smiled. "Talkative. Wondered if you had voice at all."

Neer gazed at her reflection within her sword, noticing the distant look in her dull eyes. "I used to. Now I just…don't have the care for words."

His smile faded at her shift in mood. He leaned forward with his hands together and eyed her weapon. Pointing to it, he asked, "Evaesh sword?"

She instinctively tightened her grip, protecting it from the man who asked about its nature. With careful thought, she slid the weapon safely into its sheath. "Yes."

"*Üroks* and evae share weapons?"

"Üroks?" She felt foolish for asking so many questions. Even in her extensive studies and lectures, Aragoth and the vaxros were never part of the lessons. Most texts shied away from teaching about the 'brutish beasts of the west'. Everything she, or any human, had ever heard were rumors and ghost stories.

Y'ven smiled and lifted his hands in defense. "Forgive. Have trouble with evaesh words. Ürok is weaker than evae, bigger than dreled."

A smile broke her mundane expression, realizing he was saying the word 'human'. "Why do you speak evaesh?"

He struggled to find the right word and with several attempts said, "No talk, no peace."

"You want to broker peace between your races?"

"Yes. Drimil'Rothar has"—he paused to find the right word—"*honored* me with acceptance. Childish wonderings of evae not foolish after all."

"She's evaesh?"

"Only evae accepted in Aragoth. Understand her purpose. Would not hinder her path."

"Why is she here? What does she need that's in Aragoth?"

Their conversation came to an abrupt end when Dru quickly returned. She whirled around Y'ven before hovering

69

close to his face. Her faint voice sounded like a bell chiming through the air in faint soprano melodies.

Y'ven suddenly leapt to his feet and ran into the desert with his war hammer. Stunned by his disappearance, Neer raced after him, struggling to keep up with the quick-moving warrior. While Y'ven had disappeared into the shadows, Dru's orange glow kept her in sight.

Neer huffed through tired lungs. The last thing she needed was another fight. Her body had hardly healed from her battle against the vaxros who held her captive. The wound on her shoulder was not yet scarred, and the tightness of her sun-drenched skin made every movement close to unbearable.

Her mind shifted back to her companions when a flash of heat replaced the coolness of night. Dru created a large ball of flames, and Neer was taken aback by the sight of another vaxros lying on the ground. His side was cut open, and a trail of blood spread across the ground.

Dru hovered above, pushing waves of heat and flame against his injury. The stranger grunted and twitched as Y'ven held him down, unwilling to relent as the stranger growled in agony.

"What are you doing?" Neer demanded, stricken with rage and shock. "Let him go!"

The stranger clenched his teeth, and his face twisted.

"Healing him," Y'ven explained without looking back.

The orange glow of Dru's flame slowly faded, and the shadows of night blanketed them in darkness. The now uninjured vaxros groaned before angrily pushing Y'ven away. He cut a harsh phrase and spit at him.

"What the hells?" Neer remarked, and Y'ven quickly lifted a hand to quiet her.

His eyes remained on the stranger as they spoke. The stranger gripped his freshly scarred side and struggled to sit upright.

When his gaze shifted to her, Neer realized how intensely she had been staring. Caught in the heavy glare of his orange eyes, she was filled with unease and turned away. He pointed a finger and spat in her direction.

Y'ven shook his head and stood. He placed the war hammer onto his back, and with a hard glance at the vaxros who refused to meet his gaze, he stepped away.

"What happened?" Neer asked. "We can't just leave him there!"

"We can," Y'ven snarled.

"What happened to him? Why was he spitting at us?"

He uttered an angry phrase in his native language. His lip twitched and jaw tightened. "Anger. Your kind did this."

Her eyes widened in horror. Turning to the injured vaxros, she examined the scar across his blood-soaked skin. Half a dozen fresh lacerations cut through faded yellow marks, marring his skin with razor-thin lines of red.

"A human?" her voice was quiet. It wasn't possible. Humans didn't enter the desert. The Order would never—

A flash of light ignited nearby and then Neer was thrown back by an explosion that erupted between her and Y'ven. Sharp rocks sliced into her skin as she was swept across the ground, leaving cuts across her sunburnt face and arms.

She came to a stop and lifted her eyes to the smoke and dust rising from a fresh crater. Lifting her arm, she expelled a pulse of energy that barreled through the haze. Her breath caught in her throat at the sight of a large man standing in the distance.

Dust filled the void and concealed the shadowy figure as her magic faded. Neer gasped when she was yanked by her shirt and pulled to her feet.

"Stand ürok!" Y'ven growled. "Fight!"

She was filled with strength and drew her sword from its sheath. Aching, burnt fingers gripped the hilt as she stared through the clearing dust. Her raw, blistered feet pulsed with every agonizing movement. She was running on pure adrenaline and hoped that it would see her through.

A bright glow appeared through the smog, similar to the first. She leaned closer, attempting to get a better view, when the ground erupted a second time. The blast sent waves of heat and rocks through the air that smashed against her limbs and side. She teleported aside and rolled across the dirt. Her ears rang, and her vision was blurred. The world slowly refocused, and pain pulsed through her fractured shin with every quick heartbeat.

She turned to the side and wailed as her leg twisted. Her voice carried through the now silent desert, and she fell back into the dirt.

Heavy boots vibrated the ground as the shadow appeared through the haze. Through the torture, Neer searched for her sword. Panicked eyes set on the silver handle, and she clawed for the weapon that was just out of reach. Holding her breath, she struggled to conjure her energy, but she couldn't gather the strength needed to apport her weapon.

Her teeth gritted and muscles ached as she extended beyond her fingers' reach. The coolness of the metal sat beneath her grasp, yet she was unable to pull it closer.

The sword clanked against rock as the shadow moved closer. Heavy footsteps vibrated the ground. He was coming for her. Moving quicker than she had time to prepare. Her heart thundered as she fought to grab her weapon, but she was too pained to move. Too weak and exhausted to think properly, her mind spun over what had happened and how to survive.

A dark shadow loomed overhead, and the man kicked her sword aside. His glowing white eyes were upon her as he leaned closer. Heat radiated from his metal hand, and he placed a molten-hot finger to her chin.

Her loud shriek filled the air as her skin bubbled and popped. Steam exhausted from his mechanical arm at the elbow and shoulder with a faint whistle. Neer shoved his hand away and leaned back, putting as much distance between them as she could.

She lay on the ground and whimpered as her body shook with pain. Her eyes shifted to Y'ven, and she was horrified to find him lying motionless on the ground. Dru hovered above him, igniting flames into a bleeding wound on his chest.

Neer returned her gaze to the stranger when he searched his pockets. Glass and metal clinked before he retrieved a syringe and filled it with black liquid. He brought the needle closer to her neck, and she struggled to back away.

As he leaned closer, she spotted the gleaming crossed-sword sigil of the Shadow Blades° embedded onto his breastplate. Her heart stopped as she gazed upon the familiar and wicked sigil. This man wasn't any ordinary mercenary—he was a Hunter. A magically enhanced byproduct of the Order of Saro.

The needle drew closer, and Neer met his gaze with a surge of vengeance and rage. The syringe disappeared from his grasp, and with a furious growl, he pinned her wrist to the ground just as it reappeared in her grip. She transported the syringe into her free hand and then plunged it into his neck.

Neer pressed the liquid into his body, and he pulled away from her. He snatched the half-empty syringe from his flesh, and the glass barrel shattered when he tossed it to the ground. His posture shifted and legs wobbled as he stumbled back, suddenly losing his balance.

Neer watched him with a careful eye as he swayed unevenly. His eyes crossed and shoulders slumped forward as the poison took effect. With a weak stomp in her direction, he collapsed to his knees and then fell into the dirt. The deep thud of his body trembled the ground. Dust clouded the air, causing Neer to cough and hack as it stuck to her throat.

˙ The Shadow Blade mercenaries are a band of thieves, murderers, and the altogether rotten sort. Upon Neer's disappearance, the Order lost track of her whereabouts, and the Shadow Blades, being more concerned of gold than morality or life, fought to collect the reward for her capture.

This mercenary, however, was of a different sort. He was more terrifying than the Blades she fought before. And even more dangerous.

She was immobile, unable to think or move as she stared at the hunter lying motionless in the dirt. Silence filled the air as she waited for a sign of life that never came. Surely, he was dead. If this was the poison used on her by the High Priest, the poison that blocked her energy, it would be enough to kill any normal human.

But Hunters weren't normal. And she feared it might not be enough to stop him.

She leaned closer and dug carefully through his pockets, finding empty syringes, fifty gold coins, and a crumbled wanted poster. The note read nearly the same as before,[*] though the image had been improved to show her current appearance, and the price of her head had increased by two hundred gold pieces.

"Ürok," Y'ven struggled to speak. He hobbled to her side, clutching a bloody, opened wound on his chest. "We must flee."

"I can't." She struggled to speak through the agony of her broken bone. "My leg."

"We must!" He snatched her from the ground and tossed her over his shoulder like a heavy burlap sack. With a deep, pained groan, he marched away from the hunter.

Her gaze set upon the man who tried to capture her. Beyond his body lay Avelloch's sword. In a panic, she reached out, and the weapon appeared instantly in her grasp.

---

[*] "Seeking of the highest decree: The Child of Skye. Born to the name Vaeda Vindagraav. Age 24, tan of skin, dark of hair, and teal of eyes. She has received The Mark high upon her right arm and must not be trusted. Any known whereabouts of such a demon shall be brought forth to the Order at once. Let no man fall heed to this devil's disguise. For the powers of Nizotl have drenched her soul, and she must be washed clean before entering the gates of Arcae. Reward for her capture has been increased to 300 gold pieces of any currency. Any harboring or unwillingness to bring forth her whereabouts will be met with the severest of punishments.
Go forth and carry in the Light."

The thumping in her chest slowed to a normal pace as she gripped the weapon that was nearly lost.

They traveled until Y'ven came to a slow, depleted halt. He placed Neer on the ground before collapsing to his knees in exhaustion and pain. Neer readied her sword when the faint sound of growling echoed all around. Y'ven hadn't noticed. He crawled forward, gasping and grunting.

Neer was silent, gazing upon the desert. Through the darkness came the glowing eyes of several small creatures. They stalked closer, leaping down from the large rock formations and winding carefully across the cold desert floor.

Panic fell through her. She couldn't fight, could hardly stand, yet they were coming. Sniffing and hissing, they stalked closer. Hungry snarls filled the once inaudible desert with the promise of rage and demise.

Glass vials clinked together and slipped through her shaky fingers as she searched too quickly through her leather pouch for a potion. A leathered dog leapt closer and was engulfed with flames as Dru laid her assault from above.

The creature flipped back with a pained yelp. Its body smacked against the dirt like a bag of broken bones, and as it faded to ash the others raced forward. Their claws scratched against rock and dirt as they drew nearer. Their glowing eyes filled the darkness in a wave of light.

"Start a fire!" Neer exclaimed while slicing her sword through a lunging canine. As it fell, another approached. Her sword sank deep into its skull, its veins glowing brighter with every hit. "Dru!"

The faeth jolted with attention and swiftly set a dry bush ablaze.

"Hold them off!"

Fire rained from the sky as Dru ignited the creatures with small flames. They raced around in a panic, screaming and dragging their boney, leathered faces across the ground.

Neer dripped a potion onto the burning bush, and shimmering magic rose slowly around the group, creating a wide barrier. "Come on…," she whispered. Sweat dripped from her nose as she focused on the flames. Her eyes moved to a dog running toward her, its glowing eyes hungry and open jaws ready to feast.

The heat of its breath faded when it smashed into an invisible barrier. Its body dissolved into dust and collected against the outer wall. Neer surveyed the creatures, which resolved to angrily stalking her enchanted fortress.

With a deep exhale, she fell onto her back and closed her eyes. The barrier was left open at the top, allowing smoke to filter into the cold night air. Y'ven collapsed onto his side. His heavy breaths pressed against the flames and sent embers floating through the small dome.

Dru walked across Neer's shoulder and then gently touched her cheek.

"Good work, Dru," Neer said. She gasped when pain erupted through her leg.

Dru glanced at Y'ven, who lay unconscious across the fire. Her large eyes returned sadly to Neer. She floated to her leg, preparing to heal it with flames.

"Don't," Neer warned. "Fire doesn't heal me the way it does Y'ven. You'll injure me further." As the pain swelled further, she forced herself to relax. Sweating with tremors, she turned to Dru.

"Hey," she started, and the faeth turned to her with worried eyes. "Can you speak my language?"

Twisting her hands, she regretfully shook her head.

"But you can understand me."

She nodded proudly. Flames whirled as her excitement flourished.

"Those dogs…They're creatures of darkness?"

Dru watched the fiendish dogs scratching and nipping at the barrier. With a nod, she returned her attention to Neer.

"So, they can only hunt in the shadows," she spoke to herself. "We should be safe for the night in this barrier. Is Y'ven all right?"

Dru nodded sorrowfully. Neer exhaled a relieved sigh and closed her eyes. When a soft, tiny hand touched her face, she turned to see Dru standing beside her. The faeth dragged a crinkled parchment by the paper's edge. She gazed at Neer quizzically and motioned to the picture.

"That's me," she explained. "Where I'm from, magic is forbidden. They sent that mercenary to find me. His name is Thorne."

Dru turned away as Neer became lost in thought. Thorne was the most famed and feared Hunter in all of Laeroth. Neer had heard many tales of his ruthless and cold-hearted ways. His most notable feature, and what caused Neer to instantly recognize the man she'd never met, was his metal face-plating and iron arm.

Like many other boys who were sold or taken by the Order, Thorne was discarded after failing to become a Knight, but not before the Priests sliced out his tongue. Before his execution, however, he was bought by the Shadow Blades and transformed into the fierce Hunter he was today.

Neer blinked her thoughts away when Dru lovingly rubbed her cheek. Flames brightened Neer's face as Dru set the poster ablaze. She then nestled into her hair, where she lay for the rest of the night.

CHAPTER NINE

AENWYN
Aélla

"Just as the water flows across the land and fires burn in the breeze, we must all coexist as one."
— Fyet'muskar; tome of the elements

A SHEET OF DARKNESS BLANKETED the sky, eliminating the day's light. Ash swept across the land like a gentle black snow. The wounded were healed of their ailments as they sat around a large fire in deep meditations. In their palms rested small flames. A woman, whose body resembled an evae more so than a vaxros, hovered within the tendrils of the center blaze.

Her waist-length hair wisped and twirled. Bright embers flickered strong, devouring the bodies lying idle at her feet. A swirl of fire wrapped around her, giving the illusion of a serpent glowing orange and red, constricting its way around her legs and waist.

Waves of heat brushed against the faces of those surrounding the woman. Their long hair and tattered clothes waved in its gentle, pulsating breeze as the flames grew stronger.

Aélla watched from her place in the rocks as they performed their rituals. Her eyes flittered to the cave entrance.

Most vaxros wouldn't dare live so close to the ruins. They believed them to be sacred and dangerous, meant only for those who left them behind. Stories were told over campfires of the magic and mystery haunting the ancient tombs.

Few vaxros tribes made the vow of protection and dedicate their lives to honor the sacrifice of the ancestors and prevent anyone from entering or desecrating the hallowed caves.

Aélla was lucky they overlooked her presence, focusing instead on their wounded and lost. It was a harrowing time, one she felt sorrow taking advantage of. But she understood guile would see her through this journey. It would see an end to the darkness plaguing the world.

While they were deep in their meditations, Aélla stepped through the rocks and entered the caves. Sunlight filtered inside, revealing a smooth stone slope leading further in. Jagged rocks, dripping with condensation, created a narrow tunnel leading downward into an open pit.

Following the slope, Aélla placed her hands on the damp walls. The cold rock was rough beneath her hands. Her heart pounded loudly in her ears as she slipped further into the darkness. Anaemiril was not a place for the lost or ill-prepared. Anything could be lurking beneath the surface, and though she was prepared, the First Blood had a way of guiding their intruders deep into the labyrinth, never to be seen again.

The narrow passage widened, and the slope transformed into steps that descended into a vast cave. Stalagmites and gleaming crystals filled the empty space. Glowing moss, twisting vines, and mushrooms illuminated the wide chamber. Small trees, alive with flowers and leaves, left the air fresh and warm. Water dripped from the ceiling, creating shallow pools surrounding the rock formations. The quiet trickle reverberated through the endless room. Stones of different sizes laid a crooked and uneven path at the base of the stairs. Vines twisted through deep cracks beneath Aélla's feet, wrapping around the stones and weaving them together.

Voices whispered through her mind, and the calming chimes of ghosts long past drew her further into the caverns. They spoke to her, clutching her soul like a wounded dove, cradling her thoughts with comfort and ease.

She didn't fight it, though she knew she should. But the depth of their magic was far too great for her to overcome. She was tranquil, ready to accept their guidance. Ready to follow their every whisper and plea.

Aélla followed the path and found herself deeper beneath the surface. She was utterly and entirely alone. For a moment, the crushing weight of such isolation weighed on her with the realization of how far she'd traveled, and of how much further she'd have to go.

The magic of the First Blood was more powerful than any the world had ever seen, and it all lay here, beneath the crest of the world, buried under the feet of the living.

Should she find herself in trouble, no one would come to her aid.

No one would hear her screams.

As the voices grew louder, they overpowered her thoughts. She clutched her ears, hoping to rid of the whispers echoing within her mind. Realizing the magnitude of their power and the strength of their will, she gave in.

Fighting against them was futile. If she was ever to find the rástalfür° and enter the realm of elements, she needed to trust the spirits of her ancestors. There was no other way.

Aélla pressed on, determined to find the staff and complete her mission.

At the end of the path was a wide arched doorway. Ivy and glowing flowers coiled through the stone. Beautiful, swirled patterns were etched into the frame. Their designs held no concept of age, immaculately preserved by the deep magic of the cave.

The lull of soft voices fell silent as she stepped through the opening and came to a narrow room. Sunlight poured in through a thick crack trailing across a tall ceiling. Ivy climbed

---

° A magical staff which is used as a key to open the final realm of Aenwyn.

the walls and covered the floor in a carpet of green. It traveled across the stone, wrapping around the base of a large altar like slithering snakes.

Curved half-walls surrounded the elevated statue of a woman. Her gown flowed beautifully across her feet, while her arms stretched out wide to embrace the sun. Closed eyes and a soft smile gave her a gentle, relaxed appearance.

Aélla stood in awe of the sculpture, over forty meters in height, whose sun-bleached marble illuminated beneath golden rays. Mist glistened in the evae's eyes as she carefully approached the altar.

The cracked stone was rough beneath her fingers as they slid across the ancient walls. She came to the base of the statue, inscribed with runes and ancient texts, and she knelt to touch the dry stone.

Staring up at the enormous statue, she was filled with peace and confidence. Aélla cupped her hand around the sharp edge of her dagger, and through quick breaths, she sliced her hand. The dagger dropped to the ground with a loud clink, and blood pooled across her palm.

Her trembling hand swiped across the runes, and the statue shifted. The old marble groaned, and the runes glowed. Light emitted from the cracks and swirled within the effigy. The half-walls creaked before lifting from the ground to orbit the altar.

Mystified, Aélla brought her attention to the runes below. The glowing epitaph brightened, and with another weary glance at the statue, Aélla placed her hand on the runes.

Her back straightened and neck extended as visions entered her mind. One scene after another, she watched the warning left behind.

Bubbling magma flowed deep beneath the ground, moving toward the image of a vicious draak. Resting at its feet was a pillar glowing with red energy.

The scene faded to another.

Large birds soared through the clouds. Through the mist, they came to enormous floating mountains. Winds swept through the air as the creatures careened through drifting rock and hanging vines.

A third vision revealed a dangerous jungle. Creatures of darkness lurked within the brush, hissing and screeching in their rage. An enormous Koehlaeuat° stood amidst the canopy of much smaller trees.

The last scene brought her to a valley where an ancient temple rested within the center of a stone village.

Aélla withdrew her hand from the runes as the visions faded. The statue whined and buckled as the warmth and light of its energy faded. She watched the walls shift back into place, and the magical structure once again became a lifeless statue.

Lying on the ground at her feet was a beautiful wooden staff. The weapon held four crystal shards twisted within branches along the top.

She gripped the staff and glanced at the figure. With a bow, she gave her respect to the woman for which the model was based. "Thank you, Master Aenwyn."

Her eyes were glued to the staff as she traveled through the musty, ancient cave. Touching the clear shards, she thought back to the vision she received and pondered over its meaning. While they were clear in their viewing, they held no meaning to Aélla, who had never stepped foot in the desert prior to the start of her journey.

The only knowledge she had of this quest was given by the First Blood in a temple known as the ilitran. It was there she could meditate and receive the wisdom of their magic, left behind by the wisest of sorcerers. They guided her path,

---

° Known by the humans simply as Tree.
These mysterious, mystical trees hold immense magical energy, and have been known to heal those who meditate beneath its branches.

foretelling of the dangers she would face should she start this treacherous pilgrimage.

So far, she'd traveled deep into the mountains of Uadin and to the shores of Erasin, where she entered the realms of alteration and convalescence. Now, her journey led her to a more perilous path as she searched to find the remaining realms with a sorceress she had never met.°†

A sorceress, she feared, who might be more dangerous than the prophecies foretold.

Without knowing the full extent of her journey, or how to enter the realms, she was left to find the pieces along the way. She was warned her foolish endeavors could cost her everything, yet still, she came, alone and unafraid, determined to do what was destined of her.

Sunlight brightened her skin as she stepped closer to the entrance, and large shadows became clearer within the white opening. Guards waited with their weapons in hand.

Clutching the staff tightly, Aélla stepped out into the sun and awaited the punishment for her treachery.

---

* The mountains of Uadin were once the seat of power in the ancient days of the First Blood. Though the dreleds and dwarves consider the mountains their home, they've long since moved from the rugged terrain and spread themselves throughout the continent. What was once a glorious and monumental place of power is now a wasteland of ancient ruins and inaccessible caves.
Mountainous and tropical islands, Erasin remains virtually uninhabited due to its lack of fertile soil, and its high population of territorial delvine. Though the sea creatures are unable to live on land, the beautiful and deceptive race has taken claim of the shores and outlying waters, bringing down any ships or witless boaters who find themselves passing by.

† Alteration and convalescence are two of the seven realms of magic.
Located along the rugged coastlines of Erasin, the Realm of Convalescence gifts its sorcerers with the ability of healing.
Hidden deep in the ruins of Uadin, the Realm of Alteration gifts its sorcerers with empathic and telepathic abilities.

CHAPTER TEN

FATES ALIGNED
Nerana

"Nothing is fated. Everything is a choice, and you must be strong enough to make it."

— Master Reiman

NEER RESTED IN Y'VEN'S ARMS as he carried her through the desert. Her broken leg had swollen to double its size and throbbed with pain. Cuts covered her body and slit her clothes, leaving her cloaked in thick, dry blood.

When the sun rose over the desolate plains, the creatures of night had vanished into the shadows. Thorne had yet to make another appearance, but Neer knew he was out there. A simple injection wouldn't fell the most famed and dangerous mercenary. He would find her again. It was only a matter of time.

"There," Y'ven stated. His eyes set to a village of ruins ahead.

Dru whirled around in excitement as they approached the village of Kohevar. Her aura was bright, and her wings flittered too quick to see.

Angry voices filtered through the air, and a loud scream broke through the silence. Y'ven stiffened, coming to a stop. The world was quiet as they waited, and at the sound of another shriek, Y'ven charged forward.

At the edge of the ruins, they could hear the shuffling and murmurs of the villagers. Their taunting sneers and growls cut through the atmosphere like glass.

The crack of a whip was followed by the agonizing scream of a broken woman. Neer was placed onto the ground, and she stumbled into a half-standing wall. Y'ven barreled into the city with his war hammer, and Dru was steady at his side, glowing fiercely with flames.

Neer dragged herself from one rubble home to another. Her broken leg trailed behind the other, riddled with agony. She hadn't made it three feet before collapsing into another wall. With her eyes closed, she breathed in short, pained breaths.

Shadows passed through narrow openings between the ancient walls, and she could see several vaxros standing together, shouting and growling at one another. Through gritted teeth, she exhaled a raspy breath and forced herself closer.

Coming to a crumbled home, she sat atop a slanted rock and examined the crowd. The woven trinket was held tight in her fist as she searched for a familiar face.

A tinge of hope brightened her dull eyes at the thought of reuniting with Avelloch, though she knew it was just a foolish wish. Had he been there, she knew he'd have come with Y'ven to find her. Still, she clung to the slight bit of hope, and her heart skipped at the sight of platinum hair.

The long, wavy locks were covered in blood and dirt. Leaning closer, she was crushed by the weight of disappointment when she found it wasn't Avelloch, but instead, was a woman.

Y'ven stood before her captor, growling with indignation. He pointed at the woman tied to the post. She slumped forward on her knees, bloody lashes covering her back.

"Drimil!" Y'ven exclaimed.

The villagers were silenced by his mention of this word. They stared at each other, conflicted and ashamed. As Y'ven spoke to them, the captor tightened his fists. They argued further before the woman was pulled to her feet.

Her wounds shriveled and tore, and she cried in pain. The vaxros pulled her head back, revealing her evaesh face and pointed ears. She groaned as he spoke his native language and then shoved her to the ground. Y'ven twitched, stopping himself from aiding her as she knelt on the ground, gathering her strength. Slowly, she crawled to her knees and crouched forward, looking to the villagers, who sneered and growled.

She spoke too quietly for Neer to understand. Blood glistened and slipped across the deep, red wounds on her back. The woman lifted her hand into the air, and white magic swirled around her fingers. As it brightened, the village was silent with shock. Neer couldn't believe it, though somehow it was true. Another sorceress existed, and their paths had aligned. But fate was a word she'd pushed far from her mind. After Nhamashel, she decided it was a fool's wit to believe in predestination.

Everyone carved their own path. Nothing was meant to be.

Still, she couldn't deny that being in the presence of another sorceress was far from coincidence. Her eyes were glued to the evae as she touched her back, and the wounds slowly healed.

The deepest wound continued to bleed, while shallower marks and cuts were fused into vanishing scars. Her captor stepped back. His whip fell to the ground, leaving remnants of flesh and blood along the dirt.

"I am Drimil'Rothar," the woman proclaimed as she stood. Y'ven translated her words for his people. "I do not seek passage to your village, but to tre'lan Aenwyn. By agreement of the *sin'lohai,* you must allow me passage." She stepped to the angry vaxros. Her shredded robes exposed the bloody skin along her back. "Now that you understand the truth of my identity, you *will* grant immunity."

With a furious snarl, the vaxros glanced at Y'ven and spit in his face. The evae's face twisted, but never did she respond. As soon as it appeared, her anger vanished. She was calm and reserved, watching the vaxros before her. His deep voice sawed through the air, and he placed the sharp end of a bloody spear to Y'ven's throat.

The woman grabbed his arm, and his angry eyes flashed to hers.

"Don't," she warned. Her voice was calm and fierce. "I have allowed you the honor of punishing me for my crimes, but do not underestimate the strength of my power."

The vaxros pulled away from her grasp. He turned with an angry growl and then marched through the village. The others watched her with careful eyes.

Her gaze moved from one person to the next, before landing on Neer. The calmness of her eyes shifted to shock. "Is this her?" she asked.

Y'ven glanced at Neer and gave a subtle nod.

The woman gripped her magic staff tightly, and with a deep breath, she marched to Neer's side. Neer felt the crushing weight of disappointment when she thought of Avelloch and realized he wasn't there.

"What's your name?" the woman asked.

Neer was surprised by the gentleness of her approach. Despite her fierceness and severity, she was tranquil and kind.

"Nerana," she said with a wince as pain shot through her leg.

"I'm Aélla." She smiled pleasantly.

"Wh…where is Avelloch?" Her eyes rolled aside, and she lost focus.

Aélla softly touched her arm. "Just rest, Nerana. We will speak soon."

She tried to blink away the darkness, but the pull of sleep overcame her. Staring at the woman hovering above, Neer could see only her dark blue eyes before everything disappeared.

Moonlight cast upon a sleeping world. Aurora drifted through the sky, carrying with it a luminance of green and blue. Shadowy creatures stalked the night, and fire burned within an invisible dome. Neer stirred before waking from her deep slumber. She sat up with a huff, wiping her face to rid it of her drowsiness.

Across the fire sat Aélla, who watched Neer with careful eyes. Y'ven leaned against the barrier with his arms crossed, while Dru hovered within the flames.

With a sniff, Neer ran her fingers through her hair and sat straighter. An ache in her back caused her to groan, and she bent her knee, only to realize her broken bone had healed. The blood had been cleansed to reveal her unmarked skin. She ran her fingers along her shin, feeling no scratch or lump in its place.

"How…" She looked around, before noticing the remnants of travaran nearby. With another glance to the evae, her shoulders fell. A beautiful staff with four dormant crystals glimmered in the firelight. "You're a sorceress?"

"Yes. I'm Drimil'Rothar. It is a title meaning *The Sorceress of Light*." She paused as Neer gripped her forehead. "I'm the last known magic user of my kind…the hope of peace."

Neer sighed. Her mind was muddled with sleep and confusion. "Where is Avelloch?" she asked, not interested in the life or purpose of this stranger. "Is he alive? How do you know him?"

A sympathetic smile crossed Aélla's lips. "He is alive and safe in the forest. We are…old friends."

Neer dug the trinket from her pocket and wrapped her fingers around its edges. "Why didn't he accompany you? Why did he send *this* in his stead?"

"My kind are not allowed passage through the desert."

"You're here!" Neer exclaimed. Her daring eyes met with the calm demeanor of the stranger.

"I am allowed to be for the purpose of my journey. Should the vaxros hinder my passage, my people would have reason to go to war. We do not want that."

"Your kind are attacking these villages. They attacked *my* villages."

"The klaet'il are acting on their own. As they always have."

Neer leaned forward with a huff. Her thumb rubbed along the edge of the trinket, while her eyes were distant and hard. How she wished for the simple woven circle to bring her peace, as it was believed to do.

But peace was a lie, and she wouldn't find comfort in its faith.

Breaking the heavy silence, she asked, "Why did you come for me? How did you know I'd be here?"

"I received a vision that I would meet a drimil—*a magic user*—here in the desert. I had to be sure you would not disappear."

"Well, here I am." She looked at the evae. "Now what?"

Aélla smiled. "Now, we journey together. To the forbidden realms. To the places of great power and energy."

"I've my own journey to get through."

"Yes. You seek to destroy your leaders. They've treated you as an outsider, and for that, you've had to live in isolation."

Neer's jaw tightened, and her eyes narrowed. She watched the flames and became angry. Unsettled. "Did you learn all of this in your *vision*?"

"No…Avelloch told me."

The anger faded to shock. Neer breathed quicker and wrapped her arms around her folded knees, the trinket still safely in her grasp. "You just expect me to follow you? I don't even know what you're doing. You could be working with the ones that destroyed the villages."

"I fought against the ones that destroyed the village. My journey will take me to each of the magical realms where I'll gather enough strength to put an end to the chaos and darkness that's plaguing our land."

"And you were told to do all this in a vision? You were told to find me out here and drag me along with you? Like I'm some sort of stray dog."

Aélla moved to Neer's side and lifted her hands to Neer's head. "May I?" she asked.

Through suspicious eyes, Neer agreed.

The tingling warmth of magic overcame her when their eyes met. Vivid images replaced her sight. She could hardly process one vision before the next flashed by. A glowing tree towering over a green canopy. Fires burning and the smell of blackened flesh. A cloaked shadow fading to black. A body lying in the desert. Teal eyes open. A dark shadow shrouding a crumbled, burning village.

The vision faded to white. A glowing rune came into view and rested along the side of an ancient building. The image lingered before fading to darkness.

Neer gasped when Aélla removed her hands. She gripped her forehead and closed her eyes, trying desperately to reimagine all she'd seen. "What was that?"

"It was a message, left behind by my ancestors. I was able to piece it all together over time, but some things still aren't very clear."

"How did you know that was me?"

She smiled proudly. "You are the sorceress with teal eyes. It was not hard to figure that one out."

Aélla crawled across the enclosure and retrieved a scroll from her bag. The rune from the vision marked the page, every small detail drawn perfectly on the pristine parchment. At the bottom, it read *Aenwyn* in beautiful evaesh calligraphy.

"I found this in a book written by the First Blood. This is where we need to go."

"What is it?"

"This is the gateway to the tre'lan Aenwyn. To the *Realm of Elements.*" She displayed her staff. "The crystals are meant to collect energy from each of the four elements. Fire… Rock… Water… Air…" Her blue eyes met with Neer's. "This is a key. We must collect the energy from these elements to enter the temple of Elandorr, where we can harness the full potential of our elemental energy."

90

"We?" Neer asked. "I don't have elemental energy."

Aélla smiled. "There is only one way to find out." She guided Neer's hands to the ground and directed her to close her eyes.

Neer did as she was told.

Focused on her breathing and energy, she felt a distant spark deep within her. The tug and pull of something heavy weighed her chest. Energy spiraled through her, converging with the slow rhythm of the world, and it softly pulsed like a steady heartbeat.

Every vibration chiseled through her, growing stronger the deeper her connection became. She thought of the evaesh sorceress who fought against the vaxros, and she grew fearful. To control the elements was dangerous and unpredictable. She wouldn't have the strength to carry out magic of such magnitude.

"Concentrate," Aélla warned with a soothing calmness.

Neer washed away the harrowing thoughts and focused once again on the energy pouring through her. Her body felt heavy as stone.

"Look," Aélla whispered.

Her eyes fluttered open, and she was stricken by the sight before her. Small rocks and pebbles, once lying on the ground, were now hovering inches from the dirt. They vibrated as her untrained magic kept them afloat.

She exhaled a breathless laugh and smiled widely. Her concentration waned before the weight of the world lifted from her shoulders. The pressure filling her chest erased, and the rocks fell to the ground.

Neer leaned back with a deep breath, the smile still stretched across her lips. Sweat beaded across her forehead, and the heat of magic turned her skin a shade of pink.

Aélla's smile was pleasant as she watched Neer with admiration and pride. "You are a sorceress, Nerana. There is so much that you can do."

Staring at her hands, Neer was overcome with curiosity and strength. She had the power to stop the High Priest, had the power to avenge all those she had lost. If she wanted, she could destroy all those who inflicted pain and misery upon the innocent. The world could be cleansed of their impunity and slaughter.

"How do we do it?" she asked, still staring at her hands. "How do we get the energies and unlock our potential?"

"There are four realms in Aragoth that each hold a specific elemental energy. If we can find these realms, we can extract the energy needed."

Neer looked up from her hands. "You don't know where they are?"

"Not yet. The vision given to me at the altar of Aenwyn showed a large bird flying through floating mountains. Y'ven believes this to be the k'laea.° We can get to their den if we take the *avia* to the mountains."

"*Avia*?" Neer asked.

"It's a flying boat. There is one in the city of Zaos.† We will rest for the evening, and before dawn, we will set out again." She placed the staff next to her and drank from her canteen.

Neer wondered what would come of this journey, or if she should take her chances in Laeroth. She picked up a rock from the ground and twisted it between her fingers. This evae could be leading her down a path she wasn't meant to take. She could

---

° Pronunciation: kuh-LAY-ah
Enormous bird-like creatures who dwell within the highest Peaks of Draak.
These creatures are known for their seclusion as they never leave their homes in the mountains.
Many adventurers have died in their pursuits to climb the mountains and peek at the mystical and rare k'laea, whose blood is said to reverse death and heal all wounds.

† Roughly translated to mean city of lights, Zaos was built by the y'lenae centuries ago. The desert natives worked together with the Rhyl clan of Nyn'Dira to create the magically fortified city. Some believe the pillars containing the barrier was built by the First Blood, though there is no evidence supporting such a claim.

find herself in much more peril than she would have on her own.

If she'd learned anything from her sad excuse of a life, it was that even the most honorable and kind weren't to be trusted. Everyone would betray you in the end.

Through a frustrated sigh, she tossed the rock to the ground and leaned against the barrier. Her eyes moved to the desert, which was empty with darkness.

She'd never survive in the desert on her own, and with the instability of her teleportation, she could wind up further in the wastelands should she attempt to flee with her magic. But the thought of following this stranger through unknown lands was just as unsettling.

"Nerana," Aélla started with a kind voice, "do not feel like you're forced to join me. The choice is always yours. If you ever want to leave, you may do so."

Aélla's smile eased her growing confusion, and she watched as the evae curled into a blanket and closed her eyes.

CHAPTER ELEVEN

HOPE AND RAGE

"It is a great burden to carry such energy and strength, for the fate of the world rests on the choices of its bearer."

— Rila Thrudanir, First Blood Drimil

HOURS LATER, NEER WOKE FROM a restless sleep. The fire had faded into embers, leaving the remnants of a dying heat to keep her warm. Her sleepy eyes focused on the trinket lying nearby.

She slowly grabbed it and sat with a groan. Y'ven slept soundly with Dru across the fire, while Aélla's mat was empty. Rubbing her eyes, she looked through the darkness and spotted a bright glow nearby.

Following the light, she came upon Aélla perched on the ground, resting on her knees. Her fists were pressed together as she sat in deep meditations. Three braids pulled her white hair back to expose her slender face.

Behind her, leaning against a large boulder, were bloody, shredded robes and the magical staff. Neer ran her finger along the edge of the wooden weapon, which glimmered in the moonlight.

"Good morning."

Neer flinched at the sound of Aélla's voice. She quickly stepped away and crossed her arms. "Sorry, I was just admiring your staff."

"It's all right." She fell from her meditations and gracefully picked up the staff. "Beautiful, isn't it? I had to travel into Anaemiril° to find it."

"You went into Anaemiril?"

"I had no other choice," Aélla explained. "I heard that *you* journeyed through Anaemiril as well, in the Trials of Blood. You're very fortunate to have survived."

"I don't feel very fortunate." She turned to the sky. Visions of Loryk's body, bloated and rotting, flashed through her mind. She was trapped alone with him for days after Klaud and Avelloch's departure. The smell of his corpse and blue tint of his skin were forever engraved within her mind. The emptiness of his loss still burned in her like a freshly lit fire. "It doesn't matter," she said, breaking herself from the intense memories. "What's done is done."

Aélla placed her hand atop Neer's. "We will make this right."

Neer took a deep breath and wiped her eyes, feeling a bit calmer. "So," she started, in an attempt to change the subject, "you're here to enter the realms?"

"Yes. The energy that keeps the world from falling into chaos has shifted. We are imbalanced, and only I have the capability of bringing that energy back to order."

"Sounds like shit luck. Being the savior of the world isn't as wonderful as it sounds."

Aélla's face twisted. "Yeah," she said with a scoff. "It's pretty shit."

When their eyes met, they shared a smile. It wasn't normal for Neer to come across anyone who could relate to her in such a way. She was glad to find that connection with

---

°Anaemiril is an ancient and forbidden cave system that travels beneath Laeroth. It belonged to the Ahn'Clave, or First Blood, who vanished long ago.

Neer, Loryk, and the others traveled together through a small portion of Anaemiril known as the Trials of Blood. This trial led them to Nhamashel, a cave within the system of Anaemiril.

another, especially one so similar in fate. Though Aélla was more revered as a sorcerer than condemned, she still understood the weight such power could bring. She understood the damnation and responsibility.

"Have you decided to join us?" Aélla asked.

Neer crossed her arms. She'd spent the better part of the night contemplating her fate and deciding which path to choose. "I was given a prophecy by the divine Numera. She told me to visit four trials, if energy I seek. I think she was referring to the realms." She paused in thought. "I don't know if I believe in fate anymore. If there is divine intervention, or if life is just a coincidence…but the people that I trust most believe it." Her fingers absently curled around the hilt of her sword. "If going to the realms is the only means of stopping the High Priest, then it's what I'll do."

Their eyes shifted to the sky when the shadow of a bird passed overhead. A raven batted its wings as it circled above before fading into the darkness of the sky.

"Do you meditate?" Aélla asked, her eyes falling back to Neer.

"Not really," Neer said.

With a smile, Aélla patted the ground, and Neer took her place. Aélla straightened her back and placed her fists together. "Do you know the purpose of meditation for drimil?"

"To control your energy," Neer said, now suddenly unsure.

"Partially. As full sorcerers, we're connected to the deepest levels of energy and life. We can feel the pulse of the world and taste the breath of the wind. We meditate to absorb and entwine with this energy. Once you're capable of understanding your own power, you can control it."

"Easier said than done."

"Yes, but it *can* be done." As their gazes met, Aélla comforted Neer with her soft motherly smile. "Why don't I show you?"

Neer silently agreed and followed Aélla's direction to sit straighter and press her fists together. She closed her eyes and listened as Aélla softly spoke. Her voice was hardly a whisper and soothed the unease that once filled her with doubt.

"Energy is the source of all life," Aélla explained. "What we do with it determines how it manifests."

Neer took steady, deep breaths. She focused on her connection to the world, still unable to feel the surge of energy Aélla explained. Growing frustrated by her inability, she became rigid and tense.

Aélla placed her hand on Neer's shoulder, and the unrest dissolved into relaxation. Soothed by her calm gesture, Neer retained her posture and continued with her meditations.

Aélla continued, "Ill intentions will cast dark energy, which can flourish into pain and death. Anger, vengeance, sorrow, and greed can lead us to do unforgivable things with our power." She paused, watching as Neer remained calm. "Good intentions will cast light energy, which can flourish into serenity and peace. Purity, forgiveness, joy, and kindness can lead us to do things out of compassion. Each are equally important, though the pull of dark energy is far greater and more manipulative than light. As sorcerers, we must always fight against any emotions or thoughts that could lead us to unleash our power in a destructive way.

"Every drimil can use their energy however they choose. The fate of their choices is in their hands."

Neer slowly opened her eyes as Aélla's voice faded. Calmness replaced the discontent as she sat with a stranger who understood magic far more than she ever could. "You said our fates are in our hands…," Neer started, to which

97

Aélla agreed. "What if fate has chosen a path for me?" She paused. "What if I don't *want* to let go of my anger?"

Aélla was silent. Her lips fell apart in shock and agony. A thin crease formed between her brows, and she said, "Then our only hope...is me."

CHAPTER TWELVE

STEAM AND STABLE INN

"The greatest wonders of the world can be seen through the eyes of the eagle, the fish, and the hound. 'Tis a good thing I'm all three!"

— Ronar, the great traveling dreled

TWO DAYS PASSED AS THE group trekked across the scorching desert. Neer and Aélla were covered by thin cloaks, while Y'ven and Dru remained exposed to the sunlight. Aélla walked behind them, admiring the vibrant scars across Y'ven's back that formed a circle between his shoulder blades.

"Y'ven," Aélla started, "your scars are beautiful. What do they mean?"

"They are indications of my *shelarr*." He pointed at a small design on his right-side chest. "*Atülg'shelarr*. My home. Childhood."

"And the big sun on your back?"

He reached back and ran his fingers across the faded scar. With distant eyes, he exhaled a shallow breath. "*Müz'rogg.* Mark of *al'yavan*."

"The what?" Neer asked, intrigued by their conversation.

Aélla added, "The al'yavan warriors. They are among the most brave and fierce fighters in the world." Her eyes flashed to Y'ven. "It's a privilege to be escorted by such an esteemed warrior."

Y'ven's forlorn expression brightened into a soft smile.

Neer turned away and took a gulp from her canteen, finishing off her water. The sting of her burned skin caused her to wince, and she tucked further into her cloak, trying desperately to shield herself from the sun. But the heat from its rays couldn't be quelled.

Aélla turned her attention to the sky, where the raven drifted ahead of them in wide circles.

"Is that the same raven from last night?" Neer asked.

Aélla smiled. "Yes. His name is Altvára."

"You named him?"

She nodded happily, causing Neer to fade further into confusion. "Why would you do that?"

"Altvára is a dren'seol. It means with a beautiful soul." Her eyes remained on the raven. "Evae have a special bond with nature. We can commune with animals – sometimes finding our own dren'seol that will be with us until the end."

Neer lifted her hand to block the harsh sunlight from her eyes as she looked up at the raven. "So, he's like a pet?"

"A what?" Aélla giggled, and Neer was puzzled by her confusion of such a common term.

Not wanting to perplex her further, Neer asked, "He's loyal to you? Like a companion or something?"

Aélla thought for a moment before nodding. "Yes, I suppose. Dren'seol are loyal to the person they connect with. It's a bond you form that doesn't ever go away. Sometimes, your dren'seol will also look after the people you care most about." Her smile was soft as she gazed at Altvára.

They followed Altvára to a small building perched in the middle of empty plains. The whistle and hiss of steam filled the air, escaping from several pipes along a dark gabled roof. Its green and blue walls stood out against the brown landscape. Uneven windows and a lopsided balcony made the building look hurriedly built and unstable. Two metal canisters were connected by pipes to the building.

Near the building was a stable where large upright reptiles, with short arms and large hind legs, stood inside wide stalls. Thick saddles were strapped to their backs, covering most of the glowing spots lining their spines and tails.

"Vestrils!" Aélla said of the reptiles. "I've never been so happy to see a vestril!°"

The old wooden door creaked as they stepped into the crooked building and out of the blazing sun. Neer exhaled a deep breath as cold air circulated through the small room and relieved the ache from her sunburnt skin. Shelves filled with small trinkets lined the dark walls. A wooden table with rolled parchments, unused quills, and bottled ink rested in the center of the room, making the space feel cluttered and cramped.

"*Brahg*!" a pudgy dreled with a wide smile and unshapely beard exclaimed. He stood on a tall stepstool behind a counter, making himself eye level with Aélla and Neer.

Y'ven stepped forward and spoke to the shop keep in his native language. The dreled's eyes widened, and he turned to Aélla. He disappeared behind the counter after leaping from the stool and waddled around to Aélla's side.

"Drimil," he spoke evaesh as he took her hand and bowed. "'Tis truly an honor."

"The honor is mine," she said with a genuine smile.

With another bow, he stepped back behind the counter. "Welcome to the Steam and Stable Inn! Name's Othorion Vilkas. What can I do for a fine group such as yourselves?"

"How is it so cold in here?" Neer asked. She lightly shivered and crossed her arms.

Othorion's brows pulled together, and a smile graced his lips. Neer stepped back when he slapped the counter in a fit of laughter.

"You humans and your pesky jests! Why, my dear, you're looking at the first-ever steam-powered converters!"

° Calm in nature and quick on their feet, vestrils are the main source of travel in Aragoth. Not only is their temperament ideal for even the most novice of riders, but their low appetite, high endurance, and quiet steps make them desirable amongst travelers.

Neer had never seen nor heard of such a beast. Had she been of the mind to find interest, she'd have approached the stables, but her anguish left her devoid of all emotion and intrigue.

He waved his small arm and motioned upward. Neer followed his movement and noticed copper cogs and metal pipes outlining the short ceiling. She lifted her hand and felt cool air seeping through small holes within the pipes.

"We need a room," Y'ven said, placing four small cogs onto the counter.

The dreled pushed the cogs back to the vaxros. "I could never accept cogs from Drimil'Rothar. Please. Take the top room suite. It's perfect for your…"—he eyed the trio—"*arrangement.*"

"We will take it." Y'ven placed three cogs on the counter. "And three vestrils."

The dreled moved to push the cogs away, but Aélla placed her hand atop his and looked into his eyes. He smiled and scooped the cogs into a velvet sack. Neer watched Aélla carefully, taking note of her soft eyes and caring touch as her fingers rested on the dreled's.

She caught a glimpse of the dreled's eyes and quickly turned away. Crossing her arms, she stepped further into the room.

"By the by," the shop keeper called as the group headed upstairs, "I've been hearin' rumors of the likes of your kind snippin' about. One of 'em got caught tressin' through the caves. Heard he's been sentenced to the chains.* Nasty death, that one. May be wise to pay him a visit before it's too late."

Aélla's posture fell. With a despondent nod, she climbed the stairs. Down a short hall, they came to a lonesome door.

---

* Mors'groval, a place of damnation and death known for its infamous chains which keeps its prisoners tethered to the ground until their agonizingly slow deaths.

It's a dreadful place meant for the most unworthy and dishonored. Many fallen warriors (most often those who have broken their vows to the al'yavan or more treacherously devoted their life to the Broken Order Brotherhood) now rest forever beneath the sweltering heat of a scornful, unforgiving sun.

While Aélla fiddled with the key, Neer took notice of the glowing glass orbs hanging along the walls.

"What is this place?" she asked, while reaching for an orb. It was hot to the touch, and she quickly pulled her fingers away.

"Steam power," Y'ven explained. "Invention of y'lenae."

"Of who?"

"Natives. Evae."

Aélla opened the door and ushered the group inside. Neer sat upon the fur-blanketed bed, while Y'ven stood by the window. Aélla sat in a chair by the hearth. Her usually calm eyes held deep discontent and worry as they shifted from one thing to another.

"Drimil," Y'ven said. "Are you all right?"

Breaking from her gaze, her expression remained distant. "No. The evae he spoke of…I may know him."

"I thought evae weren't allowed in the desert," Neer added.

"We aren't. And no one else but a scholar would be foolish enough to enter Anaemiril…If he's out here, I need to find him."

Y'ven leaned against the windowsill, staring over the desert. "We cannot."

Aélla stiffened. "I won't allow him to die, Y'ven. We should find out why he's here before sentencing him to death."

Y'ven turned to face Aélla, but her eyes remained focused on the floor. "Evae are forbidden, Master Drimil. It is known. Ruins forbidden. He defied our laws. Punishment is deserved."

Through several breaths, she remained calm, though the anger was evident in her dark eyes and clenched fists. Neer could sense the conflict within her, though Y'ven seemed oblivious to her increasing anguish and disgust.

Neer added, "Not everything is so black and white, Y'ven. We should figure out why he's here. If you kill without mercy, all you'll have is a sea of innocent corpses and vengeful souls."

"It is not our way!"

Aélla clutched the arms of her chair. Her face twisted, and veins swelled in her neck. "It is not *our* way," she hissed. "He will not die. Not until I have judged him for myself."

"Master Drimil —"

"Enough." She stood and closed her eyes. "Please, Y'ven. Do not make this harder than it has to be."

With a huff, he silently agreed, and Aélla swiftly left the room. Her footsteps descended down the stairs as she fled.

"Is she all right?" Neer asked.

Y'ven paced across the room, his heavy footsteps creaking against the floor. He sat in the wooden chair and leaned forward. "Cannot lose herself. Must be calm."

"No one can be calm forever."

"She struggles. Did not make it easy. Will go save her friend. Will keep her on the right path."

Neer stared at the door. She felt the sting of remorse and sorrow at Aélla's repressed anger. To be viewed upon by the world in a certain way was dismaying. Always hiding. Always pretending. It was a hellish fate, and one she didn't take pleasure in sharing with another.

As day faded into night, Aélla had yet to return, and Y'ven had made his way downstairs long ago in search of food and supplies. Neer lay in the room with Dru snuggled into the blankets by her side. The small faeth rested on her back with her mouth open. Drool slid down her cheek, and she lightly snored.

With a deep breath, Neer closed her eyes and attempted to rest, despite knowing sleep wouldn't come. It was a luxury swept away by the weight of her grief and loneliness. With firelight keeping the room aglow, she pulled Loryk's note from her boot and carefully unfolded the parchment, thankful the enchantments were keeping it preserved. She read over the words she memorized long ago. Every sideways S and elongated G were familiar and haunting.

She ran a finger down the length of the page, and with a light sniff, she tucked it safely into its place within her boot. Thinking of another, she pulled her sword from its sheath, and studied the soft glowing veins along the blade. She had never seen an enchanted weapon before and wondered what powers it held. Firelight reflected off the steel as it twisted in her hand. Her distorted reflection stretched across the blade, and she inspected her appearance. She was stunned to find her skin was tanner with light freckles across her nose.

As she stared at her reflection, a sudden quake shook the inn when an explosion erupted outside. The walls rattled, and dust rained from the ceiling. Neer dropped the sword as she braced herself in a panic. Her eyes darted to the window, where a flash of light overtook the darkness. As soon as it came, it faded, and the world fell silent and still.

Neer moved to the window and found dark smoke billowing around Aélla, who knelt beneath a shield of energy. Soot covered the ground in a layer of black, surrounding her magic.

Moonlight cast off Thorne's polished metal arm as he stepped through the haze. Neer held her breath as energy swirled within his palm and then ignited in Aélla's direction.

CHAPTER THIRTEEN

THORNE

"Find the Child, no matter the cost. Bring her to the Temple of Skye and receive your just reward."
— Bounty for the Child of Skye

HOT ENERGY SCORCHED THE GROUND as it barreled toward Aélla, who sat injured and still. A thick line of black was left in its wake as it traveled closer. When its heat touched her skin, she was tackled aside. Neer, who had teleported to her side, held her close as they rolled across the ground.

Dust and smoke swirled through the air, sending waves of soot to obscure their vision. They coughed and wheezed as the particles clung to their dry throats.

When they came to a slow halt, Neer sprang to her feet. Her eyes narrowed as she peered through the smog. Her knuckles turned white from her hard grip on her sword, which reflected the dying flames of the fresh crater nearby.

Thorne's large shadow appeared through the haze, and Neer vanished. She appeared instantly behind and swiped her sword at his back. Thorne turned, and the edge of her blade slid down his metal arm as he blocked the hit.

Fury ignited within her. She wouldn't allow the Order to steal what little remained of her life. Not even the most renowned hunter would see her to their doorstep. Not if she fought.

Not if she won.

Her arms tingled with magic and strength as she glared into the eyes of a man thrice her size. Tall as a vaxros, with muscles to match, the hunters were strong as Knights yet had the skills and adaptability of a mercenary. Thorne's lip pulled into a deep snarl. He whipped a dagger at her chest, and she vanished, reappearing to his right and slicing into his arm. Blood spilled from the incision, spattering her face and arm.

Thorne struck his fist through air and Neer disappeared. Coming to his left, she struck her sword at his ribs, and he swung his metal arm at her head. She vanished, reappearing behind, and he swung his arm back. A heavy iron hand collided with her jaw.

She fell with a great thud, landing hard on her back, unable to move from the sudden rush of pain. Specks of darkness overtook her vision, and she crawled to her feet. Every heartbeat pulsed through her red, swollen cheek. She stumbled forward and blinked her vision into focus, but the world was spinning, and she was unable to make out Thorne from the shadows dancing in her eyes.

He stepped closer—a shadow overtaking the shades of black filling the world with darkness. She knew he was there, yet she couldn't fight, couldn't bring herself out of her delirium. Her jaw ached. The taste of copper caressed her tongue. Every muscle throbbed as she had depleted her energy. She was weak. Tired. Not used to such expenditure.

His shadow towered over her, when a wave of energy suddenly knocked him aside, and Aélla ran closer. Her arm extended toward Neer, and warm magic fell over her. Cloaked in its harsh light, her wounds didn't heal, yet the pain of her ailments subsided.

The world became clearer, and she heard a powerful roar as Y'ven charged. Fireballs tore through the air as Dru sent waves of heat in Thorne's direction. Glowing fireballs created quick flashes of light, brightening the darkening world.

Thorne dove aside as the fire rushed past, colliding against the ground with smoke and flame. Dru clenched her fists and trembled with fury. Her aura brightened as she created another ball of flames.

Thorne grabbed a crossbow from his back and shot a bolt at the faeth. It flew toward her, and Y'ven swiped it away with his hammer. The bolt flipped unsteadily through the air before landing in the dirt.

The ground trembled beneath the impact of Y'ven's steps as he charged toward the hunter. With a heavy swing, his war hammer smashed into Thorne's side.

Thorne lifted his glowing palm, but the light faded when he suddenly staggered forward and gripped his throat, fighting to breathe. His bloodshot eyes glanced through the desert before settling on Neer as she sat on her knees, clutching his throat with her magic.

Anger overtook the pain in his eyes, and creases formed between his brows as he glared. He raised his hand and shot a quick, powerful blast in her direction. Her eyes widened, and she vanished. The ground erupted where she once sat. Black smoke and rocks rose from the crater in her place.

Thorne ducked beneath the war hammer swinging from behind. He kicked Y'ven in the gut, and the vaxros stumbled back. With a blow to the head, Y'ven fell to his knee. He spat out a tooth as he heaved. Blood dripped down his face, cascading over open wounds and fresh bruises.

Forgetting the vaxros, Thorne glanced quickly through the desert. He set his gaze to the east, where Neer knelt to the ground, and his eyes widened with purpose. Aélla stood before her, and a shimmering mist twisted above her palms as she lifted her hands, ready to defend.

With a growl, Thorne raised his glowing mechanical arm. Aélla waited and watched, unmoving, as the energy brightened in his grasp before it was released.

Aélla's magic formed into a protective shield that barricaded herself and Neer from the deadly blast. She fell to her knees with a shriek as her barrier was struck. Her arms trembled, but she held them firm above her, never losing her grip on the magic shielding them.

Thorne stepped closer, reloading his crossbow. He aimed for the barrier crazed with white glowing cracks. As he pulled the trigger, Y'ven struck upward against his weapon, and the bolt launched high into the air.

Aélla released the barrier and fell forward with a gasp.

Neer exhaled a pained breath. Blood dripped from a cut on her scalp and trailed over her eye, making it hard to see. Bruises formed across her face and arms where she had been struck. Her body ached from her weak and fading magic.

She glanced at Y'ven, who was caught in a battle with Thorne, and then she turned to Aélla. Fury coursed through her. "Why aren't you fighting?" she demanded. "You're a sorceress! *Kill him!*"

Before Aélla could speak, Neer vanished.

She appeared behind Thorne and slashed his side. Blood splashed across her arm and stained her clothes. She ducked below his heavy swing and spun back to put distance between them.

Y'ven struck his side, and Thorne stumbled. As Y'ven raised his weapon again, Thorne reached into his pocket and flung dark powder into his face.

Deep ragged coughs spilled from his lungs. He choked on the particles clouding his mouth and nose, dropping the hammer with a hoarse gasp and falling to his knees. Wheezed breaths entered his tightened throat, and his glowing eyes dulled as he suffocated.

"No!" Neer cried. Thorne turned to her, and she lifted her palms, slowly clenching her fists. Boiling magic raged within her. She could feel every fiber of his body — the slow beating of his heart and his rush of anger — as her energy coiled around him.

Tendrils of magic seeped into his scalp and wrapped tightly around his skull. Unable to sink her energy further and grip his brain, she twisted her hands together, like holding a ball, and slowly squeezed. She could feel the pressure of his bones in her grasp. Her face was red, and beads of sweat formed across her brow as she fought to crush his skull.

Her eyes were dark as she clenched her magic, feeling its power and rage.

Thorne gripped his head and staggered aside.

"Nerana!" Aélla screamed.

But she couldn't hear. The heat of her magic and depth of her fury were all that existed.

Thorne fell to his knees. Blood dripped from his ears and nose.

"You can't do this!" Aélla ran to Neer's side and grabbed her arms. Burning energy struck her with agony as Neer's magic flashed through her. Every muscle burned, and she fell to the ground. Her body was rigid as she lay on her back. Wide eyes rolled back as her limbs twitched.

Neer leaned forward, gripping her head from the sudden rush of energy. She noticed Aélla and fell to her side.

"Aélla!" she called while gripping her shoulders, unable to stop her convulsions. "What do I do? What do I do!"

Y'ven lay face-down in the dirt. Dru pulled his hair in an attempt to wake him.

"Come on," Neer begged. She placed her hands on Aélla's chest, but her magic was empty. Focusing harder, hoping to stop the seizing, her energy was dull and weak. It couldn't combine with Aélla's as it boiled and twisted within her.

Eventually, the twitching ceased. Her head fell aside, and her body was limp. Neer checked the pulse in her neck. A light thumping tapped beneath her finger, and she was overcome with relief.

"What's all the commotion!" the dreled called, marching outside. "I outta rip into your backside for causing such a mess!"

"We need an apothecary!" Neer demanded. "Where is the nearest town?"

His anger softened as he peered at the others. Blood and cuts covered their bodies. The dreled stepped closer, moving carefully past a smoldering crater as he approached. His eyes followed the blackened trail leading to a circle of soot. "What happened out here, lass?"

He glanced at Thorne, who was motionless on his side. Blood dripped from his nose and lips, leaving thin trails of red across his cheek that pooled atop the dirt. A light groan came from Thorne's throat, and Neer slowly turned to face him. Her skin lost its color as his eyes opened, and he slowly crawled to his knees.

"We need to leave *now!*" she demanded of the dreled.

Broken syllables sputtered from his lips, and he took a step back, watching as the hunter stood and cracked the bones in his neck.

"Get us out of here!" Neer screamed.

Trembling, the dreled nodded and transformed into a large six-legged beast. He scooped Y'ven onto the wide horn protruding from his nose, while Neer transported onto his back with Aélla and Dru. With no saddle or reins, Neer lay on her stomach and gripped a fold of thick skin on the back of his neck. She held Aélla close as the dreled stomped quickly through the desert. Dust swirled as they fled into the grueling night, and Thorne watched with dark, angry eyes.

CHAPTER FOURTEEN

THE TREE

"The ko'ehlau'at are sacred and pure, carrying energy throughout the land by way of the roots, linking all living things to its magic and power."
— Secrets of the Trees, a First Blood tome

THE DRELED RAN LATE INTO the night, his large feet pounding into the ground. Neer struggled to hold on as her arms weakened. A gash in her shoulder pulsed with every heartbeat, sending a strike of pain down her arm and making it impossible to focus. Blinking several times to clear her clouded vision, she found herself falling deeper into a state of delirium and fog.

She closed her eyes, ready to drift into a much-needed slumber, when a loud noise jolted her awake.

Something hard tugged her hair, and with a gasp, she opened her eyes. Altvára, the raven, was perched on the dreled's neck, staring at Neer with a slight tilt to his head.

He glanced at Aélla, and with a loud caw, he flew into the air. With a deep breath, Neer shook her head and blinked her drowsiness away.

In the distance, she saw a soft glow radiating along the horizon. The dome-shaped light brightened as the dreled moved closer.

Enormous rock towers and tall cacti surrounded them. Dark shadows, like pits of blackness, were created by the bright moonlight. Neer focused on the glow ahead, hoping to stay alert for the duration of the ride.

As it grew more vibrant, she shielded her eyes from its intensity. Peering through the light, she was stunned to find an enormous Tree standing tall in the middle of the desert. A web of thick roots twisted within the rocky ground, expanding away from the trunk. Glowing bulbs hovered through the wide branches, creating a canopy of light and warmth.

The luminance reflected against Neer's bloody and torn skin. Dru stared wondrously with her tiny fists held together at her open mouth. Aélla's messy hair glowed within the brightness.

The dreled stopped beneath the edge of the canopy. He gently rolled Y'ven onto the ground and took a measured step back. Neer clutched Aélla and teleported to the ground by Y'ven's side.

A flash of light created a warm breeze as the dreled transformed into his natural state. Standing completely nude, he walked to the tree and placed his hand atop a thick root.

"What is this doing here?" Neer asked. "How…?"

"'Tis truly a mystery," he said. "Some say it can heal, if you've got the strength for it. I don't believe in such nonsense. A tree's a tree."

He stepped away and walked past Neer. "I've taken ya as far as I can go. Zaos is a day north. That bugger from the inn shouldn't get a whiff of ya out here."

"Thank you," she said.

"Good luck to ya, lass." With a worried glance to Aélla, the dreled transformed into a falcon and disappeared into the sky.

Turning to the Tree, Neer closed her eyes and basked in its warmth. Hot energy stung her skin as she stepped closer. While the air was heavy and saturated with intense magic, she was calm. Serene, even, as the pressure of her own magic was lifted.

She could feel its lifeforce pulsing through the branches, like a heartbeat thumping against every twisted root and thriving flower. Drawn closer, as if being summoned, she stepped to the trunk. Its smooth bark pulsated with streams of light.

Neer closed her eyes and inhaled a calming breath. The air tingled as magic radiated from deep within the roots. Never had she noticed the strong sense of magic living within the Trees until her time in Nhamashel. With so much pent-up magic inside her, she didn't doubt it was the reason she couldn't feel the energy swirling through the air before.

Dru tugged her hair and pointed at Y'ven and Aélla as they lay motionless on the ground. Neer moved closer and knelt beside them. Nestled beneath the glowing branches, her energy burned hotter. The air vibrated and sang with a low hum.

"I don't know what to do…," she said. Thinking back to her time in Nhamashel, she knew the magic of the Tree could be used to heal them, but she had never used its power in such a way. Before then, she never knew they held such energy.

Y'ven's breaths were shallow and weak, and his skin faded into a light shade of purple as he slowly suffocated. Dru stood on his chest. Her hands twisted together as she peered at his face, tears swelling in her large eyes.

Neer carefully gripped his forearm. Her empty palm hovered over a thick root. Its energy swirled within her, coalescing with her own. Filled with its power, she became one with its strength and placed her hand on the bark.

With closed eyes, she felt the hot sting of magic moving through her. With every deep breath, the energy grew stronger. After Nhamashel, she grew sensitive to the power within the Trees and could feel it hovering around her. The sting of energy ignited within her whenever she touched the trunk or branches.

This time, however, was different. The energy tore at her soul, ripping every fiber of her being. The pain was intense. It swirled deep within, like boiling magma ready to spew.

As their energies combined, the ground beneath her knees cracked and the glowing branches withered. Her heart pulsed in rhythm with the energy flowing through the Tree. It thumped through her veins with cosmic elevation. She was no longer alive, yet she wasn't dead. Stuck somewhere in between, she converged with the energy that connected her to the Tree.

That connected her to life and the world.

Bitterness overtook the serenity. Beads of sweat formed across her forehead. She gritted her teeth and twisted her face in agony. Her body shook as fire coursed through her. Her injuries throbbed with every pulse of her heart, and with her every inhale the glowing tree illuminated, and it dimmed with every exhale.

Unable to withstand such agony, she released her grip. Her body shook, and her chest ached as she fell back with a pained gasp. She breathed in shallow, raspy breaths, and the heat within her faded.

Y'ven gasped and gripped his chest. Dru was quick to his side, her soprano voice ringing through the air as she sobbed.

"Druindarvenia…," he spoke through a raw throat.

Dru hugged his cheek. He rubbed her back with his finger, and his glowing eyes focused on Neer, who leaned forward with her head down. "Neer," he called.

She lifted her hand to quiet him. Through several deep breaths, the pain subsided. A dull ache replaced the heat that surged through her. Sitting upright, she shared a reassuring glance with Y'ven, then turned to Aélla.

She dreaded the thought of healing another, but Aélla needed it. Preparing herself for the intensity and heat, she grabbed Aélla's wrist and clutched the root.

The world outside was dark as the tree brightened. Every petal turned white as energy embraced them in a comforting warmth. Y'ven and Dru watched in silent wonder, while Neer struggled with her affliction. Her lips peeled back to reveal her gritted teeth as she fought against the agony that had stricken her.

As Aélla's small cuts melded, the glow of the tree diminished. Neer released her hold and fell back. Her chest was heavy and ached with every breath. She crawled forward with her eyes closed, reeling from the release of such energy.

Aélla exhaled, and her eyes fluttered open. She looked around in a daze, staring at the glowing petals above. Through a soft groan, she sat up and gripped her forehead.

"Drimil," Y'ven started, his voice full of worry.

"I am fine…," she said. "Where are we?"

"Still in the desert," Neer explained. She leaned against the trunk and closed her eyes. "Something happened when you touched me earlier. You fell and started convulsing." She paused with pain. "The shop keeper—that dreled—brought us here. He said some city is to the north."

"Zaos," Y'ven explained. "City of Lights. Y'lenae colony."

Aélla sat on her knees. Her eyes sparkled as she gazed upon the Tree. She touched the trunk and closed her eyes. With a deep inhale, the flowers brightened. "I have not seen a Koehlaeuat since Nyn'Dira." She took another breath. "It reminds me of home."

"It doesn't hurt you?" Neer asked.

Aélla turned with a troubled glance. "Why would it hurt?"

Neer crossed her arms, being sure not to accidentally touch the roots or trunk. "It felt like my veins were on fire. Like my soul was being torn apart."

Aélla's concern deepened. "The Koehlaeuat are places of peace. They gift the First Blood, or those with magical energy, the ability to heal. I've never known them to cause pain."

"I don't know…It felt *wrong*." Their eyes connected. "We had a Tree in Porsdur—where I live. I would sit beneath it all the time, just feeling the warmth and peace it brought. Ever since my curse was lifted, the trees feel different. *I* feel different. Freer. Stronger. Like a weight has been lifted, and I can breathe. Now I can feel the energy of the world. Its weight and power…" She eyed the branches. Warmth radiated from

116

the roots, and she hovered her hand over the bark, too afraid to touch it yet compelled to do so.

Neer ripped her hand away and clutched her wrist. With closed eyes, she exhaled.

"Have you ever regretted anything, Aélla? Done something so terrible and selfish that you aren't sure if you can live with yourself any longer? Ever since Nhamashel, all I've had is regret. I wanted to be normal. To be free...And it cost me everything." She hugged her knees. "Since meeting you, there's been something pressing on my mind, and I need you to be honest in your answer."

"Of course. What is it?"

Struggling to find the right words, Neer asked, "Did it work? Did they save her? Or did he die for nothing..."

Aélla smiled with sympathy and carefully touched Neer's hand. The weight of sorrow lifted from her chest as Aélla explained, "Yes. They saved her."

Neer nodded, and peace washed over her. His sacrifice wasn't in vain. For the first time, she wasn't as bitter over his loss, though the anger of Klaud's betrayal still weighed her with resentment and hatred.

"And Avelloch...," said Aélla, Neer quickly meeting her gaze at the mention of his name. "He's waiting for you."

Neer closed her eyes, at a loss for words. Sadness filled her with regret, yet she was wrapped in the warmth of peace and acceptance. "Thank you," she said, choosing to embrace the tranquility rather than fight it.

Aélla dug through a small satchel hanging across her chest and passed Neer her canteen. She drank the contents, not realizing how parched she was. They shared a small meal of hardtack, sausage, and cheese, thankful that Aélla had carried a small bag of food when she left to meditate. After their attack, they had left everything at the Steam and Stable Inn, leaving them with nothing but the items in Aélla's satchel and whatever lined their pockets.

"Y'ven," Neer started after washing down a bite of her dry bread with water. "I'm sorry…"

"Why apologize?" He tore off a piece of bread and handed it to Dru.

The faeth sat on his shoulder and ate her meal.[°]

"That man is a hunter named Thorne. He's here to find me."

"Why?"

Her eyes fell away as guilt and anger coursed through her. "The Order has been pursuing me since I was a child. They call me a demon. The *Child of Skye*." She paused, and a look of disgust twisted her face. "Thorne is a bounty hunter with the Shadow Blades…There is no other reason for him to be here if not for me."

"*Child of Skye?*" his words were broken as he spoke the unfamiliar phrase.

"Skye[†] is where the High Priest lives." She clutched her arm where the sigil branded her skin. "He marked and claimed me as property of the Order. The 'Child' is what they call me. Everyone understands it to mean demon." She

---

[°] While the faeth didn't require food to survive, as they receive all their sustenance from the sun or flames, Dru enjoys eating, and can typically be found stealing crumbs or leftovers from the plates of her hungry companions.

[†] Considered the capital of the human country of Laeroth. Only those with approved clearance may enter the isolated hold.

Located along the northeast corner of Laeroth, Skye shares its southern border with Llyne. The close proximity to the rebel state has left the capital to secure their borders with reinforced walls, trained guards, and mercenaries. Within the last fifteen years, 60% of the settlements along the Skye/Llyne border have been destroyed by the Order. While the residents had no association with the Brotherhood, they refused to leave their homes, and were branded traitors by the laws of the Six

.

This injustice led to an increase in the Brotherhood's numbers as the residents of Llyne joined their ranks to better defend their homes, family, and land.

exhaled a slow breath. "It isn't a title you want stamped over your head."

Y'ven and Dru shared a sorrowful gaze. The faeth slowly turned away and stared at the ground.

"Allies," Y'ven said. "We fight as one."

Neer smiled and finished her meal in silence. As Y'ven and Aélla spoke quietly, Neer focused her attention on the Tree. Never had she seen one of this magnitude, and for it to be stranded in the middle of the desert was puzzling. Nothing but rocks and dirt surrounded them as far as she could see.

She touched the trunk, feeling its smooth surface beneath her fingers, when a surge of magic flashed through her, and she was frozen in place.

The world was cold as her vision faded to darkness. Shallow water lapped beneath her knees, and memories of her time in the Trials came flooding back as she was pulled into another vision.

"Hello?" she called.

Her voice echoed far into the distance, overlapping with itself before fading to silence. A bird cawed loudly overhead, and Neer ducked with her arms raised, yet nothing flew above. The shallow water splashed quietly when she pushed herself to her feet and took careful steps forward.

Through the darkness came wide trees and thick underbrush. The water beneath her was replaced with thick grass and mud. Large birds flew overhead, and small animals scurried through the trees while rainwater dripped from the thick canopy above.

With every step, the foliage grew denser. Neer unsheathed her sword and was puzzled by its purple veins, which were now even brighter than before, though still not as prominent as they were in Avelloch's possession. Thick vines splashed her with water as she carved through the vegetation. With a final swipe of her blade, she cut through a wall of vines and stepped carefully into a clearing. Rain fell steadily from the sky, soaking into her armor and sticking her hair to her face.

She wiped the moisture from her eyes and gazed upon an enormous temple. Aged limestone steps, bordered by elegant stone columns, led to an arched double doorway.

In the center of the clearing, surrounded by thick grass and flowers, was a Tree, glowing beautifully against the dreary overcast. Its branches were vibrant and full. Damp grass pressed beneath Neer's boots as she stepped through the clearing.

Her gaze shifted to the temple, and she took a step back when her eyes set on the walls. Etched into the stone beside the large door was a glowing rune. Magic far beyond her own understanding lay active and waiting within the ancient marking. The ever-present sting of energy tugged her forward, drawing her to its power.

She stepped closer, moving up the crumbled steps and closer to the rune. Atop the stairs, she turned and examined her surroundings, searching for anything that could lead her home. But there was no escape. Wherever the Tree had brought her, this rune would take her back to the desert.

Drawn back to the glowing design, she was hesitant to touch it—not after her terrifying experiences in the Trials. Light illuminated her palm, and she struggled with her decision to activate its magic.

With a hard gulp, she withdrew her hand. Staring frightfully at the rune, as if it was a predator waiting to pounce, she turned, ready to escape in the direction she came. But the thriving rainforest, with beautiful flowers and winding streams, was now lifeless and dry.

The trees wilted before her eyes, their leaves fading to ash as they fell from cracked branches. Tall grass turned brown and then faded into grey. Darkness overshadowed the beaming sun and blanketed the world in a layer of frost.

A deep rumble shook the cold, dead air, causing large cracks formed along the walls of the temple. Neer leapt aside as thick pieces of stone fell from above, turning to smoke as they crashed to the ground.

The trees quivered and vaporized into a cloud of black. Dark mist rose from the ground as the world faded. Nothing but the bright glowing rune remained. It hovered at eye level, no longer tethered to the wall where it was carved. Its reflection rippled in darkness below.

Neer stepped closer, the force of magic too great for her to ward. Her knees were weak, and her legs trembled from fear. The yellow glow brightened her dirty face as she drew nearer. Not a sound was made when her boots pattered against the watery surface.

Standing before the symbol, she could feel its magic pulsing through the air. Without thought, her fingers lifted to the symbol. She was panicked yet couldn't move, couldn't fight the urge to set her palm upon the glowing apparition, and against her will, she touched the rune.

CHAPTER FIFTEEN

NASIR

*"For all we have lost we will regain with blood. Show no mercy.
Death is a necessary sacrifice to freedom."*
— Naisannis, Eirean of clan Klaet'il

MAGIC ENGULFED HER IN A wave of heat. She took a deep breath to quell the intense burning in her chest and fell to her knees. Voices broke the unbearable silence. They called out to her from afar, like waves brushing against the sand. Soon, they grew louder, and her vision cleared. Light replaced the darkness, and she found herself kneeling in the desert.

Aélla came to her side with Dru, who hovered in front of Neer with her head tilted slightly to the side. Purple moonlight illuminated Aélla's white hair and fair skin as she placed her hand on Neer's shoulder.

"Are you all right?" Aélla asked. Her tone exuded fear and confusion, while her eyes were focused and calm.

The uncertainty faded, and with a deep breath, Neer turned away. She noticed Y'ven standing nearby. His hard eyes were fixed above her to something behind. It was as if he hadn't noticed her presence at all.

Neer looked around in confusion, not recognizing where she was as they no longer sat beneath the large Tree the dreled had brought them to. Not even its bright glow clung to the horizon. Curious, she followed Y'ven's gaze and was stricken by the sight behind her.

Made of ancient stone, weathered and cracked, stood the temple from her vision. No longer was it encased in vines or surrounded by beautiful flora as it stood alone in the desert. The steps were corroded and missing large pieces, while the outlying pillars had crumbled to small stubs. The large double door stood proudly at the top of the stairs.

"Nerana," Aélla started, "what happened? Why did you lead us all this way?"

"What do you mean? How did I get here?"

Y'ven approached, though his gaze remained on the temple as he explained, "You walked." His eyes narrowed, heavy with suspicion. "The ruins guided you."

"No," Neer said, "it was the Tree."

"The tree?" Aélla asked. "What do you mean?"

"When I touched it, it brought me somewhere else..." Neer looked around, recalling the vivid images. "The temple...It was pristine and covered in vines." She peered at the door and then pushed herself to her feet. As she stepped closer, eager to get a closer look at the stone, Y'ven gripped her arm and pulled her back.

"No!" he growled. "We do not disturb the ruins."

"Something's led me here!" she argued. "I need to know why!"

"Only magic and death here."

Aélla came to their sides. She looked at the doors and then dug a parchment from a pouch within her robes. Holding up the paper, she revealed an image that was an exact replica of the crumbled building. Neer glanced between the page and the ruins, anxious and confused.

"This is it...," Aélla stated. "This is Elandorr.° Tre'lan Aenwyn is inside. If what you're saying is true, then the energy of the tree must've guided you here."

° An ancient monastery that once housed the most powerful elemental sorcerers and their students.

Following the disappearance of the First Blood, its doors were forever sealed, left only to be unlocked by those truly gifted in the art of elemental magic.

Aélla revealed her staff and its four clear crystal shards. "The doors are sealed. We need to harness the energy of the elements to enter. Only then will we be able to unlock them."

Neer huffed with frustration and pulled her arm from Y'ven's grasp. "You didn't receive a vision from the tree too?" she asked, and Aélla shook her head in response. Neer said, "I saw one in the Trials as well."

Aélla shook her head. "The *ko'ehlaeu'at* trees are extremely powerful. Even our most notable scholars are unable to understand them fully." She paused, and her lips pulled aside in thought. "The largest is in Nyn'Dira. They say it gives life to the entire forest, and that its energy helped to grow the other *ko'ehlaeu'at* found throughout Laeroth. Some believe they're the reason for magic's existence on our world."

Y'ven grumbled and crossed his arms. "Magic is. As life is. No purpose to question it."

Neer said, "Understanding the world and its mysteries isn't a bad thing, you know?"

"Better left unknown. We should go. Hunter will find us."

As he stepped away, Dru came to his side and sat atop his head.

He came to a halt and turned to the sky when loud screeching echoed from above. Everyone fell silent as the sudden noise faded to silence. "We must flee," Aélla said, her voice trembling with fear and urgency.

"What's happening?" Neer asked.

Aélla led the others to the temple and hid behind one of its many pillars. They tucked themselves into the shadows as large figures flew into the courtyard. The screeching was loud and overlapping as two dozen glynfir landed nearby.

Their serpent-like heads held four eyes, and their long jaws were opened, exposing two rows of sharp fangs. Long tails extended beyond the length of their bodies, and their leathered skin was various colors of red, green, blue, or orange.

Riding atop the creature's backs, nestled into small leather saddles, were evaesh warriors. Dark markings covered their faces and arms. They wore little clothes and held furious scowls.

The last of the warriors to dismount his flyer was a man dressed in dark armor with a hooded cowl that hid his face. The others waited as he walked by and climbed the steps to the entrance. He was taller than the others and held himself with a much higher poise, walking among them as more a god than man.

When they stepped beneath the awning, the leader slowly removed his cowl, and Neer silently gasped at the sight of his lifeless gaze and dark facial marking. He was the man she had encountered in the vaxros prison, the one who left his own men behind to save himself.

The one who looked into her eyes with confidence and power.

He placed his hand upon the door and spoke quietly to the others. His eyes gazed upon the dormant rune as he traced its design with his finger.

A woman came to his side. She was thin-framed with muscular arms and a vicious scowl indicative of her klaet'il roots. Her long black hair was shaven above her left ear, revealing dark markings etched across her scalp. Neer looked closer, and was frightened by the woman before her, whose appearance was nearly identical to Klaud's.

This was the evaesh sorceress who could wield elemental energy. Her slanted eyes, much like all magic users, were unnaturally vibrant in their color. While Neer had teal eyes, the stranger's were a striking shade of green. Three deep scars cracked her face, traveling above her left brow and across her cheek.

"Aélla *vos'nok tre'lan!*" the leader said.

Neer quickly glanced at Aélla, who was staring at the ground with frightened eyes. Her knuckles were white as she tightly clutched her staff. Neer returned her attention to the strangers as they marched back to the courtyard, while the leader stood alone at the rune. He touched it one last time before straightening with a deep breath and following his comrades.

They took flight, the screeching of their animals disappearing in the distance, and the group slowly exited their hiding places. Aélla was paler than usual and held a sorrowful, frightened look.

Y'ven growled angrily before speaking in his native language. He stormed down the stairs and slammed his hammer into the dirt. Aélla was quiet, gazing at her feet.

"Aélla?" Neer lightly touched her shoulder. "You okay?"

She nodded and blinked her tears away. "Yes."

"Who were those people?"

Aélla wiped her nose with a sniff and attempted to compose herself, though her discomfort and fear were as evident as the sun was bright. "They are *klaet'il.*°"

"Klaet'il? They were the ones invading Laeroth." Neer recalled her journey to Nhamashel, when the vile warriors burned several innocent villages as they sought to enter the human territories.

Aélla nodded sadly. "That man was the Nasir. He's a vicious killer."

"Who was the woman?

Aélla's eyes traveled to the sky where the klaet'il had disappeared. Studying the heavens, as if they could still hear, she explained, "Ithronél. She's a powerful blood-thirsty drimil." Her eyes fell to the others. "The klaet'il are vicious, and second to the Nasir, she is the worst. We cannot allow them here. They

---

° The oldest evaesh clan still in existence, the Klaet'il make up roughly 60% of all evaesh residents in Laeroth.

Known for their ruthless behavior, lack of empathy, and disregard for anyone outside of their clan, the Klaet'il have become known by non-humans as a terrifying, unpredictable force.

will unravel all we've worked so hard to gain. The treaty with the vaxros will be destroyed."

They realized the severity of what was to come, and the world fell silent with despair.

"What do they want?" Neer asked, breaking the long, insufferable silence.

Aélla closed her eyes.

"Me."

CHAPTER SIXTEEN

MORS'GROVAL

"Bound by chains the wicked will wait as the sun turns their flesh to dust. Beneath its heat their sins will fade, along with the life they lost."

— Vaxros tale of Mors'Groval

THE DARK WORLD WAS SILENT as they strode through the empty desert plains. Y'ven sauntered alongside Neer, slumped forward with fatigue, while Aélla walked ahead, following Altvára as he flew at an even pace. She hadn't spoken since they left the temple, and Neer was starting to worry.

Y'ven's paced slowed to a stop. He rubbed his face and exhaled an exhausted sigh.

"You good?" Neer asked.

He straightened and forced himself forward. "Yes."

"Your kind don't do well in the dark?"

"Sun-blood. Heat and flame nourish. Darkness weakens."

"That's why you worship the draak?" she asked, in reference to the scaled, fire-breathing monsters.

"Draak, first sun-blood. Masters of magic. Fire and fury."

Aélla said, ending her long reticence, "Not much is known about the draak. Even in my studies, I learned very little. They lived centuries ago. Some believe they have ties with the First Blood, but there is no proof of that."

"Draak and First Blood coexist. Fought and bled. Disappear together."

Neer's mouth fell open. Skin tingling and face pale, she struggled to form a coherent thought. Surely, the most destructive and dangerous creature to exist didn't coexist with the First Blood. Historians and scholars would have connected them long ago. It must be a mistake. The vaxros weren't known for their intelligence or archives, but the evae and scholars of Styyr were. In her time with the Brotherhood, she learned from the top minds humanity had to offer, yet still, she was never made aware of the draak's existence, or their ties to the ahn'clave.

"That can't be…" Neer said, her voice quiet.

"First Blood create tombs. Waiting. Hiding. From great draak."

She gripped her forehead. "You believe the draak extinguished the First Blood? That Anaemiril was built to hide from them?"

"That's not possible," Aélla explained and then fell back to join them. "Scholars have searched Anaemiril. They've never found a trace of the draak in their texts or ruins. Whatever happened to my ancestors… it was not because of the draak."

"Seems awfully convenient," Neer expressed. "The two most powerful races lived together and vanished. Anaemiril seems the perfect place to hide from fire-breathing monsters."

"Anaemiril was not built to hide from them," Aélla said.

As Y'ven argued, Neer couldn't focus on his words. Her mind spun from all she'd learned. The others didn't seem to notice when she stopped. Haunting memories of her nightmares came back in a flash of darkness—memories of large shadows overtaking the sky and fire devouring the world.

The abrupt call of Aélla's raven caused Neer to leap with fright. She clutched her racing heart and breathed unevenly. Fear washed over her, and her skin tingled and stung. Staring at Altvára, who soared high above, Neer was frozen, unable to think, imagining a horrible beast fifty times its size.

Altvára soared from the sky, resting on Aélla's shoulder, and she rubbed his neck to calm him.

"We are close," Y'ven stated. "Just ahead."

Aélla set her eyes on the horizon as figures emerged in the darkness. The others were silent as they stalked forward, crunching over old bones. Their eyes widened as several hundred cracked and eroded structures came into view. Buzzards circled the sky, and Neer curled her nose as the putrid smell of death lingered in the air.

Stopping at the edge of a dense boneyard, Aélla stepped to the nearest pillar.

"What's going on?" Neer asked. "What is this place?"

"*Mors'groval,*" Y'ven stated. "Place for *nesiat.*"

"For what?"

His glowing eyes stared at the boneyard, and an unsettling chill fell through her as he explained, "Banished...*lost.*"

Terror-stricken and full of sorrow, Neer returned her gaze to the desolate ruins. Aélla moved further through the skeletons, and with a deep exhale, she closed her eyes. Light steps carried her through the valley where hundreds of bodies had been left to rot. Their faces were shriveled and sunken, dried from the heat.

Deep symbols marked their foreheads, and trails of blood stained their faces like blackened tears. Aélla knelt before a sun-scorched vaxros and touched the symbol.

"What is this?" she asked.

Y'ven hesitated. Glowing eyes shifted from one body to the next as he explained, "Traitor."

Aélla's head fell in sorrow. She withdrew her hand and clutched her wrist. "This must be where the *kanavin*[*] are coming from. If we don't contain their energy, they will all manifest."

"Too many. No time."

---

[*] Pronunciation: kah-nah-veen
In the language of the evae, kanavin is a term that loosely translates to *creature of darkness.*

"If enough anger and vengeance is set upon this place, it will manifest greater creatures. Your people will be in danger."

He agreed and with a sad nod said, "No time."

Aélla exhaled a sad breath and looked up at the sky. Altvára circled around before leading them north, further into the land of the dead. Without speaking, Aélla stood and followed him.

Neer and Y'ven shared a worried glance. They didn't want to venture further into the graves. It wasn't the deceased who concerned them, but the creatures that feasted upon their bones; the creatures that attacked them on their journey to meet with Aélla. Should they see themselves ambushed a second time, they'd become nothing but more souls lost in the sea of dishonored.

But this was Aélla's quest, and she would see it through with or without them.

Stepping over decaying corpses, Neer was reminded of her encounter with the undead twins of Galacia. She imagined their torn flesh and rotten limbs racing toward her, ready to rip her apart in their undying fury.

She watched the dead with a careful eye, taking note of the chains binding their wrists to the ground. Buzzards picked at the leathered skin of a small man, one Neer assumed to be evaesh or human, while many others had become dry bones and forgotten souls.

With every step forward, voices whispered through her mind. She shook her head before scratching her ears, trying desperately to quell the noises. Emotions that weren't her own filled her with dread and anger. Loss and regret. Heavy sorrow weighed her feet, and she slowly stopped.

While Aélla searched for the living and knelt with the dead, Neer stood alone, engulfed in misery. She gripped her aching head, whimpering and begging the voices to stop. For the pain to end. Lifting her mist-filled eyes, searching for the source of her agony, she spotted a familiar figure perched in the distance. Visions of her nights in Nhamashel, when she was forced to sit with Loryk's rotten and contorted corpse, entered her mind. For an instant, the pain was overshadowed. Breath caught in her lungs as she stared at the figure, hoping for a miracle.

The voices consuming her were quieted by her longing and shock. She stepped closer to the man chained to the ground, his body becoming clearer with every stride. Her body trembled at the sight of his bleeding skull and slumped body. It wasn't real. She knew this wasn't him. He was buried six months past, and she had sat in the crypts at his tomb for weeks, wishing for death herself. No, this couldn't be Loryk. In her mind, she knew, yet her heart spoke differently.

A tear fell from her eye as she stared at the friend she lost so long ago. Whatever magic was cast on this place must've placed him here, whether by illusion or physical matter, she didn't know. But she had to see him. She needed him to know her regret.

She touched his shoulder, ready to confess her sorrow and guilt, and the figure shifted. A slight movement by most would go unnoticed, but Neer felt it. She backed away, staring at the man before her. The chains rattled as he moved and slowly lifted his head.

She fell back, staring into a stranger's eyes as he pleaded for help. Heartbroken over this revelation, Neer could do nothing but stare into his eyes. This wasn't Loryk, though they looked eerily similar. No, this man wasn't her friend, but he wasn't entirely a stranger, either. Her sorrow faded into shock as she recognized him from their meeting in a tavern just weeks before.

"Thallon!" Aélla called in a panic. She overshadowed the moonlight, racing to his side and removing his binds.

"Drimil!" Y'ven exclaimed as he barreled closer.

Aélla ignored his outburst and forced magic into the dying man. Her arms were straight as she pressed her hands against his chest, white magic glowing beneath her palms. She grunted and struggled as his wounds were healed. While her body became frail and lifeless, his regained its fullness and strength.

His shriveled skin and blanched hair slowly returned to their natural ivory and light brown color. Injuries formed into scars that disappeared into smooth skin. His eyes opened, and he inhaled a deep breath while sitting up in a panic.

Aélla fell back with a shallow exhale. Dark circles under her eyes and sunken cheeks gave her a sickly appearance. She'd lost her muscle tone and whimpered with every breath.

He breathed heavily and looked around, scanning the desert. Bloody, dirt-filled hair tangled in his fingers when he leaned forward and closed his eyes. He struggled for a moment, his composure shifting from shock to relief, before he breathed in a slow, steady rhythm. "Aélla?" he asked, turning to the frail and sickly woman at his side. "What are you doing here? Did the eirean[*] —"

"No…I'm here alone."

He gazed upon the place of his imprisonment. A dark red stain from the previous gash in his skull covered the ground. "Guess it's my lucky day." He pushed himself up and helped her to her feet. Dusting his trousers, he turned to the others that stood nearby. "Wow. A vaxros, faeth, and lanathess. Just need a dreled, and you'll have the whole collection."

Aélla's eyes struggled to stay open, and she swayed on wobbling legs. Y'ven stepped to her side and calmly pulled her into his arms. Thallon met Y'ven's gaze and nodded in a

---

[*] The eirean are a conclave of leaders from each of the five clans of Nyn'Dira. These include Klaet'il, Rhyl, Y'darus, Gorn, and Saevrala. While the clans live in separate territories, and have adopted their own set of rules, guidelines and customs, the eirean will come together in times of great importance.

Aélla's pilgrimage, for example, was a matter handled by the eirean, for her journey has consequences that may affect the entirety of the forest, rather than her clan alone.

silent greeting. Before the vaxros had time to appease the gesture, the stranger set his eyes to Neer.

A light smile pulled his lips as he stared at her in shock. "Small world, huh?" he said.

"I'll say," she remarked.

When Y'ven stepped away, the others followed. As they wandered through the valley, the whispering voices plagued Neer's mind. Their sorrow and fear tugged her heart, blending with her own to create an even heavier weight within her chest.

"What's your name?" Thallon asked, and for a moment, the pain lifted as she envisioned another standing next to her. The resemblance of his appearance gave her a peace she hadn't felt in a long time, but with it came the sting of despair and longing.

"Neer," she said, her voice bleak and emotionless.

His face twisted in humor. "Do all your people name their children after adjectives?"

His sense of humor was familiar, and he chuckled when a smile pulled her lips. "It's Nerana," she explained.

"Nerana...that's nice. You should've led with that one."

Her eyes remained on Thallon as they walked in a comfortable silence. His build and height were similar enough to Loryk's that Neer confused them when she looked away, and their faces were eerily the same. The man was evaesh, yet still, he resembled her friend enough that it was painful to look in his direction.

Painful...and comforting.

CHAPTER SEVENTEEN

THE RUINS

"Through darkness and shadow, the Light remains, untethered by sorrow or pain. To release the strife sets the world alight with new hope and promise to gain."
— Vow of Drimil'Rothar

THROUGH THE LONG AND QUIET night, they moved onward toward their destination. Altvára, who drifted calmly through the skies, came urgently to Aélla's side. Her tired eyes widened as he ruffled his feathers and cawed with distress.

"Something's wrong," she said.

Loud screeches shattered the silence, and seven figures appeared in the distance. Their long wings moved like liquid shadows against the sky. Aélla stumbled back, watching as they drew closer. Still weak from the energy transference that saved Thallon, she was unable to fight. Her sunken cheeks and cracked lips portrayed the health she had given to aid him.

"Come," Y'ven said. He carefully scooped Aélla into his arms and, beneath the shadow of darkness, led the others into the ruins of a destroyed village. Sharpened posts outlined the settlement where bandits and thieves would frequent. Many of the lost homes of the desert were taken by force or abandoned by their *shelarr*, or tribe.

The village was silent and empty, which proved in favor of the group as they were able to slip into a nearby stable undetected. Moonlight filtered through crevices along the walls and ceiling. Aélla rested against the wall with closed eyes, while the others peered through the cracks and watched the sky as klaet'il riders flew overhead.

Their shadows faded as they moved out of sight.

"*Kila!*" Thallon exclaimed, breaking the heavy silence. "Why haven't they been stopped yet?"

"Why are they here?" Y'ven growled.

Thallon paced the small area and rubbed his face in frustration. "They're looking for something."

"For what?"

"I can't…I can't tell you." He stepped back as the angry vaxros approached.

Towering over him, Y'ven glared with menacing eyes. His thick fists hardened, and his chest puffed in anger. "They kill my people! They break the pact!"

"Calm down, all right? This isn't my choice!"

A deep, sawing growl vibrated in Y'ven's throat. He grabbed Thallon by the shirt collar and slammed him against the wall. His feet hovered above the ground as Y'ven held him at eye-level, watching as he squirmed and fought.

"If I tell you, then my people will kill me!" Thallon explained. "I'm here under strict orders from the *Eirean* to find what the klaet'il searching for before they get it!"

"If it is vaxros, then—"

"It's not a vaxros item…It's First Blood."

Y'ven's eyes widened. A deep, infuriated scowl twisted his face, and Thallon became truly frightened. "You desecrate the ruins!" Leaning inches from Thallon's face, Y'ven began shouting in his native language.

"No! I don't *desecrate* anything. I'm a scholar! It's my duty to—"

He recoiled when Y'ven raised his fist.

Neer quickly grabbed Y'ven's arm. "Knock it off," she warned. "If those evae come back, we won't have the strength to fight them. Save your energy for something that matters."

Y'ven seethed. His fiery eyes burned into Thallon's before he dropped him to the ground and stomped away. Dru dashed to Thallon's face and angrily pointed her finger at him before following Y'ven.

Neer caught a glimpse of Thallon's eyes and then stepped across the stable. She dug through her pack and retrieved a barrier potion and enchanted flint. With a few strikes of the flint, a small flame appeared, and she dripped the dark liquid into its heat.

Shimmering magic formed into a large invisible dome extending beyond the walls of their shelter. Curling into her cloak, she kept to herself, watching as the flames whirled and popped.

Thallon leaned against the wall of the barrier. With a grunt, he swiped a few rocks aside and got comfortable. His legs were extended and ankles crossed, allowing his feet to warm by the enchanted flames. His eyes were on Neer, and she closed her eyes, growing tired of purposefully avoiding his gaze.

Late into the night, everyone rested in silence. Dru was asleep next to Y'ven, who snored loudly in his slumber, while Neer lay on her side, bundled in her cloak with her eyes closed. Light shuffling came from across the flames as Aélla slowly rose. She rubbed her head with a groan and accepted a canteen Thallon offered to her.

"Hey, A," he said. "You all right?"

She nodded with a deep, exhausted sigh. Water spilled down her chin as she finished off the drink. "Thallon," she started weakly, "why are you here? What happened?"

"I could ask the same of you. I thought you were forgoing this great and noble quest."

With a weak sigh, she closed her eyes and leaned back against the barrier. Dark circles rested beneath her eyes, giving her a deathly appearance. Her skin had grown paler, and her bones were more prominent. "Why were you in

Mors'groval?" she asked, ignoring his attempt to change the subject.

"Why else? The damn vaxros assumed I was trouble and sentenced me to death."

She turned to him with sour vexation, unwilling to take part in his dramatics. "I know you're entering the ruins." He turned away with a huff as she reprimanded him like a child. "Our people have enough strife with the vaxros. You shouldn't—"

"He's searching for something." The words rolled over hers and made them silent. "The Nasir. He didn't come here for you or the vaxros or a war. He's looking for a First Blood item called *clavía muínsii*. We can't let him get it."

"Why does he want a First Blood artifact? What does it do?"

He hesitated for a moment. Dark blue eyes peered to the vaxros and human as they lay perfectly still in their sleep. With a deep breath, he leaned closer, and anxiously explained, "I can't tell you. Not with the others around. The Eirean don't want anyone to know it exists." He paused with a deep sigh. "Just trust me, Aélla. If he finds it…it's all over."

Her gaze shifted to the ground, and she was consumed with sorrow and fear.

"Anaemiril stretches beneath the entire continent. How could you possibly know where to look?" she asked.

He ran his fingers through his dirty, matted hair. "That's the thing…They destroyed my notebook when they captured me. I know it's deep beneath the surface. Probably in a tomb of some great leader, or hidden behind walls of enchantments or traps."

She crossed her arms to vanquish the swell of agony filling her chest. "He'd have no issue sacrificing all of his people in order to find it," she said of the Nasir.

"Yeah, I know. That's why I have to do it. I know these caves and their traps better than anyone."

"Where is the next cave?"

He made an inarticulate gesture. "I don't know. I'll need to find a map."

"We're going to Zaos. I'm sure you can find a map or library there."

He nodded silently. The lines pulling his face inward vanished, and his shoulders were released of their tension. "Thanks for saving me out there," he said. "I know it's been a long time since we've seen each other. I really owe you one."

Darkness overtook the moonlight when Altvára perched himself on the broken wall. His dark eyes sparkled in the firelight as he looked through the stable with quiet intent.

Thallon chuckled breathlessly. "Should've known he'd send that bird out here to watch over you. I can't remember a time when you two weren't together. Seems like yesterday we were all just kids, doesn't it? Running through the willows and playing at *aesgrot.*"

Aélla smiled. "*Aesgrot* was *your* secret hideout. I was never allowed, remember?"

"Oh, yeah. *Boys only.* Can't say we never broke *that* rule." He laughed. "Crazy where we all wound up, isn't it? You're on this pilgrimage, he's out fighting the war, and I'm here getting enslaved by these *diafahl.* *" He gestured toward Y'ven.

"Thallon!" Aélla remarked in deep offense.

"Sorry." He leaned forward. His hair tangled as he raked his fingers through the dirty locks. "After being left out there for days, it's hard to overlook such puerility."

"You shouldn't harbor such hostility, Thallon. We need to work together."

---

* A slang term used by the evae to mean devil. The klaet'il, in particular, have used this phrase against the vaxros since the War of Fury, when the vaxros invaded Aragoth and forced the evae into a bloody, brutal war.

After the vaxros victory they declared the land as rightfully their own and sealed their borders to all evae. The Klaet'il have held a vindictive grudge that's lasted several centuries, while the other clans harbor resentment and anger toward the diafahl race, and still refer to them as such.

With a sigh, he rubbed his face. "Yeah, yeah. Save the speech." He paused with consideration. "So, what's with the lanathess? I've never seen one up close like this before. Not a wild one, anyway."

"She isn't *wild*!"

He raised his hands in defense. "I only meant that I've never spoken to someone from *their* land. Are the stories true? Do they really feast on evaesh flesh or speak in grunts?"

"No! They're nothing like that!"

He laughed. "Why are you getting so worked up?"

"Those stories are barbaric and unbecoming. Nerana is not an animal, and she doesn't eat evae!"

"How can we know for sure? I mean, maybe she's planning her recipe right now. Fresh evaesh stew with a side of vaxros meat. Garnish with a faeth, and she's got herself one tasty meal." Aélla glared at Thallon as he playfully wiggled his fingers and laughed. "Come on, A, where's your sense of humor?"

Aélla sighed with indignity. "We need to try to get along. None of us will survive if we don't."

"All right, I hear ya." With a sigh, he settled into his blanket. "I think I'm going to sleep. Should we keep an eye on these two?"

"No. They can be trusted."

"All right. Get some rest. You need to heal as much as you can."

As their conversation ended, the world filled with the sound of Y'ven's sawing snore.

Morning came, and the group headed further north toward their destination of Zaos. Aélla, who had gained a bit of her strength and color during her sleep, walked alongside Thallon. They kept a quiet conversation as the others trailed behind.

Neer was silent most of the walk. Her skin burned beneath the thin protection of her cloak, and the throbbing of her blistered feet was unbearable. The inner soles of her boots had worn through, and every step struck her with sharp pain.

Unable to go any further, she leaned forward with her hands on her knees. She then sat atop the dirt, removed her boots, and found half a dozen ripped and oozing blisters beneath the worn holes of her socks. The bottom sole had rubbed off her left shoe at the heel, allowing dirt and rocks to rattle inside.

"Fuck…," she groaned, cursing the desert and its arid heat. She flung her boots aside in anger, and the contents of her bag spilled as she went through her things, too impatient to sift through them within their leather confines.

Her blisters and sores sizzled as she sprinkled a clear healing potion over her feet. Gray mist swirled above the fusing wounds.

The pain faded, and she wrapped her feet in bandages to prevent further blistering. She glanced at the group as they walked further ahead, unbeknownst of her departure. With a sigh she stood and collected her boots from where she'd thrown them.

As she lifted her shoe, she noticed deep red stains spattered across the ground in large puddles of dried blood. Searching her surroundings, she found no signs of a struggle or remnants of battle. But through the wind came haunting voices stricken with anger and pain.

"Nerana!" Aélla called, causing her to jump.

"Does she always wander off like this?" Thallon asked.

"Something's here," Neer said. The voices grew louder as she stepped ahead to the edge of a shallow vale. They gripped her mind and tore her soul. She could feel nothing but pain. Misery.

Death.

She collapsed to her knees as the others came to her side and stared at the village below. Ancient ruins rested at the base of the valley, surrounding a large cave opening where skull-adorned stakes had been staged as a warning for intruders.

But it wasn't the cave that stole their breath. Not the ancient ruins or the forbidden entrance to First Blood territory. It was the bodies of the villagers lying in pools of blood. Vaxros men, women, and children lay lifeless beneath the endless heat of the sun. Blood dripped down their faces from their eyes, noses, mouths, and ears, leaving an underscore of streaks across their faces. Their homes of stretched leather and wooden poles smoldered with ash and smoke.

Y'ven stood with his fists clenched and chest puffed. The tension erased from his shoulders when Aélla took his hand, and his gaze fell to the ground. Dru peered at the village with wide, sorrowful eyes.

"What happened?" Thallon asked. His voice was silent, unrecognizable in his shock and grief. "How did they die like this?"

Aélla's jaw clenched as she stared at the village, studying every face and trail of blood. She understood this was the doing of the klaet'il, as they left their mark scorched in the stone, just as they did to every village they massacred.

The mark of the nesiat. The soulless and lost.

She inhaled a deep breath and then treaded slowly into the village. Y'ven followed, keeping steady pace with Aélla, who walked with forced confidence. Her blue eyes were hard, and her lips were pursed together as she withheld her sorrow.

Neer stepped back, unable to venture forward as agony and rage consumed her. Clutching her ears, she sank to her knees.

Kill them!

Protect the ruins!

Die with honor…

The gruff, angry voices were those of the vaxros who were slain. They overlapped in her mind, creating a haze of noise and screams.

In the village, Aélla stumbled forward, stricken with sudden pain. The voices whispered softly through her mind, yet she could never make out their words. Her breath caught in her throat, and she repressed the agony building up inside.

After a few forced breaths, she continued forward, and came to the village center. Y'ven approached the slain villagers, kneeling beside them and touching their faces as he searched for survivors.

"There are none," Aélla said without a glance in his direction. She didn't have to look. The village was small enough for her to feel their energy. If anyone was still alive, she would know.

"I must be sure."

A tear fell from Aélla's eye as she knelt to the ground. With her fists together, she forced the pain aside and focused on her magic. Heat radiated from within, erasing the dread plaguing her, softening the voices of the dead.

As her magic grew, its heat expanded, covering the village with its warm sting. Y'ven was overcome by its warmth and looked around in confusion. Turning to Aélla, he became aware of her intent and slowly stood, watching.

Beads of sweat dripped down her face. Her teeth were clenched so hard they could crack. Jaw aching, arms burning, she remained calm, lost in her meditations.

Shimmering magic enveloped the village, like waves of heat rippling across the ground. Neer and Thallon watched as it grew larger, covering the fallen warriors and their broken homes.

Magic settled over the somber ruins, and Aélla opened her eyes. Her irises glowed with whiteness. She turned to the sky, and the shimmering magic rose like mist. As it faded from view, she closed her eyes and fell from her meditative posture, leaning forward onto her hands.

Neer sat back, thankful the voices had stopped. No longer did they claw her mind, beckoning her to relive their anguish and misery. "What was that?" she asked, placing a hand on her wet forehead.

"She released their energy," he explained while looking at Neer. "They'll no longer manifest into creatures of darkness."

CHAPTER EIGHTEEN

TIAT'MÉVIN

"Bring to me the broken and I shall restore them anew."

— Drimil'Leirin

AT DUSK, THE GROUP FOUND themselves at the edge of an enormous city. Beautiful, curved pillars towered over tall buildings and homes. Grass, trees, and streams surrounded the community, while the world around remained lifeless and empty.

They followed a narrow path winding through steep drop-offs and jagged cliffsides as they journeyed closer. Neer was silent, gazing upon the spectacular city.

The light dirt path faded into beautiful cobblestones at the city entrance. A large stable full of vestrils sat to the far left. The animals trilled and pulled at their reins when the group passed by.

Neer watched curiously as two humans, a man and woman, stood at a stall petting a vestril's nose. The woman giggled as she ran her fingers down its snout. "I want one!" she begged.

He scoffed while shaking his head. "No, Nicolette. We can't take the vestrils home."

She pouted before feeding the vestril a desert fern.

Before Neer could ask how, or why, the humans had made it this far into the desert, a vaxros guard marched forward to block her path. He spoke with aggression and confidence as his gaze set to Y'ven, who was calm as he spoke to the guard.

"Drimil'Rothar," Y'ven explained, and the sentry glanced at Aélla.

His lip twitched, and a rumbling growl escaped his throat. Unable to refuse her entry, he turned around and marched down the cobblestone path to a small arched bridge. He placed his palms firmly together, and a low whisper seeped from his lips before he raised his right hand into the air before him.

A thick scar across his palm glowed and the air around it vaporized into shimmering mist, creating an opening in the invisible barrier that protected the city. The guard stepped aside and watched with anger as the group walked past him and into the city.

Cool air embraced them with a touch of relief that soothed their burnt skin. Beautiful trees, butterflies, daisies, and streams wove through the buildings and homes. The barrier resealed itself, and the heat of the desert vanished. The guard stood confidently by its entrance with an axe in hand.

"What is this place?" Neer asked, her wide eyes scanning every detail of the immaculate city as they wandered into a large, round courtyard surrounded by stalls and buildings. People bustled through the shops, casting disgusted glances at the strangers huddled together.

The villagers, with dark tan skin and short pointed ears, stood a head shorter than Neer. Women and men wearing fine jewelry and gowns of satin walked by the filth-ridden out-siders with vocal disdain. Their jeering tone portrayed a sense of hierarchy, placing everyone else at the bottom beneath their feet.

Starvation displayed across the boney frames of beggars standing at the edge of the alleyways. They wore dingy rags and had no shoes to cover their callused feet. Gown wearers purposefully ignored the children in rags, who peddled flow-ers or potions for measly prices.

The affluent members gathered in the western wing of the city, where an elegant stairway was surrounded by a lush garden of colorful flowers and glowing bulbs. At the top of the stairs, the road weaved through beautiful cobblestone homes and small yards of grass.

To the east, across the narrow stream, the cobblestone road was cracked and uneven. The homes were made of tin or clay and held lopsided walls with crooked pipes. Colorful tents of canvas and linen gathered along the roadside in the dirt. Wet clothes hung on lines while children splashed in the stream nearby.

In the center of the courtyard, six children raced through the streets, playing tag. They smacked the head of a young child sitting in a wagon. Their taunting laughter echoed above the murmur of voices as they teased him.

The boy, no older than seven, wiped his teary eyes. His face was red as he silently wept.

"What are they saying?" Neer asked as the others teased and poked him.

Y'ven replied with repressed anger, "Cannot stand. They tease him."

"What?" Neer stomped forward, ready to chastise the insolent children, when a young woman broke through the crowd. Her angry voice cracked as she shouted at the older boys. Gathering her dress at the hips, she marched forward and then scooped the crippled child into her arms.

She turned, ready to carry him away, but when her eyes met with Aélla's, she froze. Her pursed lips parted, and her anger vanished.

"Drimil'Rothar?" she asked. The others caught sound of her title and turned to the evae. Her platinum hair and radiant poise were enough to distinguish her from the others, yet she remained calm and humble in their admiration.

The mother stepped closer. Tears stung her eyes as she pleaded and wept, and Aélla's confidence diminished into sorrow. She leaned forward with her eyes set on the ground, and the mother gently took her arm. "Please," she begged in broken evaesh. "*Please!*"

147

Aélla gazed at the boy curled against his mother's chest. With a subtle nod, she agreed to help, and the mother gasped with relief. Hugging her child, she closed her eyes and sobbed. *"Tíat'mëvin,"* she said. *"Tíat'mëvin…"*

More villagers gathered, and a hush fell over the city. The mother sat in the midst of the crowded street, cradling her still-weeping child. Speaking softly, she cupped his face in her hands and lovingly kissed his forehead.

Aélla's jaw tensed, and she held her breath. The woman met her gaze and nodded. With a deep exhale, Aélla's shoulders fell, and she knelt by the mother and child. With a long, sorrowful gaze into the mother's eyes, Aélla awaited her approval. The mother gently clutched her arm, and with a smile, she gave one last nod.

Placing a hand each to the mother's and son's legs, Aélla closed her eyes. The boy whimpered and cried as strong, painful magic coursed through him. His mother clutched him tighter, her clenched teeth exposed beneath her stretched lips as she withheld a violent scream.

Her body trembled with pain as the fullness and color of her legs slowly diminished. Tears streamed down her face, and she gently stroked her son's hair, whispering softly into his ear.

Neer watched in wonderment as Aélla transferred the boy's ailments to his mother. She stepped forward, admiring the magic she'd never witnessed before. Aélla had a unique variation of healing that allowed her to fuse, or even transfer, injuries without causing harm to herself. She had also healed herself of sunburns and small wounds, all things that Neer had never had the capability to do.

Staring at her own hands, Neer wondered if she, too, could harness such abilities. But the thought eluded her as Aélla slowly opened her eyes and removed her hands. The mother remained clutched around her son. Her breaths were uneven and raw.

"Mama?" the boy said.

He pushed himself from her grasp, and she fell aside. Catching herself on weak arms, she withheld her tears. The boy shuffled and turned to his feet. His eyes widened in excitement and horror as he wiggled his toes.

"Mama!"

The mother smiled as she wept. Reaching out to Aélla, she took her hands. "Tíat'mëvin…"

A smile broke Aélla's lips as she sniffed. "You're welcome."

The boy stood on shaky legs and fell into his mother, who quickly caught him. They laughed and cried as they embraced. The villagers knelt and bowed to Aélla in admiration and respect.

She slowly stood and gazed around her, staring at them with glistening eyes. Everyone stood as excited strangers flooded the streets, reaching for Aélla, begging for her help. Neer, Y'ven, and Thallon were pushed aside by the stampede and stumbled back. Dru's red aura brightened as she glared at the crowd. Her small fists rested by her sides.

"Dru…," Y'ven started, pulling her closer. He spoke to her in their native tongue, and her anger deepened. She pointed vehemently at the crowd before snubbing her nose and quickly flying away.

"Come," Y'ven said, slipping away from the masses.

Thallon and Neer followed close behind, glancing back at Aélla, who smiled at the villagers before healing their wounds. Neer set her gaze ahead and focused on the city. Lampposts with large glowing bulbs lined the roads and kept the darkening world alight.

Y'ven opened the door to a small shop and was brushed aside by two gown-wearing women who snubbed their noses at him.

Neer huffed with anger and watched the women disappear into a sea of nameless faces. She stepped angrily into the shop and trailed behind Y'ven as he moved carefully through the narrow room. Cool air blew from the pipes along the ceiling and brushed his hair aside.

He paid no attention to the sneering patrons as he meandered through the room, searching the glass shelves and tables. Neer followed as he fingered through small vials of potions, rocks, and alchemical items.

Poking through a box of shining gems, Neer stiffened when Thallon stepped to her side. He cleared his throat and turned to her with a sly smile. "I guess I should thank you for finding me out there," he said.

"Guess you should."

He shook his head. "Seems the rumors are true. Your kind really *don't* like to coexist with ours."

She hadn't meant to sound so dull or uninterested, but in her months of loneliness, it had become her natural tone. And in his presence, it was easy to be hostile. Automatic, even. For it wasn't a stranger that stood next to her, spilling useless words into the air as if speaking was essential to his existence. He was a ghost. A haunting memory of the friend she'd never see again.

"I'm sorry," she said. "You just…remind me of someone I knew."

"He must've been handsome, then." She didn't return his playful smile. "By the way you've been avoiding me, I'd say you either hated or loved him too much."

The gems clinked as she closed the drawer and rummaged through a shelf. Thallon was a step behind, unconvincingly picking through a box of trinkets, awaiting her response. She wasn't used to such games, and her time alone had made her impatient.

"Do you always talk this much?" she asked with sudden hostility.

He chuckled. "I spend most of my time alone underground. I suppose I have a lot of words to share."

She focused on the various items on the shelf. "How I envy those tombs."

"Funny," he said with a laugh. "I never knew Ianathess could jest."

"I never knew a scholar could be so thick."

"Ouch." He placed his hand over his heart. "That stung a little."

With a suspicious side eye, she ignored his playfulness, choosing instead to keep her guard up. He was too kind. Too talkative. Too much like *him*.

Her attention moved to Y'ven, who grunted as glass vials clinked and rolled against a shelf. His large hands scrambled to pick them up and, in his haste, managed to topple several more.

Neer wove through the crowd and came to his side, while Thallon walked through the shop before eventually finding his way outside. Neer placed a hand on Y'ven's arm and carefully reassembled the vials. He straightened and looked at the shoppers, who stared at him with patronizing eyes. Dru, who had found her way back to the group only moments ago, twisted her face in anger. She crossed her arms and stuck out her tongue at the strangers. They recoiled in offense and turned away before leaving.

"Bring a vaxros into a glass house," Neer teased, standing the last vial in its place. "What are we doing here, anyway?"

"Supplies. Healing. Wards. Poison."

"Yes, yes, I get it." Neer stepped aside when a young girl walked past. The youngster gave a polite smile before her mother rushed her aside and put distance between them and the outsiders. "Why are we here anyway? In this city?"

"*Avia* is here. Will take us to mountains," Y'ven explained, peering through the shelves.

"Where Aélla can obtain the energy of wind?"

"Yes."

Neer looked through the shelves and spotted a beautiful decanter of dark purple wine. The crystal vessel sparkled as light from the overhead bulbs glistened against its polished edges. She smiled and pulled the item from the shelf and removed the stopper. With a satisfying pop, the top separated from the base, and the decadent aroma of m'yashk filled her nose.

She closed her eyes and breathed in the familiar scent. While licking her lips, she swirled the contents, wishing desperately to take a sip.

"Come," Y'ven said, pulling a vial from a wooden box.

Neer reluctantly placed the wine back onto the shelf, and with a final glance at it, she followed Y'ven. They stood in line behind three others, waiting to pay for their items. She couldn't stop herself from glancing at the wine, and with each passing shopper, she worried they'd take it before she had the chance.

"What do you see?" Y'ven asked.

"The m'yashk," she said, her eyes still glued to the purple wine. "Reiman and I used to drink it from a decanter similar to that one. We'd stay up by the fire, telling stories or reading."

"M'yashk valuable. For wealthy only."

She smiled. "I know. One of the best parts of having a powerful father is reaping the rewards of his connections. He knows people all over the continent, and he's got more money than I've ever seen."

"Who is he?"

Neer hid her smile, relishing in the secret of who her father was. Y'ven was part of the Brotherhood, and she knew he would know her father. Not wanting to draw the attention to herself, she decided against telling him for now. "Just a man," she explained.

Y'ven didn't bother to question her as they stepped to the counter. He paid for his item, and they shuffled through the shop.

Outside, they met up with Thallon. Behind him, voices echoed from the courtyard where a larger crowd had gathered around Aélla. She placed her hand on a woman's face, and the people bowed and cried as she healed her superficial wounds.

"Why is she healing them?" Neer asked.

"Why not?" Thallon responded.

She crossed her arms. "No one's that nice."

"If you've got the power to do good, why not use it? Seems like you could find a little kindness yourself, lanathess."

With a spiteful glare, she explained, "I've got something better." She pulled back her cloak to reveal the m'yashk hidden safely inside.

"What are you doing?" Y'ven growled.

"Aélla's got her magic, and I've got mine." She smiled. "What do you say, Y'ven? Want to enjoy this delicious, rare drink with me?"

He snatched the decanter and peered through the street. The passersby glanced at him with caution.

Thallon gave a prideful laugh. "Come on, Red. You can't be as stiff as the others."

Y'ven rubbed his forehead and looked at the emptying streets.

"Well...?" Neer pressed, raising her hand and giving the decanter a light shake.

Y'ven's eyes widened with confusion. He looked at his hand and then reached for the wine she stole with her magic. Neer vanished and reappeared several feet back. With a laugh, she took a swig of the expensive drink.

"Lighten up, big guy," Thallon said. "It isn't like you've got much left to lose, right?"

Neer raised her brows with a smile. Turning away, Y'ven's tension fell, and he bound closer to Neer, snatching the decanter. She laughed with glee when he huffed and then gulped the stolen drink.

CHAPTER NINETEEN

M'YASHK
Nerana

"What's life without a bit of fun?"

— Loryk Vaughan

AFTER STEPPING THROUGH THE MISTING force field and into the desert, the group untied three vestrils from the nearby stable. The animals stomped and trilled as they mounted the saddles and gripped the leather reins.

"Want to race?" Thallon asked, coming to Neer's side.

She smiled with excitement and snapped the reins. Y'ven's laughter echoed above the hard thumping of the vestril's feet as he quickly caught up to the others when they sped away.

Neer pulled the reins to the right, and her vestril smacked into Y'ven's. He playfully kicked her away with a roaring laugh. Her vestril shrieked and thrashed its head, causing the trio to roar with laughter.

Y'ven leaned forward and commanded his steed to hasten. Neer was close behind as they wound through steep rocky hillsides. He rounded a sharp turn, and she lost sight of him. Thallon trailed close behind as they moved carefully up the hills before finding Y'ven at a large tree. He dismounted and tied the reins to the trunk.

He turned to Neer and Thallon, grinning from ear to ear, as they strode to his side. Thallon dismounted first and went to Neer's aid. He reached up to help guide her from the saddle, and with a smirk, she vanished.

Thallon stepped back, astonished at her disappearance. A curious smile pulled his lips before he turned around at the sound of scraping boots. She stood several paces behind him, and with a knowing smile, she took a drink of wine.

They moved to the edge of a steep cliff and hung their feet over the edge. Neer sat between them and passed the decanter to Thallon. He was quiet, overlooking the city in the distance. Purple moonlight illuminated against the enormous, curved pillars and gave a soft glow to the barrier shielding the city.

Neer shifted her gaze to the stars, which overlapped to create a thick line across the dark sky. She took a sip of wine when it was passed back to her and then wiped her lips with a refreshed sigh. The sweet juice was reminiscent of what her father used to drink, and she could almost hear his soft voice and the warmth of the hearth as she took another sip.

The moment eluded her when Y'ven removed the decanter from her hands and took several gulps. He passed the container back, and after another sip, she passed it to Thallon.

He drank his share and wiped his lips. "So, where are you from?" he asked.

Accepting this gesture of friendship, Neer said, "Styyr. I spent my childhood in the colleges."

"Really? Did you learn anything useful?"

She smiled. "Just how to sneak through the corridors and prank the professors."

He laughed with red cheeks, the drink clearly taking its effect on him. "What about you, big guy?"

"Wait, wait!" Neer said with a drunken giggle. She touched Y'ven's forehead and merged her energy with his. As the swell of magic decreased, she opened her eyes and smiled. "Go on *big guy*. Talk in your native tongue."

He gave her a curious look, and asked, "What did you do?"

She smiled brightly and attempted to speak his gruff, raspy language. The words were broken and hard to understand. With a deep laugh, she explained in evaesh, "I can understand you."

He rubbed his forehead while shaking his head. "I come from atülg'shelarr."

Thallon smiled. "I'm sure your people don't like you leading us through the desert."

"I don't care."

"Oh?"

Y'ven stared at the wine as it swirled within the container. "I was a warrior of the *al'yavan.*° If you survive the rites, you must take the oath of the warrior."

"The oath is about sun-blood and honor, yes? You can't have a family, right?"

Y'ven exhaled a deep, harrowed sigh. Staring over the edge of the cliff, he recited the unbreakable vows.

> "I am now a warrior of flame.
> Ancestors, gift me your strength.
> Blood of my brothers, honor my valor.
> Heat of the flame, fuel my rage.
> I give my life to the people's defense.
> I am the shield in the sun. The axe in the night.
> I will not cower in defeat.
> Victory is my honor and blood my sacrifice.
> I shall bear no children. I shall take no mate.
> I give my life, and my death, to the al'yavan.
> Until the sun fades to ash, shall my oath remain."

° An esteemed and highly respected warrior pact. Those who survive the brutal and threatening rites are gifted with the mark of the warrior. They are regarded as the fiercest, strongest, and bravest of their people. The al'yavan are free to live in seclusion or within a shelarr of their choosing. They dedicate their lives to protecting their people and land.

Neer mulled over the words, taking much longer in her inebriation to understand them, before coming to a damning conclusion.

"That's pretty harsh." The words spewed from her mouth in a slur of anger and aggression. "No one should have to make that sacrifice."

"I was young. I didn't understand the weight of my decision…I didn't know the truth of pain." He took another gulp of wine. "Calla was my bond mate. I forsook the vows to be with her. It brought great shame to our family, and I was exiled."

"Where is she now?"

"She left with our young son after learning of my betrayal… I lost everything."

Neer turned away and closed her eyes. She understood the loss that came with losing the person you love. With another sip of wine, she retrieved her sword from the sheath on her side and was astonished to find its glow had once again disappeared. Moonlight reflected against the blade, brightening her dirty face. Her fingers grazed the pristine metal, desperate to know its secrets.

"Damn," Thallon said. "That's…heavy. What about you, Neer? Do you have any family back in…What was it called? Styyr? I'm sure your stories are better than his, right?"

She shook her head and sheathed her sword. "No. All my family is dead."

Thallon's expression fell. "Wow…" At a loss for words, he took a drink of wine.

"What about you? I'm sure you've got a story you're just dying to tell us."

"Not really. I grew up in the forest. Have two brothers. They're both warriors with the avel.° Elidyr's earned his own nickname, so he's got a life many would envy."

"A nickname?"

° The most esteemed and well-trained warriors of Nyn'Dira.

"When a warrior is known throughout the forest, they tend to have names associated with them. Through rumors and stories—whatever the case. Elidyr earned his after he single-handedly fought off a band of klaet'il. *Aen'mysvaral*. It means *with a mark upon his face*. After the fight, he was injured. Took the *nes'seil* a long time to heal him. We didn't expect him to come out of it."

"Do all fighters earn these names?"

"No. Just those who have enough reputation to be known throughout the forest. Nasir is the most notorious. His name means *bringer of death*. Chilling, right?" With another sip of wine, he exhaled loudly. His eyes moved to the sky, where hundreds of stars overlapped in a beautifully glowing line. "Beautiful here, isn't it?"

Neer lay on her back, and Thallon followed. Y'ven remained in his place, becoming lost in thought.

With her hands beneath her head, Neer gazed at the stars and brightly glowing moons. "The stars don't look like this in Laeroth," she said.

Thallon chuckled. "This is *all* Laeroth, you know?"

"I know that!" Her cheeks burned. While non-humans referred to the entirety of the continent as Laeroth, the humans used the name in reference to their lands, and Neer was embarrassed to have been called out on the distinction. "I'm referring to my country, not the continent."

"Oh, yeah. You humans started your own civilization and just cut us out, huh?"

Her lips pulled together in a scrunched smile when their eyes met. "I suppose that's good for you, seeing how we like to feast on evaesh flesh and speak in grunts."

With a light chuckle, he turned away. Long fingers covered his face as he fell into a fit of laughter. "I'm sure your kind have *plenty* of stories about the evae."

"Maybe one or two."

"Who knew that all it would take to cut you loose would be some fine evaesh wine?"

"There's more to me than meets the eye, Ebbar—" Her happiness faded to misery. She sat up and gripped her head. With a sigh, she closed her eyes and took another drink of wine. "Sorry."

"It's okay." He sat up with her. "You said I remind you of someone you knew. What was his name?"

She wiped her tears and wrapped her arms around her knees. "Loryk."

He lifted the decanter and met her gaze. With a soft smile, he proclaimed, "To Loryk." Wine splashed in the near-empty vase when he took a gulp. "And to everyone else we've lost." With a nod to Y'ven, he passed the wine around.

Neer finished off the drink and looked out over the horizon.

She stared into the darkness with a stiff throat and tight jaw. When a tear fell, she relinquished her festering emotions and heaved the beautiful decanter over the cliff. Thallon's laughter broke the intense silence as the shimmering crystals faded from view before a faint shatter echoed from below.

"That's more like it!" He playfully smacked her shoulder. She turned away to wipe her eyes while he stood. "Come on. I want to show you something."

She took his hand and rose to her feet. Her face was red, and her body was warm with the tingle of strong wine. Thallon quickly caught her as she stumbled forward, and they laughed too hard at her drunken mishap.

"You coming, Red?" Thallon glanced at Y'ven and found the vaxros asleep at the cliffside. When his eyes met with Neer's, they erupted with uncontrolled laughter. "He can't even handle a little m'yashk!" Thallon said with a cackle, and leaned forward onto his knees while Neer covered her face, tears rolling down their reddened faces.

Each time their eyes met, they fell into another fit of laughter, and clutching her aching stomach, Neer avoided Thallon's gaze.

"Come on," she said with a giggle. "We should move him away from the ledge."

"We can try."

With wide smiles, they began pulling at Y'ven's arms, but the vaxros was dense as stone as he lay snoring and motionless. Neer and Thallon laughed, pushing and heaving until he was no longer close enough to fall.

"Come on, *Tioval*." Thallon took Neer's hand and pulled her behind as he made his way up the cliffs. He released his grip and climbed over a large rock before turning around and extending his hand to her, offering his aid. With a playful glare, she smacked him away and made the climb herself. He smiled proudly as she stood next to him. "You aren't like the other lanathess, are you?"

"I'm not like *anyone*."

His smile grew wider, and he led her carefully through the rocky summit before coming to a long-abandoned temple. Large stone pillars directed them to the tall and narrow building where a path was carved into elegant patterns, trailing to the closed doorway.

"What is this?" she asked.

"The y'lenae call it *caelum'naos. One with the wind and sky*."

"How did you know it was here? On top of this mountain?"

"I'm a scholar," he chuckled. "It's what I do."

She took a step closer, touching a pillar. The stone was rough with age beneath her fingers. "Is it dangerous?"

"Maybe. We can take a look inside, if you want."

"If the vaxros didn't hate you enough before, they will now."

He smiled with a cunning grin and reached for her hand. "That's only if they find out."

With a nervous glance to the temple, she contemplated her decision. Turning back to Thallon, she was reminded of the friend she lost and of the adventures they shared. Fear never held her back before, and she wouldn't let it now. She straightened with confidence and took his hand.

Inside the ancient, well-preserved building, they came to a large empty room. Three long windows rested on each of the opposing walls and filtered moonlight into the narrow corridor. A large statue of a man stood proudly in the center, a timepiece held in his right hand. His left hand was paused in front of his chest with a thumb and finger curled inward to make a circle. His robes opened at the waist to reveal the puffy trousers beneath.

Neer touched the ancient stone. "This looks like a statue of the divine, Vethar."

"*Divine*?" His voice was broken as he spoke the foreign word.

"He's the divine of history and prophecy. Seers would speak with him to foretell the future. It's the reason he and his teachings were banished from the Order. His temple in Styyr was destroyed long before I was born."

"The *Order* are your leaders, right?"

She smiled, happy to have someone familiar with her culture. "Yes."

He turned back to the statue, staring up at its massive size. "This is a statue of An'feindro'l. He was a First Blood scholar of energy and time."

She turned back to the statue and studied his face. His long features and slanted eyes showcased his evaesh roots, but the fullness of his face and his low cheekbones resembled a human, making his evaesh features easy to overlook. Inspecting further, Neer was surprised to find long ears protruding from his hair.

"Interesting," she thought aloud, "that your scholar and my divine would have such similarities."

Thallon shrugged before stepping away. Parchment crinkled as he shuffled through drawers and shelves. "There is so much history to be discovered in this world. So much of the

First Blood is left to mystery. It wouldn't be so far-fetched to believe that our ancestors coexisted."

Neer scoffed. "I doubt that. The Order is firm in their belief that anyone not of pure human blood is sacrilege and demonic."

"What about you?" he asked, without turning away from the book he absently flipped through. "You're lanathess, right? But you're magic." His eyes shifted to hers. "Is that considered pure in the eyes of your *divines*?"

"No," she said. "I'm demonic. Same as you."

His gaze returned to the book. "Yeah. I thought so. I've never known of a human drimil. Only the First Blood, their ancestors, and the eólin° have ever possessed magic."

"So, what? You're agreeing with my people? That I'm a monster born of human disguise?"

"No. Just saying it's odd, is all." He continued flipping through the book. "*Something* gave you magical energy. Who's to say it wasn't your *divines*?"

She crossed her arms and glanced at the statue. The powerful First Blood scholar was intimidating and strong. She couldn't shake the familiarity between this man and the divine, but in her diluted mind, she hadn't the will to think of it much further. They were similar and nothing more.

Wanting to rid herself of this conversation, Neer focused on the temple. The small room held several bookshelves and tables along the walls where thick dust collected atop the ancient books and scrolls. "What is this place used for?"

"Well, it isn't used anymore. Says here, this was a sanctuary built to honor An'feindro'l. Travelers would climb this mountain on each solstice to pay their respects."

Behind the statue, Neer spotted light etchings in the stone wall. She ran her fingers along the rough surface and leaned

---

° Mentioned before in chapter seven, the eóilin are those who were not born of magic, yet still hold its abilities.

closer to get a better look. Peering through the darkness, she was able to make out the faint foreign markings. The symbols were written in a language she didn't know, yet she could read them with clarity.

"What'd you find?" Thallon asked, coming to her side.

Neer jumped back, frightened by his sudden appearance. He glanced at the markings, and a puzzled look pulled his face.

"This is First Blood text," he drunkenly said. Inching closer, he read them aloud, reciting the familiar prophecy Neer received long ago.

"A heart of gold turned to stone…A familiar embrace in arms unknown…Four trials you must take if energy you seek…Many years shall pass, but few will you need…Shadows fall upon a sleeping land…Stay close to the light…" He struggled to read the last of the foreign words,

"*Aerón'dok'fan.*"

Chapter Twenty

Above the Clouds

"K'relök mruvaan Atria'Erquiseaan farvakal twi'liek."
Through wind and air, we shall conquer the lands that were taken.

— Sayings of the Y'lenae

THE STREETS OF ZAOS WERE calm as early risers carried on with their morning tasks. Merchants rose with the sun, unlocking their doors and polishing shop windows, preparing for the day. Bakers lit fires in their ovens, sending the aroma of burnt wood and ash through the air. Chickens squawked as butchers placed them onto a chopping block, and Neer shuddered at the sound of a cleaver hacking through their brittle necks. She crossed her arms and turned away.

The group stopped as Aélla approached a stall owner who called her aside. Wrinkles creased the woman's face as she smiled to the evae. She stood much smaller than the others due to the hunch of her back.

Leading Aélla back to her stall, the woman placed a silver platter atop the counter and lifted the dome cover to reveal pastry tarts. Neer eyed the day's old treats as if she had never seen food before.

The woman pushed the tray to Aélla, but she was reluctant to take it.

"Come on," Thallon whispered harshly, "use your status for good. We're starving." While they had provisions, and were regularly eating foul-tasting meals, the lure of a pastry tart was too good to pass.

Aélla turned to the woman, who smiled with admiration, and politely bowed before accepting the offering of food. Everyone grabbed a tart, gave their thanks to the kind stranger, and continued on their way.

Neer bit into her breakfast and relished in the taste of sweet berries, while Y'ven recoiled in disgust. She chuckled before taking another bite. "Not used to nice-tasting food, Y'ven?"

He huffed and shoved the tart into his mouth before swallowing it in just a few quick bites. Neer watched him with amusement and understanding. The fruits of the desert growing beyond the protection of this city were bitter and bland.

As they moved further through the village, the streets came alive with voices and soft music. A band sat in a small alcove, playing woodwind instruments. Their tunes were soft and harmonious, perfect for a wakening world.

Children raced by, pushing wooden wheels with sticks, while adults spoke quietly to one another. Aélla smiled at the residents as they bowed to her. Y'ven tensed and moved to her side as the strangers began pulling at her clothes and begging her to heal them.

Neer watched her, thinking of her kindness and gentle approach as Aélla refused their pleas with an apologetic smile. "Is she always treated this way?" Neer asked.

Thallon responded with a full mouth. "Kind of. She's the last living full-blooded sorceress…Well, last living aside from you. A lot of our people think her being here is fated."

"What do you think?"

He shrugged and swallowed his food. "I'm a scholar. I don't believe in fate."

The group came to a halt when a carriage crossed their path. The large black vehicle carried several passengers from one side of town to the other. Steam rose from the exhaust pipes as it cut through the dense horde of villagers.

Through the thick crowds and luring merchants, the group found themselves at the edge of the city, where empty desert stretched for miles beyond the invisible protective barrier. A small crowd gathered in the empty courtyard, while Neer stood along the outskirts with her group.

"I've been thinking," Thallon started as he came to her side, "about that inscription. I get the feeling you know what it means."

"No," she lied, staring ahead to purposefully avoid his gaze. The last thing she needed was a stranger interpreting her fate through ancient prophecies and riddles.

His eyes narrowed as he examined her hardened expression. *"Shadows fall upon a sleeping land,"* he started, reciting the ancient words, *"stay close to the light…or all shall end."*

Her heart stopped at his translation. For hours, she would lay awake during the night, wondering what the words could mean.

He asked, "That sounds like a warning, don't you think?"

Not wanting to express her concern or fall into a conversation he cleverly tried to trap her in, she smoothly stated, "Who knows? You're the scholar."

He smiled at her attempt to undermine his conclusion. With another bite of his tart, he ended the conversation, though his sly grin never faded.

The soft murmur of the crowd fell silent as a large shadow blanketed the courtyard in darkness. Gripping the hilt of her sword, Neer lifted her eyes and found it wasn't a creature or enemy that came from above. It was something different. Something metal and loud descending from the sky.

As it grew closer, strong winds swept across the courtyard. Everyone gathered and quickly stepped aside, clearing the wide space to allow the floating machine to land before them.

It touched the ground with a metallic screech. The floating mechanism resembled a giant rowboat with round windows across its bow. Two long blimps were tethered to each of its sides with tight metal strings. Large cogs, tall metal canisters, and two large pipes billowing with thick steam made up the back of the flying boat. Behind the mechanisms, still spinning as the machine landed, was a giant fan.

Neer and Aélla stared in amazement as the flying boat landed before them. A rope ladder unrolled down the side, and a group of twenty people climbed from the ship.

"This"—Neer stepped closer, her eyes wide as she fell speechless and amazed—"is magnificent…"

"Ürok and evae have no *avia*?°" Y'ven asked.

Aélla said, "The only way to soar the sky is with the glyn-fir."

Silence overtook the once noisy courtyard as the avia stilled and the winds subsided. Heavy boots thudded across the ground as a dreled waddled to the awaiting crowd. He was a short, pudgy man who smiled through an unkempt beard.

He spoke a language native to the y'lenae, and the strangers passed him handfuls of golden cogs. The dreled fingered through them with a delighted grin.

As he approached the group, speaking in the same native language, Aélla politely smiled.

"I am sorry," she explained in evaesh. "Do you speak the common tongue of the evae?"

With his hands to his hips, the dreled puffed out his chest and proclaimed, "Apologies, young evae! Name's Reuhnar Vilkas! Have you come to scurry an adventure atop the Great Mastiff? I tell you, 'tis a journey like no other. Can take you halfway across the desert in just two days' time!

° Roughly translated: airship.
The Great Mastiff is an avia, or airship, powered by steam and wind turbines. Three avia exist in Aragoth and were created by the y'lenae as a way to travel between the three major cities of Zaos, Kelua, and Rhynd.

"O'course, there's the matter of a small, wee little price of just twenty cogs each."

Y'ven snarled. "Asked fifteen from others."

The dreled gripped his stomach and roared with laughter. "Oh, dear. You're a clever one, aren't ya? All right, best I can do is seventeen cogs each, but I can't go any lower!" He pointed a stubby finger at Y'ven.

"Actually," Aélla started. "We seek to find the k'laea.°"

His eyes widened in terror. "Why would you want to go to a place such as that?"

"I am Drimil'Rothar. Gaining trust with the k'laea will grant me passage to tre'lan Aenwyn."

The man trembled before bowing on his knees. "My lady," he said. "'Tis truly an honor to meet you."

She smiled pleasantly. "The honor is mine."

The dreled's excited eyes turned to the crowd of paying customers gathered by the airship. He waddled hastily to their sides with flailing arms. "Sorry! Shops closed! You'll need to return tomorrow! Go on! Get!"

Cogs were thrown at the crowd as he shooed them from the courtyard. The angry villagers protested with spite, and in his anger, the dreled transformed into a mammoth. He reared back and trumpeted a loud warning from his long snout, causing the crowd to trip over one another as they fled in terror.

Neer chuckled as the crowd ran past them and into the village. She was reminded of Gil and his antics when others would cause him trouble.

"Right this way, Master Drimil." The dreled motioned to the avia before sliding large goggles over his eyes. "Come on then, we aren't getting any younger!"

They climbed the long, unstable rope ladder while the dreled transformed into a bird and flew to the top. Aélla was first to board, followed soon by the others. Thallon reached

---

° Mentioned in chapter ten, the k'laea are enormous bird-like creatures who dwell within the highest Peaks of Draak.

over the edge for Neer's hand as she came to the top. With a huff, she accepted his offer, and was pulled up.

"Take care not to fall off," the dreled explained as he stepped to the back toward the large fan and canisters. Fifteen seats were in the center of the boat, bolted to the flooring. "'Tis a long way down!"

He disappeared through a trapdoor while the others remained on the top deck. Neer stepped to the railing and looked at the city below. She could see far into the bustling village and streets.

The ship shifted and caused her to stumble aside as the large turbine slowly rotated and steam whistled from small holes in the pipes.

Pressure nudged them downward when the avia lifted from the ground. Wind swept across the large ship as they floated higher into the air. Aélla came to Neer's side, and they looked over the edge to the dwindling city below. The two giggled like children, pointing out the large buildings and specks of people.

A wave of heat overcame them when they passed through the barrier. Neer had forgotten how intense the desert was and longed to be back within the cool, protected village.

She turned back, ready to invite Y'ven over, when she noticed him meditating at the bow of the ship. The sun gleamed against his skin and illuminated his yellow scars. Behind him, Thallon dug through a metal box filled with crossbow bolts.

"Oh, look!" Aélla exclaimed, pointing to a vibrant forest in the midst of brown rock and dirt. "Isn't it beautiful?"

"What is that?" Neer asked. "How is it so green?"

"That's Fru'skomir. It's protected by enchantments to keep it alive."

Neer stared in wonder at the beautiful trees. Too involved in her fascination to ask questions, she gazed upon the world below. Small black dots cast long shadows as people wandered the vast desert plains. Villages of tents and clay homes rested all throughout the open canvas. Staring down to the inhabitants, she noticed a large crowd of people gathered in a small village.

Sunlight glinted with white specks as they swung weapons at each other. Neer watched them for a moment, feeling puzzled and overwhelmed by the fight. Unable to see who was involved, she leaned further over the railing.

The air cooled as they moved higher, and she lost sight of the world below when clouds overtook the sky. Moisture dampened their clothes and skin, soothing their mild sunburn. Neer backed away with a deep huff. She turned to Aélla, who stood with her eyes closed as the winds swept through her long hair.

Not wanting to break her tranquility, Neer kept to herself as she thought of the fight below. It wasn't unlike the vaxros to find themselves in large battles against one another. But she couldn't erase the unease sifting through her.

Something felt different. It felt… *wrong.*

Her thoughts were broken when a loud, animalistic screech chiseled through the frosted air. Neer turned, searching for what could have made such a noise, but was met with undisturbed skies. Turning back, she noticed Y'ven was still in his meditations, but Aélla had a look far more frightening.

Her fair skin had become paler as she gazed wide-eyed into the clouds, watching as the klaet'il emerged from the mist.

CHAPTER TWENTY-ONE

PURSUIT

THE CLOUDS SWIRLED, AND BLOOD-CURDLING screeches overlapped from every direction, drowning out the sound of the powerful turbines and wind. Aélla created a barrier as arrows emerged from the clouds. She grunted and winced as they struck her magic, creating small white cracks in the air before her.

A screech echoed nearby, and Neer turned with her arms out, ready to use her magic, when the quick flash of a dark green creature flew past, and she withdrew in shock. Large wings stretched open as it hovered nearby, and the clouds disappeared to reveal a winged beast of the klaet'il. Its green, leathered skin held yellow spots, and its bird-like talons curled beneath its long body.

"*Drimil'caal!*" The rider called with an intimidating growl. His gaze was fixed on Aélla as he spoke to her in his native tongue.

Neer readied her arms as half a dozen flyers appeared through the clouds. Each of the riders had the same tattooed skin, dark hair, and fierce scowls. Neer scanned their faces and was eased by the absence of the Nasir and Ithronél, the elemental sorceress.

Aélla was quiet as the man pointed his spear at her, and his comrades released several arrows in her direction.

The weapons struck against her magic, fragmenting the air with white lines. Aélla screamed and fell to her knees, stricken with agony as her energy was punctured. Shaky arms struggled to maintain the barrier, and as it faded, Neer turned to the nearest flyer. He drew back an arrow, ready to strike down the fallen evae, when Neer teleported behind him on the saddle. He choked a silent gasp, blood spewing from his mouth, when her sword struck through his back. Faint purple veins illuminated across the blade.

As he slid from the saddle, falling lifelessly through the thick clouds, his flyer began to thrash in opposition, and Neer transported back to the ship. Unable to properly control her magic, she rolled across the floor. Dru prepared a fireball in her hands as a klaet'il rider swooped over Neer and slashed his sword across her back.

She unleashed a shriek as she collapsed to the ground, blood draining into a shallow puddle around her. Dru's fireball was released from her grasp and slammed into the face of the glynfir. It let out a screech as it spiraled through the air. The klaet'il rider quickly leapt onto the avia as his flyer descended through the clouds and out of sight.

Thallon stood above Neer with a crossbow in hand and a long metal shield on his arm. His robes waved violently in the wind as he aimed his weapon at the klaet'il who stood on the avia with them. The bolt released and sank deep into his chest, and a deep explosion tore him apart as the weapon ignited. Thallon shielded himself and Neer as blood and innards rained from above.

Neer peeked around the shield in horror, her eyes glued to the remnants of a man that once fought to kill her. "What was that?" she asked, her voice trembling.

Thallon gulped down his emotions, and then carefully retrieved a bolt from the quiver on his back. Inspecting them further, he noticed bright yellow veins pulsing across the metal shaft. "They're enchanted…" he remarked.

"You didn't notice before?"

"I had just found this when the klaet'il attacked! Sorry to jump in the line of fire to save you instead of inspecting the weaponry!"

With a huff he glanced aside and noticed Aélla sitting on her knees across the platform. The evae struggled to use her energy as two klaet'il rained arrows down from above. A klaet'il with a bone necklace watched her with prideful eyes as she was pinned behind her magic, unable to fight against them as arrows slammed against her barrier from every direction. His permanent scowl was deep and intimidating. He called to a female rider and pointed at the ship. The woman nodded and commanded her glynfir forward with a snap of the reins.

As Neer lifted her hand, ready to use her magic to help Aélla, the flash of another glynfir moved overhead. Thallon pulled her aside and ducked beneath the shield. The purple glynfir reeled in its wings and moved quicker through the air, toward Y'ven and Dru. Its klaet'il rider stood on her saddle and drew back her sword. As she closed in, ready to make the deadly swipe, Neer shoved Thallon aside and blasted the klaet'il back with a powerful wave of energy.

The purple glynfir spun through the air, its wings flailing wildly as its rider struggled to hold on. Her sword dropped onto the airship as the glynfir screeched and cawed. The animal clawed through the air, attempting to grab a hold of anything it could find, and as it passed by the air canisters, its sharp talons scratched into the iron pipes.

Hot steam whistled from the pipes and scalded its leg. With a loud scream, the glynfir withdrew its arms, and the pressure of the steam released in a thick, expanding cloud. The klaet'il rider fell from the saddle and rolled across the ship before tumbling over the edge.

Her commander snarled in disgust as he watched her fall through the clouds.

Y'ven shouted and gripped his hammer, while Dru hovered nearby, tossing small flames at the klaet'il who landed on the avia and ran toward them. The nimble fighter dodged her attacks as he moved toward Y'ven. Neer fell forward in agony as her back bled and throbbed. Thallon struggled to aim his weapon, knowing the wrong strike could destroy the avia. As the fighter closed in, Y'ven raised his hammer, and the klaet'il slid beneath his powerful swing, slicing his sword deep into Y'ven's leg.

Jumping to his feet, the klaet'il slashed at Y'ven's back, but the vaxros dodged the attack and swung his hammer.

The klaet'il spun to evade the weapon that moved past his cheek. With a smirk, he twisted his sword and spoke viciously to the vaxros.

Flames brightened his face as another fireball blasted toward him. In the same motion, he spun aside and threw a dagger at the faeth.

"Dru!" Y'ven called while reaching out for her. The klaet'il slashed his arm, and he roared in agony. Blood spattered onto the avia as he stumbled aside. With a deep, opened gash in his arm, Y'ven lifted his hammer and blocked a deadly strike to the chest.

The dagger moved quickly through the air, hurtling toward Dru, who was stricken with terror as the sharp weapon hurled closer. The coolness of its metal blade touched her skin, before vanishing from the air. She glanced aside as Neer tossed the dagger to the ground and extended her arms toward the klaet'il fighting Y'ven. But her strength was overshadowed by pain, and she hunched forward, blood slithering down her back and pooling around her knees. She struggled to lift her arm and use her magic.

Y'ven kicked the klaet'il back and swung his hammer. With a backward roll, the klaet'il evaded the deadly hit and slashed his sword. As the blade made contact with Y'ven's arm, it disappeared, and the klaet'il stumbled aside.

Y'ven lifted his hammer and smashed it deep into the klaet'il's skull. The crack of his head splitting open vibrated through the air before Y'ven kicked him back and removed the weapon. Hot blood spattered across Neer's face. She dropped the klaet'il's sword and leaned forward onto her fists.

Warmth filled her body as light swirled around her. She looked at her arms before turning back to view Aélla, who reached out to her before turning away as more arrows fell from the sky. As the magic around Neer faded, the pain of her injury decreased, and she sent a pulse of energy to the arrows descending over Aélla. They flipped through the air and disappeared into the clouds.

The commander shouted in anger and threw his spear. Y'ven tackled Aélla aside and roared in agony as the spear sank deep into his leg. Through a deep, raspy cry, he removed the blood-soaked weapon, and a fierce glare overtook his expression. He leapt to his feet and turned to the klaet'il with a menacing glare. Hobbled steps quickened as he moved to the edge of the avia and pulled back his arm with a furious cry.

The klaet'il watched him with a light smirk. His fists were hard on the reins as he prepared to evade the attack. As Y'ven heaved the weapon, the commander's arrogance faded to shock. His hardened eyes were fierce as the spear was thrown to the right and thrust into the stomach of an archer. The arrow fell from his grasp as he was hurled through the air.

With an angered growl, the commander flew to Aélla, who sat with an arrow in her arm.

Dru tossed weak fireballs to the glynfir, who easily evaded the attacks.

"Drimil!" Y'ven roared.

As the klaet'il raced closer, Neer ran forward and, with a deep breath, teleported herself onto the back of the glynfir. The creature swayed and screeched as she stood on the flaps of its large wings.

The sudden movement caused the glynfir to bypass Aélla. Neer grabbed the klaet'il long hair to steady herself, and blood splashed across her face when her sword sank deep into his back.

Before he could fight back, she teleported away and rolled across the avia. Weakened from her magic, she couldn't catch herself as she tumbled to the edge. Tumbling closer, she could feel the cold rush of air coming from the mountain as the avia approached its surface.

Just as she reached the edge of the ship, a shadow enveloped her in darkness, and the weight of Thallon's body pressed her against the wooden flooring as he grabbed her from behind. With a grunt, he moved them away from the edge and sat on his knees.

Neer glanced at him, watching as a stream of red glided down his temple. She winced as pain throbbed in her back, coursing through her like fire. Slowly, her grip on Avelloch's bloody sword loosened as her body fell limp, and she closed her eyes.

CHAPTER TWENTY-TWO

AIR
AÉLLA

THE SHIP DESCENDED INTO THE mountains, steam billowing from its busted pipes. The misty air laid patterns of frost along the bow as it moved through the peaks and closer to the ground. Y'ven fell to his knees, wincing as blood poured down his arm and leg. White breath clouded his face as he exhaled deep, exhausted breaths.

Aélla was flung aside as the avia ripped through dense pine trees. She grunted and crawled to her feet. Taking Y'ven's arm, she urged him to follow as she gathered around Neer, who laid unconscious at the bolted seats. Thallon was knelt beside her, clutching the wound on his head. Aélla took hold of a chair to steady herself and then closed her eyes. Her lips stretched and teeth clenched as she struggled to create a small barrier to protect them against the harsh winds.

Heavy snow and pine needles hailed past the weak barrier as it formed around them. The ship barreled through the mountains, and with a sudden jolt, it collided atop the icy ground. Everyone was lurched aside as the ship came to a rumbling halt.

Aélla collapsed to the floor and the barrier disappeared. The bitter cold kiss of snow layered over them, soaking into their clothes and skin. Steam filled the air as the avia settled with a loud, grinding creak.

Orange light and heat came from the left when Dru pushed bright flames into Y'ven's injuries. He groaned through clenched teeth as she mended his deep wounds.

The clunk of footsteps pounded against the wooden surface as the dreled made his way to their sides.

"You spriggots all right?" he asked. "My! What happened to ya? Best get inside and away from the cold! Come on now!" He tugged Aélla's arm, and she crawled to her feet. Y'ven carried Neer as everyone followed the dreled into the lower-level bunks.

The small room was cramped and narrow, with wooden bunkbeds lining the walls and a small table near the door. Too large to fit on the beds, Y'ven bundled within three quilts on the floor, while Aélla and Thallon sat at the table. Neer lay unconscious on a bed, and Dru snuggled next to her in the fur blankets.

"Bit of a nasty landing," the dreled said, climbing onto the chair next to Thallon. "What was goin' on out there? Why're you all busted up?"

The ship was silent as they refused to speak. Harsh winds pressed against the outer walls as the snowstorm grew stronger. Y'ven leaned forward, and the avia creaked with a loud whine. The bundled blankets made his natural form look even thicker.

"Can you fix?" he asked.

"Sure hope so! Lest you've got another way off these rocks." He glanced between the passengers sitting quietly in their somber trances. "Didn't think so. I won't be able to check the damage 'til morn. Best we get some shut eye 'til then."

The dreled looked between them before quietly taking his leave. Hanging lanterns swayed lightly from the low ceiling, casting a soft flicker of candlelight that reflected against the crystals of Aélla's staff.

Thallon leaned forward and blew warm air into his hands. "So, this is where tre'lan Aenwyn is? At the top of a freezing mountain…" He spoke through a busted, swollen lip. "Couldn't have been on a warm shore, or in the forest?"

"What do you know of tre'lan Aenwyn?" Aélla asked. She rubbed her hands together as the tips of her fingers started to turn blue.

"Not much. Each element is a different realm. You can't use any magic other than the element which it holds—in this case, air—and if you survive, you're able to use that energy more powerfully." His voice faded into harsh shivers. "But the realms are full of magic. Everyone will have a different test— like the *avour'il*°—with illusions and magic."

"Illusions of what?"

He rubbed his hands together and breathed out a puff of white air. "I don't know. I think the realm works off of your fears and memories. It'll use your own emotions against you." He huddled further into his cloak. "*Kila!* It's cold!"

Aélla bundled tighter into her cloaks as well. "I just hope we are able to get through this before the klaet'il find me."

Thallon's eyes were set on Neer as she slept. "The klaet'il…," he started apprehensively, "they aren't here for you."

Aélla's tired eyes shifted to him. "If they aren't after me, then why did they attack us?"

"If I'm being honest…I'm not so sure it's *you* they're trying to take."

A small line formed between her brows. With a hesitant sigh, Thallon dropped his arms to the table. Slowly, his gaze shifted to Neer, and the color drained from Aélla's face. Her wide eyes were set on Neer as she became lost by the revelation. "But they…Why would he…"

"The same reason *you* want her."

° A dangerous and forbidden test of strength, will, and spirit. Located deep within the forest of Nyn'Dira, this test is used by the klaet'il to train their soldiers. All other clans have banished any from entering the avour'il, as many who enter are never seen again.

"I'm trying to *save* her!"

He raised an eyebrow. With another glance to Neer, he leaned back in his chair and closed his eyes. "We all know how this is going to play out, Aélla. A human with magic is unheard of. She's dangerous."

"*You* are dangerous! The klaet'il and eirean and triandal! Any person with a *sword* is dangerous!" Her face turned red. "Nerana is not what they think her to be! So long as she's with me, she's safe!"

"For how long? The Nasir and klaet'il have power beyond our measure. They'll know how to keep her magic contained."

Aélla scoffed. Her eyes set upon the table as she fell into deep thought. "Avelloch told me that she is being hunted by her people. They consider her *dro'fahmel.*° But he trusts her…and so will I."

Thallon shook his head in disgust. "The day that I trust that *nesiat* is the day I —"

"Enough." Her grim voice shook him. A furious scowl pulled her face with a shade of darkness she'd rarely shown. Beneath the weight of her sudden fury, Thallon withdrew from his anger. "Say what you will about Nerana or myself…but you will not speak of him that way."

His lip twitched as emotions tore through him. With a deep growl, he marched from the ship and swiftly fled into the frozen night.

At his departure, Aélla exhaled a deep breath. Her anger lingered for a moment as she gazed upon the room. With a long glance to Neer, she sadly turned away and spent the rest of the night embraced by sorrow and fear.

° Dro'fahmel is an evaesh phrase meaning *soul of the damned*. This dangerous and often unsaid phrase is given to those who are deemed unworthy of this world. Even the most ruthless and vile of evae, the Nasir, has yet to earn such a condemnatory title.

Hours later, a glimpse of morning sunlight broke through the rugged peaks, filtering pink and orange light across the quiet mountains. Aélla sat atop the snowy bow of the avia. The fur of her thick cloak swayed against the cold morning breeze. Warm magic twisted and burned within her as she meditated.

A glint of sunlight brightened her face and revealed a small scar, nearly invisible unless seen in the perfect light, that lay beneath her left eye. It was the only imperfection she seemed to carry, though she wouldn't consider it an imperfection at all, as it was caused when she and her brother were playing as children. She always thought it made her look tough, like him.

With a soft breath, she relaxed her shoulders and opened her eyes. Sunlight sparkled against the pines weeping beneath the weight of snow.

Darkness blocked out the sun and sent a wave of cold over her skin as a shadow passed overhead. Hovering above, moving slowly to the north, were hundreds of red-feathered k'laea. Their large, wide wings cast long shadows over the quiet peaks.

She had heard many stories of the k'laea, the most widely known being that certain First Blood clans revered them as gods, giving them praise and offering sacrifices to be burnt at the stake. Aélla didn't believe in such atrocities, but the legend of the k'laea had survived many centuries, and to be in their presence was truly a gift.

As the last of the k'laea migrated by, she gathered her staff and set off into the mountains. Sunlight glistened against the snow as it swirled through the air with a gentle breeze.

The short walk took hours as she climbed through deep snow and over steep peaks. As she came to a hidden vale, the overlapping sound of hundreds of k'laea filled the air. Large red feathers lay atop the snow as the animals perched in their nests on the ground.

Her eyes scanned the valley before setting upon a great white k'laea nestled within a shallow cave. She closed her eyes and took several calming breaths. Any wrong movement could send them flying, and she couldn't take that chance.

As her deep breaths slowed, she nodded to herself and stepped into their den. Snow crunched beneath her feet as she moved further into their home, and the k'laea flapped their wings in defense. Bright orange fledglings perched in their nests as their parents reared in opposition.

Aélla remained calm and relaxed, though the urge to run wasn't far from her mind. She held the panic deep within her chest, unable to breathe for fear of it releasing.

She paused in her step as a bird lunged forward. Its sharp beak opened close to her face as it squawked with fury. Continuing forward, she approached the cave, and the white k'laea flapped its wings defensively. The enormous creature stepped forward, and Aélla stumbled back, gulping down the fear mounting in her throat.

"Please…" She bowed. "I do not wish to harm you."

The k'laea examined her. Their gazes met as she timidly lifted her eyes, and the creature stepped back before lifting its wings to showcase its wide span. Sunlight glistened against its beautiful white feathers.

Aélla took a careful step forward. The k'laea wiggled and moved its wings to assert its impeccable dominance. Aélla was instantly still but never broke eye contact. She had learned from her studies how to appease the great k'laea, and remaining confident and alert was the only way to ensure her survival.

With another step, the creature stiffened. She moved half a step at a time, her feet sliding across the snow. When she stood only inches away, the k'laea looked down to her. Her heart thudded hard against her chest as she hesitantly reached out and touched its chest.

Her eyes closed as their energies intertwined, sending a surge of heat swirling through her. The purity of its magic touched her own, and she smiled brightly. When the k'laea shifted, Aélla slowly stepped back. The large bird brought its head close to hers, and she could see her reflection in its eye as it examined her.

Retracting its wings, the k'laea bowed, and Aélla calmly stroked its head before mounting onto its back. It stood tall, and she quickly wrapped around its neck to keep from falling. The others were quiet as the white k'laea opened its wings and took flight.

Cold winds brushed through Aélla's hair as they soared above the peaks. Sunlight brightened the snow-covered mountains and gave warmth to the frigid air. Animals wandering through the sparse trees left trails in the deep snow. Elk and moose ate leaves and berries while direwolves hunted for prey.

The k'laea climbed higher into the clouds, and Aélla curled into its back. Its feathers were soft and kept her warm. As they broke through the heavy clouds, they came to an enormous floating mountain range. The rock formations were broken into hundreds of islands covered in grass, snow, and waterfalls. Sunlight was cast into several rays, shining through the smaller rocks and thick vines.

The k'laea called out as it soared through the sky. It flew around a smaller mountain before approaching its tallest peak. Landing atop the snowy surface, it bowed its head, allowing Aélla to dismount. She stood atop the enormous floating mountain. Trees and snow surrounded her at every turn. Had she not witnessed the magnificence of the Sky Mountains for herself, she would believe she was standing back on the mountains in Aragoth.

The k'laea rested in the snow as the evae looked around. Aélla smiled to the great creature before trekking through the mysterious lands. With no path to guide her, she broke several limbs of the snow-covered pines to keep track of where she had been.

The forest grew thinner, and sunlight sprayed through the trees. A light breeze swept across the mountain, sending waves of loose powder glistening through the air. Her eyes fell to stone steps that were laid beneath the snow, leading to a higher peak. She bundled tighter into her cloak and followed the half-buried steps.

"Aélla…" a voice whispered through the wind, echoing over itself as it faded with the breeze.

She turned with a gasp, searching for the one who called her. It was a long-forgotten voice, but one she recognized clearly.

Finding herself alone, she gulped down the knot in her throat and continued up the steps. The winds increased the higher she climbed. Her cloak waved hard and slipped beneath her fingers. She clutched it tightly in her fist and held it to her chest.

Ice formed along her cheeks and her skin burned against the intensely cold winds. She pushed through the heavy currents, struggling to take a step, when she was thrust aside and slid on the snow, nearly losing her footing. Her cloak was ripped from her grasp by a freezing gust of wind and drifted through the air.

Her eyes followed as it moved further away before disappearing into the mist of swirling snow. Looking around, she caught sight of a shadow slumped in the distance. Aélla clutched to the trees as she fought to move closer and was perplexed when three others came into view. They towered over a woman knelt before them, their silver armor shimmering against the whiteness of snow. Golden scapulars hung from their waists, giving no ebb to the winds sweeping around them. Black liquid dripped from a syringe laid at their feet.

"Please…," the woman pleaded. "Don't take him!"

Aélla's breath caught in her throat. She stepped forward, eyeing the woman she never thought she'd see again. Her white hair was matted with dirt and blood, and in her arms was a boy. He trembled and shook, staring at the men threatening him.

"He has no magic," the woman demanded. "I'll be of more value than this child!"

As the knight drew his sword, Aélla raced forward. Struggling to conjure even the most miniscule strength of energy, she found there was none left. She was void of all magic. Empty of its power.

The knight struck his sword at the woman and child, and the shadows faded to smoke.

"No!" Aélla screamed. She reached for the black mist dispersing into the sky. "Mother..."

Misty eyes stared at the place her mother once sat. It was a vision from the past, and one that always haunted her dreams. It was the day she lost everything. Misty-eyed and stricken with grief, Aélla looked around, wondering how the vision came to be.

"It's a test..." She reminded herself of her conversation with Thallon. The realms took one's darkest memories and fears and brought them to life. It was more than a test of magical strength or endurance...it was a test of will.

Shifting her gaze from the snow to the mountain peak, she spotted a light glistening from the summit. It was faint and hardly noticeable behind the thicket of snow and mist.

With her eyes on the light, she pushed through the heartache, and moved past the place her mother once sat. Moving closer to the summit, voices began whispering through her mind. Some familiar, others unknown. They were distant and soft as they spoke to her, warning her of the journey ahead.

Demanding her to turn back.

A shadow lurked nearby, moving quickly from one tree to the next. Aélla paid it no mind. She wouldn't succumb to the illusions of this place. Her goal was set. She would reach the summit and obtain the energy. It was the only way to end this suffering.

"Aélla!" The familiar voice of an old friend called out to her. It was panicked and scared. She couldn't escape his pain as he cried out. Glancing quickly through the forest, she remembered it was an illusion, and covered her ears to quell his screams. A hard gust of wind pushed her aside, and she lost her footing.

Slipping from the icy step, she tumbled down the sloped hillside. She clawed through the snow and halfway down caught a thick curved root. The winds battered and beat her into the ground. She winced and crawled forward, snow clinging to her face and burning her skin.

Clutching the root, she curled into her knees to keep herself warm. Every gust of wind took her breath away. She could feel every vibration of the wind as she fought for the spark of warmth to ignite in her chest.

But no energy was present, other than the sharp sting that came from every hard gust of wind. She winced and cried, unable to escape the weight of its magic as she was pressed further to the ground.

She closed her eyes and fought against the magic that compressed her. Focused on her energy, she allowed every tendril and spark to pass through her. Her magic slowly converged with the wind, twisting and tightening like a rope as they melded into one. And for a moment she was weightless. The breath of the world filled her with life and power. Every fiber—every push—increased her connection. It moved through her like a ripple on the shore, growing stronger with every shift of the wind.

Energy coursed through her like a freshly lit fire. She was alive. The weight of magic filled her with purpose. Like a warm coat covering her cold and damp skin, she was comforted and whole. The void within her filled as energy sparked in her chest.

The winds pushed and pulled as she reached out to grasp its strength, fighting to contain such wild and forceful power. It slipped through her fingers like an angry eel, but she managed to find her grip and took hold of the wind.

Hot, burning magic coursed through her as their energies entangled.

Curled into the ground, she fought to control it. Beads of sweat dripped from her red face. Her jaw ached from the tension as she forcefully willed the energy to obey.

Slowly, the winds reduced. The snow whipping through the air fell calmly from the sky, and a light breeze replaced the raging gale.

Lifting her eyes, she could see the light at the summit. Through pained, exhausted breaths, she kept hold of the wind and climbed the slope.

At the peak, she came to an altar of tall rock pillars bordering a circular stone platform. The aged stone, which held remnants of a design etched into its surface, was cracked and battered beneath her feet. Unable to withhold the energy, she released her grip, and the winds unleashed through the air

She fell to her knees and crawled across the stone. The winds surrounded the altar, sweeping with pines and snow in a vortex that circled the undisturbed platform.

Resting in the center of the altar was a narrow rock pillar. Aélla clutched her aching chest as she crawled to her feet and approached the monolith. She ran her fingers along the recess at its apex and noticed it was the size of the crystals in her staff.

As she reached for a shard, the twisted branches holding it into place slithered open, allowing her to receive it. She carefully removed the crystal shard and placed it into the recess. The platform creaked and shifted as the cracks of the pillar brightened with light. Its luminescence traveled through the platform and the ancient symbols at her feet glowed brightly.

Aélla stepped back, mesmerized, as the winds surrounding the altar came together high above and funneled down into the pillar. The force of wind pushed her back, and she was blown aside before rolling across the platform. Lying on her stomach, she watched the winds being vacuumed into the crystal.

Winds tore pines from the trees and swept snow high into the air. The cold stung her skin as she gazed at the vortex in awe. The funnel dwindled before being absorbed completely into the crystal, and the world fell deathly silent. Aélla didn't breathe, gazing upon the shard, which now glowed a vibrant white.

She stood and hesitantly retrieved the crystal. The opened branches slowly tightened around the shard as Aélla placed it back onto the staff. She glanced at the pillar and found the glowing cracks and symbols were once again dormant.

A loud shriek came from the distance. Its reverberating sound chiseled through the cold air. Climbing through the rocks, Aélla peered through the clouds, when a dragon broke through the mist. Its white scales glistened as it twisted and wove through the sky. A dark shadow rose over the altar, and two monstrous claws gripped onto the peaks of the towering rocks formation.

Bright blue eyes met with hers, and she was frozen in place. The dragon lifted its wings and took flight. Aélla fell back from the pressure of wind. Its large wings dipped beneath the clouds and spread open, breaking the heavy mist. Aélla stared in wonderment at the mythical creature, when her gaze fell upon the world below, and her heart stopped.

Fires scorched the forests and fields as smoke filled the sky, shrouding it with darkness and ash. Deep cracks fragmented the ground, and dark mist rose from the depths of the world, giving birth to vicious creatures and ancient magic.

The thick clouds came back together, and the world faded along with the dragon. Aélla stared at the ground in anguish and fear. Visions of the world, burning and scorched, were all she could see. She wondered of the importance of such an illusion, and the presence of a dragon, powerful and extinct, filled her with dread.

Her thoughts were broken as light and warmth radiated from behind. She slowly turned around and was met with the apparition of her mother, who smiled and reached for her hand. Her white robes cascaded down in several layers.

Aélla stepped closer, staring at a face she could only recall through memory shards and visions. Her mother's voice whispered through the air, yet her lips never moved. It was clear and beautiful, just as it had always been.

"Do not fall victim to the darkness of this world," she warned. "You cannot fail." Their eyes connected, and Aélla was overcome with fear. "You must save us all."

Winds swept, and the vision of her mother disappeared. With tears in her eyes, Aélla reached for a woman who was no longer there.

Glowing now at the center of the pillar was an ancient rune, written in the forgotten text of the First Blood. Her heart thudded hard as she reached out to touch the rune, and then disappeared in a flash of light.

CHAPTER TWENTY-THREE

CITY OF LIGHTS

"In this life, there'll be no rest, child. They'll hunt and prowl until you are found. Make peace with it, for it is your fate. You'll stumble and fall, but you mustn't forget: never let them catch you."

— Gilbrich to Nerana

SUNLIGHT REFLECTED AGAINST THE DEEP snow, creating a blinding brightness across the mountaintops. Neer stood on the deck of the avia and peered through the trees in search of Aélla. Hours had passed since the others awoke to find her missing without a trace.

Shallow impressions of her footsteps trailed into the woods. Neer had spent the better part of the morning following the faded path, which ended at a vale of red feathers and empty nests.

Her eyes fixated on the trees where Aélla's footpath led. Dru came to her side and rested atop her shoulder. The faeth rubbed her hands together nervously and looked at the empty mountains.

"Do you think the klaet'il took her?" Neer asked Thallon, who sat along the edge of the deck and leaned against the railing.

"No," he said. "The glynfir aren't hunters. They wouldn't be able to track us this deep in the mountains."

Y'ven stepped forward. "We failed. Could not protect her."

"She's fine, big guy. Aélla is more capable than you think," Thallon stated, though his voice was full of worry. "She entered the k'laea den. I'm sure she is in the realm right now."

With a deep exhale, Neer got comfortable beside Thallon. The wooden flooring of the deck shifted as Y'ven stepped across the platform. He sat beneath a column of sunlight and closed his eyes.

Thallon leaned against the railing on folded arms. Sunlight brightened his fair skin and dark hair. Even with their differences, his resemblance to Loryk was unmistakable. Neer wondered if it was fate that brought them together, either as a way for her to fill the gap left behind by her loss, or as a cruel joke from the merciless Divines.

When he turned, her thoughts were broken, and she quickly looked away. A sly smile pulled his lips. "You checking me out, Ianathess?"

She snorted. "You wish, elf."

He chuckled. "What? You aren't into the evaesh type?"

Feeling slightly uncomfortable with his playful flirting, she purposefully changed the subject. "How do you know Aélla?"

His smile grew, and she avoided his gaze. Turning back to the forest, he said, "We're from the same village. I was best friends with her brother as a kid."

"She has a brother?"

"Yeah. He's a piece of work too. Nothing at all like her. I can't stand the bastard." He paused. "What about you? You don't strike me as the type to trust easily. How did you come to join Aélla on her journey of death?"

"She knows someone that I trust. Someone that told her to find me."

"Really? You've got friends from Nyn'Dira?"

"Yeah, he —"

Their conversation was ended when a flash of energy radiated from behind. Rippling magic spliced open the air above the deck, and Aélla fell through the portal. She landed atop the ship with a hard thud. The rift of shimmering light hovered in the air before collapsing in on itself and disappearing.

"Drimil!" Y'ven called, racing to her side.

Aélla stood and gripped her forehead. "I am all right."

"Where were you?" he asked.

Aélla smiled at his fatherly temperament. "The k'laea came while I was meditating. I couldn't let them slip away."

Neer stepped closer. "Did you get it?" she asked.

Aélla proudly displayed her staff, which held three dormant crystals and one glowing.

"I thought we had to do this together," Neer stated. "Shouldn't I have entered the realm to strengthen my magic too?"

"No," she explained. "The purpose of these realms is to obtain the energy so that we may enter the final realm. Even if we went together, the realm would split us apart and place us in separate planes." She secured the staff onto her back. "Once we gather each of the elements, we will both enter the temple of Elandorr. That is where we will be gifted with the strength of all the elemental energies combined."

"We'll be stronger than that elemental mage?"

"She's been training her entire life. Eólin aren't usually as powerful as Ithronél, but we'll be stronger and have more capabilities without the need to train or master them."

Thallon crossed his arms. "That's great and all, but say something next time." His voice was sour and scolding. "We have been worried sick!"

"I'm sorry. I didn't mean to worry you."

They turned when loud boots clunked against the platform, and Reuhnar, the dreled, stepped forward. He wiped his blistered hands onto wet overalls and shook the mist from his frizzy hair. His rosy cheeks lifted into a large smile as he asked, "Ready to head home?"

The group sat atop the snow-covered platform as the turbines spun. Winds swept snow through the air, and they lifted from the ground, leaving the frigid mountains.

The sun rose higher as they returned to Zaos and walked through the crowded streets. Aélla smiled at the villagers as they bowed and touched her arms.

Neer walked alongside Thallon and stared at the beautifully inscribed bar strapped to his forearm. "What is that?" she asked.

"This?" he lifted his arm. "It's a shield."

"That's a shield?"

With a sly smile, he pressed a blue stone button in the center of the bar and metal plating emerged from the contraption, creating the shield he used on the avia. Its metalwork was immaculate, with golden trim woven through its thick steel plating. "Nice, huh?" he said, before pressing a button in its interior, causing the shield to fold in on itself and disappear into the thin bar on his arm. "It's a First Blood weapon made of alveryan steel."

"You found it on the avia?"

"Yeah. The dreled said I could keep it. Guess traveling with Aélla comes with some perks."

Neer turned aside as Aélla approached. "Where do we go from here?" Neer asked.

"I am not sure," Aélla said. "The vision I received showed the k'laea standing tall. There was also a temple of stone, a jungle, and lava…I do not know what it could mean."

"Maybe there is a volcano or something nearby."

"No," Y'ven explained. "No volcano in Aragoth."

"A temple of stone?" Thallon said with a finger to his lip. "It could be *Althidon*. It's a temple in the heart of I'vasaar."

"Where is I'vasaar?" Aélla asked.

"Far," he said. "Past Sandir."

While they fell into a deep conversation about their journey, Neer turned her gaze to the city gates. The guard, who was now dressed in a dark cloak, opened the entrance and stepped into the city. She watched with suspicion as he marched across the bridge with great purpose.

Stepping closer to view him clearer, she wondered if he was vaxros at all. His build was large, but still, he was different. His arms were smaller and height was shorter than a typical native.

She curled her fingers around the hilt of her sword and stepped back when he raised his metal arm toward the crowd, a white light emitting from his palm.

As the light brightened, Neer teleported to Aélla's side and then transported them several yards away as a heavy blast erupted in the courtyard. Bricks and dust pelted their skin as they rolled through an alley. Blood painted them with red, spraying through the air with severed limbs and twisted bodies.

Desperate cries and panicked screams overtook murmurs of the city. A man pulled himself forward, leaving a red trail in his wake as his partially severed legs dragged behind. Innards hung from lamp posts and dripped blood onto the bodies lying in the streets.

Smoke rose from the deep crater created by the powerful blast. Jagged rocks and uneven cobbles surrounded its perimeter.

Aélla crawled through the alley toward the street. Her eyes were wide as she moved absently over lifeless bodies and puddles of blood. It coated her hands and stained her robes as she crept closer to the smoke and chaos. Her body trembled, and blood dripped from her ears.

Neer stood and gripped her head. Stumbling into a wall, she groaned with pain, every heartbeat throbbing in her temples. The world spun, and her vision blurred. Loud screams were muffled in her ears.

Pushing through the disorientation, she stepped closer to the street and came upon the devastation. Bodies were piled in the streets, leaving survivors covered in blood and wailing in agony. Peering slowly through the rubble, Neer's breath caught in her throat when she spotted Thallon lying at the edge of another alley, gripping his exposed ribs.

Blood coated his shaky hands as he grasped the torn flesh, howling in agony. Light illuminated to the left where Thorne prepared another attack. Without thinking—without feeling—Neer teleported ahead, grabbed Thallon, and rolled aside as a second explosion shook the street where he laid.

A sharp rock cut deep into Neer's cheek as she rolled into the alley. Smoke and dust filled the city as people wailed and shrieked. Neer clutched her side and crawled to her knees. Hot blood filled her mouth from the wound that cut through to the inside. Thallon wailed and clutched his broken ribs.

People raced through the streets, trampling over one another as they fled.

Aélla pushed through the crowds and blocked the stampede with a weak barrier, aiding those who had fallen. Thorne appeared through the smoke behind the horde. The metal plating in his face reflected with firelight as he came into view.

Neer turned to Aélla, and as their gazes met, she pointed to Thallon. "Help him!"

Aélla rushed to their sides. "What's happening?" she asked. Thallon screamed as she pressed her hands to his chest. Magic burned through them as she healed his wounds.

"We have to fight him," Neer stated. "I can't do this on my own!"

Aélla couldn't respond as she was filled with pain, using her own health to mend Thallon's deep injuries. His bones cracked as they mended and snapped into place. Without healing him entirely, she waited for the bleeding to stop, and then leaned back. Blue veins formed around her eyes, and her skin paled.

"Can you fight?" Neer asked.

Aélla nodded breathlessly as her eyes closed with exhaustion.

"Get Thallon somewhere safe. I can't hold him off for long!"

Before Aélla could respond, Neer raced into the street. Tripping over large rocks and loose cobbles, she arrived in the clearing smog as Thorne approached from the haze. His boots thudded against the ground, drawing nearer with every agonizing stride.

Neer unsheathed her weapon as he stood several paces away. The crowds had passed, leaving the streets littered with the bodies of the dead and injured. Neer snarled, her vengeful eyes set to the hunter.

She growled under her breath, and her fingers wriggled against the hilt of her sword. Shaking her head, she was overcome with fury, and with a deep breath, she vanished.

Appearing behind Thorne, she struck her sword toward his back. He turned and swiped her blade with his metal arm, causing her to stagger aside. Energy ignited within his palm as he lifted it toward her. She teleported several paces back and lifted her hands defensively.

As the energy of his hand brightened, so too did the magic inside her, and she formed a half-shield around him as he expelled his energy forward. The explosion collided with her barrier, sending shockwaves of fire through her veins.

Neer fell to her knees with a horrid shriek. Pained, shallow breaths entered her lungs as she fought to stand.

Black vapor rose, and Thorne stepped closer. His skin was singed from the explosion, and the metal plating on his arm and face glowed orange from heat. The space between them dwindled with every step. Neer swiped her sword from the ground where she dropped it, then teleported closer and plunged her blade into his gut.

He groaned with a hateful sneer. As their eyes met, she twisted the blade, and a deep, sinister growl rumbled in his throat. With a hard kick to her stomach, Neer crashed to the ground.

Thorne's flesh squelched, and blood poured from his stomach when he pulled the sword from his gut. The blood-coated steel dripped with crimson as he stepped closer.

When fire rained from above, illuminating his face, he lifted his metal arm and shielded himself from the fireballs being cast from the sky, where Dru hovered above the destruction. Smoke filled the air as his cloak caught fire, and with a violent tear, he ripped the cloth from his back.

A powerful shout vibrated from Y'ven as he ran at Thorne from behind. Lifting his hammer, he brought the weapon to his head. Thorne grabbed his crossbow and ducked beneath the swing then shot a bolt into Y'ven's arm. The vaxros growled and raised his hammer again. The steel bolt ripped his skin as he swung at Thorne's chest.

Thorne stepped aside and kicked Y'ven in the gut. Y'ven stumbled back with a deep grunt, and Thorne thrust Neer's sword to his stomach.

His empty fist met with Y'ven's skin, and he turned in sudden puzzlement. Staring at Neer, he was stunned to find the weapon was held firmly in her grasp.

Thorne, ready to send a powerful blast her way, stumbled suddenly with a wheezed gasp. His gaze set to Aélla, who stood in the alley with her arms stretched toward him. Ash and dust swirled through the air as she pulled the air from his lungs.

His movements slowed as he gasped for breath. His face turned red as Aélla twisted her palms, pulling them inward toward her chest. Blue tinged his skin, and veins swelled in his neck as he fought to breathe.

Their eyes locked, and her hands started to shake. With the shallowest of breaths, he raised his arm, and the weaponized limb started to glow.

She pulled harder, strengthening the magic that slowly depleted. Energy brightened in his hand. The light glistened in her eyes as heat radiated from his limb.

Neer ran to his side and swiped her sword to his neck. As the blade swept closer to his skin, he lifted his arm and grabbed her by the throat. He squeezed tight, still unbreathing as Aélla continued her assault, and Neer was unable to free herself from his iron grip.

Her fingernails ripped when she clawed at his hand. She kicked and pushed against his body, but he never flinched. Never once showed an ounce of hesitation or weakness.

Dropping her sword, she clutched his wrist and focused on her magic. But her energy was unstable as she fought to breathe. She kicked her legs to free herself, unable to quell the panic raging inside.

Redness overtook his eyes as he suffocated, but they remained strong as they shifted to Aélla. Thorne's eyes narrowed as the energy released from his palm, and Y'ven collided his war hammer against his metal shoulder. The ground cracked as his blast eviscerated the street, flinging rocks and dust through the air.

The powerful blast shook the city, and Y'ven was launched backward, smashing into the side of a building. He fell to the ground in a motionless slump. A deep, cracked impression lay in the wall where he hit.

Neer flipped across the ground and into the fresh pit formed by Thorne's explosion. Her body smashed against smoldering rocks and sharp edges when she fell. Blood poured down her face, running across her eye and down her cheek.

She whimpered, unable to move as her skin was burnt and laced with lacerations. Darkness cloaked the sun as a shadow stood in the haze above her. Barely breathing and hardly awake, she was powerless to fight.

Released of Aélla's hold, Thorne stood tall and collected a needle and vial of black liquid from his pocket. Neer recognized this from her time with the High Priest. She knew it to be a poison that blocked her energy.

As the syringe was filled with the dark liquid, Neer closed her eyes and disappeared. Landing ten yards away, she rolled across the blood-soaked street. The usage of her magic was unbearable. Searing pain coursed through her, and she grunted, withholding her agony through clenched teeth. She crawled on her stomach and reached for her sword.

Bone fragments and piles of flesh squished as her body was covered in the remnants of the dead. Their blood dripped down her face and into her eyes.

Shaky, burnt hands reached for Avelloch's sword as she inched closer. Her strength depleted, she struggled to grip its handle. She touched the worn leather with her fingertips, unable to grasp it.

Blackness filled her vision, and her body grew numb. Her lungs ached for a breath she could never fully draw. She crawled, her mind dreary and body weak, in one final effort to take her weapon and then collapsed to the ground.

Thorne climbed from the crater and inhaled a frustrated breath. He stomped over bleeding citizens and splashed through puddles of blood, following Neer's feeble attempt to escape.

She was motionless as the thick needle sank into her neck. As the glass vial slowly emptied her body went limp, and she was slung over his shoulder.

Firelight brightened Avelloch's blood-soaked sword as it lay in the street, left behind as Thorne escaped the demolished city.

CHAPTER TWENTY-FOUR

FIRE AND BLOOD
Y'ven

"Y't yoven grúkataa reymüak."
Through the flames we will rise again.

— Words of the Vaxros

ASH FELL LIKE GREY SNOWFLAKES atop the crumbled streets. Silent weeps and broken dreams lay scattered across the burnt and blackened homes. A monument of the dead, scorched and alone, while the living aided the wounded.

Aélla was motionless on the ground. Her body lay beneath rock and dust. Blood that wasn't her own puddled around her, soaking her clothes and painting her ash-covered skin a shade of crimson.

A sea of red-robed men and women marched through the crowds, kneeling beside the dead and gathering the injured onto stretchers. Cries of desperation wept from mothers scouring the ashes, searching for their loved ones. Metal carts creaked beneath the weight of battered, lifeless bodies as they were collected from the streets.

Aélla was lifted from the ground, and the village fell silent. Deathly silent, as the grieving and forlorn looked at their savior. She was placed onto a stretcher and carried through the village. Onlookers knelt in a respectful bow. The red robed workers moved quickly through the somber streets, while the others remained silent and still.

Y'ven sat on the ground, coughing and wheezing, watching them move hurriedly past.

Ash and dust swirled as he sat up. Streaks of red overlapped across his back and arms. A razor-thin line stretched across his forehead, covering his face in a mask of blood.

Clearing himself of the filth, he was stricken with a sharp, stabbing pain in his thigh where a deep wound opened his skin. He leaned back and clutched his leg, breathing through tightly clenched teeth. Blood and spit spewed from his lips as he grunted with agony.

Peering through the streets, he searched for the others. Villagers scoured the debris, uncovering bodies layered with ash. The glowing blue veins of Neer's sword illuminated from the street. His eyes shifted to the left of the sword, where an ash-covered body lay broken and bleeding.

With a pained growl, Y'ven crawled to his feet. Blood drained from his leg as he hobbled closer. Ash flurried into the air, and he grabbed the sword, then turned to the body. Stricken with grief, he carefully uncovered the ash blanketing their skin.

Through a deep, relieved sigh, he leaned back, thankful it wasn't Neer. Scanning the crowds and debris, he noticed Thallon lying in an alley. Aélla's bloody cloak covered his body as he cried with pain.

Y'ven stumbled forward and forced the villagers aside. They scoffed and sneered as he brushed past and made his way into the alley. Thallon whimpered as he was lifted into Y'ven's arms and carried away.

With slow, limping steps, Y'ven came to a stairwell leading to a basement door. At the base of the stairs, he crumbled into the wall in agony.

With a deep breath, he forced himself forward and approached the stone door. Glancing to the alley above to be sure

no one was lurking by, he pulled the unlit sconce, and a glowing rune illuminated on the wall behind.

He pressed his shoulder against the rune, and a hidden
door appeared. The stone scraped against the ground as he
pushed it open, and then stepped inside a dark, empty tunnel.
Y'ven dragged his injured leg, blood collecting in his armor
and sticking the material to his skin.

The short walk became longer as he paused to rest. His
eyes set ahead where orange light filtered in from an open
doorway at the end of the tunnel. Aromas of freshly cooked
meat, boiling stew, and fresh vegetables filled the air as he approached the doorway and stepped into the hidden sanctuary
of the Broken Order Brotherhood.

Small homes were nestled together within a vast cave.
Banners displaying the Broken Order sigil hung throughout
the streets, and each person that stepped by had the Broken
Order pin fastened to their tunics and armor.

Y'lenae and vaxros walked alongside each other, carrying
the injured into a gathering of small, windowless buildings.
They rushed to Y'ven's side as he limped through the streets,
and two men pulled Thallon from his arms before placing him
onto a stretcher.

Y'ven followed as they carried Thallon to the cluster of
buildings. Inside, the singular room was filled with beds lined
against the wall where men and women covered in blood lay
atop the sheets. Buckets of excrements, blood, and tissue were
placed between each of the beds.

A woman pulled back a white curtain to reveal a clean,
empty bed at the end of the room. "Lay him here," she instructed the men carrying Thallon. Vials clinked as she rummaged through cabinets, retrieving a thick paste and yellow
elixir. "All right, hold him still while I—"

Her voice faded when she turned to Y'ven but found he
was no longer there.

Y'ven left Thallon behind as he marched through the sanctuary and back to the city. Stepping out of the hidden

doorway in the alley, he returned to the chaos of Zaos, where men and women displaying the Broken Order sigil ran through the streets, giving aid to those in need. While many were treated for their ailments in the alleys, the most severe were taken to the *hipera*° across town.

He glanced at his thigh and knew he'd never make the journey without aid. Kneeling painfully by a small flame, he cupped his hands around the heat and carried it to his deep wound. He pressed the fire into his skin and growled with pain.

Through clenched teeth, he exhaled deep, raspy breaths. As his skin fused into a bright yellow scar, he leaned back with a sigh of relief. Taking time to recuperate, he examined the scene around him, watching as small flames crawled through the wreckage around two deep craters.

He pushed through his anguish and walked through the busy streets. Across town, he approached the *hipera*, and stepped into the halls flooded with injured civilians. Eyes gaze shifted to a man sitting on the floor, crying. His legs were both severed beneath the knees.

He reached for Y'ven, wailing in agony. Unable to give him aid, Y'ven sadly pulled away, and the man fell aside. Still searching for the faces of his companions, Y'ven scanned over the sick and wounded, unveiling the cloaked bodies.

An orange spark caught his attention as it flittered at the end of the hall, becoming larger as it raced toward him. He stepped back as the glow smacked into his cheek with a gentle thud, and a smile broke his sullen expression when Dru hugged him. She backed away and berated him for taking so long to find her.

° Institution providing medical care for the sick or injured.
While there are no hipera throughout vaxros territory, the y'lenea cities each have one of their own. Filled with electricity and apothecaries, they're much more functional, safe, and renowned than the hipera of the forest regions.

"Where is Aélla?" he asked in his native language. "Have you seen Neer?"

Her gaze fell to the floor and shoulders slumped before she led him through the crowded halls and into a quiet room where Aélla rested beneath a thin blanket. Her weapons were placed atop a table across the room. Y'ven put Avelloch's filthy sword onto the table with the others and then slowly turned to his friend.

Dru walked across Aélla's pillow and touched her cheek. Turning to Y'ven, she sorrowfully shook her head. He moved to Aélla's side and placed his hand on her arm.

"Drimil…Aélla…" He gently shook her, but she didn't wake. With a defeated sigh, he pulled a wooden chair from the corner and then sat beside the bed, waiting for her to wake.

Hours passed before Aélla woke from her dreamless sleep. Dreary eyes struggled to open as light filled her vision. Heaviness pulled her arms, making it impossible to move. Turning aside, she found the source of her wakening as Y'ven snored with the voraciousness of a hungry boar.

Nestled in the blankets, Dru shuffled in her sleep. With a great yawn, her large eyes fluttered open, and as they slowly met with Aélla's, she was filled with excitement. Her red aura glowed as she flew happily into the air, moving to Y'ven's side. With several angry tugs of his hair, the vaxros woke.

He sat up with a deep breath and looked at Dru, who pointed eagerly at Aélla. The sleep faded from his eyes as he leaned forward with relief. "Drimil," he said. "You are all right?"

She nodded weakly. "Nerana? Thallon?" Her voice was hardly a whisper.

Y'ven's head fell between his shoulders. He closed his eyes and explained, "Evae safe. Healing. Ürok…gone. Taken."

Falling back into her pillow, Aélla stared at the ceiling. "The others? The village?"

"Destroyed, Master Drimil. Many wounded."

"My magic…needs time to heal…" She paused. "Find her, Y'ven."

"Drimil, I—"

"Altvára will guide you." Her tired eyes met with his as she warned, "We cannot let her get away."

CHAPTER TWENTY-FIVE

BROKEN DREAMS
Y'ven

"Through blood and flame, I shall defend. These walls are mine to uphold. The people—mine to protect."

—   Oath of the Griadrok

BLACK CLOUDS SHADOWED THE SUN as they rose from the great city of lights. Beneath the painted colors of dusk, Y'ven rode quickly across the empty desert atop a large, six-legged beast. Its thick grey skin was hidden beneath a leather saddle, and three horns, freshly sharpened the night before, sat atop its head.

The beast struggled to keep pace with the quick moving raven as it followed Altvára's path. Y'ven leaned forward, his large fists clutching the reins. He paid no mind to the wanderers or passing warriors as he barreled through the wasteland. One village stood nearby, and he was sure this was where he'd find them.

As darkness settled across the land, his mount thundered across a wide stone bridge. The canyon below held the remnants of a once-flowing river where shards of bones and animal skulls lay scattered along the dried riverbed. Serpents and *khiut*, shadowy canines, made the canyon their home as they crept through the darkness.

Y'ven's beast slowed as it neared the end of the long passage, and he gazed upon the remnants of an abandoned village with sorrow and guilt. The village was a small collection of old square homes. Stairs were carved into the side walls leading to the rooftops, and stone streets were coated with thick layers of dust. Deep cracks and erosion painted the homes with dark lines in their abandonment.

The ghosts of his past haunted the quiet streets. He could still hear their laughter and voices as if they'd never left. As if they weren't forced from their homes after his betrayal destroyed their lives.

At the end of the crossing, Altvára perched atop a tall cairn of stacked stones. His glassy eyes peered over the village nearby, watching with intent while Y'ven dismounted and tied his steed to a hitching post.

Stepping to the monument, he gazed upon its height. Each stone represented a new leader. A person who would protect the village and grow its prosperity. The tablets at the base of the cairn had blackened with age. They were thick and sturdy, bearing the weight of all those who came after.

The edges of the stones were beveled and uneven with dark markings of old blood staining their exterior. It came from the ritual performed by the villagers when the new leader was inaugurated. Standing in Y'ven's place before the cairn, the successor wore a crown of bones and was painted with the blood of their people.

One by one, the villagers would slice their palm and give them a new design. Each new successor had more than the last as the settlement grew. The bond-mate of the previous leader would then pass the next stone to the man or woman who would take their loved one's place.

Y'ven touched the stone resting at the top. His fingers slid across the rugged and sharp edges, remembering how long and tireless it had been to mine and shape. The scar on his hand revealed his sacrifice. He had sliced his palm, just like all the others, and smeared the stone with blood that still stained the edges.

His eyes shifted from the monument to the village resting beneath a blanket of silence and devastation. Crumbled half-walls surrounded the once bustling community. The alleys and streets where children once played were now cracked and muddled.

Altvára cawed before taking flight, but Y'ven didn't notice. His mind was set upon the village he once called home, a place where he vowed himself to Calla and raised his son. It was a place of peace and finality. The place he believed he would live out his days with his mate and their children.

But being a vaxros, he understood peace would never last, and so, he now walked through the forgotten streets alone, carrying the weight of his heresy and guilt.

Every step brought him further into the past. Roh, the blacksmith, lived in the first home on the left. Her forge once filled the village with the smell of coal and steel. It gave a hardiness to the peaceful village and kept passersby from wandering too far into their borders.

Y'ven's fingers trailed across the soot-covered stones as he passed by. Closing his eyes, he breathed in the lingering scent of the life he once knew.

Further through the village, he came to the courtyard, which housed a large firepit that was never without flame. It was a sacred place, one that saw the residents at its location each night to give thanks to the sun, the flames, and the world. To see it devoid of any heat or life left him heavy with grief.

Glancing through the empty, dilapidated homes, he stepped to the pit and came upon a damning word etched deep into the stone.

Traitor.

He became lost in his misery, forgetting for a moment why he was there and what he was after. Forgetting there was another he needed to find.

Never expecting to return to his village, he was anguished to find it in ruins. To know that his family and life would never return.

Altvára cawed while landing atop a broken roof, and Y'ven turned to find the raven perched above his home.

"Fate has brought us here," Y'ven whispered, reciting the vows he took so long ago. Moving closer to the home, he was filled with memories. "'To give us strength…" He continued the vow as he passed the courtyard where his son took his first steps.

"To give us peace…"

Past the gate leading to his home, where he and Calla shared their first night as bond-mates.

"To give us life…"

Standing at the door, he touched the handle. His jaw clenched, and he closed his eyes, remembering the day she left and took everything he lived for.

"To give my soul… to you."

Through a deep, pained breath, he turned the handle and forced the door open. The empty home was full of memories and voices. He could see every moment of his life flash before him, as if his family was standing inside, waiting. His son toddled for the door with his arms open, ready to be held by his father.

Calla was always a step behind, sharpening weapons or preparing dinner. The bookshelves were just as they left them, covered in dust and frozen in time.

He touched the bed that was once his and slowly closed his eyes.

Quiet steps etched across the floor behind, breaking him of his desolation. His ears perked and eyes opened. With sudden urgency, he turned and swung his battle axe toward the intruder.

A large shadow ducked beneath his swing and rolled backward across the floor, lifting a metal arm. A blast of energy exploded at Y'ven's feet. He was flung into the desert as the walls of his home collapsed. Dust collected in his throat as he heaved and coughed.

A light broke through the haze, and he rolled aside as an explosion shook the ground. Smoke and flames rose from the place he once lay. Grabbing his axe, he took several deep breaths and jumped to his feet.

He staggered aside and then quickly regained his balance as Thorne stepped through the smog. A faint click sounded from his direction, and a bolt was released from his crossbow. Y'ven swung his axe forward. The steel of his chipped blade collided with the bolt and flew it off course.

Gripping his weapon tight, he glared at the enemy. Slow steps carried them in a wide circle. Their gaze never broke, fury increasing with every stride. Smoke and dust twisted through the air as the flurry of the blast swept through the village.

Fueled with rage, Y'ven broadened his shoulders, clutched the iron shaft of his battle axe, and charged. With a wide swipe, his weapon whipped through the air. Thorne leapt back, and the chipped steel scraped against his metal face-plating with a loud hiss.

Jabbing from the left, Thorne struck at Y'ven's stomach. The vaxros turned and blocked the hit with his axe. With a heaved kick, he sent the hunter back. Thorne quickly regained his posture and dipped his hand into his pocket.

Black powder slid between his fingers as he retrieved the deadly poison. Y'ven recognized it— the dust that nearly choked the life from him during their last encounter at the Steam and Stable Inn.

With a furious snarl, Y'ven tackled Thorne and slammed him to the ground. His knuckles bled as his fist met with the hunter's jaw. Bruises and blood painted his iron-plated face. The bent metal created sharp edges that cut into Y'ven's skin.

Thorne kicked Y'ven aside, causing him to roll across the dirt. As he crawled to his knees, the faint click of Thorne's crossbow was followed by a dull pain when a bolt plunged into Y'ven's side. He crawled forward and groaned with fury. Shaky hands tugged at the bolt, and he recoiled with a thunderous growl as the barbed head sliced and pulled.

Filled with rage, he stared into the eyes of his enemy. Every hot breath was a reminder of all he'd lost. Should he die here, it would be with honor, not regret. He would protect his vows to the bitter end.

When Thorne lifted his metal arm, Y'ven unleashed a hellish battle cry and charged. Thunderous steps shook the village as he approached the unmoving man. Thorne's energy brightened, illuminating his metal plated face. Y'ven struck the metal palm with his battle axe as the energy grew.

A spark of magic ignited like lightning before a deep blast detonated from his arm. Y'ven was thrown back. Harsh winds and hot air rushed past as he fumbled across the ground. Old stones crumbled and creaked beneath his intense weight as he slammed into a home. His vision darkened as he lay motionless on the ground.

Every beat of his heart thumped hard throughout his body. The sharp, broken handle of his battle axe was gripped tight in his fist, devoid of its bladed head.

With a thunderous growl, he sat on his knees. Pain erupted through him, tearing at every fiber and eviscerating his soul.

Thick black smoke rose from the explosion site. Thorne knelt in the clearing haze, a dark shadow slumped forward and unmoving. His metal limb was blown off just above the elbow. Sharp, serrated splinters edged the broken limb.

Y'ven bowed his head, thankful it was over. That he had survived.

Blood squelched between his fingers as he gripped his throbbing side. He muttered a curse beneath his breath and shook his head to rid himself of the agony. Orange veins glowed against his dark skin where the bolt sat deeper in his side.

He was poisoned, and it was quickly taking its effect.

Glowing yellow eyes remained unfocused as he fought to stay conscious. Glancing back to the shadow kneeling nearby, he was astonished to find Thorne was no longer there. Not a trace of him was left behind, and Y'ven realized he had fled the village.

He scoffed through a deep, exhausted breath, disgusted that he was defeated twice by the human assailant. Both times by way of poison. A *coward's* weapon.

His breathing shallowed, and darkness pulled the edges of his vision. He closed his eyes and accepted his defeat. There was no sorrow or regret in dying with such honor. Every warrior wishes to die by the blade. Death was easy, and long had he been ready for its eternal release.

Y'ven thought of his family, of the son he'd never see again, and whispered a quiet goodbye.

Altvára's caw broke his trance, and it was then he realized death was too peaceful a fate for a fallen warrior like him. He wouldn't find peace in its unending embrace. His fate was far from over.

His eyes slid open when the thud of muffled steps came closer. A shadow crept overhead, and Y'ven lifted his eyes to the stranger before him, wearing a dark cloak that shadowed their face.

This stranger wasn't Thorne, and Y'ven began to wonder if it was Neer that had come to his aid. Glass vials clinked as the shadow dug through their pack, before drawing back their hood.

Y'ven's eyes widened as he saw a stranger. An evae. Faint wrinkles surrounded his light blue eyes, depicting his age. Small, pointed ears were revealed beneath golden hair that fell just below his shoulders. A short beard covered his face, making it look smaller and more human-like.

Kneeling beside Y'ven, he filled a syringe with clear liquid and pushed the needle into his thick skin. The man was silent while Y'ven grimaced and howled.

As the potion emptied, he lightly tapped Y'ven's arm. "You will make it," he spoke the native language of the vaxros.

Y'ven turned to him with daring eyes and clutched his aching side. He remained silent as the stranger leaned closer and with great confidence demanded, "Now…take me to the human."

CHAPTER TWENTY-SIX

WORDS OF CAUTION
Aélla

"This world is not meant for such darkness and strife. When the sun is buried in shadow, it is I who shall carry the torch."

— Vow of Drimil'Rothar

AÉLLA WALKED BENEATH THE SHADOW of a cloak. Led closely by Dru, she wandered through the smoldering city. Her eyes were heavy, focusing on the dark blood stains and broken cobbles that filled the roads. Just that morning, she had been a victim of the horrific attack, and now she walked alone, wondering about the fate of her friends.

She followed when Dru disappeared around a corner and led her down a long alley. Coming to the narrow steps of the Brotherhood sanctuary, she instructed Aélla how to open the secret doorway. The evae pulled the sconce, and a rune brightened on the wall behind.

She pushed hard against the stone wall, and the door slid open with a loud scrape. Inside, she followed Dru through the dark passages before entering the enormous hidden city.

Hundreds of people scurried around, their voices filling the wide chamber in a flurry of noise.

"Excuse me," Aélla called as she passed by several strangers. They walked hurriedly by without the slightest glance in her direction. Her eyes fixed on a familiar, haunting symbol pinned to their chests. It was cracked and broken.

From the left came the wail of a mother cradling her child. A man dressed in red robes stood over her, rubbing her shoulder. His clothes and face were stained with blood. More injured and nes'seil walked through the cluster of small medical buildings.

Aélla kindly passed through the bustling streets and made her way to the mournful mother.

"Excuse me," she said to the *nes'seil*,* who held a deeply sorrowful gaze. "Have you seen another evae? He has dark hair and green robes."

His face pulled together in confusion. While shaking his head, he struggled to understand her language. Her blue eyes focused on the *hipera*, or medical buildings, which were overflowing with injured civilians.

She pushed through the crowded halls and whimpering patients of the first three hipera, then entered the fourth. Checking each room, she found bandaged and bleeding strangers lying in their beds. Buckets of waste, blood, and severed limbs lined the halls, and dirty clothes were left in piles across the flooring. Her eyes watered at the smell of defecation and decay lingering in the air.

Red-robed healers walked briskly through the corridors, moving from room to room as they checked on their patients.

Stepping over a man who lay in the hall beneath a sheet, Aélla opened the next door. Its iron hinges creaked as she looked inside. Six beds rested within the cramped and quiet room. Two of the patients had sheets over their faces. Thick blood spatters painted the linen in shades of red.

A woman was nearest the door, her blond hair singed unevenly. Deep burns crawled from beneath the bandages wrapping her face and neck. Every shallow breath was followed by a whimper.

---

* A person who is trained in the art of potion mastery, medicinal science, and healing.
Among the humans, the nes'seil is known as an apothecary.

Dru moved across the room, inspecting each patient. As she approached a man lying beneath the window, she lifted into the air with an excited spin. Tiny embers trailed from her glowing body as she pointed at the bed.

Aélla lifted her cloak and raced through the maze of beds, coming to his side. She leaned over Thallon and examined his injuries. A deep cut disfigured his top lip, while shallow marks covered his arms. Bloody bandages wrapped his chest where his ribs were once exposed.

He breathed at a steady, shallow pace. She touched his arm and allowed the sting of magic to radiate through her, extending beyond her palms and into his body, healing his minor injuries. She winced as the pain of his ailments coursed through her.

A deep scar replaced the cut on his lip, while the marks across his arms left no trace of their existence. She gazed at his chest, where beneath the blood-stained bandages his ribs were slowly healing. With no one to transfer the deeper injuries to, and her magic being incredibly weakened after the fight, he was left to suffer his ailments until they healed naturally.

An orange light expanded when Dru hovered nearby, and Aélla turned as she pointed at the door when someone stepped inside. With a final glance to Thallon, unmoving and asleep, Aélla returned her attention to the door.

A man wearing a large headdress of bones and feathers squeezed into the narrow doorway. Large muscles and vibrant eyes belied the hunch of his walk and age of his voice. His staff bore stacked skulls atop its crown with several hanging from thin ropes. Beautiful scars laid circular patterns across his chest and face.

"Blood of evae," he started in a gruff, vibrating voice. "Is it truth? Are you Drimil'Rothar? Daughter of the First Blood. Bringer of peace and light."

Aélla straightened, and with a bow, she said, "Yes. My name is Aélla, and I'm here to enter tre'lan'Aenwyn." She

216

spoke her native language and was elated to find he understood, though he responded in his own tongue.

"This is a harrowing task you seek. The *grudagh*° are meant for only the most gifted of drimil."

"I am the last of my kind. There is no one else to take on this journey but me."

He nodded. With a glance to Thallon, he stepped further into the room and stared down at the evae, transfixed on the bandages that wrapped his chest. "He is with you?"

"Yes. I found him in Mors'groval. He was excavating the ruins when your people captured him."

With an angry growl, he turned away. "It is forbidden to enter the ruins. Sacrilege."

"The ruins of my ancestors are by right mine to enter. Thallon was only doing what he was told by me," she lied, hoping it would be enough to squander his growing opposition.

She was relieved when he closed his eyes and exhaled a defeated sigh. "Come, Master Drimil. There is much to discuss."

With a respectful bow to the stranger, she followed him through the crowded halls of the hipera. He walked kindly by the patients and healers, allowing them to pass him by each time they crossed paths.

Out of the building and into the streets of the hidden sanctuary, the passing vaxros bowed as he walked by. He gave a respectful nod to each of them.

"You are a dül?" Aélla asked, though she already knew the answer. The symbolic headdress and tribal scars were evidence enough of his position.

"I am Dregorn. Dül of Zurág'shelarr."

"I had no idea your people could live underground."

"We are weakened by darkness. But in times of uncertainty, we must take such risks."

° Vax for magical realms

"Times of uncertainty?"

He placed his arm before her, and they came to a stop, waiting patiently as two nes'seil marched by carrying an injured man on a stretcher. The y'lenae victim's arm had been severed and his face slashed. He wailed while clutching the stub of his arm as the healers raced to the overcrowded hipera.

"Yes," the dül continued, reminding Aélla of their conversation. "It is known that *shadosalaan* haunt our world. The energies are shifting. Balance is askew."

"I'm working to rectify that."

"While you take the path of redemption, we must do what we can to secure our borders. The evae have begun invading. They are targeting marak'shelarr. These are villages that protect the ruins."

"They are klaet'il. No other clan would ever seek war with your people."

"Evae is evae. One sword speaks for a thousand men. Should you raise your arms to attack, we will raise ours to defend."

"You plan to attack the forest?"

Grim eyes glanced at her before he refocused on the road ahead, which had become less congested as they moved further into the underground city. Fires burned in large pits, and the smell of wax and coal filled the air.

Peeking into a window, Aélla spotted a woman crafting molten glass into a beautiful decanter. Across the street, covered in soot, was a blacksmith. Water bubbled when he placed a red-hot axe into a deep wooden tub.

After traveling through the dense village, they approached a large building. Nestled within many smaller shops, it sat beneath the glow of streetlamps. Thick steps led them to a beautiful double door, whose surface was etched with elegant, swirled designs.

Dül'Dregorn opened the door and, with a wave of his hand, invited Aélla inside. Entering the large chamber, they came to a beautiful library, where across the room an enormous hearth of bricks rose to the tall ceiling. Bookshelves filled with tomes and scrolls lined the walls, and wooden stairs led to the second and third story platforms.

A sofa and two chairs sat in front of the fireplace, while glowing light illuminated from a low-hanging chandelier.

Several people walked quietly through the expansive library. While some carried books, others sat at desks, writing or reading. Golden pendants glistened along each of their breasts, and Aélla paused with concern.

"Where are we?" she asked. "Why are you all wearing that symbol?"

Dül'Dregon sighed and rested in a large chair. Opening a side table drawer, he retrieved a long wooden pipe and box of tobacco. He drew in several small puffs and exhaled a steady stream of smoke.

Aélla sat at the edge of the oversized leather chair to his side. "Dül'Dregorn," she pressed.

Smoke wisped from his pipe, and he stared into the hearth. "Long ago, the üroks came. It was a massacre. Children were struck down by men on horses. Warriors fought against foreign soldiers of the same size and strength. I was there, witnessing it all. My people. My *home*…reduced to ashes. For nothing more than the land beneath our feet. It wasn't slaves or fear that drove them to kill us…It was their thirst for power. Greed led them to genocide.

"Forty-one of our bordering shelarr were destroyed. They were farmsteads, mostly. Larger shelarr were meant to protect them, but they were distracted by battles of their own.

"We were lost. Their numbers were too great. Their militia too powerful. We were not prepared for such devastation. The vaxros would have seen defeat at the hands of the ürok had it not been for the Brotherhood. They came and fought alongside our people. Drove the enemy away.

"Many of my people are not easy to forgive. We are hard. Warriors. But those of us who were there—who lost everything—we understand the debt that is owed."

His glowing eyes finally blinked. They shifted to his pipe, which had burned out. Leaning forward, he reached into the fire and extracted a flame, relighting his pipe and taking several shallow puffs. Then, he leaned back and continued, "This is a sanctuary for the Broken Order Brotherhood. We wear these pins to show our loyalty. It is not the ürok that wishes to see our end, but their leaders."

"I don't understand," Aélla said. "The Broken Order Brotherhood is a human movement. Why would vaxros and y'lenae want to join their ranks?"

"The üroks are leading us down a path of no return. They must be stopped."

Aélla's hands twisted in her lap. She stared at her fingers as her mind raced. "You want to fight the humans?"

"We will protect our borders first. The Brotherhood understands the fate of the world lies in more than the destruction of the ürok leaders. We will fight alongside our brothers to conquer the evae invading our lands."

"Do you know what they're after?"

Smoke filled the air when he exhaled another puff of his pipe. He turned aside when a young vaxros woman approached. In her arms was a large book. She spoke quietly to the dül, who responded in an equally silent voice. Aélla paid no mind to their conversation, becoming lost in her own thoughts.

The klaet'il wouldn't risk sending the evae and vaxros to war for no reason. It had been centuries since the War of Ashes, when the vaxros first came to the desert and caused conflict between themselves and the evae.

The treaty that followed such a bloody conflict allowed Aélla passage into their lands, but the klaet'il were not permitted under any circumstance.

As dül'Dregorn leaned back into his seat, his eyes moved to the hearth. "The Nasir seeks power," he said. "But he will not find it. Hidden beneath the sands where bones grow cold and lava scorches the air, it waits."

Aélla leaned back when their gazes met.

"Do not seek what has been concealed by those more powerful and wise," he warned. "Turn back, Master Drimil. Undo what has yet to be done." He paused with apprehension. His lips shook, and his eyes were wide as he struggled through his fear. "Turn back…before it's too late."

CHAPTER TWENTY-SEVEN

BROTHER
Y'ven

"We are all brothers here."

— Words of the Broken Order Brotherhood

Y'VEN STOOD BEFORE THE EVAE. Shoulders square and lip curled, he stared hatefully into his fierce eyes.

The evae was strong and confident, never faltering beneath the stone-cold glare of the angry vaxros. Altvára took flight, and the warriors maintained eye contact. Boots shuffled across the floor when the evae stepped closer. Y'ven groaned and straightened. The bolt tugged at his skin, tearing the wound and spilling with blood.

"Where is she?" the stranger demanded.

Y'ven was silent, the hardness of his eyes yet to disappear. With a snarl, the evae looked around. The room was silent and empty, destroyed by the hunter.

"Is this your doing, vaxros? What does a warrior of the flame want with a lanathess?"

Y'ven glared, unprovoked by the evae's deadly eyes. "What does an evae want with her?"

The stranger stepped closer. His eyes moved to the bolt in Y'ven's side. Hot blood spilled from his wound, and the slight arch of his posture displayed his weakness against the agile and furious warrior.

Their gazes met, and the evae warned, "If she is harmed, I will come for *you.*"

Y'ven's lip twisted into a hateful snarl. His glowering eyes followed as the evae fled the home and strode through the village, determined to find Neer. He searched empty rooms and overturned the furniture, relentless in his pursuit.

As he entered Y'ven's abandoned, destroyed home, the vaxros stepped closer, watching carefully as objects and furniture were tossed aside. The evae's shadow moved frantically from one room to the next.

Y'ven reached for his axe, which lay at his feet, and painfully gripped his side. Every breath was another wave of agony as his flesh was pulled and torn. His eyes flashed to his home as the evae departed to search another. Y'ven couldn't allow him to find her, but neither could he fight.

With a groan, he clutched the fletching of the blood-coated bolt and inhaled a deep breath before forcing it deeper into his flesh. He leaned against the wall, choking and wincing, pushing hard through clenched teeth. His arms began to shake as he struggled to pierce through his thick skin. The sharp arrow ripped through his flesh, and he released a thunderous cry. Gripping the arrowhead, he took several shallow breaths, and with a forceful pull, he yanked the bolt from his body.

Blood sprayed onto the floor, and he collapsed into the wall. The bolt slipped from his wet, sticky fingers and fell to the ground with a loud clack. He gripped his side, pain throbbing with every quick, jolting heartbeat.

A shadow entered the home as the evae returned. His light, shoulder-length hair was in disarray, and the paleness of his face had shifted into a deep shade of red. His gaze fell to the bloody bolt. Shaking his head, he walked past Y'ven to the far side of the room.

The silver pommel of a longsword displayed from beneath his cloak.

Y'ven gazed upon it for several seconds, noticing the pommel was made into the sigil of the Broken Order Brotherhood. With another groan, he leaned against the wall with his eyes closed. "You are with the Brotherhood?" he asked. He was silent with intrigue as the stranger stepped closer. Y'ven groaned when the evae pulled his shoulder to examine his scars and took note of the Broken Order sigil along his collar.

Their gazes met, and the evae reached for Y'ven's hand. "Brother."

Y'ven gripped his forearm, and they shared a uniting nod. The evae stepped away, and Y'ven leaned back into the wall. "Why are you here? What do you want with the ürok?"

"She's important to the Brotherhood."

"There are many vaxros who may search for her. Many in the Brotherhood that—"

"She's important to *me*." His deadly glare transcended to fear and panic. Turing away, he regained his composure and stepped through the empty home. Y'ven's heavy steps scraped across the ground as he followed. With every stride forward, he exhaled another pained breath.

Stepping outside, he noticed the evae staring at Altvára, who was perched atop a roof.

"This is a *dren'seol*?" he asked of the raven. "A companion. It's loyal to someone."

"Yes," Y'ven explained. "It leads me to her."

The evae nodded with purpose. He started to speak, but as he turned to Y'ven, his gaze fell to the blood dripping from his side. Digging through his bag, he approached the vaxros and procured a jar of travaran, passing the thick brown potion to his brother. Y'ven shook his head in opposition.

"It won't work," he explained. "I need flame and heat."

Long fingers wrapped around the jar as the evae retracted his offering. Lost in thought, he glanced through the village. His eyes set upon the dormant firepit, and Y'ven followed his gaze. With just a single spark, a new fire would ignite and burn until sunrise.

The evae stepped to the pit and gathered a flint from his pack, when Y'ven stormed over, crashing into him. The vaxros gripped his wrist, and deep breaths escaped through clenched teeth as he warned, "Do not light it."

"You need to heal, brother. If this wound isn't—"

"I will get help at the sanctuary. *Do not light it.*"

The evae sighed. "Your pride gives rise to imprudence. Is your life worth less than the dishonor of lighting this pit?"

Y'ven turned away. He fell into deep thought as he gazed upon the sacred pit. Rekindling the fire once it had gone out was the responsibility of the *i'ghor*, or leader. To bring life back to a place he destroyed would bring him unforgiveable, tormenting shame.

Touching his wounded side, he was reminded of the severity of his injury. Thick blood coated his fingers and hardened in his clothes. He wouldn't survive the journey back to Zaos.

"A man can either die by his honor," the evae started, "or he can live by his wisdom. There isn't a ghost you will find that has changed the world without disgrace." Their gazes met. "I will light this fire, and you will heal yourself. There is no glory in dying of obstinance."

Shaken, Y'ven ripped away from his heavy gaze. He stared longingly into the pit, torn by his indecision. It would do no good to die by such a fate. To be left for dead in a village of ghosts and memories. His purpose was clear. The path to restoring his honor wasn't by dying to respect old customs.

His grip released on the evae's wrist, and he pulled away. Brightness filled the night when the flint was struck, and a roaring fire engulfed the pit. Y'ven leaned against the stone wall containing the fire. Mist filled his eyes as he gazed upon the flames, watching as they danced. It was the same as it had always been, yet now, standing alone, it was different.

With closed eyes, he reached into the blaze and collected a tendril of flame. The heat whirred and hissed, hovering within his palms. Placing the fire to his side, he pressed it into his wound. His body convulsed and throat tightened as the heat sank deep into his tissue.

It traveled into his back and through his side. The fire tugged his perforated muscles and organs. He pressed hard against his skin, trapping the heat inside.

As the flames healed his wounds, he exhaled a deep, hoarse breath. Collapsing to his knees, he breathed in long draws, and the evae knelt before him.

"You did well," he said. "Honor is not bestowed by the integrity of your beliefs, but the valor of your adversity." The hint of a smile tugged the edge of his lip. "You have my respect, brother. Now come. Let us find the girl before it's too late."

He pulled Y'ven to his feet and patted his shoulder. With a glance through the village, his gaze paused on Altvára. The raven's head shifted from one direction to the next, before it took flight, and the evae wasted no time following him.

The glow of firelight became a speck on the horizon as they rushed into the desert. Behind lonesome rock columns and jagged boulders, they found a small campsite of ashen logs and an empty cooking cauldron.

Altvára landed atop the rocks, while the others climbed through the deep and narrow crevices. Nestled within the rocks, hidden by dark shadows, was a small canvas tent. Residue of a recent meal lined the small cauldron.

"Nerana?" the evae called, slipping into the tent.

Y'ven strode across the camp, finding six gold coins, leather strips, several vials of black liquid, and a clear crystal lying on the ground.

Light shuffling came from behind, and he turned his attention to the evae as he stepped from the tent with Neer in his arms. Her body was limp and eyes were closed. Y'ven marched to his side. Furious and confused, he reached for Neer, but was met with hostility.

"Why do you search for her?" Y'ven demanded. "How do you know her name?"

The evae pulled Neer closer as he gazed into Y'ven's eyes and explained with great confidence, "I'm her father."

CHAPTER TWENTY-EIGHT

CONFIDENCE AND POWER
Y'ven

*"We are not blood, but I will care for you as if you were my child...
and protect you just as fiercely."*

—   Reiman to Nerana

Y'VEN WALKED ALONGSIDE THE EVAE carrying Neer. She
lay unconscious in his arms, and he worried about her safety.
With several glances in her direction, he forced the intruding
thoughts of death from his mind and instead focused on the
evae.

The pommel of his sword revealed his loyalty to the Brotherhood, but still, Y'ven was curious. There was only one evae
known to be part of the rebel guild, and surely Y'ven wasn't
in the presence of such a man.

The evae held no expression, focusing on the unending
horizon. His blond hair, matted with dirt and blood, hung
messily over his shoulders. His dark cloak had faded into a
shade of light grey after its many days beneath the unrelenting
sun. Being nearly twenty sun-cycles from the border, Y'ven
knew this stranger had been in Aragoth for some time. His
survival became a question of strength or luck, as no outsider
had ever survived on their own so far in the desert.

Y'ven turned away and set his eyes on the horizon. "You
are with the Brotherhood?"

With a hard blink, the evae refocused his gaze and turned to Y'ven. "Yes."

"What is your name?"

Without the hint of hesitancy or guile, he said, "Reiman."

Y'ven was speechless. His mouth opened and closed again with no words spoken. Bright eyes gazed at the notorious leader. "Master Reiman…," he said, "it is truly an honor."

With a sideways glance, Reiman's lips curled into a subtle smile. "The honor is mine, brother."

"You…you are here in Aragoth? You seek Neer?"

"Yes. I couldn't allow her to succumb to the dangers of this place."

"She is evae? This is why she is magic?"

Reiman glanced at Neer. "She's human. I don't know how she came to possess such energy."

"Ürok's are not born with magic. She must be evae. Or cursed."

"She isn't cursed." He straightened his neck and held his chin high. "Have you ever been told the history of the First Blood and humans? It's a troubling tale of bloodlust and rage. Long before the vaxros came to the desert or the evae were banished from their lands, this continent belonged to the First Blood. Powerful and elusive, they kept their secrets hidden from the world.

"The humans slowly left their home of Aeshan[*] to find a better life, and the First Blood welcomed them with open arms. The races coexisted for many years, but peace isn't imperishable, and the humans' desire of freedom was merely a concealment of their true intentions.

---

[*] The continent northeast of Laeroth is known mostly as a place of kingdoms, war, slavers, and poverty.

Since the time of King Benjamin IV, aeshan natives have seen a constant decline of wealth and power in their homeland. Refusing the aid of their neighboring continents, and for fear of losing his reign to foreign invaders, King Benjamin VII sealed his borders from defectors and outsiders fifty years ago.

"They seduced the First Blood into relationships, and thus the reign of half-human sorcerers began. This mutation eventually led to humans birthing full sorcerers without the use of First Blood lineage. Impatient for power, the humans revolted. They fought against the very people who not a century before had given them refuge in their hour of need.

"The First Blood were masters of the arcane and proved to be superior in all aspects of battle, magic, and wit. The humans who fought against them—and those who bore magical energy—were eradicated."

Y'ven pondered for a moment, taking in the story and all its details. "Neer is a descendant of these humans? The magic was passed to her through her ancestors?"

"I do not know. Magic in humans isn't impossible but is extraordinarily rare and can be even more dangerous. Their race isn't meant to withhold such energy. Many who are born with her abilities die soon after." His eyes shifted to Neer as she lay in his arms. "The actuality of her survival only proves her strength. She's meant for greatness. So long as she's guided toward the right path."

Their conversation ended, and the world fell silent. Slow footsteps shuffled against the dirt as they wandered throughout the night. Shadows lurked in the distance, followed soon by vicious howling and snarls. Y'ven held his battle axe and focused on the desert, while Reiman kept his poise.

"You do not fear the creatures of night?" Y'ven asked.

"Once you've lived as long as I have, fear becomes acquiescent. What may be, may be. In the end, it is all the same. You fight, or you die."

"I heard the tales of your prowess and glory. You led the Brotherhood in the battle of the gorge.° You saved my people from the üroks."

° A deadly battle which resulted in the loss of thousands of innocent vaxros lives after human invaders ambushed their unprotected villages and settlements.

"This world does not belong to one. We are all a collective being. Coexistence is the only future we have."

"This is why you fight with them? Why you have left your people behind?"

"There are many reasons I chose to leave the forest." He smiled with thought. "And what of you? Protecting a human and traveling alongside an evae is strictly forbidden, yet here you are, in open defiance of such laws."

"My people and I haven't seen eye to eye for a long time."

"I noticed the marking across your back. The one blemishing the sun scar of the al'yavan."

Y'ven turned away. His eyes focused on the ground in sorrow, and his shoulders slumped forward. Reiman took note of this change and inhaled a soft breath.

"I, too, bear the mark of a traitor," he explained. "Sometimes, even the most noble of actions can be misconceived by others. It isn't what you do with your injustice, but how you do it. I could've sought revenge or lived a life of seclusion — two of the things expected most of those deemed *nesiat*. But instead, I chose a different path. One of virtue and consideration."

"My actions were not noble. I forsook my vows. Brought shame to my family…to my son. They will never outlive such dishonor."

"I am a lost evaesh warrior who leads a rebellion of humans with his adopted human sorceress…" Their eyes met. "If there is anyone here undeserving of such titles as noble and heroic, it is I."

"You are not undeserving, Master Reiman."

Reiman smiled knowingly. "Nor are you."

They walked in a comfortable silence beneath the glow of the prominent moons. Y'ven's scars glowed under their

---

The aftermath of this battle, which lasted two years, gave further proof of the vaxros' need to seal their borders, and has led to an increase in armed forces guarding their lands at the edge of the Reinwald Gorge.

purple luminance, displaying his successes and failures as a warrior. The intentional designs were overlapped with battle marks. The *muz'rogg*[*] engraved across his upper back was a mark of high esteem and valor. To have it eviscerated with the branding of a traitor left him alone and outcast.

He took comfort in Reiman's words, knowing greatness would be given to those who sought to redeem themselves. Though, he feared redemption might never come.

As the sun began to rise, the sky bloomed with pastels of orange and pink. Y'ven squinted beneath the harsh light as it shone into his eyes. He relished in the warmth and power of its energy, while Reiman began to slow, and fatigue overtook his confident stride. Y'ven examined his appearance, which was red with exhaustion.

"I will carry her," Y'ven suggested.

He reached for Neer, and Reiman promptly pulled her away. Rejected, Y'ven understood his position and focused on the journey.

Sunlight sprayed against the curved pillars protecting Zaos as the city became clear in the distance. Reiman exhaled a deep breath of relief, and his energy had seemed to return as he walked with hurried steps.

"Why did you search for her?" he asked, drawing nearer to the city.

Y'ven kept his pace. "We travel together."

"Why?" He came to a sudden halt. Turning to the vaxros, the tiredness of his eyes had become dark and hard. "What does a fallen vaxros warrior want with a human sorceress?"

"We are with another. She is Drimil'Rothar."

Reiman's eyes widened. With a quick glance to Neer, he stiffened and continued toward Zaos without another word.

The city was left in shambles and without proper guard, allowing Reiman and Y'ven to enter without persecution.

---

[*] The mark of a warrior that resembles the sun.

The muz'rogg signifies one's position as an al'yavan warrior, the fiercest and most feared of vaxros fighters.

Waves of heat lifted the cool air of the city as the barrier was left broken upon its entry. Loose stones tumbled beneath their feet as they stepped across the cobble bridge.

The natives and Brotherhood associates worked together to restore the crumbled homes and devastated streets where dark, dry blood covered the cobbles in thick spatters. Reiman slowly stopped as a young boy approached. His dirty rags were singed, and the deep cut across his cheek caused his face to swell and drip with pus. The boy stared at him with wide eyes, impetrating help.

Reiman's eyes softened at the boy's silent plea. He looked at Neer, who not long ago carried the same sorrow and fear. Memories of their first encounter entered his mind. She was small and frail, just as the boy before him. But in her eyes was strength and purpose, something most children lacked. He saw in her that day what many would otherwise overlook. A simple, yet courageous trait that would carry her to victory.

Hope.

This child didn't carry that same spark, yet still, he needed rescue. Glancing to Y'ven, Reiman motioned to the boy. Y'ven nodded with understanding and placed a hand on the youngling's back. Leading him through the streets, they approached the hidden entrance of the Brotherhood sanctuary at the base of the stairs.

Within the corridors of the sanctuary, Y'ven followed Reiman as he strode to the center of town. Members stopped and stared as he walked past, their eyes gleaming and lips parted at the sudden appearance of their leader. Whispers of his arrival spread throughout the city, and the streets grew full of onlookers and admirers.

Y'ven glanced to Reiman as he stared above the others as if they weren't there at all, not with arrogance or pride, but confidence and poise. Even in his disheveled, exhausted state, his presence was a step above the rest. The hardness of his eyes and fortitude of his posture gave rise to his position as a great and noble leader.

As he approached the city center, Aélla stepped forward to block his path, and Reiman's chin lifted slightly as he looked down to the woman standing confidently before him.

A peculiar spark settled in his eyes as he gazed at her, knowing exactly who she was without needing introduction, though they had already met once before.

Her fingers laced together in front of her waist as she examined the stranger carrying her friend. When their eyes connected, she raised a curious brow, and he knew she recognized him from their previous encounter not so long ago.

"It's good to see you again," she said, her voice smooth with assurance and strength, *"Master Reiman."*

CHAPTER TWENTY-NINE

POSITION OF POWER
Aélla

"Those with authority will bow to the one who wields true power."

— Words of the First Blood

REIMAN SAT IN A LEATHER CHAIR nestled before a crackling hearth, in his hands a mug of steaming cider. Leaning forward, he retrieved a mulling stone from the fire and dropped it into his beverage. The cider bubbled and hissed with the scent of cloves and cinnamon.

As he leaned back, blowing the steam of his drink, he glanced at Neer, who lay motionless atop a cushioned bench. Firelight brightened the dark bruises across her face, and burns covered her throat in overlapping blisters where Thorne had gripped her with his hot iron hand while she was in his captivity.

Aélla sat on a stool next to her, gently smearing ointment across her shallow cuts. She hesitated over the deep split that opened her cheek. Shifting her eyes to the ointment, she knew it wouldn't be enough to heal such an injury.

As she covered the last mark, she wiped her hands clean with a linen cloth and sat in a chair opposite Reiman. He offered a glass of cider, and she kindly refused. She leaned forward with her hands in her lap and eyed the man next to her. His chin was high as he focused his gaze on the hearth.

"You are their leader?" she asked after several minutes of silence. Reiman nodded in response, yet never met her gaze. "Why were you so elusive when we met? You mentioned the *human sorceress* but failed to tell me that she's your daughter."

He straightened and turned his glass upward, finishing his drink. The cup thudded against the hard grain of a wooden table as he placed it aside. "Master Drimil, you must forgive me. It would do no good for you or anyone else to know that she is directly connected to the rebellion's leader. To know that my kin is considered demonic by her people."

"Why are you here, Master Reiman? It's quite convenient you show up when disaster strikes."

A half-smile tugged the edge of his lip. "I'm the leader of the largest organization in Laeroth, second only to the Order. Make no mistake of my intentions, Master Drimil. I'm here to see that Nerana takes the right path."

"You had me believe you were here to stop the klaet'il from creating war with the vaxros," she said, referring to the conversation they had long ago. Aélla had met Reiman only once before and learned of his identity through her time with the Brotherhood in their sanctuary. The two had fought against the klaet'il, who ambushed a vaxros village.

"Another lie, I'm afraid. To protect myself." He paused with purpose. "To protect her."

Aélla leaned closer and gazed daringly into his unflinching eyes. "Protect her from *what*?"

Orange light cast across the dark room when a log split. Embers sprayed into the air as the woodpile shifted beneath dancing flames. Reiman stared unblinking at Aélla, who matched his gaze. She could see he wasn't familiar with being challenged, and the provocation of a stranger filled him with curiosity and ire.

The intensity of their glare diminished when the door opened, and Aélla turned away, undeterred by his authoritative demeanor.

Her eyes shifted to Thallon as he entered the room. He grunted with every slow step and leaned against a cane of solid oak with gold embellishments near the handle. Clutching his bandaged ribs, which were little more than healing scars and bruises, he moved to Aélla's side.

"Hey. What's going on?" he asked. Since his arrival in the sanctuary, he had been confined to the medical rooms. Only now, three days since the attack, was he able to withstand the pain of walking.

Aélla was silent as he turned to Neer, and the softness of his eyes faded to horror at the sight of her patched and injured face. Hobbling to her side, he examined her injuries. "Will she make it?" he asked.

Aélla took a moment, then stepped across the room to his side. "Yes. She's alive but weak."

"Who was that man? How did he destroy the city like that?"

"His name is Thorne," Reiman explained. His silhouette could be seen from the edge of the chair as he stared into the fire.

Thallon glanced at Aélla with a peculiar gaze. The cushioned bench squeaked beneath his weight as he sat down and then leaned aside to better view the stranger he had yet to meet.

"Thorne?" Thallon asked.

Reiman's shadow enveloped the room when he stepped in front of the hearth. Moving to a desk, he began digging through his satchel. "He's a bounty hunter with the Shadow Blades. They're a mercenary group contracted with the Order of Saro." With a small mortar in hand, he mixed herbs and potions together. They watched silently while he focused on his concoction. "He was searching for Nerana."

"Well, that's obvious," Thallon said with a scoff.

"Why are her people coming into the desert?" Aélla asked. "Surely, they wouldn't risk war with the vaxros for her capture."

The pestle clinked as he mashed the contents into a pungent paste. "Luckily for the humans, the vaxros are distracted with the klaet'il. Otherwise, they'd…"

His voice was silenced when Neer began to wheeze and panic as she woke. Her wide eyes glanced from one person to the next as everyone crowded her side. She reached out to them, unable to speak through her injured throat. Strained words were all that came from her lips.

"Hush now," Reiman said, breaking through the others to take her hand, and Neer stared at him with wide eyes, shocked to see him so suddenly after months of separation. "You're all right, child."

"Child?" Thallon remarked. "Who are you?"

Reiman brushed Neer's hair back and looked into her eyes. "Do not speak. You are very injured, Nerana, but you will survive."

"Who is this?" Thallon remarked.

Aélla glanced between Neer and Reiman. "He is her father."

"*Father*?" His voice was heavy with confusion, as if he'd never heard the phrase before. "She's evaesh?"

Reiman paid them no mind and raced back to the desk. Neer reached for Aélla's hands, her bloodshot eyes pleading for relief.

"I'm sorry," Aélla said. "I cannot heal you."

"Why not?" Thallon remarked. "Give her your energy!"

"I'm still too weak," Aélla sorrowfully explained. "If I give more of my energy, it could compromise us both."

Neer's arms shook as she gripped Aélla tighter. Writhing with agony, she tensed, unbreathing.

Reiman pulled Aélla away and took her place. He mixed the paste one last time before scooping it onto his fingers. "Do not scream," he warned and smeared the paste across Neer's neck.

Neer's body shook, and her face turned a deep shade of red as she withheld the painful, burning agony of travaran.

She clutched his arms while searing pain tore through her wounds. The suffering of scorched heat over flayed skin would've been a pleasantry to the agony she endured.

"What's happening?" Thallon argued. "What are you—"

"It's travaran," Reiman explained, without turning from Neer. "She could damage her throat further by expelling her pain. It could also lead to her magic being inadvertently unleashed. She must contain it."

Her nails dug into his arms, and her body tensed. After several minutes of grueling torture, she exhaled a deep breath and collapsed into the cushions. Aélla and Thallon hovered closer while Reiman removed the paste from her now healing wounds. The blisters overlapping on her skin had dissolved, and the welts had diminished significantly.

"You all right?" Thallon asked. He gently rubbed her arm with the affection of a worried parent.

Neer touched her neck and closed her eyes. With a gentle nod, she silently answered his question.

Reiman wiped his hands clean on a handkerchief. "Travaran is effective but incredibly painful. She will recover."

As he stepped back to the desk, his gaze fell to Thallon's wrapped wounds.

The scholar lifted his hands and quickly objected. "I'll just heal naturally," he said.

Reiman placed the mortar onto the desk and hadn't the slightest concern when Aélla marched angrily to his side. Her scornful gaze went unnoticed as he rummaged through his things.

"Travaran has been banned for a reason!" she spewed. "Forcing her to withhold that amount of pain is—"

"It was the only way." His dark eyes met with hers, and she was instantly silenced. Reiman turned back to the desk and quietly sifted through his things as if the altercation never took place.

She watched him with disbelief and repulsion. The redness of her face was blanketed by the orange glow of the room. With a heavy, defeated sigh, she moved back to Neer's side. Grabbing a fur pelt from a basket, she draped it over her body.

"That was pretty tough," Thallon said. "You're just full of surprises, aren't you?"

Neer cut him a sideways glance, which came off harsher than she intended. Thallon laughed it off. He gripped his side with a groan, and the joyful sounds became groans of pain.

"Your ribs…" Neer started, remembering his horrific injury. Her wheezed voice was made silent as she touched her cheek, stricken with pain.

With a wince, he straightened, portraying the act of strength as he withheld his agony. "Oh, uh, yeah. It's nothing."

Her eyes drifted to his cane, which he leaned heavily on for support. Their eyes reconnected, and she lifted a brow, challenging his argument. With a hidden smile, he turned away.

"I'm a scholar. Using a cane is part of the job."

The blankets shifted as she sat up. "Just need some wrinkles and a beard," she wheezed.

He chuckled and lightly gripped his chest. "If that's the kind of thing you're into…" His brows lifted in a playfully suggestive manor.

The cut to her face burned as her lips pulled together when she withheld a smile. Aélla watched her with careful eyes, noticing the rosiness of her cheeks. With a quiet sigh, her gaze averted to Avelloch's sword, and she fell into quiet contempt. Thallon got comfortable by Neer's side and exhaled a deep breath, sinking into the cushions. With his eyes closed, he leaned back, basking in relief.

"Master Drimil," Reiman started, pulling Aélla's attention away from Thallon and Neer, "what is it you're here for? Why have you allied yourself with Nerana?"

Aélla stiffened at his calm approach as he leaned against the desk with his palms flat. The firelight shone against his back, creating a shadow that shrouded his face in darkness. With a quiet sigh, she released her disaffection and reminded herself that he could be trusted. "We seek tre'lan Aenwyn," she explained, referring to the realm of elements.

"And you need Nerana for this?"

The rigidness returned as she met his gaze. "Yes. You understand my duty. Having two full sorcerers is much better than one."

"You understand that Nerana is human."

"Yes, I—"

Her voice was cut off when the door burst open, and everyone turned as light filled the dark, firelit space. Dru darted through the room with a flash of orange light, and Y'ven's shadow darkened the entry. Embers spewed as the faeth raced to the hearth and dove into the flames. A wave of heat brightened the mantle as she absorbed the fire's energy.

Heavy footsteps bounded through the room as Y'ven stepped inside with an armful of books and scrolls. Aélla helped Neer to her feet as everyone crowded the desk. Objects clattered and fell to the floor when Y'ven spilled his armful onto the cluttered surface.

"This is where you've been?" Aélla asked, while lifting the cover of a book. The vaxros nodded as the others dug through the pile of tomes.

"Library," he explained in evaesh. "Books of Aenwyn."

Thallon leafed through a thick book with a black leather cover. His eyes squinted and shifted from left to right, following the trail of words. "This is in vax, Y'ven. We can't read any of it!"

With a gruff snarl, Y'ven snatched the book away. Paper crinkled beneath his finger as he whisked roughly through the pages, stopping near the end. Slamming the book onto the desk he read aloud in his native language, "Tre'lan Aenwyn is a sacred place of power. To fully obtain its energy, you must survive each of the four elemental realms. Located throughout

D'windlemer, the drimil must accept passion, peace, strength, freedom, and sacrifice.

"Collect each energy into the rástalfür° and enter the sacred chambers of Elandorr, where strength and energy will be forever combined."

The room fell heavy with silence as they stared at the book, firelight dancing across their faces. Each held distinctive expressions of confusion and intrigue. Aélla's lips contorted, not quite into a frown, yet not also a smile. It was somewhere in between. As her brows pulled together, the nature of her confusion was made clearer.

"Y'ven," she started, rubbing her forehead in dismay, "this doesn't answer any of our questions. We know to retrieve the elements."

He flipped the page and her jaw dropped. Scribbled over the words in dark charcoal was an outlined map of the desert. The lines were uneven and tattered, as if written in a hurry.

Small circles were scattered throughout the empty sketch.

"Whoa!" Thallon snatched the book and examined the drawings. "These are all the known locations of the realms! Look!" He pointed to a village just north of Zaos. "This is I'vasaar. It's only a five-day walk from here!"

"That's too long," Reiman stated. "We do not have time to waste. Not while the klaet'il are in the desert, and the humans are in the forest." Taking the book from Thallon, he pressed a finger to the page. "If we pass through Sandir, we'll save days from our trip."

"You're coming?" Neer asked. Her voice cracked and caused her to cough.

Aélla quickly passed her a canteen of water.

"Don't want an old man tagging along?" Reiman playfully teased.

° The enchanted staff Aélla collected from Aneamiril that can contain each of the four elemental energies and use them as a key to enter Elandorr, where she will gain the full strength of her elemental abilities.

She lightly smiled before taking another sip of water.

Thallon shook his head. "No way are we going through Sandir. There has to be another way."

"What is Sandir?" Aélla asked.

"A cursed place. The ground looks solid, but it'll pull you under like quicksand if you step in the wrong spot. The First Blood had them placed all around the desert. They're too dangerous—we aren't cutting through it!"

"Why would the First Blood create places like that?"

Thallon leaned against the table with a wince, carefully gripping his ribs as he explained, "I don't know. It could be protecting something, or are just used as a way to guard certain areas of the desert. Whatever it's meant for, it's extremely dangerous. Once you get pulled under, you never come back out." He leaned against his cane with another grimace. "If you're going that way, then count me out. I'm not dying just to get someplace quicker."

Y'ven agreed, and spoke evaesh as he said, "Sandir deadly. Many die."

Reiman straightened. "We have two sorceresses and warriors. Should we come to trouble, I've no doubt we'll see our way through."

"Well, good luck to you because I'm not going," Thallon argued.

"Thallon…" Aélla begged.

"Sorry, but there is no way you're dragging me across Sandir. You're all *fyet* if you think otherwise."

"Then stay behind," Reiman suggested, gathering his things. "This is the quickest way to I'vasaar, and time is of the essence."

Neer stood by Thallon, staring at the map. "Is there another way?" she asked.

Thallon glanced at her, then focused on the book. A crease formed between his brows as he studied the poorly drawn map further. Tracing across the page, he explained, "We can swing left and head through the outskirts of the jungle. Or we can go right, which will take even longer, and cut through the foothills of the mountains."

Neer pondered for a moment, before reluctantly stating, "Sandir does seem easier."

"It's quicker, not easier. I'm telling you, going through that place is a deathtrap."

Aélla bit her lip and furrowed her brow. The room fell into a bitter silence. Reiman wasn't bothered by their argument as he collected his things into a large pack. With a light exhale, Aélla stated, "We should stick together. If Y'ven and Thallon believe Sandir to be too dangerous, then I think we should listen to them."

Neer agreed, and Reiman stiffened. His hard eyes focused on hers, and she returned the deadly stare. He wasn't familiar with being at the mercy of another's command. But to have Neer question his judgement — or worse — side with another, sparked him with quiet vexation.

"It's settled, then," Aélla remarked, breaking them of their long gaze. "Once we've healed, we'll head for the jungle. At the least, it'll give us a few days of shade and protection."

Thallon closed the book and stuffed it safely into his pack.

With a final glance to her father, who remained still in his displeasure, Neer turned away. She took her place on the bench, while the others fell into silent projects. Her gaze was set on Reiman as he stood at the table in deep thought.

She worried for him, though she wasn't entirely sure why. He had always been respected and obeyed. It came with being a leader. Amongst their people, he was considered of the highest esteem, a ruthless warrior and hallowed savior. A god among men. He was the only evae any human truly respected. Yet now, he was at the mercy of someone far younger, and far greater, than himself.

With a confident gaze across the room, Reiman took his mug, gathered a few books, and got comfortable once again in front of the fire, where he sat in a tranquil silence for the remainder of the night.

CHAPTER THIRTY

A FATHER'S LOVE
Nerana

"Do not be consumed by what once was. Look ahead, and you shall find peace for your pain."

— Vethad, the Book of Time

THE NEXT MORNING, NEER SHUFFLED through the crowded streets of the underground city. People walked by without a glance in her direction. Their voices were pleasant as they carried on with their daily routines. She eyed each passerby, taking note of their calm expressions and the warm familiarity they shared with one another.

Her eyes moved to the pendants and scars of each of the Brotherhood members. It was commonplace for those who swore allegiance to the Brotherhood to carry the sigil, though Neer chose to forego hers long ago. Her eyes were proof enough of her heresy. She didn't need to further display her identity by wearing a symbol of defiance and rebellion.

Watching the people wander by, she was reminded of Porsdur, and it filled her with an ache that came from being too far from home. She longed for the intimacy of friendship and trust. Of knowing each face that passed by and not having to glance over her shoulder.

Gone were the days of peace and comfortability. The path that lay ahead was brutal and unknown, but she knew she must take it. For it wasn't but the taste of revenge that gave her the comfort she would always be without.

With darkness shrouding her every thought, she was happy to pass by a young girl selling flowers in front of a large stall. Overcome by the scent of lilies, which were her favorite, she smiled. Stepping to the stall, she was greeted by a young woman with a wide smile and large round eyes. She looked much like all the other y'lenae—short, slim, and dark-skinned.

Neer looked through potted and hanging plants before kneeling in front of the girl and picking a white lily from her small basket. "How much?" she asked pleasantly.

The girl's large eyes were full of confusion, and she turned to the woman behind the counter as they spoke kindly in a foreign language, undoubtedly of Neer. Neer reached into her pocket, retrieved two copper cogs, and placed them into the girl's hand.

With a smile, the girl bowed. Neer sniffed the flower before walking further into the street. The scent of coal filled the air as she walked past the smithy, and she was happier still to have the lily, which aided in masking the stench of smelted steel and soot.

As she walked by, she brought her attention to a vaxros smithy wearing long sleeves and a thick leather apron. Metal clinked as he pounded hot, malleable steel into an axe. He placed the half-made weapon into a slack tub, causing the water to sizzle. Steam clouded his arms and face as he held the metal beneath the water with tongs.

Neer curiously watched as Reiman stepped to the smithy with his hands laced together at his waist. She smiled as his familiar authoritative voice reigned over the others. His poise was that of a man in charge. Even a stranger could tell his position.

The vaxros exhaled a hard breath from his nose and tilted his head directedly to his apprentice. A younger vaxros, with smaller musculature and much fewer scars, stood at a table sorting weapons. Reiman gave a respectful nod to the smith and glided to his apprentice with ease.

246

As Reiman spoke to the boy, who even in his youth stood taller than the evae, he picked through the freshly forged items, and the boy cut him a daring look. Reiman didn't notice, focusing on the weapons. When their eyes met, Reiman's voice faded.

The apprentice stiffly nodded, picked up a longsword from a shelf, and slowly unsheathed it from the scabbard. Reiman ran a finger down the smooth edge of the blade. He accepted the sword and placed a handful of cogs into the boy's hand.

As the boy refused, Reiman kindly curled his fingers around the cogs, and with a gentle tap to his hand, he bid the smiths farewell.

He stepped onto the street and caught sight of Neer, who watched him from nearby. With a smile, he fastened his sword to his belt and approached her. "I didn't expect to see you out so early."

"Hard to be a night owl when you can't see the sun," she jested with a grin, and winced when a spark of pain flashed through her injured cheek. Her raspy voice, caused by the wounds still healing in her throat, was unrecognizable.

"It's good to see you smiling." He touched her face, carefully examining the deep bruises. She winced as he grazed the bandage covering her left cheek. A thick red line stretched across the white linen, matching the shape of the wound beneath. "I was certain you were lost..." His eyes lost their light as he stared through her, reliving the pain of finding her unconscious and beaten in the desert. She knew his thoughts by the manner of his sorrow and wrapped around him in a tight embrace.

Comfort filled her with peace as he accepted her loving gesture. Folding his arms around her back, he kissed her head and backed away. With a sniff, she hid her emotions. Reiman knew better than to press her on them, and she was glad when he made no mention of her tears.

Instead, he focused on more pressing matters, and she wasn't the least bit surprised at his change in subject. "Come now. There is much to discuss."

She followed him through the bustling city streets. He kept a slow pace as they wandered past residents who bowed their heads in his honor. Ignoring their respectful gestures, he walked past them without a glance in their direction.

Neer had never seen such admiration for her father. The humans of Porsdur understood his position as their leader, but never did they treat him differently. Here, it was as if he was royalty, or a divine.

Through the winding roads and into a small neighborhood of dome-shaped houses, they entered the quiet residence they called home. Inside, Reiman struck a flint and lit the logs within the hearth. The room was aglow with warm, flickering light, and Neer took a seat on the bench. The worn leather cushion sank comfortably beneath her weight.

The seat shifted as Reiman got comfortable next to her.

"How did you know I was here?" she asked.

Reiman withheld a smile and leaned further back with a knowing look to his eyes. Though she didn't ask his intentions, she knew he came to find her. Reiman never moved without calculation, and since her time in Nhamashel, she knew it wasn't fate that would've brought them together so conveniently.

"After all this time," he started, with a sly grin, "I figured you'd know me by now."

Their eyes met, and she couldn't hide her smile. With a slight chuckle, she shook her head. Reiman wasn't an overly proud man, but he was powerful, and it was something he was never too shy to enlighten her about. No matter the occasion—whether it was his daughter finding herself in peril, the Order destroying another village, or the elves invading the country—Reiman always seemed to know about it, and anytime she'd ask how he knew, his answer was always the same. *I've got eyes everywhere.*

248

"Why are you here?" she pressed. It wasn't like him to follow her. Over the years, she'd gotten herself in harrowing situations that Reiman never saw fit to see her out of. This time was different, and she needed to understand why.

A deep pit formed in her stomach when their eyes met, and she could sense the reprisal that was to come. His look of authority and intimidation used to frighten her. Now, it felt more like a challenge.

"Why are *you* here?" he asked. The friendly tone they once exchanged had become heavy and reprimanding. "You were meant to go to the colleges of Styyr to train your magic with the scholars. Why were you in Ravinshire, and now Aragoth?"

She turned away to avoid his gaze. The colleges of Styyr, her intended destination, were burned down long ago. But Reiman and the Brotherhood had connections to the scholars who lived nearby. They were willing to teach Neer everything they knew of magic.

The intimidation of his tone overpowered the confidence she once felt, and she became a child stammering over her words in the presence of a scornful parent.

"*Nerana*," he demanded coldly.

With a huff, she released the anxiety festering within her chest. Reiman must've known of her fight with the Priest. There would be no other reason for him to be here.

"I know you know." Her voice was sharp as glass. "I'm sure the whole world knows by now, right? Is that why you're here? To tell me that what I did was foolish? I know that! But he was killing innocent people! There was a child and—"

"And you are a *sorceress*!" he snapped. "A *demon* to these ingrates! Did it ever occur to you that by saving these people, you put the others at risk? It was because of your impulsiveness that the entire village was burned to the ground! Every man, woman, and child in Morinth was accused of harboring a sorceress and were put to death in the streets!"

Horror overcame her. Emptiness and guilt filled her with despair. She could do nothing but stare at him as the words repeated in her mind, and she hoped against all odds that they weren't true.

Reiman stared into her eyes with a look of condemnation and reproach. Hidden beneath his disapproval was shame and sorrow, but he'd never fully express it. It wasn't his way to have a gentle hand or loving nature. Neer understood this, though now more than ever, she wished for him to be more a father than a mentor.

"You *must* control yourself," Reiman said. "Not only have you sent the entire hold of Ravinshire into panic, but your actions have fueled war between the evae and lanathess!"

"What?" her hollow voice cracked. Large eyes, full of regret, stared at her father.

With a sigh, Reiman leaned forward and rubbed his forehead. "The Order is furious. They want blood. They know that you were traveling with evae and believe you to be in the forest. As retribution for your treason, the citizens of Ravinshire have been sent to find you. Should they bring you back—dead or alive—their hold will be pardoned of all charges."

"I...I didn't mean for—"

"But you did. You have always been impulsive. I should've never trusted you to go out on your own. Not so soon after Loryk's death. It was a risk that we shouldn't have taken."

"Loryk has nothing to do with this!" Her guilt turned to anger. Deep, vengeful anger. Her face was hot as she stared at her father, daring him to speak another word. Reiman and Loryk never had the best of relationships, but even he knew not to overstep his bounds.

Beneath the weight of her fury, Reiman's scornful gaze remained. He wasn't afraid, even with all her power and strength. "You will never truly master your skills if you cannot control your emotions."

Her voice cracked and faded as her anger increased. "I couldn't just let them die!"

"Your actions will always have consequences, Nerana. Too many times have you allowed yourself to be compelled by your emotions, when your wit should've told you otherwise." He touched her arm, becoming instantly calm. "Don't forget our goal. Once the High Priest is dead, we will be free from his reign. You cannot save everyone. All that we can do now is prevent *more* from dying."

Filled with anger, she marched to the door, and he quickly took her hand. She turned to him, ready to push him back with a powerful force of energy, when their eyes met, and she became powerless. It wasn't rage or disappointment looming in his eyes, but something she was all too familiar with.

Regret.

Tears filled her eyes when he pulled her into a loving embrace. Her chin shook, and her chest was heavy with grief.

"You aren't alone," he said. With a deep breath, he backed away.

Neer wiped her face and watched as he dug through his pocket. Firelight glistened off of a memory shard he procured from his cloak. Dark energy swirled inside the crystal shard like angry clouds. He placed it into her hand and curled her fingers around its edges.

"May this see you through troubled times."

With a kiss to her head, he quietly exited the room.

Gazing upon the shard, she was overcome with fear. Whatever memory was housed inside, she was unsure if she wanted to relive it. Surely, he wouldn't gift her with anything painful, but she knew that any memory within these shards would be from her childhood, as they were extracted upon her arrival to the Brotherhood eleven years ago, and the thought of reliving her past was almost too much to bear.

Shoving the crystal into her pocket, she marched from the room and shuffled through the crowds, wandering aimlessly through the unknown streets. Passersby recoiled at her harsh approach as she brushed past without a glance in their direction.

Eventually, her path led to a lush garden. She came to a stop and gazed upon its beauty, perplexed at how such a place could exist within a cave. Lifting her eyes, she found an orb of enchanted light hovering above, giving life to the thick grass and tall trees. A gentle moving stream wove through the shrubs, and glowing bulbs hovered over flowerbeds of orange, pink, and blue.

Stepping through the quiet gardens, Neer found herself secluded beneath the canopy of a tall willow tree. With her knees to her chest, she examined the clouded shard. Hard eyes looked at the stone she was reluctant to use. It reminded her of the simple truth that all she had now were memories.

Through anger and sadness, she shoved it back into her pocket. Now wasn't the time for such reminiscing. As she sat alone, her mind tugging between acceptance and fear, her curiosity outweighed her strength, and with a huff, she cupped her hands around the crystal and closed her eyes.

The warm tingle of magic swirled through her as visions appeared in her mind.

Sunlight filtered through stalks of wheat as she ran through a field of grain. Kernels fell from above, cascading across her shoulders and filling her curly blond hair with seeds.

At the edge of the field, her tiny hands pulled open a wall of grain to reveal a working farmstead. She breathed in the aroma of fresh lumber and pressed seeds. Pigs snorted as a farmer led them down the road to a newly built pen. Hinges whined when the gate opened, and the swine raced inside.

Behind the pen was a wheat mill where the O'Dowry family lived. Standing in the fields was a man. With a heave, he drove a hoe into the dirt and raked it back. A thick layer of dust covered his overalls, revealing his long day beneath the sun. He wiped the sweat from his brow and drove the tool back into the ground.

With a smile, Neer escaped the wheatfield and ran to the mill. Near the wooden toolshed, she grabbed a cup and pumped water through a spigot. The cold liquid spilled over the edges as she approached the man's side. His short brown hair stuck to his forehead in wet patches. With an exhausted sigh, he stood and wiped his forehead with the back of his arm.

Green eyes met with hers as she passed the cup, and a wide smile elated his tired appearance. "Vaeda," he said with a chuckle, before guzzling the drink. Feeling refreshed, he leaned onto the hoe with folded arms. "What are you doing out here? And why are you so filthy?"

"I was playing in the fields with Matilda and Erik."

His smile never faded. "Go wash up for dinner. Your mother is making your favorite tonight. It is your seventh birthday, after all."

The girl bounced on her toes, and with a squeal, she wrapped tight around her father's waist. He stumbled back with a laugh. Dropping to his knees, he pulled her tight into his arms. "I love you, sweetheart." With a kiss to her head, he lovingly patted her back. "Now, run along. Papa's got work to do."

The vision faded as she skipped away. Silent tears fell from her eyes, and she clutched hard to the crystal in her grasp.

For hours, she sat alone, forgetting the world as she re-played the memory and wished for the family she'd never see again.

CHAPTER THIRTY-ONE

STRICKEN

"Water is calm and flowing, gifting the world with patience and grace. Air is free and light, giving hope and life. Rock is strong, it carries your burdens. But fire … fire is angry and alive. If given the choice, it will consume until there is nothing left."

— Numerian; the Book of Nature and Elements

NEER STOOD BESIDE Y'VEN, PACKING her things. It would be a long journey to I'vasaar, where they planned to collect the energy of rock, and she was in great haste to see this quest through. Every second she spent in this desert was another second of resentment and restlessness. Her hatred of such a place was unmatched by any other. Not only for its arid climate and brutally cold nights, but its inhabitants and deadly creatures that stalked the night.

Shaking her head to rid herself of the intrusive thoughts, her eyes wandered to Dru as she walked across the desk. The small faeth carried a single vial like a heavy log before placing it with Y'ven's things.

Her good deed went unnoticed by the vaxros, who was shoving various necessities into his pack. His movements were slow as he'd gone for too long without the sun's heat and energy.

Neer glanced at Thallon as the scholar came to Y'ven's side and flipped through a book. He asked Y'ven to translate certain words, and with a look of disapproval, Y'ven snatched his belongings from the table and bounded across the room.

"What?" Thallon griped at his refusal to help. Sharing a glance with Neer, he turned away, suddenly aware of his foul mood. "This place is getting to us. We need some air."

Quietly, she slung her pack over her shoulder and approached the weapons rack, retrieving her sword. The polished evaesh steel glinted with firelight, sending waves of orange through the dark space. Glowing purple lines crazed the length of the blade, shimmering like an aurora in the night sky.

She touched the smooth edge, becoming lost in her memories, and she thought of how it came into her possession. As doubt crept into her mind about his disappearance, she reached into her pocket and clutched the trinket he gifted her. Holding it close to her chest, she closed her eyes and inhaled a deep breath.

Carefully, as if not to scratch or otherwise obscure its beauty, she slid the sword into the scabbard on her belt and gently placed the trinket into her pocket.

"Ready to go?" Reiman asked.

A scrunched half-smile eased the sorrow of her face. It had been years since she and Reiman saw fit to travel together. To have him accompany her on such a harrowing journey was a relief as much a comfort.

His skin creased along the edge of his eyes when he smiled. "Come then," he announced. "There is no time to waste."

The room fell to darkness when they snuffed the fire and left the home.

Through a quiet neighborhood of small homes, and past the city center, they moved to the far end of the cave. Along the jagged, uneven wall was an arched doorway leading to a dark tunnel. Yellow crystals swirled along the walls, keeping the corridor dimly lit. The tunnel was made of carved stone, which had been eroded and made uneven with time. The floor sat in shallow waves, making it easy to trip and stumble.

The warm air of the sanctuary fell colder as the light of the entry diminished. Reiman held a torch and led them through the quiet underpass. Deep scratches rested along the walls. Dark stains, reminiscent of blood, spattered the stone.

"What happened here?" Aélla asked, her voice echoing softly down the lonesome hall.

Reiman answered without averting his gaze from the path. "This was once a sanctuary for the y'lenae during the War of Ashes.* They built this cave to protect themselves from the vaxros and evae that had stricken their land and laid claim to their home. Some were caught escaping into the tunnels."

She touched the wall. "How did it become a sanctuary?"

"Once the treaty of peace was signed, the vaxros gave refuge to the y'lenae. Eventually, they built the city of Zaos over the cave. The Brotherhood has used it as their base since."

---

* A deadly, brutal war between the vaxros and klaet'il that ended with the vaxros taking claim to the desert region.

The War of Ashes first began after the vaxros fled to Aragoth when the volcano of Iziazan erupted and destroyed their home. Caught between friction and unease with the native y'lenae, war was inevitable. Calling upon their cousins to the east, the y'lenae sought the aid of the Klaet'il, who were hungry for battle.

A swift attack that was meant to see the vaxros out of their land soon became a bloodbath of honor and arrogance as neither side were willing to see a truce.

Fifteen years of war left Aragoth in a state of disarray and cast a dark stain upon the vaxros as they were viewed as vicious and fight-ready brutes.

By the end of the war, the klaet'il realized they couldn't see victory in the wastelands and retreated back to the forest with resentment and vengeance. Never forgetting their failure, they've held a deep mistrust and hatred toward the vaxros, while the latter banished all outside races from their land.

In respect and honor of the original inhabitants, the Treaty of Peace was enacted between the vaxros and y'lenae which allows the desert natives to coexist.

Thallon hobbled closer, still using a cane, though his face no longer contorted in agony with each step. "Are you two talking about the War of Ashes?"

"The sanctuary," Aélla explained.

"Oh, yes. The sanctuary. For a vaxros-inclusive human group led by a defector evae with the intent of killing their proud and prosperous leader." He gave her a look of disapproval and suspicion. "Hey, Reiman...?" he asked, clearly unsure of the warrior's name but wasting no time to find if it was accurate. "Why is it that the evae aren't invited into this underground faction of yours? Seems to me if you really want to kill off the human leader, you'd get the forest clans to join. I don't know anyone who hates their kind more than we do."

Reiman's shoulders fell slightly forward with a deep exhale. "Our kind is too primitive. They hold onto the old ways, never wanting to coexist or see beyond our borders."

"Yeah, because forcing children to pop their own eyes out in service of a higher power is much more sophisticated."

Neer crossed her arms at his mention of such a vile and horrific ritual, which included having young teenage girls willfully—though more by coercion or fear—remove their own eyes and devote themselves to the temple as servants to the Divines.

"My people are misguided," Neer explained. "They're manipulated and afraid. The soldiers and commonfolk shouldn't be made responsible for the actions of their leaders. The Order of Saro has to be destroyed. Their teachings are barbaric and indoctrinating."

"All right." Thallon pressed a finger to his lips. "But tell me this...if these people are so blinded by your leader that they willingly sell their own children off to be mutilated and disfigured,[*] do you really think they'd see you as a hero for destroying the only belief they've ever known?"

---

[*] The Reaping.

She paused with anger and remorse. "I've been viewed as a demon my entire life. I expect no different once all this is done."

The conversation faded into a heavy, uncomfortable silence.

Moving further through the tunnels, the beautifully carved walls became natural and uneven. Moisture created the scent of damp rock and mold. Rats scurried underfoot as the group marched through shallow puddles and slick rock.

Moonlight lifted the darkness as they came to a narrow opening at the end of the hall. Their dampened skin shimmered with its ambient glow. Neer bundled into a thin cloak, climbing through the passage and into the desert. Reiman took her hand and pulled her from the trenches.

Cold air seeped into her bones as night left a blanket of frost over the barren plains. Miles behind, lingering against the horizon, was the glowing city of Zaos.

Thallon was guided carefully from the cave. Leaning against his cane, he exhaled several deep breaths. The others continued onward, but Aélla stayed behind. Her eyes glistened as she admired the shimmering city. With a sorrowful gaze, she bowed and turned to catch up with the group.

"We should really take a rest," Thallon groaned, gripping his chest.

"You should've stayed behind," Neer suggested. "They would've accepted you in the sanctuary until you've healed."

"Not a chance. We're in too deep. I can't leave that place and make it back to Nyn'Dira on my own."

"I'm not sure you can make it to I'vasaar."

Taken by the Order of Saro as infants, either by trade or force, young boys were genetically modified and brutally trained to be the largest and strongest among humankind.

Only males were allowed to join their ranks, and just after acceptance, while still too young to speak, their tongues were sliced from their mouths, forcing them to communicate to only one another through arm and hand gestures.

He playfully scoffed. "If you think I'm going to let a la-nathess best me, then think again."

They came to an old campsite of ashen logs and half-standing tents. Thallon leaned against a rock while the others dug through their supplies. Reiman passed around jerky and fruit, while Y'ven and Dru started a fire.

Aélla sat beside Neer and raised her palms to the flames. The orange glow brightened with her every inhale and dimmed with each exhale.

"You're controlling the fire?" Neer asked with the hint of excitement clinging to her voice.

Aélla fell from her trance and lowered her hands. "I'm not very good," she admitted. "Why don't you try?"

Reiman interjected, "Nerana should not be dabbling in the lost arts of the arcane. She needs a proper teacher."

"She has me."

"Forgive me, Master Drimil, but you—"

"You are forgiven."

Everyone glanced between them with timidness and discomfort. The sweetness of Aélla's eyes masked her strength and solidity. Beneath his pressuring glare, she felt no trepidation or unease. In fact, she seemed to grow in confidence from it.

"Aélla," Neer started, breaking the long and unbearable tension, "are you sure I can do this? I've never used elemental magic before. I didn't even know I could before you showed me."

"You will be fine." She guided Neer's hands to the fire.

The group was silent as Neer concentrated on the flame. Heat stung her palms when she held them close to the fire, and boiling magic coursed through her veins like hot fizz. Every muscle burned. Her skin gleamed red as sweat glistened across her body. Muscles tightened in her neck as she struggled against the raging agony.

Unable to withstand the torture, she opened her eyes with a sharp gasp, and the flames exploded into a quick flash of heat and smoke. She fell back with a crash while the others shielded their eyes. Lying on the ground, staring at the sky, she was overcome with relief. No longer was she gripped by the searing agony of her magic.

As the others shifted, she was reminded of their presence and slowly sat up. Gripping her forehead, she eyed the fire, which still burned atop the logs.

"What happened?" Aélla asked. "Are you all right?"

"Yeah…," Neer said with a huff. "It was painful. Like my blood was evaporating. Everything hurt."

Thallon added, "You controlled it, though."

"What?" She lifted her head in surprise.

"Yes," Reiman stated. He stared longingly into the flames, perplexed and concerned. "They grew stronger until bursting when you released your hold."

Neer turned her palms upright, coursed with confusion that made her sick and unnerved. "I don't want to do that again."

"Fire wasn't the wisest of choices," Reiman explained. "It's unstable. Alive. You should focus your strength on an easier, more controlled element. This is why she needs a proper instructor. Someone who understands her abilities and what she can or can't control."

Aélla argued, "If she was given these tools earlier then—"

"Stop," Neer interrupted dejectedly. "I couldn't train my magic before. The Order could sense it. They used it to track me." She turned to her father with admiration and respect. "Reiman did the best he could with what he was given."

A faint smile brightened his eyes, and with a subtle nod, he quietly returned to his meal.

Late into the evening, Neer stared at the sky, thinking of her life and what had become of it. She wondered about the secrets her existence held, and if her path truly lay in

260

releasing the country of its leader. Or if she could be meant for something more. Something far greater.

As her thoughts led from one troubling thing to the next, she was shaken by the sound of rustling paper as Thallon dug through his pack. He unrolled a map next to the fire and examined the faded lines.

His brows furrowed in concentration as he plotted several courses with his fingertip. "I've got it," he said. "It looks like we came out of the caves here. If we head north, we should hit the canyon by sunrise. Walking its base will protect us from the sun and keep us close to fresh water." He trailed up the winding river. "We can come up here at the edge of Sandir and go west to the jungle."

"You think that'll work?" Aélla asked.

"Yes. The canyon will protect us from any kanavin too."

Neer shivered at his mention of the kanavin, or creatures of darkness. Her eyes shifted to the world around them, watching for any creatures that could be lingering in the shadows.

Huddling over the map, Aélla and Thallon continued speaking of their journey. "We just have to be careful walking so close to the tree line," he said.

"Why?" Aélla asked.

"They say it is haunted. Wispers and ghosts stalk the undergrowth. Apparently, it's a place of the damned."

"Wispers and ghosts are kanavin. They wouldn't be there if not for a shift in balance."

Thallon shook his head. "Aragoth used to be a jungle. Inhabited by the First Blood. Fru'skogmír is all that is left behind, guarded by enchantments and traps."

"What?" Neer asked, interrupting their conversation. "Aragoth was a jungle?"

"That's right. No one knows how it turned into this dusty pile of shit, but it was once a beautiful forest." He spread his arms wide, indicating their surroundings. "All that's left is Fru'skogmír, or land of the dead. Legends say that wispers, ghosts, and powerful magic dwell within the trees."

Aélla unconsciously twisted her hands. "The last element is there. We'll have to enter the jungle to obtain it."

His face turned pale. "Aélla...even walking along the tree line is dangerous. We should find another way. I'm sure there is another realm of water." Neer leaned over his shoulder, watching as he traced over the page. "*Kila!*" he hissed. "The only other water realm is south of Gul'frir.°"

"That's too far," Aélla stated. "We have to go into the jungle."

Neer studied the map. Eying the city of Gul'frir, partially hidden beneath Thallon's finger, she realized it would take weeks to travel such a distance. The thought of facing vicious, harrowing creatures like a wisper was nothing compared to spending weeks longer in the desert. Neer understood the dangers of wispers, and she knew she could fight them alone.

While Aélla and Thallon discussed their options, and drew closer to making the long journey south, Neer said, "I'll do it." They turned to her with questioning eyes. "I'll go to the jungle alone. The more people we have, the more dangerous it'll be."

"But Nerana—" Aélla started and was quickly interrupted.

"I've fought ghosts and wispers before. I can do it again."

Thallon rubbed his forehead. "Are you sure about this? The creatures you've faced aren't anything like these,

---

° Gul'frir, like its sister, Zaos, is an enormous city protected by enchantments and magic.

Being closest to the desert border, Gul'frir has been a target for most attacks, as outsiders want to either destroy or steal their technology, enchantments, and airships.

To better protect their land, the vaxros have constructed several villages around its perimeter, which has been effective in reducing the attempts of outsiders.

Neer. They've been conjured by the First Blood. They're meant to entrap anyone that steps foot beyond the trees."

With a deep breath, she came to the decision. She knew it was their best chance. "I can do it," she said. "Once we get the elements of rock and fire, you go to the temple. I'll meet you there once I've obtained the energy of water, and we'll unlock the doors together."

CHAPTER THIRTY-TWO

BEWARE THE CHILD

"The sun brings life and power where the shadows bring death and deceit."

— Words of the vaxros

NEER STOOD ALONE BENEATH THE glow of the moons. The luminance of a campfire flickered in the distance where the others lay asleep. Sweat dripped from her brow as she slashed her sword through the air, fighting the demons in her mind. Every swipe of her blade drew black mist as the creatures bled smoke. Teleporting back, she plunged her weapon forward with a quiet grunt.

Swiping full circle, she was startled to find the shadow approaching. She held her sword and waited, exhaling a long breath as Reiman's silhouette came into view. Moonlight shone against his longsword, and a smile flashed across Neer's face.

"What are you doing out here?" she asked. Stepping back, she raised her sword, ready for a challenge.

"I heard you from camp," he remarked and slashed his blade. Teleporting aside, she appeared behind him. He turned back with his weapon drawn to block her strike. His proud smile gave her confidence. "Using magic, are you?" he remarked with a curious gaze.

With an assertive shrug, she struck her weapon forward. Steel clashed as he caught her blade. He pushed her aside, and she appeared to his left, slashing her blade to his neck. He drew his sword to block the attack.

She disappeared again, this time appearing several yards away, hidden within the shadow of darkness. Covering her mouth to stifle a laugh, she watched him scramble to find her. With his weapon drawn close, his eyes darted from one place to the next, unaware of her next move.

Neer tossed a rock to the east, and Reiman became aware of her position. As he marched closer, she appeared before him, touching his chest with her blade. The seriousness of his eyes obscured his faint smirk. "Think that's funny, do you?" he quipped.

"A little bit." She laughed.

With their eyes still connected, he raised his chin with a knowing gaze, and her confidence faltered. She fell into a state of confusion as she realized his elation wasn't of pride for her victory but was instead condemning.

"Look down," he suggested.

Still perplexed, she glanced at her waist, where he held a dagger to her stomach. Turning back to her father, she couldn't contain her smile. The quickness of his draw out-matched the unpredictability of her magic. "I thought this was a sword fight," she said.

"Never underestimate your opponent." He slid the dagger into a sheath hidden beneath his cloak. The longsword was still gripped tight in his right hand.

Glimpsing her sword, his eyes widened, and she instinctually drew back the weapon as he touched its blade. "Where did you come upon a weapon like this?"

"Why?" she asked, much harsher than intended.

"This is a First Blood sword. No one has seen such a weapon in centuries."

"How can you tell?" She twisted the weapon, whose steel looked as normal as any other. Reiman sheathed his sword and reached for hers, but Neer cradled it close to her chest. "What are you doing?" she asked defensively.

"I'll show you." He made an inarticulate gesture with his hands, beckoning her to hand it over. With a nervous glimpse to the sword, she placed it into his hands. He twisted the weapon and ran his finger against the smooth edge of the blade. "These veins," he started, "they're enchantments. No other material has this capability."

"What can it do?"

"I'm not sure. Clearly, striking your subject or waving it through the air doesn't affect its abilities. It may need to be activated by a First Blood."

Neer studied the sword, never remembering it holding any magic as Avelloch used it. As they spoke of its power, the purple glow vanished, leaving behind dull, empty veins. Neer staggered back, perplexed by the sudden change. "Maybe my magic is disturbing it," she said. "It never lost its glow before."

"No…this is what it's meant to do. We just don't know why, yet." Reiman lifted the weapon and twisted it through the air with several flicks of his wrist. The movements were fluid, as if the weapon was dancing through the air. "Feel its weight," he said. "It's lighter than most steel. More durable."

Neer watched in horror as he slid his dagger against the blade. Breath caught in her throat as the metals scraped together. Once finished, he turned the sword from side-to-side, allowing the moonlight to cast off the polished steel.

"No scratches," he remarked. "Fascinating."

Neer collected the weapon and secured it into the scabbard on her belt.

"Where did you find such a weapon?" he asked.

Not wanting to admit it was left behind by Avelloch, as Reiman had already given her enough grief about giving such devotion to a stranger, she lied. "I found it in Nhamashel."

"Keep it close to you," he warned. "If others hear of its existence, they may try to take it for themselves."

"What's so special about it?"

"First Blood weapons are made with alveryan steel. It's the strongest metal in the world. That, alongside its ability to absorb enchantments, make it desirable."

"Can't they just make their own?"

They walked back to camp, and Reiman held a light smile. "Alveryan steel is only accessible through Anaemiril. That doesn't mean the foolish haven't tried searching for it. Even so, the process of mining and smelting such a delicate material is an art most smithies don't possess. The First Blood understood its properties. They are the only known smelters of alveryan steel."

"How can a race so advanced and powerful just vanish?" she wondered aloud. "It doesn't make sense."

"I suppose that's a great mystery which may never be solved." His face illuminated with firelight as they approached camp. "Whatever happened to the First Blood—they made sure we could never find out."

At camp, everyone woke, gathered their belongings, and continued on their journey. Neer groaned as the blisters on her feet rubbed against the worn leather of her boots.

Reiman's shadow became invisible along the horizon as he carried onward, leaving the others to follow. Neer was conditioned to his otherworldly position, as if he ruled the dirt beneath their feet and air in their lungs, and for as long as she had known him, there was no one who questioned this portrayal of esteem.

No one, that is, except Aélla, who gawked at him as if he were walking without a head. Neer had never questioned his authority until now when it was Aélla who was meant to lead this journey across the desert, not her father.

Her thoughts dissolved when Aélla passed her a large red fruit and jerky, and Neer thankfully accepted her breakfast.

"Are you all right?" she asked of Neer's limping.

"I'm good," she said with a wince.

Aélla's face pulled inward sympathetically, before she calmly touched Neer's arm and allowed the slow warmth of magic to heal the wounds on her feet.

"Thanks," Neer said with a sigh of relief. "Why are we walking instead of riding?"

Thallon came to their side, map in hand. "There is a village up ahead. Maybe they have stables."

"No," Y'ven remarked. "We avoid the *bor*.°"

"We can't walk the desert, big guy. Your skin may be thick and calloused, but ours isn't."

Y'ven turned to him with a growl, and then stood before the much smaller evae, blocking his path. His glowing yellow eyes burned like fire. "We do not go."

Aélla touched Y'ven's shoulder, and with a deep exhalation, he walked away.

"Bastard," Thallon muttered, shoving the map into his satchel. Parchment crinkled, and glass vials clinked within the full pack. "What's his problem?"

"Just let it go," Aélla said with sincerity.

Thallon sneered while crossing his arms. "You know, sometimes your constant forgiveness and happiness is a real pain in the ass."

She smiled with a hint of sadness. "You have no idea."

Ignoring his obvious look of confusion, she focused on Reiman's torchlight, which grew brighter as he stood motionless up ahead. As they moved closer, the heavy odor of decay filled the air with its pungent smell. Neer covered her nose, while Thallon gagged.

"*Kila!*" he exclaimed. "Is this another boneyard?"

Neer was stricken with overwhelming, foreign rage. Stumbling forward, she gripped her burning chest when voices

---

° In the language of the humans, bor translates directly to mean village. With no organized form of government or politics surrounding the desert or vaxros community, there are no documented numbers of bor, or vaxros villages, though it believed to be well over 5,000, with nearly 500 shelarr, or tribes.

shouted in her mind. They spoke a language she didn't understand as they unleashed their fury.

"Neer?" Thallon called.

Her face was red, and her skin was hot. Peering forward, through the blackness of night, she caught the silhouette of four vaxros lying on the ground. Their innards were strewn across the dirt, heaped in steaming piles of meat and blood. Their flesh was open with deep lacerations. Bite marks and deep wounds were layered across their arms and thighs.

"This wasn't Klaet'il," Reiman explained while inspecting the bite marks. "Something else is out here. Be on your guard." Stepping through the wreckage, his torch light brightened over a fallen merchant's cart. Furs, empty crystals, and shattered clay pots were spilled across the ground.

Y'ven knelt beside a victim, whose arm had been ripped off below the elbow, and he growled a phrase in his language. Clenching his fist, he stood and exhaled a deep thunderous roar. His voice quivered with fury and pain. Dru ducked behind Aélla, watching sorrowfully as he was consumed with grief.

"We must burn them," Aélla said. "Before their energies manifest."

Neer coughed and fell to her knees, sweat dripping from her face as pain coursed through her. Her fingernails dug into the ground as she clenched her fists.

"What's going on?" Thallon asked. "Why is she acting like that?"

Reiman pushed the others aside and came to her aid. He lifted her chin and looked into her eyes, which were black as coal. Puzzlement flashed through him as he examined her reaction, which was furious and pained.

"She can feel their emotions," Aélla explained. "Whatever thoughts and feelings they had as they were dying…we experience them."

"What?" Thallon asked. "Why doesn't it hurt you like this?"

She watched Neer writhe and shiver. "I don't know." Stepping to a body, she hovered her palm over their remains. Closing her eyes, she inhaled a deep, ragged breath. "Burning them isn't enough. I need to absorb their energy into a vessel. Crystals or a magical receptacle. Somewhere it can be contained."

"Why?"

"Their anger has culminated into dark energy."

"Do we have anything like that? Maybe we should check the cart."

"Wait." Reiman clutched his arm as he stepped away. Staring into the desert, he waited, watching with purposeful intent. His eyes were fixed on the horizon, like a hawk watching its prey. The others were quiet, scanning the desert for any possible intruder, when the faint sound of a weeping child filled the silence.

No one spoke. There were no words. The haunting sound chilled them. It was a quiet, sorrowful reminder of the pain inflicted upon the bodies scattered at their feet, a vicious realization of what was to come.

Aélla stepped forward, ready to find the child and bring them comfort, but came to a stop as Y'ven touched her shoulder. He gazed into the darkness where the whimpering child lay.

Silently, he followed the harrowing sound, when a shadow cradled by darkness came into view. It knelt over the body of a vaxros warrior, and Y'ven stiffened with remorse.

Another step closer, he reached out and touched their shoulder, and the child sniffed. Their body shook beneath his touch, and he felt something odd. It wasn't the smooth, tough skin he had anticipated. It was cold as ice and rigid as bone.

Between each cry came the sound of tearing flesh. The snap and slop turned his stomach. He pulled the child's shoulder, and then fell back as it snapped its head in his direction. Crashing to the ground, a creature, with calloused skin covering its eyes and a large mouth full of sharp teeth, released a shrieking scream. Vibrating sounds of falsetto and tenor rang through the air in a childlike voice.

Blood and bits of flesh covered the torn skin of its sunken face. The liver of the fallen vaxros was still clutched in its claws as it stood over Y'ven, who was too stunned to react. With another snap, the creature sank its teeth deep into Y'ven's forearm.

He roared with agony as it pulled a chunk of meat from his limb. With another scream, it slashed its claws across his face. Y'ven unleashed a pained cry as three red lines were stretched from scalp to jaw.

The creature opened its wide mouth as it leaned closer. Its hot breath pressed against Y'ven's skin as it mimicked his roar. Thick slime fell from its teeth and slid across Y'ven's neck. He was stiffened with agony as it leaned closer, bringing its razor-sharp teeth to his throat, when it was thrust aside by a powerful wave of magic.

It flipped across the ground like a bag of crunching bones, mimicking Y'ven's roar. Aélla rushed to Y'ven's side, inspecting his injury as he lay on his back, trembling in pain.

The faint sound of crunching bones and shifting limbs crept through the air as the creature stood. Deep, throaty clicks vibrated from its throat, becoming louder as its scream increased. The hoarse noise penetrated the silence, and everyone was stiff with terror.

Standing tall, with thick spines along its back, was a wisper. Gray leathered skin, like that of a mummified corpse, covered its frail, boney figure. The calluses over its eyes extended back into two thick horns atop its misshapen head.

Reiman pulled Neer to her feet and shoved her sword into her hands. "Fight," he demanded.

The wisper's shadow was blurred against the dark horizon as it turned to the sky and raised its long arms. A deep roar shook from its throat.

Neer pushed through the agony that had stricken her and watched as the wisper stalked forward, following the scent of decay. Clutching hard to her sword, she waited until it was within closer range, and then she vanished.

The wisper turned with a hard swipe of its claws as she appeared behind it. Dodging its attack, she plunged her sword through its chest, narrowly missing its heart. With a loud shriek, it struck again, clipping her ear. She teleported back to give them distance. Hot blood trickled down her neck, and a flash of pain moved through her like a strike of lightning.

She stumbled forward and gripped her wound. The light shuffle caught the attention of the wisper, who turned sharply in her direction. Another shriek erupted from its wide mouth before it charged forward.

Neer waited as the creature sped close, sharp teeth exposed within its open jaws, and hot breath spewing repugnant odor across her face.

As they came face to face, Neer released a furious scream and pushed her sword through the wisper's heart. The mimicked sound of her own wail rumbled in its throat as it became motionless and heavy on her blade.

She ripped her sword from its chest, and the wisper faded to ash at her feet.

CHAPTER THIRTY-THREE

THE FARMER

"There is no greater victory than to live and die by the axe and flame."

— Sayings of the vaxros

NEER STUMBLED BACK AND COLLAPSED to her knees. Gripping her throbbing ear and fighting against the voices of the dead, she curled to the ground. Bright light engulfed her with the sting of magic, and the ailments that afflicted her were suddenly absolved.

As her injuries numbed, and the anger of the departed passed, the light slowly faded. Peering through the darkness, she spotted Aélla extending her palm in her direction. With a reassuring nod, the evae returned her attention to Y'ven and focused her healing on him.

Neer pressed a hand on her chest, where the weight of anguish and energy once encumbered her with pain. The slice to her ear had been healed, along with the black veins growing from the injury.

"Nerana."

She was silent as her father came to her side and touched her shoulder. "Are you all right?" he asked.

With a breathless nod, she silently answered. For a moment, she was free from the constraint of magic and emotion. She was far enough from the wreckage to no longer be immobilized by the deceased and basked in the quietness. "Why does that happen to me?" she asked. "My head…I can hear them. It's like they're shredding my mind."

"I don't know. But now isn't the time for such conjecture. Wispers feed off the dead. If there was one, there are surely more."

Thallon paced around while clutching his forehead. His wide eyes were set on the ground as he shuffled back and forth, becoming unhinged. "What was that?" he exclaimed. "What in the world was that thing!"

"Calm down." Reiman stood next to Thallon and spoke calmly, like a father to his unruly child. "We can't disturb the energy here. It'll only call upon more. Aélla," he called, "you mentioned containing their energies into a receptacle?"

She wrapped Y'ven's bleeding arm in a thick bandage. Without turning away, she answered, "Yes."

"You," he turned to Thallon, clearly forgetting his name, "there are several crystals by the cart. Gather them for her."

"You're jesting. In case you don't remember, that *thing* was by the cart! We should get out of here!"

"Thallon," Aélla begged.

They held a long, insufferable gaze as she pleaded against his anger. With a defeated huff, Thallon resolved to obeying, though he didn't do so quietly as he muttered an incoherent phrase. Reiman gazed through the desert with a watchful eye. Being sure they were alone, he returned to Neer's side.

"You did well," he stated. "Wispers aren't easily defeated."

She sat forward with her elbows on her knees. "I saw a leg-hold trap in Llyne a long time ago. I just…I had no idea things were this bad." She turned away with a sigh. "The men I was with before. The evae. They spoke of something called *naik'avel*. Said it was the reason creatures of darkness are spawning."

"Yes. A lot of my kind believe naik'avel to be *the end*. When darkness shifts the balance and fires rain from the sky."

"You don't believe it?"

He got comfortable next to her and wiped the dust from his hands. "I think my people are reluctant to move on from old traditions and outdated beliefs. Naik'avel is nothing more than a children's tale. A way to explain the disappearance of the First Blood and keep uncontrollable children in line."

"They seemed pretty convinced," Neer said of her old companions.

"They're deluded, Nerana. Made to follow in the guise of their leaders."

She peered to the bodies and watched as Aélla knelt over each of them. Holding an empty crystal close to their chests, she closed her eyes and became still. Dark energy filled the crystal with swirling light—some darker than others, some lesser in quantity, but all were dark.

The quiet whispers ringing through Neer's mind slowly faded to silence while Aélla moved from one person to the next. Neer gripped her forehead in relief. "Something has to be conjuring these creatures," she said. "There has to be a reason for mine and Aélla's existence."

"Not everything has purpose or meaning. Some things simply *are*." He gave a half-hearted smile before standing and reaching for her hand. She took it and stood, then brushed off her trousers.

Her gazed shifted to the north where several torches appeared in the distance, drifting like fireflies through an endless sea of blackness.

"Look!" Neer pointed.

The brightness grew as six vaxros shadows appeared.

Dru hovered several yards ahead and squinted her eyes beneath her hand. When an angry voice echoed from the intruder, the faeth flinched and darted quickly into the safety of Y'ven's disheveled hair.

Neer shared in Reiman's puzzlement as the vaxros came trudging from the darkness. Strong fires blazed upon their torches, irradiating the yellow scars across their faces and chests. The steel blade of a scythe glimmered when a farmer stepped forward and spoke gruffly while pointing to the cart.

The vaxros lifted their eyes to the outsiders, and deep scowls overtook the worry they first expressed. Lifting their weapons, the vaxros sneered at the strangers before them.

As Y'ven crawled to his feet and stumbled back, still affected by the ailments of his attack, two warriors swiftly placed their spears to his neck.

"Why do you travel with these *grot'méget?*°" A warrior with a waist-length braid growled in their native language.

Y'ven took several deep, pained breaths. Low grunts escaped his throat, and his eyes rolled back. He collapsed to the ground with a hard thud. Aélla stepped forward and was met with a spear pressed to her throat. The braided warrior snarled his lip as he held her captive.

"We didn't kill your people," she started in his native language, and the warrior pressed the weapons harder to her skin. A thin line of red appeared along the blade's edge. "Please," she begged. Her words were broken and hard to understand. "I am Drimil'Rothar. We came upon the wreckage and found a creature of darkness. Erm…" She stumbled over her words before spouting the correct phrase. "*Shadosalaan!*"

The pressure of his blade faltered as he considered her words. Glancing behind her, where the bodies of his kin rested, he was disturbed by his loss and uncertainty.

The discontent was short-lived. He stiffened with fury and pressed the spear firmer to her neck.

"There is no blood on our hands. We are not here to cause conflict. Under the treaty of *sin'lohai,* I am able to enter your land."

° In the language of the humans, grot'méget can be interpreted to mean bastards of the night.

Being sun-blood, the vaxros rely heavily on sunlight and flame to nourish their bodies. Other races are referred to as night-blood, as they can walk among the darkness without losing their energy or strength.

"Not with others," he said. Before she could speak, to plead their innocence, another voice interrupted the silence.

"Y'ven?" a vaxros called, seemingly unsure of himself as he crept closer to the fallen warrior. The curious vaxros had short black hair and minimal scarring compared to the others. He carried a scythe with bits of grain stuck in the chipped edges of the blade.

He knelt beside Y'ven and brightened his face with the torch.

"You know this warrior?" a female vaxros asked.

"Yes…" He touched Y'ven's face. "He is my brother." Turning to Aélla, he asked, "What happened here?"

Reiman straightened his chest piece and stood taller. Voice resounding with confidence, he explained, "They were attacked by a wisper. It most likely lured them as it lured your brother—by mimicking the cries of a child."

"Where is this beast?" the braided warrior before Aélla said with a growl.

"It's dead. Lying in a pile of ashes in that direction." He pointed into the desert. "These bodies must be burned, or others will come."

A huff grumbled in the vaxros's throat. With a look to his comrades, he ordered them forward with a silent nod. Two warriors marched quickly into the desert to investigate the ashes.

"Vrogrün." The brother said as he approached the vaxros holding his spear to Aélla. "Allow me to take him to my village. He should be treated for his injuries."

With a heavy snarl, the spear was removed from Aélla's throat. Her shoulders relaxed as the warrior stepped away. Pushing his comrades aside with a forceful grunt, he moved to Y'ven's side.

Staring down at the fallen warrior, Vrogün's lip twitched with fury. "He comes with me."

"Killing him will not avenge your sister or nephew! It will not restore their honor."

Vrogrün cut him a sharp look, and the brother stepped back. Nodding to Y'ven, Vrogrün commanded the others to collect Y'ven, and they did so without question.

The thud of heavy boots broke the deep silence as Vrogrün paced in front of the group. A deep scar laid the pattern of a sun across his upper back, indicating his pact with the al'yavan warriors. Beneath it was another design made of ten separate cuts, some more faded than others.

His glowing orange eyes flashed to Aélla. "The treaty allows *you* entry to our borders, Drimil'Rothar," he said, "but it does *not* allow theirs."

She stiffened. "They are with me. I cannot do this alone."

He marched forward, and she stood straighter, staring up at his massive size. "I am the leader of the al'yavan. I will not allow traitors into our lands. You will turn back, Drimil, or there will be blood."

Aélla matched his intimidating gaze, which only deepened his fury. "You already have an enemy with the klaet'il," she said, her eyes burning with contempt, "Do not make an enemy of me."

Vrogrün's expression ignited with hatred. His thick arms hardened as he clutched his spear. She knew he understood the weight of her power, but he'd never acknowledge defeat. It wasn't the way of the warriors of flame. He would fight to protect his pride and honor.

Aélla was prepared to fight, and she was prepared to win.

He drew back his spear, and she stepped back with her arms raised defensively, ready to use her magic. As he drew a breath and tightened his grip, his comrades returned from the desert.

"Vrogrün," a vaxros with one eye said. He placed his hand on his leader's shoulder, and Vrogrün roared with vengeance. The one-eyed warrior gasped as the spear plunged deep into his stomach. Lifted from the ground, he choked for breath as Vrogrün held him up, shaking with rage.

Tossing him aside, Vrogrün glanced at Aélla, who stood with purposeful confidence, though in her eyes was unconcealed terror. The others were silent as the injured man laid in agony, the spear still in his gut.

Vrogrün spat at Aélla's feet. With a gruff exhale he turned, snatched the spear from his victim, and marched back in the direction he came. His allies gathered the one-eyed man and Y'ven, and then followed their leader into the shadow of darkness.

"What are you doing?" Thallon argued, marching to Aélla's side. "We can't let them take him!"

"Enough!" Aélla snapped. Her voice was hoarse with pain and rage. "We are in no condition to fight. We will respect their customs and allow Y'ven to go…but I will not let him die."

Y'ven's brother slowly approached Aélla. His shoulders were wide as he stood before her, staring down at the woman who challenged their famed and respected warrior. "Vrogrün will have revenge for your heresy." His eyes fell away as sadness overtook his expression. "Come. My home is safe. You can rest there."

Aélla respectfully bowed and waved the others forward. Reiman touched Neer's back, urging her to follow. Stepping over the bodies, they quietly trailed their leader.

The short walk felt long, blanketed with a deep silence. It was a silence of regret and anger. Of vengeance and sorrow. They each felt it, yet they said nothing. Words weren't fitting for a time of such anguish.

Neer crossed her arms to repress the emotions swelling in her chest. She would get him back. He wouldn't be forever taken. She wouldn't lose another friend.

They walked further, and the scent of wheat replaced the aroma of dirt and rock. Neer was brought back to her childhood and quickly lifted her eyes. The imprudent hope that she'd somehow wound up back home—back to her family—

was squandered at the sight of wheat fields growing in the desert.

Resting within the center of the fields was a tall barn made of clay and rock. The dome roof was spattered with several holes, revealing its weathered age. Bright firelight flickered through the windows, casting an orange glow into the fields.

Y'ven's brother leaned his scythe against a large table of tools as he walked by. At the home, he slowly opened the door and invited everyone inside. They shuffled in and stood together.

A firepit lay in the center of the floor, brightening the entirety of the room and illuminating the long hall to the right. A deep cauldron, with remnants of dark stew stuck to its edges, hung over the fire. Furs and weapons lined the walls in no discernable order.

The brother led them to a cushioned bench and chairs to the left side of the room.

"Papa?" a child called. Her light footsteps came to a stop as she approached the end of the hall. She wore a yellow nightgown and sleepily rubbed her eyes.

He moved to her side and led her back to her room. The others were quiet until he returned and took his place in a wide chair.

"Where have they taken him?" Aélla asked.

The brother leaned forward with a sigh. "He will be in atülg'shelarr. It was our childhood home."

Neer asked in a hurry, and Reiman easily translated, "If they wanted to imprison him, why wait until now?"

"He travels with *grot'méget*...the unwelcome. Outlanders. It is forbidden. He will be judged for this, and they will not show mercy."

The grave silence darkened. No one shared a glance as the weight of his conviction set in. Aélla shifted in her seat, breaking many of their deep, harrowing thoughts. "What is your name?" she asked.

"Torvüg."

"Y'ven is your brother?"

He nodded. "Older brother. My only brother." His eyes fell away, staring at nothing as he was lost in sorrow. "I have not seen him in many cycles. Since before the birth of my third child."

"Who was that man? The one who took him."

"Vrogrün. He's the leader of the al'yavan…and brother to Calla, Y'ven's bond-mate."

Reiman continued to translate as Thallon added, "Y'ven said she left long ago. After he was exiled."

"They are mated for life. She carries the weight of his dishonor—just as I do. Just as Vrogrün does. She and their son Zarender survived the raid on their village and have been living under the protection of Vrogrün since."

Neer huffed with fury. "This is just for revenge. Y'ven wouldn't have been carried away had he not broken his oath."

"That's right," Torvüg explained. "Vrogrün will most likely challenge Y'ven to *vitru*…and in his condition, my brother will surely lose."

"Vitru?" Aélla asked.

Torvüg was hesitant. His gaze shifted to the fire. The flames illuminated in his eyes as he regretfully, and painfully, explained, "A duel to the death."

CHAPTER THIRTY-FOUR

HONOR AND BLOOD
Aélla

CLOAKED BENEATH THE SHADOW OF silence and moon-light, Aélla and Torvüg walked alone to *atülg'shelarr,* where Y'ven was being held captive.

To the disaffection of the others, Torvüg had asked that the rest of the group stay behind, explaining their presence would only hinder Y'ven's safety.

With a shiver, Aélla bundled into a thick cloak. Trailing behind Torvug, she took note of the scars along his back. There weren't many, half a dozen at most, but they were just as prominent and beautiful as all the others she'd seen.

One in particular caught her eye. It rested between his shoulder blades and was in the shape of a scythe. She presumed this to be his occupation, as warriors bore the symbol of the al'yavan in the same position on their backs.

"Torvüg," she said in his native language, still broken and hard to understand, "what should we expect when we get to the village?"

"Many will resent your presence, but as Drimil'Rothar, they will not protest. We will go to the *gaelrog* in the village center. This is where Y'ven will be."

Aélla understood gaelrog to mean fighting ring, and it was there that Y'ven would fight Vrogrün to the death. Her eyes burned with tears that never fell. She wouldn't allow them to. Not when strength was needed.

With a deep exhale, she straightened her shoulders and asked, "Why are you loyal to him?"

"I'm sorry?" Deep lines formed between his brows.

"He's viewed as a traitor for his dishonor to the al'yavan. His bond-mate abandoned him. His people too. Surely, they would see anyone who gives him respect as a traitor."

Torvüg nodded stiffly. He paused for a moment, staring at the village in the distance. "He is my brother. I will never abandon him. It is not my way."

Aélla was filled with sadness and respect. She understood the weight such heresy could bring. Living beneath the shadow of her own brother, she was made to endure the suffering of his shame after his banishment. And while their people had abandoned him, she never would.

She had hoped that by taking the oath and fulfilling the title of Drimil'Rothar, his past would be absolved, but it was only Aélla who saw redemption. She was viewed as more of a savior for her bravery in the face of such adversity and shame.

"That's incredibly noble," she said, continuing their conversation. "To show him loyalty, even if it casts shame upon your family."

"I am a farmer, Master Drimil. My family was born into great shame."

Sorrow washed her expression. She eyed the scar on his back, marking him as lower class. Unworthy.

Dishonored.

"There is no dishonor in choosing a life of simplicity."

He scoffed, though she couldn't tell if it was from amusement or anger. "No one chooses this path. As a child, I was injured. A warrior cannot fight with a twisted foot. He cannot win."

They approached a village and came to a collection of small stone houses bordered by a tall canyon wall. Torvüg eyed the rough-built structures with desperate eyes. Low chatter filtered from the windows of each brightly lit home. Shadows stalked the street as residents disturbed the silence of morning.

Standing tall within the packed village was a large temple. Heavy smoke billowed from the center of the roof and disappeared into the sky. No windows were present on the outer walls, leaving Aélla to wonder what such a building was used for.

As if reading her mind, Torvüg explained, "That's the temple of the dül. She will join us today."

Aélla's eyes were glued to the building before it disappeared behind a wall of tall shops.

Firelight brightened the village as they stepped to a crowded courtyard. A wide circle of torches lit up a large arena where dozens of vaxros gathered. They cheered and hollered as two warriors brawled with ferocity and pride. Blood laid trails of red down their faces.

"What's this?" Aélla asked.

"*Tozhug.* It is a test of strength and will."

Vaxros jeered and scowled at Aélla as she shuffled through the crowd and came to the outer edge of the fighting ring. Yellow scars illuminated across the dark skin of the warriors, and they circled around with their fists up.

Torvüg explained, "We only battle at night, when we are at our weakest."

Her attention moved to the fight as a vaxros with a nose dripping in blood taunted his opponent.

The opponent, who had a swollen eye and bleeding cheek, snarled. He jabbed with his right hand, then hooked with his left. The bloody nose opponent ducked and struck him with a powerful uppercut. Swollen Eye stumbled back, and the crowd cheered wildly.

Before his rival regained his footing, Bloody Nose struck him hard in the stomach. He bent over, holding his ribs, and a final blow to the face sent him to the ground. He lay unmoving atop the ring. The dirt faded into a darker shade of red as blood spilled from his injuries.

Aélla stepped back when the champion lifted his arms and roared victoriously. The courtyard was alive with cheering and praise. His busted knuckles dripped with blood, trailing across his wrist.

The victor knelt in the center of the arena and leaned forward to broaden his back. A female vaxros with many scars of her own stepped behind him. She pulled a curved dagger from its sheath on her side and the crowd cheered.

"What is she doing?" Aélla asked.

"Mark of a warrior. One mark for ten battles won."

The victor didn't flinch as the dagger slid across his skin. The fresh mark connected nine others into a completed design. It matched the same design etched on Vrogrün, the al'yavan leader's, back. The same marking that remained forever incomplete on Y'ven.

The female stepped back, and the warrior stood. Everyone, including Torvüg, bowed to him. His prideful eyes looked down to those at his feet. With a sinister smile, he stepped through the crowd and made his way into town.

Chains rattled beneath the sudden growling and hostility of the crowd as Y'ven was marched forward. Led by Vrogrün, with thick chains binding his wrists, his tired eyes remained on the ground, never daring to meet those of the people spitting and jeering in his direction. Bandages wrapping the deep bite wound on his forearm had turned a dark shade of red. Black veins crawled outward across his skin from beneath the blood-soaked linen.

"He cannot fight like this!" Aélla demanded, and Torvüg grabbed her wrist as she stepped closer to the ring. "This is unfair! He's been poisoned!"

"Calm yourself, evae," Torvüg's gruff voice vibrated as he harshly warned her. "This is our way."

Redness painted her face with anger. Her eyes shifted to Y'ven as his chains were removed and he was thrust to his knees in the center of the ring. Vrogrün kicked downward onto his spine, and he collapsed into the dirt. The others cheered, while Aélla and Torvüg turned away.

"Brothers and sisters of atülg'shelarr," Vrogrün called with his arms wide. His voice echoed against the canyon wall and sounded through the village. "Today, we rid our name of this traitor! The scourge of his existence will not be remembered. Today, brothers and sisters, I will defeat this fallen warrior and reclaim the honor that he has stolen from us!"

Everyone erupted in cheers and shouts. They stomped rhythmically against the ground, sending a tremble through the village.

"Y'ven," Vrogrün started, "I will give you the choice. Fight for your honor, or die by the axe."

Y'ven stared at the ground. His weight was pressed against his uninjured arm, while the other was curled inward toward his chest.

"Brother." Torvüg knelt along the edge of the ring. "There is no honor in death. You can do no more harm to your reputation by refusing this fight. Walk away. Live."

Y'ven shook with anger. "I will fight and restore honor back to my family…to Calla and Zarender."

"They are not coming back, Y'ven! Dying by his hands will not change that! You will fight for them, even after they abandoned you?"

Y'ven glared hatefully into Torvüg's eyes. "I will *always* fight for them."

Torvüg watched in horror as Y'ven crawled to his knees. Wobbling and unsteady, he came to his feet. Blood seeped from his filthy bandage.

Vrogrün's thin lips pulled together as he growled furiously. Y'ven held an equally powerful glare, though the darkness of his eyes was shrouded by the ill effects of the poison coursing through him.

The village fell silent as the dül parted the crowd. Wearing a necklace of fur and feathers, the aged vaxros stepped into the ring and stood between the warriors. Her robes dragged the ground and covered her body like a layered veil of dark leather.

She touched each of their shoulders and looked above the crowd. Her voice was calm and gruff. "By a warrior's honor, I will now commence the sacred battle of *vitru*. Under protection of vax law, the victor shall be absolved of any past crimes. Weapons are not permitted. Aid is not permitted." She turned to Vrogrün, who stood tall and proud. "A sacrifice must be made by the challenger to honor this battle."

She passed him a long, curved dagger. His chest puffed with confidence as he accepted the weapon. Staring into Y'ven's heavy eyes, Vrogrün placed the dagger to his own ear, and made a clean slice through his flesh. With a deep grumble, he passed the dagger and his ear to the dül. Blood covered his neck and shoulder, but he stood angry and proud, not showing an ounce of pain in his furious eyes.

The dül bowed respectfully, held the ear up high, and said, "This is a fight to the death, and to the death shall you fight."

She stepped a toe out of the ring, and Vrogrün struck Y'ven with his fist. Y'ven staggered back. Blood poured from his nose as he stumbled to the edge of the ring.

A menacing smile tugged Vrogrün's lip. "You will die here, Y'ven. Only then will Calla have peace! Only then will the shame of your betrayal be washed from her name."

With a deadly glare, Y'ven stepped forward. Vrogrün roared with anger and charged. Y'ven leapt aside and swung his fist. His knuckles collided with Vrogrün's jaw. The hard crack went unnoticed by the fuming warrior as he grappled Y'ven's waist and lifted him from the ground. With a roar, Vrogrün flipped him backward.

Y'ven wheezed with a raspy grunt as he landed hard atop the dirt.

Vrogrün knelt over him and swiped at his face. Y'ven dodged the attack and shifted his weight to the left, causing

Vrogrün to tumble aside. Jumping to their feet, they stood across from one another.

"You couldn't even protect your own family!" Vrogrün taunted, striking his fist.

Y'ven spun and jabbed at Vrogrün's side with his uninjured arm. Vrogrün leapt back to dodge the attack.

"They are greater for your loss!"

Vrogrün ducked when Y'ven swung at his head. With a swift kick, he struck Y'ven's ribs and smiled at the sound of a crack. Y'ven stumbled aside with a deep grunt. Vrogrün leapt forward and struck Y'ven beneath his jaw.

As he fell back, Vrogrün kicked his chest, and the ground shook as Y'ven collapsed. He exhaled a deep breath, the air pushed from his lungs. Vrogrün stood above him with a disappointed snarl.

"Get up!" he sneered, while kicking Y'ven in the side, further cracking his broken ribs.

Y'ven gasped and grunted in agony. Blood splashed from his lips, and he rolled onto his side. His teeth were stained with red when he crawled to his knees.

"You are worthless!" Vrogrün shouted with another kick. "Pathetic!"

Y'ven grunted when the heavy boot was shoved against his stomach.

"Your son will always know what a disgrace you were!"

Y'ven's eyes widened with rage. His fingers curled into the dirt. As Vrogrün lifted his boot to Y'ven's face, Y'ven grabbed his leg and yanked him aside. Vrogrün tumbled over with an angry snarl. Y'ven tackled him and smashed his head into the ground.

Vrogrün's angry, hoarse scream echoed through the village as Y'ven beat him with a heavy fist. Blood splashed from his face and covered the ground. His teeth were knocked loose and flung through the air.

Unable to fight him off, Vrogrün gathered a fist full of dirt and tossed it into Y'ven's eyes. Y'ven backed away and clutched his face. Vrogrün pinned him down and held him in a tight head lock. His thick fist met several times with Y'ven's face.

Y'ven bit deep into Vrogrün's arm. Blood filled his mouth, and he spit a chunk of flesh to the ground. With a loud roar, Vrogrün released his hold and staggered aside.

He stumbled out of the ring, and Y'ven's eyes narrowed with hatred.

"You cannot step out of the ring!" Torvüg called. "It is a dishonor to—"

Vrogrün silenced him with a disgusted, taunting laugh. He snatched a spear from an onlooker and turned to Y'ven with a sadistic gaze. "There is no *honor* in fighting a disgrace like you! Only a true warrior will step out of this alive."

Before the dül could step forward and end the fight, Vrogrün charged forward with a raging growl. His footsteps vibrated against the dirt as he moved closer. Blood-coated teeth were exposed beneath his pulled lips, and he released a hellish scream.

Y'ven leapt aside, but the spear sliced into his shoulder. With a furious cry, he kicked Vrogrün in the stomach. Vrogrün staggered and turned sharply, swinging the spear to Y'ven's chest.

As the weapon came around, Y'ven caught it with his injured arm. Blood seeped through the bandage as he pulled Vrogrün closer, intentionally smashing their foreheads together.

Winded and in a daze, Vrogrün stepped back. Blood coated his fingers as he grazed the fresh cut across his scalp.

Y'ven snatched the spear and snapped it over his knee. The broken weapon clattered against the dirt when he angrily tossed it aside. Orange sunlight peeked over the ridge, filling the village with light and warmth. Deep cuts and glistening blood were revealed across Y'ven's skin beneath the light. His shoulders rose and fell with every hard breath as he glared at his opponent.

With a deep exhale through his nose, he charged. Still dazed from his attack, Vrogrün was slow to move and crashed to the ground when Y'ven tackled him. Kneeling over his enemy, Y'ven's fist collided with Vrogrün's face again. Bones cracked beneath the weight of his fury as he struck him without pause. Blood sprayed onto Y'ven's face, and he roared with anger.

Vrogrün fell silent and still, and Y'ven slowly backed away. He turned to the sky and unleashed a deep, furious roar. Sunlight reflected against the blood trailing down his face and arms. He sat on his knees, staring at the sky.

His body trembled with regret and hatred. Closing his eyes, he exhaled a deep breath. Y'ven pushed himself away, stumbling through the crowd, uncaring of their angry stares. Vengeful eyes were upon him, yet they never spoke a word.

Aélla watched with sorrow as he pushed through the crowds. He took confident strides, walking through the village he once called home.

No longer burdened by the weight of his heresy.

No longer labeled as a traitor.

CHAPTER THIRTY-FIVE

SECRETS AND LIES
Nerana

"Give yourself to thee and unbind the shackles which imprison your soul. Drench your spirit in the Light to be absolved of your past transgressions and live forever in the comfort of peace, grace, and Light."

— Rotharion, the Book of Light

FIRE CRACKLED AND POPPED WITHIN the confines of Torvüg's silent home where Neer sat with her head in her hands. No one had spoken since Aélla and Torvüg's departure, and there was silence. A deep, unbreakable silence.

Thoughts pressed against her mind and caused an ache beneath her forehead. With a huff, she stood and strode across the room, where she knelt in a corner alone and meditated.

Warmth and energy coursed through her, but she struggled to clear her mind as heaviness weighed her thoughts. They grew dark and painful, clawing at the deepest reaches of her soul, sending frost and agony through her veins. She could see Y'ven lying amidst the fallen vaxros warriors, his face slashed by the wisper, his arm weak with necrosis from its poison.

Different images flashed like a dying flame, shifting between darkness and light. She envisioned her mother burning in the street. Avelloch's kiss and the heat of his body. Loryk's laughter and the sound of his final cries.

She saw the world engulfed in waves of smoke and flame. Not a soul was left as darkness crept over like a slow-moving shadow, devouring all in its path.

"Neer," Thallon said for the fifth time. Only now did she hear his voice break through the harrowing visions.

With a gasp, she fell back. Sweat dripped down her forehead. For a moment, she was lost. With a glance to Thallon, who reminded her much of the face in her visions, she turned away.

"They're back."

Just then, the front door opened, and Torvüg stumbled inside with Y'ven on his arm. His brother's head fell aside, and his feet dragged the ground. His jaw was twisted, and skin was covered in open wounds.

Reiman rushed to their sides and draped Y'ven's injured arm around his shoulders. Together with Torvüg, they made haste to the table.

Dru, who had spent her time weeping in the firepit, sprung to life at the sight of her friend. She darted from the embers in a ribbon of red light, before smacking into Y'ven's chest with a burst of flames. She nuzzled into his skin and held him close while the others marched him across the room.

"Rhax!" Torvüg called. Soon after, his bond-mate appeared from the hall. Her expression shifted from confusion to worry as she turned to view Y'ven. Coming to their sides, she helped lift him onto the table. "He is poisoned by a wisper. We have to extract the arm," Torvug stated.

"What!" Neer exclaimed, though he couldn't understand. She leaned against the table as the others cut his bandages. "You can't do that!"

His large head was close to hers as he growled. "Stand back, ürok. This is not your place."

Dru walked across Y'ven's neck and gently touched his face. Her body trembled before she collapsed to her knees in a fit of tears.

"He is not dead yet, little faeth," Rhax, Torvüg's bond-mate, explained. She mixed several herbs and pastes together into a glass vase.

The pungent odor of pus and rot filled the room when Y'ven's bandages were removed. The deep wound in his arm was yellow with infection, and black veins stretched away from the bite mark, crawling up his elbow and down to his wrist.

Reiman leaned closer, inspecting the gash with a keen eye. "If we can eradicate the infection and remove the poison, he can keep his arm."

"We cannot risk it." Torvüg turned to a boy who was taller than Neer yet had the look of an adolescent. The boy passed Torvüg a sharpened axe. Another child, a girl, who was smaller than her brother, wrapped a tourniquet around Y'ven's bicep. Torvug placed the blade to Y'ven's skin. His hands trembled in hesitation.

"Wait." Aélla kindly touched his arm, and with a deep breath, his shoulders relaxed. "We shouldn't make any harsh decisions." Her words were broken as she spoke his language.

"This is our way, Drimil," he explained. The panic and fear in his voice had vanished.

"But it is not mine." Hard eyes bore into his, and he slowly stepped away. Without blinking, he walked across the room and sat on the sofa. Neer watched him curiously, perplexed by his sudden shift in mood. She studied him for a moment, wondering why he so willingly stepped away from his brother. With a glance to Aélla, she pushed aside her suspicions, choosing instead to focus on more pressing matters.

Aélla stood with her palms over Y'ven's injuries. With a deep breath, she closed her eyes, and carefully clutched his arm. Her breathing was ragged as her grip tightened. She winced and groaned with pain, yet there were no markings on her body.

Neer watched curiously, noticing that his injury wasn't transferred into Aélla as it slowly wove together. Thallon soaked the blood and pus into a rag as Y'ven's thick skin formed into a deep, unsightly scar. Layers of uneven skin covered the now closed injury.

Reiman pulled Aélla away. Her body was frail and skin translucent. Sunken eyes and cracked lips replaced her once full and healthy appearance. Dark veins had formed around her eyes, and Neer came to a sudden realization.

"What's wrong with her?" Thallon asked.

Neer touched Aélla's arm and felt her cold skin. "She was giving her energy to save him. Just as she did with you in Mors'groval. I didn't realize it then…"

"She can do that?"

"I've done it…" Neer turned her palms upright. "All this time, I thought our abilities were different. I thought that I was limited like the others…But… Do we have the same magic?" Neer had no guidance by way of her magic, and in the few things she did understand, healing was one of her most useful and dangerous incantations. While Aélla possessed the ability to heal without injuring herself—and could even transfer injuries from one person to the next—Neer could only heal by gifting another with her own health. To witness Aélla perform magic that Neer could do herself made her question the magnitude of her abilities. Most importantly, she needed to know if she could heal without injuring herself, just as Aella had done. If so, then it would prove what she had believed for so long…

That fate was never on her side, and had she known the truth of her power, maybe she could have saved the people she lost.

Looking at the others, her gaze fell to a fresh cut on Thallon's arm. The small wound was filled with hardened blood. Touching it, she concentrated her magic, focused on healing rather than transferring her energy.

She winced as the sharp sting of a blade slicing just beneath the skin burned through her. As the pain faded, and the sweltering heat lifted from her bones, she slowly opened her eyes. Thallon watched curiously, a light smile tugging his lips.

She removed her hands to find the open wound was gone. Not a trace of it was left behind. Neer stepped back, gazing desperately at her hands, wondering how she could hold such power.

"Looks like you're more powerful than you think, *drimil*," Thallon said with a smile.

"How…" Her voice faded. "Did you know this?" She turned to Reiman, who avoided her gaze as he led Aélla to a chair across the room. "Reiman!" she demanded.

He turned to her with condemning eyes, and she knew. "Why didn't you tell me?" she demanded. "I've been living with this, and you never said a word!"

"Calm yourself."

Rage boiled inside her. It consumed her with betrayal and deceit. "Tell me!"

"It was unwise for you to know your true potential. To know that you have abilities you will never be able to use. Not until the curse was lifted." He peered into her furious eyes. "Had you known of your power, you would have misused it in ways that would crumble all we've worked so hard to gain."

She screamed, her voice cracking, as she said, "Had I learned to control it, I could've saved him!"

The home trembled as her eyes darkened. Stepping calmly to her side, Reiman placed his hands to her shoulders, and with genuine regret, he said, "I did what was best for *you*. Had you practiced your magic, the Order would've pursued you. Captured you." He paused. "Some things in life cannot be changed. His death will always be."

The darkness of her eyes faded, and she fell into angry tears. She pushed him away and marched from the home. Outside, she breathed in the cool morning air and smell of fresh grain. Rubbing her face, she exhaled a deep, sorrowful breath. Her eyes moved to the sky, where the blue and green aurora danced high above.

She thought of the Divines and how they could see fit to bring such injustice and cruelty to those so undeserving. Arcae, the plane of existence for all those who had departed this world and transcended to the next, was currently believed to be elsewhere, far from Erolith or the mortal plane.

But the Old Ways, the beliefs that Neer would cling to had she any belief at all, said that those who departed lived forevermore in the sky,° far above the reaches of Erolith. She liked to think their souls came together in the lights that danced above her. Their ambience filled her with a peace she hadn't felt in many years.

Wherever he was, she knew Loryk wasn't there. Her mother and father. All those she lost. They were gone. Drifting further away with every passing day. Their hold on her slipping like water through her fingers. The sound of her mother's voice was silenced long ago, becoming one she didn't recognize as time made her forget. She feared this would be true of everyone she lost. Their faces, their warmth…their songs.

Neer wiped her eyes and pushed the thoughts aside. It did her no good to dwell on such misery. She knew this. Yet still, she stood alone, embraced by her solitude, comforted by her anguish. She couldn't let it go. Didn't want to. Grief and anger were all that kept them alive. It was all she had left of those she loved.

Light obscured her view of the sky as the door behind opened. With a soft exhale, she was freed of her thoughts, and she closed her eyes, waiting as another came to her side.

° Both the old ways and new hold true to the belief that some souls are damned to one of the seven layers of hell.

The darkness of their soul dictates the depths they're condemned. Each layer is worse than the last, and crimes such as renouncing the Divines, or simply questioning their existence at all, would see them in the torturous pits for all eternity.

While the Old Ways stated those with redeemable hearts could eventually be granted peace in Arcae, the New Ways condemn you forever.

"Hey," Thallon said. "You all right?"

With a nod, she wiped her eyes. "Yeah." Her voice betrayed her forced confidence. "I'm good."

She avoided his eyes, which focused sorrowfully on the tears gliding over the fresh scar stretching across her cheek. He leaned against his cane and followed her gaze to the sky. "Pretty. We don't see this in Nyn'Dira." He glanced at her, waiting for a response that never came. Turning back to the sky, he said, "When I was a kid, my brothers and I would always climb this big tree. We thought it was the biggest one in the entire forest. I was smallest, so they always had to me help up. We'd get to the top, teetering on the thin branches, and would look at the stars.

"My brother, N'iossae, believes that if we can touch the sky, we can look down and learn the secrets of the world. There is a saying with my people. *Mii frandír no'ami.* Do you know what that means?"

Her eyes shifted from the sky to his, and she shook her head in silence.

"*In the shadows we wait.* There is so much we don't understand about this world. But if we were up there"—he pointed to the sky—"high above the clouds, looking down...we would see ourselves. Our lives. Our homes. The world." He lightly smiled. "So, lanathess...what would you see?"

Returning her gaze to the sky, she became lost in the lights. "I'd see..." Her voice faded as she pictured her life. What could've been yet would never be. She imagined Arcae and the Divines supping with those she lost. They were happy and together, free from the pain of this world. A tear fell from her eye. "Everything."

He placed a hand on her shoulder, and the visions she'd wrapped herself in faded. "Come inside," he said. "You don't want a crippled scholar watching your back if the *kanavin* show up."

She recognized this phrase to mean *creatures of darkness,* and the harrowing thought sent chills down her spine.

As he stepped to the house, she quickly took his arm. "Thallon!" Her voice was unexpectedly harsh, and with calmer resolve, she continued, "Thank you."

With a bright smile, he extended a bent arm. She accepted his thoughtful gesture, thinking more of her old friend than of the new one before her, and wrapped her elbow with his.

Stepping inside, they found Aélla lying motionless on the bench, while Torvüg and his family paced the living space. Another child, no older than three, stood by his mother. She patted his head and led him down the hall.

A deep groan came from across the room as Y'ven slowly woke. He lifted himself with a huff and leaned over the edge of the table. Fresh, bright yellow scars lay across his arms and face. Purple bruises left dark patches along his chest and jaw.

"Y'ven!" his young niece cheered. She giggled as he ruffled her hair.

Torvüg came to his side, and the brothers gripped arms in a firm shake. "Brother," Torvüg said, "you are alive."

Y'ven grunted in response. His face twisted as he gripped the deep bruises on his chest. "We cannot stay. They will come."

"You are absolved of your treason. They will not—"

"I have shamed them, Torvüg. Their leader is dead. They will not forgive this." He exhaled a deep, pained breath. "I will not be the cause of your suffering."

Torvüg paced the room. With a growl, he shook his head. "You will stay. Rest. At midday, I will lead you to the canyons."

Y'ven agreed with an angry huff. His brother gathered his family and disappeared down the hall. Dru's glowing aura brightened Y'ven's fresh scars as she hovered in front of him. With a wail, she smacked hard into his cheek, embracing him. He lovingly rubbed her back with his fingertip.

Neer sat on a bench by her father. They exchanged an apologetic glance and remained wordlessly in their forgiveness. It wasn't often that she argued with Reiman, and while this instance would've been ordinarily hard to let go of, she was in short supply of family and knew that, above all else, he always had her best interests in mind.

Leaning onto his shoulder, she closed her eyes and was comforted by his embrace as he wrapped his arm around her back. They sat in a comfortable silence for the rest of the morning, and for the first time in months, she knew she wasn't alone.

Chapter Thirty-Six

Erot'myen
Nerana

"We are beckoned to walk the path of our ancestors, searching for answers they could never find. But do not give in to the temptation of fate, my daughter. Forge your own path, and live by the way of your spirit, not of those long passed."

— Merethyl Líadrinel to Aélla

As midday came, the group set out across the desert. Mountain ranges lined the horizon, creating breaks in the sunlight that shone like orange columns against the sky.

Y'ven walked alongside his brother, and together, they led the others. Their gruff voices were muffled to Neer, who trailed far behind the group with Aélla. In the hours since Y'ven's return, she had regained most of her color, though her sunken cheeks and dark circled eyes gave her a sickly appearance.

"Aélla," Neer started, "what magic do you have?"

She tucked her hair back to better see her friend. "I'm a descendant of the First Blood, which means that I hold the energy of each of the realms of magic."

"You're First Blood?" Neer was shocked by this revelation.

Aélla nodded proudly. "My mother was First Blood. She was a powerful sorceress too. All women were."

"Men didn't carry magical energy?"

"Not as commonly. My mother could have done great things with her magic. She could have become Drimil'Rothar, too, and gone on this pilgrimage, but she chose to have a family instead." She smiled with the hint of sorrow and grief. It was a look Neer knew all too well. *"Aes'prínehn fortaal nuala…We are what we choose to be.* My mother died when I was very young. I don't remember much of her, but she did gift me with a memory shard, and in it, she said that.

"As First Blood, there is much expected of us. My mother forged her own path, despite the advice and pressure of others. They wanted her to do greater things, but she wanted a simple life with her partner and children. I admire her for this. She was what she chose to be, just as I have chosen to take on the responsibility of being drimil'Rothar."

Neer thought of her own mother, and how she'd given the same advice. Lying in bed as a child, Neer would stare out of her window, wondering when the Order would find her. Wondering if her life would ever be normal. Her mother would lay with her and brush back her hair.

You are not what they claim you to be. They're afraid of what's different, but being different is what makes you so important. Don't let them take away your light, my sweet, beautiful, child.

Don't let them change you.

The words were haunting as she thought back to her childhood. To a time she now struggled to recollect. Brushing the thoughts away, she inhaled a deep breath. "Your mother sounds like a kind woman."

Aélla smiled. "She was. The world is lesser for her loss."

Neer nodded and crossed her arms. Returning to their original conversation, she asked, "You said there are realms of magic?"

"Yes." Aélla straightened and cleared her throat. "There are seven realms that exist on this world, and each holds their own form of energy that keeps everything alive and in balance—health, nature, mortality, time, illusion, light, and dark."

"And you can do all of that? Because you're First Blood?"

Aélla nodded in response.

Neer looked at her hands, more confused than ever, and wondered of her identity and existence. She'd never felt as though she truly belonged. Even in the Brotherhood, among friends and family, she was different. She was magic. A sorceress. A human born of demonic blood.

"Does that mean that *I'm* First Blood too?" She glanced at Aélla, whose worry unsettled her further.

"No…I don't think so."

"Why not?"

"Because humans and First Blood cannot have children together."

Neer huffed in frustration. Knowing it's better not to dwell on things she might never understand, she asked, "Is that why you're going to the realms? To master these energies?"

Aélla nodded. "I must enter each realm in order to unlock the final Realm of Light, or *Tre'lan Rothar*. It's there that I'll be able to bring balance back to the world."

"Why has it fallen out of balance?"

Their eyes met before Aélla slowly turned away. "I don't know. But we're going to try to find out and stop it from happening again."

Day was fading into darkness when they reached the deep, desolate canyon. Trekking carefully down a winding path, they came to the base of the chasm, where a slow-moving river drifted through the rock and stone. The gorge created a tall barricade, keeping them safe from the predators lurking above.

Following the river, they found themselves at an ancient, decrepit village. The waters carved through the center of what was once a vast, immaculate city. Weathered stone, destroyed by centuries of rain and sun, were nothing more than lumps of grey.

Half-standing walls created a maze through the ruins. Streams of light illuminated within the water, keeping the village bright. They stepped through the forgotten homes. Nestled in the center of the village was a large pool of fresh water. Each ripple and wave crashed with blue bioluminescence, just as it did in the river nearby. Thick pillars that once upheld a sturdy roof surrounded the pool like proud knights guarding its perimeter.

"What is this?" Aélla asked, approaching the water.

"*Frot'myen,*" Thallon explained. "A bathhouse."

Neer knelt by the water's edge and dipped her fingers beneath the surface. She was surprised to find it was warm. A gentle stream flowed from the river basin to feed fresh water into the pool and exited through another stream on its opposite side.

Thallon continued, "They were a luxury of the First Blood. Scholars have found them all across the accessible caves of Anaemiril. We believe they were extremely sacred."

"Why?" Neer asked.

"Here you must be your most vulnerable. Musical instruments were found throughout the rooms, which suggests it was a place of relaxation, but there were also ancient texts of magic, battles, and runes."

Reiman touched a tall, weathered pillar. "The y'lenae must have coexisted with the First Blood."

"Or the First Blood lived here first," Thallon stated.

Aélla stepped to the water and dipped her palm beneath the surface. Staring at the liquid in her hand, she said, "There is magic in this water. Surely it is a place of great healing. We should stay here for the night. Regain our strength and continue before sunrise."

The others agreed, while Torvüg vehemently denied. Y'ven reached out to his brother, but he stepped away with a furious huff. With slumped shoulders, Y'ven watched him march through the city.

Y'ven sat on a rock nearby, not daring to step foot into the pool. He lifted his bitten arm and struggled to bend his fingers. Thick yellow scars and faded black veins covered his skin in overlapping patterns.

"What was that about?" Neer asked, undressing to her undergarments and stepping into the water. The tingling warmth of the pool filled her with ease. She sank beneath its depths and closed her eyes. Leaning with her head against the edge of the pool, she exhaled a deep breath.

"Ruins forbidden," Y'ven explained. "Will not stay."

Thallon added, "If it's against your beliefs to stay here, then you should go with him."

"Best to stay. Protect."

"You are a man of great honor, Y'ven," Reiman announced. "The Brotherhood is greater to have you."

Y'ven smiled, though his eyes revealed pain and regret. Neer leaned back and spread her arms across the ledge behind. She looked through the long-forgotten city. There was a calmness to such isolation, and she wondered how far they were from civilization. "What was this place?" she asked.

"Y'dris," Y'ven explained. "Ancient city."

"I thought the y'lenae couldn't survive in the desert...Why would they build a city way out here?"

Reiman said, "The y'lenae are evae who once lived in a great rainforest known as *D'windlemer.*" He paused. "Long ago, this entire desert was a thick forest, much like Nyn'Dira. There is much speculation as to its destruction. Some blame the humans, while others the First Blood. Even the vaxros have been blamed, but in all the stories there holds one truth—the forest that once existed for millennia has simply vanished. It is now the wasteland you see today."

Neer added, "There must be answers somewhere."

"We've tried to find them," Aélla said. "Scholars have searched all throughout the texts. They've even entered sealed portions of Anaemiril…but there are none. Whatever happened, it is not known."

Y'ven added, "Ateus. Most feared and powerful draak. Unleashed vengeance."

Neer remembered the draak to be enormous creatures her people referred to as dragons. The vaxros revered them as an icon of power and fury. Her mind scurried as she replayed all she'd learned in her head.

Her thoughts shifted to Ateus, who she had learned about from the Order of Saro, but before she could make a connection between the fallen divine and the draak, Reiman said, "There is much unknown about this world and its histories. It is important to understand but more important to focus on the future. Will we reach the jungle soon?"

"Two sun cycles, we reach *Fru'skogmir*°," Y'ven stated.

"Are we close to Sandir?" Reiman asked of the formidable, enchanted plains.

"Above the ridge."

Neer moved her arms softly atop the surface of the water. The rippling waves reflected against her skin, healing it of its many fresh cuts and stinging sunburns.

As the night grew colder, everyone exited the pool. Neer wrapped in a dry cloak and set off to find a warm place to rest. Being far from the others, she felt a sense of peace. She found some time for herself, to be alone in her thoughts.

Her wet footprints were left behind when she stepped through the quiet ruins. Nestled within the confines of a half-standing home, she emptied her pack and created an alchemic fire to keep her warm. Dripping a potion into the enchanted

---

° A small jungle notoriously located within the dry wastelands of Aragoth. While many scholars have tried their best at finding the source of such abundant plant life, there has yet to be an answer. Many have left its mysteries to the First Blood, whom they believe enchanted the last piece of the extinct and forgotten rainforest, D'windlemer.

flames, a barrier formed around her that protected her from the cold night air.

The shield cascaded through the wall to the other side. Deep ridges lay in the stone, making it uncomfortable to lean against. She turned back to clear the wall of any debris, when she noticed deep markings carved into the smooth surface.

Rigid stone scraped beneath her fingers as she traced the indentations. Placing her palm to the wall, she focused her energy and was able to read the foreign symbols.

> *"Fires rained, and then it came.*
> *Its soul is lost with naught to gain*
> *We fought and bled and choked and pled.*
> *Now, we lie in crypts with the dead."*

Neer read the words until they were burned into memory. She searched the remaining walls but found them barren of any marks or etchings. Turning back to the note, she ran her fingers across the words and spent the remainder of the night wondering of the fate of this village.

Hours later, the stillness of night lightened as the world welcomed a new dawn. Neer, who had yet to find even an hour's worth of sleep, quietly gathered the others. They woke from their slumber with heavy eyes and aching backs.

"We have to get moving," she said, while pushing Y'ven's shoulders.

The large vaxros growled in opposition as he rolled over. Dru hovered in front of his face and pulled his eyelid open. She looked into his large pupil with a light tilt to her head. With a deep sigh, he sat up and rubbed his head.

Everyone gathered, and they set off deeper into the canyon. The moonlight faded into light blue as dawn lingered along the horizon. The coolness of night was slowly replaced with the dry heat of another day, and Neer wrapped into her cloak, dreading more walking beneath the burning sun.

She examined the quiet city before pausing her gaze upon the home she slept in. The haunting words replayed in her mind, and she became lost in the riddle.

"Is something troubling you?" Aélla asked, but Neer was jolted from her thoughts and turned away with crossed arms. "Are you all right?"

Her lips pressed into a hard line as she scanned the village and decided against telling its secrets. There were more important things to focus on, and a conversation of such weight wasn't one to have so early in the morning. Avoiding Aélla's gaze, she explained, "Just ready to get out of here."

Neer brushed passed Thallon as he greeted with her a smile. He watched with discontent as she continued onward, paying no mind to the man she'd so callously ignored.

"Everything all right?" he asked, turning to Aélla.

She straightened her posture and gripped her staff. With a reassuring nod, she followed the others as they walked quietly through the village.

Thallon's gaze set on Neer, who walked several paces ahead. His eyes shifted to Aélla when she stepped to his side.

"Do not pursue her," she warned. "We are not here for such things. You must focus. We are all depending on each other."

His chin lifted while a wide grin brightened his face, stretching the scar that disfigured his lip. "Don't worry, A. I'm as focused as ever."

Large, pleading eyes gazed at him, before she slowly nodded and turned away. Thallon's gaze shifted to the sword strapped to Neer's hip, and his eyes narrowed in suspicion. With a scoff, he shook his head.

"That's Avelloch's sword, isn't it?"

Aélla's fingers fidgeted along her staff, and she stared at the ground, unwilling to face the eyes boring into her.

Thallon crossed his arms and faced her. "Your loyalty is to the people. To protect them." Aélla remained quiet. "But my loyalty…is to the truth."

"You can't!"

His glare deepened at her fearful outburst. "If Neer is going to trust us, then she deserves to know who he is. What he's done…Who he is to *you*."

Aélla straightened her back and puffed her chest. With newfound confidence, she matched his intimidating gaze. "Whatever secrets kept are between them. It is not our place to decide how they're told."

With a sly smile, Thallon stepped away. Aélla's knuckles cracked as her grip tightened around her staff. Altvára, the raven, swooped down from above and landed on her shoulder. His black wings flittered as he positioned himself, settling into place.

The anger released from her eyes when she gently rubbed Altvára's chest and walked along the path of her friends, watching closely as Thallon made his way to Neer's side.

They trekked quietly through the abandoned city. Neer curled tighter into her cloak as the dark sky brightened. The water created a draft, keeping the ravine cold and damp. The group refilled their canteens and dipped their cloaks beneath the surface of the river before climbing a natural stairway to the top of the cliff.

Halfway up, Neer glanced at the valley. To the left was the abandoned village, which she could see in its entirety. Its layout was complex and intricate, and the eroded walls created a beautiful pattern around the river, which passed beneath her and flowed to the right.

"There is Torvüg," Y'ven explained as they drew closer to the top of the cliff.

The shadow of a man hovered close to the edge of the canyon. His large cloak swayed in the breeze, and Neer thought it odd he'd be wearing such a garment. It wasn't typical for the vaxros to wear their cloaks so close to daybreak.

As they reached the top, the shadow came into view, and they found it wasn't Torvüg who awaited their arrival.

Standing silently, they gazed upon a long, tattered cape thrown over a thin iron pole.

Fresh sunlight glinted against thick blood dripping down the shaft and soaking into the dirt. Neer stepped closer, and Y'ven quickly pulled her back. His eyes were hard as he stared at the cape. Dark red blood soaked through the material where it covered a large, lumped object at the top of the pole.

"Y'ven…," Aélla started in a broken voice.

The world was silent as he stared at the cloak. With forced steps, he approached it and gathered the loose material in his fist. His jaw clenched, and he took several deep breaths, before ripping it from its place.

The heavy, blood-soaked material fell to the ground. Dirt shuffled beneath its weight as it settled into place. Sunlight reflected against the blood dripping from Torvüg's empty eye sockets. His jaw hung open, and blood drained from his neck, painting the pole with the colors of crimson.

Loud, panting breaths filled the silence as Y'ven touched a symbol carved into his brother's forehead. It matched the one he bore across his back. A symbol that brought him deep shame and would now forever be engraved on his brother's name.

Traitor.

CHAPTER THIRTY-SEVEN

TRAITOR

THEY GAZED UPON TORVÜG'S SEVERED head, and Y'ven fell to his knees with a deep, ground-trembling thud. His yellow eyes glowed with fury and hatred. Large muscles swelled with veins as his arms tightened and chest heaved. He spoke in a rough, furious voice and stared at his brother, cursing those who betrayed him.

A light breeze lifted dirt into the air. The dust became lost in Torvüg's hair and clung to the lines of red dripping down the post.

The deafening silence lifted at the sound of distant shouts where six vaxros wandered the desert. Blood spattered their dirt-coated skin and dripped from their weapons like molasses.

Y'ven turned to the strangers who walked nearby, but they didn't glance in his direction, it was as if they were entirely unaware of his presence. Furious, he collected the axe from his back and marched in their direction.

Aélla reached out for him, but her fingers swept through the empty air as he moved too quickly for her to grasp. "You can't!" she warned.

Neer stepped in front of Aélla to block her path. "What are you doing?" Neer argued. "His brother was beheaded, and you're telling him not to fight?"

"This isn't the way!"

"That was his brother!"

"There are other ways of justice than murder!"

Neer stepped closer. Her face was red, and her eyes were hard. "There is no justice in this world. You fight or you die."

Aélla's jaw dropped. The confidence she once held faded to fear.

They averted their attention to Y'ven as he unleashed a deep, voracious growl.

Sunlight blazed with orange against the sharp edge of his axe as it was lifted into the air and struck through the neck of the nearest warrior. Blood sprayed as his head rolled across the ground.

Y'ven gripped his weapon tighter, and the others turned to him with wide eyes. They charged forward, battle axes and spears gleaming with fresh blood. Y'ven dodged the first swing of a smaller vaxros. With a hard kick, he pushed the youngling back and then raised his axe to block the attack of another.

"You killed him!" Y'ven growled with ferocity and grief. "My brother!"

Holding off his attacker, he couldn't react when a third warrior came from aside. Bolstering a spear, the female warrior drove the blade closer to his side.

Neer transported to her side and slashed her sword across the warrior's arm.

With a deep, pained growl, the warrior spun aside and lifted her spear. A fresh mark stretched across her arm, exposing the fat and muscle beneath. Neer stood several paces back, her eyes fixed on the much larger vaxros that threatened her.

Hearing the footsteps of another, Neer quickly ducked beneath the heavy swing of a battle axe coming from behind. As he slashed his weapon downward, she disappeared.

Y'ven kicked away his enemy and cut his throat with a quick swipe. The warrior stumbled back, fingers sliding into

311

his neck as blood poured from his skin like a waterfall. Dropping to his knees, the warrior choked and spewed blood across the ground.

Y'ven turned back and slashed at the female warrior lunging forward with her spear. Their weapons collided with a loud clash. She lurched forward and smashed her forehead against his. Specks of white flashed behind Y'ven's eyes.

The warrior drew back her weapon, ready to strike his chest, when he cracked her jaw with his fist. The female staggered aside, and with another hit, she fell to the ground.

As Y'ven stood over her, seething with rage and grief, the youngling charged at him. Neer ran forward and raised her sword, but before her blade met with his skin, the young vaxros was thrown aside by a powerful gust of magic. His war hammer fell from his grasp as he rolled across the desert floor.

Neer turned quickly, searching for his attacker, when her eyes fell to Aélla. The evae spun aside as a vaxros swiped his battle axe at her chest. The sharp edge of his blade clipped her arm when she dodged his attack. Spinning her non-magical wooden staff, she struck his head.

He stumbled back, and she cracked her weapon against his chest. The staff spun quickly in her hand as she danced around him, striking from the side.

She lunged forward, and he grabbed the staff as it moved closer toward his face. Through a heavy glare, he spat out a mouthful of blood and angrily snatched the staff from her grip.

"Drimil'Rothar," he sneered. "You will die today."

"We don't have to fight!" she begged with assertion. "Lay down your arms. Go back to your shelarr and tell them of your treason."

"Treason!" he laughed with disgust. "You ambushed us. You killed my brothers."

"You beheaded an innocent man!"

"We beheaded *no one*!" As he struck with her staff, it disappeared from his grip. Turning back, he was hit in the jaw

312

as Neer teleported behind and struck him with the weapon she stole. A tooth flung from his lips, and he staggered aside.

She vanished and came up behind him with her sword in hand. The warrior turned and blocked her hit with his axe. She stabbed his arm and then jabbed for his chest, but the vaxros grabbed her arm. Her bones ached as his grip tightened. She couldn't teleport within his grasp without bringing him with her. The use of such magic was dangerous. Deadly, even. But being his captive was worse.

As he lifted his axe, a sinister grin pulled his lips. Looking into his deadly eyes, Neer enveloped them with magic, and they vanished.

She brought them high above the ground, and the vaxros's heavy weight dragged them quickly down. In his panic, he released his grip and fell quickly to the world below. Neer vanished before hitting the dirt and rolled across the ground.

She coughed and wheezed as her chest burned. Unable to crawl to her knees, she lay on the ground, watching as the others fought nearby.

Her attention moved to the warm liquid seeping into her clothes, and she followed a trail of blood that led to the vaxros who fell from the sky. His skull had smashed against a rock and was left open to expose his brain.

Turning away, she rested her head onto the ground as her body ached with the tenderness of battle and depletion. Heavy eyes struggled to stay open, and darkness loomed in the corner of her vision.

As she swayed between the realms of consciousness and sleep, the ground beneath her started to quake with slow tremors that vibrated through her with magic and power.

Struck with a sense of urgency, her eyes opened, and she forced herself to sit upright on her knees.

Her attention moved from the ground to the fight, and she wondered if the battle could be causing such a disturbance. Reiman was nearby, dancing around two warriors. As a vaxros jabbed at his feet, the other struck for his neck. He dipped and spun through their slow, predictable movements like a flowing river, moving with grace and precision. Their faces were somehow redder with fury as they moved faster, becoming sloppier with every swing.

Thallon knelt behind the safety of a shimmering barrier. Vials and herbs collected around his knees as he poured the contents of a freshly made potion into a glass orb. With a quick shake, the mixture turned into a black mist, and he threw the potion into the midst of the battle.

Black vapor rolled across the ground when the vial shattered, and tendrils wisped into the air, catching in the throats of those within its grasp. The vaxros moved slower, their movements becoming more predictable and without purpose. Reiman, unphased by Thallon's potion, dodged an unhurried strike and then swept his blade across the throat of the female warrior he fought against.

In the same motion that cut her throat, he jabbed through the chest of the second warrior. Blood coated his face as it spilled from his victim's body.

The battle came to a finish, and Neer crawled forward, but the dirt beneath her shifted with a hard jolt, causing her to fall back. She landed on the ground and noticed the hard rock that once lay beneath her had become soft and fragmented, like thick dust.

Lying on her back, she felt the warm tug of the dirt pulling her under. The sting of magic shrouded her with warmth and pressure. She closed her eyes, hoping to focus her magic and escape, but she was weak. Depleted. Unable to fight against the force dragging her slowly beneath the surface.

"Nerana!" Reiman called, his voice laced with fear and panic.

As he rushed closer, she quickly pushed him back with a weak blast of energy. The air caught in her throat as she exerted magic she didn't have. Her bones felt weaker, and her mind grew weary as she slowly sank into the ground.

Reiman stumbled back as the dirt shifted in a wide circle around her. He stepped closer, prepared to save her, when she exclaimed, "Don't!" Her voice was raw with guilt and sorrow. The pits were impossible to survive. She wouldn't have him become entrapped as well.

"Take this!"

Aélla reached with her staff, and Neer gripped it with her free hand. Y'ven, affected by Thallon's potion, slowly bounded over, and together, they attempted to pull her free. In his weakened state, Y'ven could hardly hold a grip to the wooden shaft.

"Use your magic!" Thallon demanded. "Come on, Neer!"

Beneath the crushing weight, she couldn't find the strength to free herself. Her energy blended with the magic pulling her under. It tugged at the strands of her existence. She felt every vibration and wave of heat that tore through the ground, and she realized the magic encasing her was far beyond the power of her own.

Aélla knelt to the ground and placed her palms to the dirt. For a moment, the magic surrounding Neer shifted, and a surge of energy, like a violent shockwave of electricity and fire, tore through her. Aélla closed her eyes and pressed harder to the ground, and Neer released a horrific shriek of agony. Aélla quickly released her hold, and the fire coursing through Neer ceased.

Descending further, the weight of the world was crushing. Hot magic stung her skin, filling her with dread and unrest. She was paralyzed. Immobile. Stuck as the writhing magic pulled her further until she was swallowed, and the surface became solid once again.

CHAPTER THIRTY-EIGHT

SHADOWS AND DARKNESS
Nerana

"Into the land of fire and vengeance. Tempered in flame. Forged by pain. This is how you gain your strength."

— First Blood Proverb

ROCKS COMPRESSED HER BONES AS she sank further into the crust of the world. Magic swirled within her chest. It burned and stung as it fused with the energy pulling her under. She couldn't control it. Couldn't use it to free herself.

She was trapped, unable to take even the shallowest of breaths. Her life was slipping away like slow mist from a morning leaf, carrying with it her thoughts and warmth.

Deep grinding vibrated through the ground as the enchantments dragged her deeper. Rocks and dust scraped against her skin, painting her body with razor-thin lines of red. Cold and alone, she began to suffocate. Her thoughts drifted from one thing to the next as the pain turned to numbness.

Further down, the deafening grinds tapered. Her arm slid through the dirt and into warm, open air. Slowly, she was released from the grip constricting her and fell into darkness.

Warm winds swept past as she descended. Slithering between life and death, memories flashed through her mind. All that she had lived through came back in a convolution of emotion and color. The images overlapped in a blur, yet she could see them with clarity, reliving piece by piece every detail of her life.

The warm embrace of her father's strong arms. Her mother's voice when she whispered goodnight. The laughter of her friends and touch of those she loved. She reached out, grasping desperately at the life she once knew. Hoping to find the peace she deserved.

But peace was unattainable and happiness a lie.

Screams fractured her thoughts, shattering the memories holding her close. Devoid of her comfort, she could feel only pain as frost settled into her bones, and she crashed to the ground.

Lying unconscious, she was quiet and still, unaware of the affliction gripping her. Shallow cracks left her skull bleeding and open. Her arm was twisted beneath her, shattered from the fall.

A ball of light drifted through the air, descending toward the unmoving sorceress. Its brightness shimmered against the blood encasing her body as it gravitated closer. The sting of magic absorbed into her chest, and she was filled with heat.

A voice whispered to her through the rampant noises of her mind, and Reiman appeared in shadows of her thoughts. Scratches and cuts drew blood across his face. His cloak and armor were shredded to reveal thick lacerations across his arms and chest.

He reached out to her with blistered hands, and with fatherly comfort, he said, "It is not your time."

She stared desperately into his nurturing eyes. Her fingers slid into his hand, and her thoughts dwindled to blackness.

Creaking bones shifted as her shattered tibia pulled itself back through her bloody and ripped skin. Her body twitched, and her bones popped into place. The marks along her face that cut through her cheeks wove together.

As the scratches on her skin disappeared, her teal eyes opened, and she inhaled a deep, raspy breath.

Panicked, she sat up and choked. Dust spewed from her throat as she coughed and wheezed. Reaching through the darkness, she searched for anything to relinquish the rawness paining her.

Her hands pressed against shards of bone, and she glanced around to find herself crouched in a sea of corpses. Withdrawing her hands, she peered through the blackness surrounding her. Far above was the underbelly of Sandir. Falling dust came together in several downward-facing cones descending like a constant rain.

Slowly, her vision focused, and she could see through the thick darkness. Jagged rock walls created a wide cavern. The light glow of stones and algae kept the hollow illuminated with dull light. A pungent smell of sulfur clung to the air. She gagged and retched, unable to suppress the sickness that overcame her.

Lying beneath her was the body of a vaxros warrior. His wide, glassy eyes gazed above, staring at nothing. Blood dripped from his parted lips. His limbs were twisted and broken. Blood and brains spilled from the gash in his skull.

Voices slowly whispered through the air. They weren't panicked or fearful. There was no pain tugging her chest. Instead, they were calm and peaceful, caressing her with their softly spoken words.

They uttered an ancient language, but she understood every word.

"Tré muíllryen ark'valla…"

Through flame and shadow the power remains…

"Dö'nui'e for vóla…"

Face the void…unbroken. Untamed.

"Nors'vektha a'kalla Rotharí…"

Shrouded the sun. Carry the Light…

A subtle pull beckoned her to a dark corner. Bones clattered and snapped as she tripped through the cave, following the warm sting of its essence. Ancient armor and weapons lay in pieces across the ground. Flesh sloughed from corpses and covered her boots in putrid filth.

The voices grew louder as she climbed through the bodies, and then fell suddenly silent when she reached the edge of the cave. Peering through the darkness, she found an enormous portrait hanging along a smooth stone wall.

The thick golden frame was adorned with beautifully swirled patterns shimmering in the pale luminance of algae and stone. Painted onto thick canvas, shrouded in shadows and darkness, was a woman. A wide smile stretched her lips in a way that was both unsettling and peaceful. White, wavy hair hung across her narrow shoulders.

In her hands was a black ring crazed with white glowing cracks. She held it outright as an offering to her audience. Behind her, fires burned with madness. Scorched bones rested at her feet. Her flowing gown was singed unevenly at her knees.

Neer ran her finger along the striations of tempera and found it wasn't oil or water that created such a masterpiece.

It was blood. Ancient, hardened blood.

She took half a step back, and the voices that were once silent grew louder, shouting with anger. Speaking too fast for her to understand, she was lost to the noises and consumed by their words.

A burning halo formed within the center of the portrait, crawling across every brush stroke and uneven line as it grew. The heat expanded, and the portrait was engulfed with flames. Leaves of scorched canvas drifted into the air and fell to the ground.

The flames climbed higher, casting light throughout the desolate cave. As soon as it had started, the flames quickly died, and the room was cold with darkness. Not a scent or sound filled the empty air. White air clouded Neer's face with every exhale. Chills covered her skin, though she couldn't tell if it was from the terror or frost.

Light appeared through the golden frame, like a window revealing another part of the cave. Crossing her arms to rid them of the chill that overcame her, she took several steps forward. As she approached the frame, a flash of energy created a frigid breeze behind her.

She turned with her arms out and attempted to use her magic, but the familiar spark never burned in her chest. Her attention shifted from the emptiness inside to a shadow approaching from ahead.

Neer was frozen as a woman stepped through the darkness. A wide smile stretched her lips. Curly blond hair hung across her shoulders. Her green dress was singed at her knees, and burns covered her arms and blackened her feet.

In her hands was a ring, held outright as an offering.

But Neer didn't notice her gesture. She didn't see the similarities of this woman and the one from the portrait as she stared into her eyes. This was a face the world was never meant to see.

A face with condemning eyes of teal.

The voices whispered, while Vaeda smiled. It was sinister yet calm. Peaceful and forced.

Neer stepped back, and waves of heat engulfed the room, yet there were no flames. The voices shouted, clawing through her mind. She could no longer understand their words as they overlapped into a plethora of unattainable sounds.

She fell to her knees and gripped her ears. But the voices came from within. Her face grew red, and she fought against their angry pull. She held her breath and clenched her teeth. Dirty fingernails dug into her scalp as she screamed.

The world fell deathly silent when the voices came to a sudden halt. Their sounds lingered in her mind, drifting from her thoughts like a quiet breeze.

Trembling hands were slowly removed from her ears, and she exhaled a deep breath, relieved to be rid of the noise and chaos. Her mind was her own, no longer gripped by the magic that scourged the cave.

Her solace was short-lived, however, as Vaeda stepped closer. Her footsteps were silent, a shadow with movements smooth as silk. She stopped just steps away, her smile never fading. Teal eyes never blinking. She was frozen, holding the ring out as if it were a gift to be received.

The vibrant color of her eyes darkened. They grew lifeless and cold as frost settled into the air once again.

Her smile never faded.

Rocks creaked and moaned as the cave shook. Dust and stone fell from above, crashing violently against the sea of bones. Neer didn't move. She didn't blink nor breathe as her focus remained on her former self. The girl she once was stood before her now as an adult.

Vaeda's black eyes widened as the cavern quaked.

Neer stumbled back when Vaeda vanished into a cloud of black mist. The rumbling ceased, and the cold lifted. A frigid wind moved past as the apparition appeared behind Neer, and she was frozen with fear.

The phantom whispered softly in the voice of the ancients, *"Fohl'nok melän..."*

Free us.

The faint clatter of metal clinked against stone as the ring dropped to the ground, and the ghost disappeared.

CHAPTER THIRTY-NINE

FIRE
Nerana

FUMBLING THROUGH THE DARKNESS, NEER found the ring. She slipped it safely into her pocket and peered through the frame. Light flickered through the opening, yet the cave inside remained black and void. With several deep breaths, she pushed through the fear and stepped through.

Waves of heat distorted her vision as she came to a room filled with boiling magma. Fires burned and scorched the stone, singeing her skin. She turned around, hoping to escape the sweltering blaze, but was met with solid rock where there was once an opening.

Standing against the wall, she gazed upon the enormous cavern. The walls were carved perfectly smooth, and arched bridges extended above a river of flowing lava. In the center of the room, nestled within a moat of liquid flame, stood a statue of a draak. Black scales glistened with orange light. Fire spewed toward the high ceiling from its opened mouth. Long, crooked arms were outstretched to showcase thin wings, and its thick hindlegs stood on clawed feet.

Resting in front of its legs, atop the island surrounded by lava, was a pillar of the Divines.* The pillar, which stood as

---

*A place of great power, faith, and sanctuary. The Pillars can be found all throughout the continent, with most being in the plains and woodlands of the human territories.

tall as a full-grown man, was dwarfed by the large sculpture at its back.

The lava from the slow-moving river bubbled and popped, and Neer stepped back. She glanced around, searching for an escape, but the only path was impeded by flames rising from cracks in the ground.

Magic pulled her toward the pillar, like an invisible rope tugging the very essence of her soul. She could feel its grip increasing, and she took a measured step back, putting distance between them. But she couldn't escape its hold. Whatever called her there, be it the Divines or magic, she knew she had to follow.

The fires grew more violent, whirling and popping as she stepped closer. Jumping back, she shielded herself from the embers and heat, and the raging fire slowly dwindled back to its calmer dance. She'd have to teleport across, but her magic was weak and diminished beneath the weight of energy engulfing the cave.

Resting on her knees, she placed her fists together and exhaled. Breathing slow, she fell into a harrowing, deep meditation. Her face was red as she reached deep into her soul, struggling to find an ounce of energy that was no longer there. Her chest was empty, void of anything but fire and rage. She couldn't teleport herself to the pillar.

She'd have to control the flames.

Her mind went back to her first time controlling the heat of the firepit and the pain that it caused. Hesitant to relive such agony, she knew this was her only hope of survival and forced herself to focus.

She pressed her fists harder together and closed her eyes tightly. The scorching heat was unbearable. Every wisp and flare of the growing flames pulsed through her like a steady beating drum. Vibrating into her core, resounding into a crescendo of strength and fury. Through a deep scream, her energy ignited, and blistering heat boiled in her veins.

She fell forward, gasping in agony. The energy started to fade, and she knew she had to push forward. She needed to endure the torture to return to the surface.

With a pained gasp, she returned to her meditative posture and forced herself to continue. A loud, raw scream escaped through clenched teeth as her blood was set ablaze, and heat raged through her.

The flames rose with her agony, becoming hotter and spraying soot through the cave like black snow. She opened her eyes, watching the flames that were now tamed by her energy. Drawing in a deep breath, she opened her aching fists and placed her palms to the ground. Slowly, she exhaled and forced the flames to withdraw.

The raging fires sitting before her transcended into waves of blue heat. She could see now the patterns before her created a path outlined in fire.

Her chest burned hotter as she stood and held on to the energy quelling the fire's heat. Forcing herself through the path, she remained calm in her steps, not daring to lose focus and allow the deadly flames to reignite.

Over the arched bridge, she came to the base of the statue. Falling to her knees, she released her hold of the flames, and the cave ignited once again in a firestorm of heat.

Weak and trembling, she crawled to the pillar. She touched the impression where the crystal would fit, and a sinking, harrowing reality tore her soul.

She didn't have the staff.

Without it, she couldn't contain the energy. She was trapped, stuck far beneath the surface where she'd waste away in a pit of fire.

This was truly hell.

The thought put a sour smile to her face. Caught between delirium and insanity, she began to laugh. Hysterical, distraught laughter erupted from her throat, causing tears to fall from her eyes. Her smile never faded while amusement and bitterness shredded her soul.

She turned around and slumped against the pillar, watching the fires and lava. She dug through her pockets, searching for the ring, hoping it could lead her to safety, but instead, she found something different. Something she knew could save her…but with a heavy price.

Orange light reflected against the smooth edge of the memory shard as she pulled it from her pocket. This was her way out. She could use the shard as a vessel to contain the energy. But doing so would erase the memory inside, releasing her of its hold. Further eliminating any part of the life she so desperately held on to.

There wasn't much she remembered of her childhood, and she feared this memory could be the last piece of her old life. Relinquishing it would not only erase the memory but also its effect on her. She would remove it completely from existence. It would be as if the moment never happened at all.

She scoffed at the twisted cruelty of her fate, to sacrifice one of her last memories in order to survive. Tears slid down her face as she was overcome with grief. Her lips curled, and her chin shook as she lost herself. The Divines weren't through with her yet. Whatever games they were playing…she officially lost. This was the end.

Neer wondered if they were this cruel, or if she truly was deserving of such injustice and hatred.

Holding the shard to her forehead, she closed her eyes and sank into her sadness. The memory replayed several times over. She hoped it would be enough to keep it alive after it was gone. But it was a fool's wish. Nothing would bring back the images once they'd been released. Even the memory she would hold from watching the vision would be lifted from her mind.

Her tears mixed with sweat as they dripped from her chin. Her lungs ached for the touch of a fresh, cold breath. She had to leave this place, and she couldn't go without securing the element.

"Fuck you…," she growled, repeating the phrase several times as anger consumed her. Fires spewed and popped as her fury ignited. She spoke to the Divines. To life. To fate. To everyone who forced her into this miserable existence.

Through her anger, she pushed herself up and forced the shard into the hollow depression. She stumbled aside as fires swept through the air, creating a vortex that spun into the memory shard.

A dull ache filled her mind with darkness and ice as black mist rose from the vessel. She fell back and clutched her head as pressure swelled deep inside. The memory shard that once swirled with dark energy lightened with fires as her memory evaporated from its center.

As the vortex absorbed into the shard, the flames and magma turned cold, and the cave darkened.

Emptiness filled her where comfort was once present. The memory she cherished more than anything had disappeared completely. The mark it left behind was gone, and she felt alone, unable to remember his face or name. He didn't exist, and it left her with nothing but emptiness.

Pushing through the desolation, she turned to the memory shard, which now glowed with flames, and took it in her hand. The statue of the draak stood proudly above, its opened mouth devoid of fire and heat.

She stepped back as a rune appeared on the stone beneath her feet. It glowed orange and radiated with warmth. Filled with agony, she pressed her palm to its surface, and the world disappeared.

CHAPTER FORTY

STRENGTH AND POWER

"No matter how lost or broken or afraid, call out to me… and I will find you."

— Reiman to Nerana

THE WORLD WAS COLD WITH darkness and silence. Altvára cawed from high above as he circled the empty air. His dark shadow was a blur against the moonlit sky.

Neer lay burned and tired atop the cold ground. Her body was limp, and her eyes were heavy with exhaustion and pain.

Rolling onto her back, she exhaled and closed her weary eyes. A hard lump pressed into her back, and she fumbled through the dirt before retrieving the memory shard. Emptiness lingered within her as she struggled to retain any semblance of the memory it once held. She knew it belonged to her but couldn't recall even the slightest feeling it gave. Any trace of the memory, both from its origin and any recollection from the shard, had been erased from her mind.

Whatever it held, she knew it was important as it left a void inside her that couldn't be quelled. Sickness and sorrow filled her at the thought of losing such an important piece of her history. She longed to have it back, to fill the vacancy and ice that dwelled inside. But it would never be. It was a dangerous thing to release the magic within a memory shard, and she dreaded the rebuttal she knew was to come from her father.

Father. The word held little meaning. It felt hollow and empty. She knew what it once meant, but now…it was lost in the wind. Untethered and broken.

As if her thoughts had called upon him, Reiman came to her side. He knelt over her and inspected the burns across her skin. Red, blistered wounds were outlined in black. Her shoulder had a deep burn into the muscle where a pop of magma seared through her armor.

Tattered clothes and singed hair showcased her torture beneath the surface. She whimpered as he checked her injuries. Light blue eyes met with hers, and for a moment, she felt relief.

He leaned closer, carefully brushed back her hair, and whispered, "You're all right. Rest now. You did well."

She opened her palm, and his gaze shifted to the glowing shard in her grasp. With a deep inhale, his shoulders rose. A grave look crossed his eye as he collected the vessel and placed it carefully into his cloak.

Neer sank into his arms, unconscious, as he carried her to an abandoned village. Half the homes had collapsed, while the others were left to bake in solitude beneath the relentless heat of the desert sun.

Y'ven sat atop a crumbled half-wall and sharpened his axe. His eyes widened at the sight of his leader carrying their lost friend. Dru darted to Neer and touched her face. Reiman paid the faeth no mind as she looked at him for answers.

The coolness of night subsided as he stepped into the half-standing home that had become their hideout. The roof was caved in and collapsed on the left side, while the walls were intact and secure. Reiman stepped across the small room and placed Neer onto a cracked stone table.

"What happened?" Aélla asked, rushing to her side. "How did she get here? Where did these burns come from?"

"Drimil." Reiman placed a hand on her shoulder. "You must remain calm."

Aélla exhaled a slow breath, though the fear hadn't fully erased from her eyes. Turning back to Neer, she clutched her burned arm and slowly healed her outer wounds.

As the shallow blisters healed, Aélla leaned back with an exhausted huff. Wiping her brow, she dug through her leather pack and collected several herbal ingredients into a mortar. She mashed the ingredients together and then smeared the paste over Neer's deeper wounds.

Reiman brushed back Neer's singed, uneven hair to reveal the trails of dried blood that lay across her face and neck. His caring eyes examined the ash and filth matting her hair.

"How did she survive?" Thallon asked as he entered the home. "We saw her get pulled under. No one has ever made it out."

"She had this," Reiman said, exposing the fiery shard. The others were silent with confusion and surprise. Aélla stepped closer and carefully took the crystal into her hands.

"This…is a memory shard. How did she use it to collect the energy?"

Reiman leaned with his back against the wall and closed his eyes. Pinching the bridge of his nose, he became somber and quiet. "It was released," he said. His voice wavered and shook with grief. With a sharp breath, he composed himself and looked at the others with forced confidence. "She forfeited the memory inside."

They glanced at Neer with sorrow. "What was it?" Thallon asked quietly.

With another wavering exhale, Reiman explained, "Her father."

Aélla covered her mouth with a silent gasp, and the room was deathly silent with the weight of despair.

Reiman cleared his throat and stood tall. Stepping to Neer, he placed a hand on her shoulder and whispered, "I'm sorry…"

The others watched in silence as he briskly fled the home.

Morning drifted over the slumbering world as the moons dipped beyond the edge of the horizon, allowing the sun to brighten the sky.

Neer lay atop the table, just as she had all night. Her body was motionless and weak, while her mind soared. Fires burned, and heat blazed through her. She was standing alone in a pit of flames. Voices called out to her, screaming for aid. Searching for an end.

They burned hotter, overtaking her mind and devouring her whole.

Waking from her nightmare, she shot up with a gasp. Clutching her aching chest, she gazed at her surroundings. Sunlight beamed into the room, casting light across the dust-coated floors and empty walls. Weapons, bags, and other items belonging to her and the others lay on a table nearby, and she exhaled a deep breath, thankful to be back with her group.

Wiping the sweat from her brow, she touched her body, wondering if this was real. If she had truly survived, or if this was another test.

White bandages wrapped her skin where blistering wounds healed beneath. Blood caked her tattered, ash-covered armor and skin. The air was heavy with dry heat and dust. Magic weighed her chest in the way it always had, and she knew this was reality.

Slinging her legs over the edge of the table, she spotted a leather pouch and fresh fruit lying on a stool next to the table. She stumbled across the cold floor, snatched the canteen, and drank the water inside. Liquid spilled down her face as the contents ran dry.

She leaned against the wall and slid down until she sat on the ground. Biting into the fruit, she became aware of her hunger and quickly devoured her small meal.

Her eyes averted to the doorway as a shadow darkened the entry. She was tense for a moment, until Aélla stepped inside.

The evae smiled pleasantly, striding across the room to Neer's side. "Hey. How are you feeling?" she asked.

Neer groaned with stiffness and sat straighter. "Better. Did you heal me?"

Aélla nodded in response. She got comfortable by Neer's side and twisted the glowing memory shard between her fingers. "You released the memory inside?"

"I had to. There was no other way."

Her lips pursed together, and she stared unblinking at the fiery shard. "Reiman said it was yours?"

Neer crossed her arms. "Yes."

"This is dangerous. Releasing the energy of a memory is—"

"I know." Neer curled into her knees. Dirty hair was caught between her fingers as she raked them across her scalp. "We had no way of knowing the element lay beneath the surface. I'd call it luck that we found it at all, but…" Her words faded as the emptiness increased. She inhaled, hoping for it to squander. Memories of her time underground came to fruition, and she was puzzled by a teeming thought. "Did you heal me after I was pulled under?"

"After you were pulled under?" The wrinkles along Aélla's brow deepened as their gazes met. "No. We all thought you were gone, Neer. I cannot heal those that I can't see."

Neer turned away. Fear and doubt crept through her mind. "I was dying…My body couldn't move, I…I felt myself slipping away. Then, I wasn't. Something healed me. There were hundreds of bones and bodies down there. I shouldn't have survived."

"There is one possibility." The hint of terror clung to her voice. "But I have only heard of it in rumors and myth."

"What is it?"

With a nervous exhale, she gained the courage to speak and did so while looking into the eyes of her friend. "*Nrët morvrën*; it's a dangerous curse."

"You think I'm cursed? With what? By who?"

Before Aélla could answer, their intense conversation was broken by Y'ven as he stepped into the home. Dru fluttered to Neer's side and hovered before her face. The faeth stared quizzically at her, then turned to Y'ven with a thumbs up.

The vaxros nodded, and with a shout, he called, "Master Reiman! She is awake."

Reiman burst into the home and came to Neer's side. He inspected her arms and face. With a deep exhale, his head fell between his shoulders. "Nerana. It is good to see your eyes. Master Drimil"—he turned to Aélla—"my deepest thanks. You are a trusted ally."

With a genuine smile, Aélla bowed her head, Reiman returned his eyes to Neer, who was brooding in silence.

Her eyes shifted to Thallon as he stepped to her side, scanning over her bloody and torn appearance. "You look terrible," he said.

She turned away, rejecting his attempt at humor. Closing her eyes, she pushed herself up and stepped across the room. Her sword lay on a table with everyone's belongings, and she ran her fingers down the length of the blade, thankful it wasn't lost in the fight.

"What happened down there?" Thallon asked. "Aélla said you retrieved the energy of fire. Sandir must be a portal into the realm."

Neer turned to him and found everyone watching her. She leaned against the table and crossed her arms, not yet ready to relive the harrowing events of the caves.

With a shake of her head, she attempted to brush away the confusion. "A vision appeared. She was my age…and she looked like me when I was younger. Before I changed my appearance."

"Did she say anything?" Aélla asked.

Neer thought for a moment. Her mind scrambled as she replayed every moment of her time in the realm. "There were voices. They spoke a language I've never heard…but I could understand them."

"What did they say?" Thallon asked, the words spilling from his mouth with excitement.

Aélla placed her hand on his shoulder, and he became calmer in his approach. Turning back to Neer, they waited in silence.

She shifted with discomfort. Her lips pulled aside while her eyes moved from one place to another, never focusing on anything. "I can't…I can't remember everything. Something about power and facing the void. Carrying a light…" She huffed in frustration. "I don't know what it means!"

"That's all right." Reiman placed his hands on her shoulders and gave an easy smile. "You did well, child. I'm proud of you."

A faint smile pulled her lips. She leaned back against the table, when something tugged in her pocket. Her heart sank as she retrieved the ring and held it between her finger and thumb. Examining the glowing lines sprawling the black metal, she was stricken with flashes of darkness and pain.

Jumping back, she dropped the ring and gripped her head. The others turned to her with worry.

"Neer?" Thallon came to her side. "Are you…" His voice trailed to silence as his gaze shifted to the ring lying next to her. Carefully, without moving too quickly, he clutched the band between his fingers and lifted it from the table. The color washed from his face, and his eyes became distant, holding no life as they stared forward, unblinking.

"What is it?" Aélla asked, coming to their sides.

Thallon gasped and placed the ring back onto the table. "This…is what I am searching for. It is the ring the Eirean sent me here to find." His eyes averted to Neer, and she stood quietly with her hand on her head. "Where did you get this?"

"In the realm," Neer explained. "A woman in a portrait was holding it."

"A portrait?" Thallon asked, seemingly unconvinced. "What do you—"

"I don't know!" She thrust the words out with a rush of frustration. "She was in the portrait one second and then standing behind me the next! When she disappeared, the ring stayed behind."

"Do you know what this is? How close you came to unleashing such rage and unrest?"

"It's a ring!"

"This is not just a ring, Neer. This is something far more dangerous than you or I understand." He rushed to the table and hastily dug through his things. Tossing items and clothing aside, he retrieved a small leather pouch from his pack and slipped the ring inside. He tied off the top to ensure it was secure and slid the small pouch into his pocket. "I have to go," he said. "The Eirean asked me to find this and return it to them immediately."

"What is it?" Aélla asked. "You shouldn't leave on your own!"

"I don't know what it is. They only said that it's extremely dangerous, and that *no one* should know of its existence." He shook his head while shoving his things into his pack. Beneath his breath, he sneered and cursed that a human was the finder of such a relic.

"Hold on," Aélla argued. "Thallon, please. Do not leave."

He stopped and exhaled a deep breath. "If anyone else gets this—"

"They won't. Just keep it safe. No one here is going to take it, and we won't tell anyone of its existence, right?" Everyone silently agreed, so she touched his shoulders and looked into his eyes. "Once we are finished, I will take you directly to the Eirean myself. Please. Do not go off on your own."

He turned away with a sigh and closed his eyes. "You are lucky the vaxros who imprisoned me took everything that I had, including the *n'aeth.*° Otherwise, I would be gone." With a glance to the others, he sneered and ripped away from Aélla's grasp. "Let's go."

Everyone followed as he gathered his belongings and left the village behind.

The desert heat was relentless as they trekked a long and tireless path. Barren plains of rock and dust stretched for miles in every direction. Green didn't exist there. No animals, villages, ruins, or caves. The world was empty and forgotten. A wasteland of scorched dirt.

Neer had long grown tired of the smell of dust and the color of brown. But most of all, she hated the heat. Her skin brightened with a shade of red, and it shriveled and burned beneath her cloak.

As the day faded to dusk, the mundane aroma of a lifeless desert was replaced with the refreshing scent of rain and trees. It was a sweet, woodsy smell of wildflowers and grass. She inhaled a deep breath and smiled with relief.

Stepping over a ridge, they came to the edge of an enormous, dense jungle. Tall trees created a thick canopy that partially shadowed the sun, allowing life to flourish in the understory and brush. Branches rustled as colorful birds took flight. Vines slithered through large limbs and hung from branches.

"We can't get too close," Thallon explained, staring in wonder, as if he had never seen a forest or green before. "Fru'skogmir is a dangerous place. Protected by ancient enchantments. Do not touch the leaves. Do not drink the water from the vines."

"What's so bad about it?" Neer asked. "We need to refill our canteens, and —"

° An uncommon, mystical artifact which may transport its traveler instantly from one place to the other. Only able to be used once, the n'aeth, or transporting stone, loses its magical energy after its incantation has been said.

"No," he said decisively, while looking into her eyes. "The jungle is not to be trifled with. It is dangerous."

Aélla stepped closer, and asked, "How is it dangerous? Do others live there?"

Thallon sighed with frustration. Rubbing his forehead, he explained, "There are enchantments protecting it from outsiders. I've only heard stories, but we should take caution."

"Agreed," Y'ven said. "Don't enter. Don't touch. Stay on path."

"Thanks," Thallon said with a half-smile. With a glance to the others, who were ready to spew more questions, he turned and led them to the tree line.

Beneath the edge of the canopy, the world was cool with mist. Magic hovered in the air, pricking their skin with its soft sting. Aélla stared into the forest. Neer watched her for a moment, noticing the sadness and longing in her eyes.

"*Vaeda…*"

Her ears perked, and her head lifted at the sound of a faint whisper. Turning to the trees, Neer slowly stopped. She could see nothing through the dense leaves and shrubs around the jungle's perimeter. The canopy repelled the dwindling sunlight and left the jungle dark with its shadow.

"Neer!" Thallon's voice broke her concentration, and she jumped at the sound of his voice. He came quickly to her side and pulled her away. "We must stick together."

"I heard someone," she explained.

"It's the enchantments. They are like wispers or ghosts. Do not listen to them. They will deceive you. Pull you further into the jungle, and you will never come out."

Following the others, they came to a stop when Reiman lifted his hand. The collective, overlapping sounds of shrieks and raspy growls broke through the quiet dusk. They came from the desert, while the jungle was peaceful and calm.

Dark shadows lurked nearby as khiut, the fiendish dogs of shadow and death, rose from their daily slumber. The cry of an animal shrieking in pain filled the air. Its horrified call was silenced by an influx of hissing and hungry growls.

"We must stop," Reiman said. "We'll rest beneath a barrier."

Aélla protested. "It's too dangerous. If many of them attack at once—"

"A pack of khiut follow the scent and sound of their prey. Should we continue walking, they will find us. If we mask our scent, they will lurk beyond the barrier but never attack it."

"If they see us inside—"

"They will not attack us." He spoke with great resonance and authority, and his dark eyes burned into hers. "Now, shall you set up the barrier, or I?"

Aélla inhaled a cautious breath. She glanced to her companions, who were silent beneath Reiman's intimidating glare, and then agreed to create a barrier. With everyone huddled together, she placed four drops of clear potion around them and lifted her arms. Shimmering, translucent energy formed above her hands and cascaded downward until reaching the ground, where the magic collided with the potion and became invisible.

As the night grew longer, more khiut stalked the land. Dozens of the fiendish, snarling creatures wandered past the barrier. Their noises were made silent, while their glowing eyes were bright. Aélla watched as one of the dogs sniffed behind her. Its leathered snout moved along the barrier's edge as it searched for its prey.

Her eyes lingered on the creature as it remained in its place, still sniffing and searching.

"You are of clan Rhyl?" Reiman asked. While the others had fallen to sleep, he and Aélla remained awake.

"Yes," she said, finally breaking her gaze from the khiut and focusing on Reiman. "As are you?"

He nodded. "I was. Long ago."

"Humans and evae do not typically coexist. We do not join armies or other races for a common cause."

He smiled, and for a moment, his icy exterior grew warm and inviting. "Is that not your own goal, Drimil'Rothar?"

"My goal is far beyond the scope of racial quarrels."

"Yet, somehow, it involves Nerana. The only known human sorcerer since Ateus." Their gaze was heavy and dark. The warmth brightening his expression faded. Not the trace of a smile clung to his lips. "Why have you allied yourself with her?"

Aélla's eyes narrowed. She tensed beneath the weight of his conceit.

"You must know the evae she traveled with before," he continued. "The two that fought with her…that betrayed her."

"They didn't betray her!"

He lifted a hand to quiet her. "I understand their reasoning. I do. Losing you would be a great tragedy. As an evae, I recognize the importance of your birthright."

"Klaud did not intend to betray her. He left her with the potion that could cure her. He'd have never fallen to such unforgiveable measures had there been another choice."

Reiman glanced at Neer, who lay slumped against Thallon in a deep slumber. "Does she know who they are to you? Why you've come to find her?"

Aélla turned away. "No. Not yet."

"Good. Don't tell her." Their gaze met, and Aélla was shocked by his suggestion. "Should she know the truth, whatever trust she holds in you would be squandered. Get through your journey here. Go to the forest. Allow her to figure things out on her own."

"I don't like lying to her. I never wanted to form an alliance under false pretenses."

His cold eyes hardened. "I know your reasons for seeking her out."

"You know *nothing* of my intentions."

"You are powerful, Master Drimil. But make no mistake, should any harm come to Nerana—should you and your comrades seek to provide illness or death upon her—I will show you the strength of *true* power."

Aélla matched his gaze with a darkness of her own. One she didn't often show. This man was still a stranger, one she had yet to fully understand. She wanted to trust him, to see him for the wise and noble leader that he was, but she couldn't. Not yet. Not while he remained so elusive in his reasonings for holding such power.

Not while he remained so resolute in challenging her fate.

"Nerana is my friend," she explained. "Should any harm come to her, it will not be of my hands, nor of those that I trust." The silence lingered as their gazes fell colder. "Do not mistake my kindness for weakness, Master Reiman. You may believe you understand the meaning of power, but should you threaten me again, you will come to know the verity of its strength." Her low voice faded, and they were left with silence as they spoke not a word for the rest of the night.

Chapter Forty-One

I'VASAAR

"Reist frigga lyeü'o'kavén lor tük."
This land is sacred. Do not disturb its peace.

— Aldír Nälevarta'e

TIRED LEGS BURNED AS NEER walked beneath the gentle hum of pattering rain. Thick leaves blocked the sky and drizzled water atop her head. A rush of warmth poured across the desert in a wave of golden light when the sun peeked beyond the horizon. She blocked the brightness from her eyes with her hand.

"We're here!" Thallon called from far ahead.

Gathering along the edge of a hillside, they came to a slow stop. In the distance, surrounded by barren desert, was a large, sprawling city. Hundreds of square clay homes and buildings were collected together in a wide circle formation.

Enormous rock pillars rose above the city like ribs and cast deep shadows that brought shade to many of the streets and homes. A slow-moving river carved through the center of town and gave life to small palm trees and thin grass. Streams broke away and slithered beneath bridges and through patches of green.

Tall clay walls surrounded the city with large gates along its perimeter. Sentry stood guard with bows and spears at each of the wall's fortifications and watchtowers.

Within the confines of the densely packed city was an inner barrier with less fortifications. Elevated above the rest of the city, the larger buildings surrounded a temple.

Thick pillars, a wide doorway, and hundreds of stairs led to the entrance of the ancient and cracked sanctuary. Y'lenae residents filtered through as they entered and exited the ruins.

"Is that it?" Neer asked of the temple.

"Yes," Aélla stated. "That's where tre'lan Aenwyn˚ resides for the energy of rock."

"It looks like a working temple. Will they let us in?"

Thallon added, "These are the only ruins the vaxros have permitted for entry. Look." He pointed to different sections of the city. "The shadows are where the y'lenae live. The vaxros stay in the sun. They coexist."

Reiman placed his hands to his hips. "We should get moving. The longer we're in the desert, the longer the fight remains in Nyn'Dira."

As he stepped away, the others slowly trailed behind, never removing their eyes from the civilization below. While y'lenae residents farmed or worked the shops, the vaxros forged weapons in smithies and laid bricks for new foundations.

"Nerana," Aélla started, "you need to train with your elemental energy. We can find time in the village to practice."

"Are you sure we should be using our energy on training? I'm powerful enough with the magic that I have. If—"

"You are a sorceress. The stronger you are in all your magics, the more powerful you will be."

Thallon gave a worried look that went unnoticed by the others as they focused on their conversation. He turned away with hard eyes and pressed his lips together in a straight line. Setting his gaze to Reiman, he scurried ahead and caught up

---

˚ Tre'lan Aenwyn translates to The Realm of Elements

to the much older evae. Reiman cast a quiet glance in Thallon's direction before returning his gaze to the trail ahead.

"So, you're Neer's father?" Thallon asked. "She's half-evae?"

"Adoptive father," he corrected. "She came into my care at fourteen years old."

Thallon raised a curious eyebrow. "Since when did an evae keep track of age?"

"Just another reason to leave." Reiman smiled as he turned to the scholar. "The humans, in all their faults and setbacks, understand the value of organized civilization. Evae, as a society, are unprogressive. We have not moved forward with the rest of the world. It's the reason we live in trees and hunt for our food while more advanced races have farmsteads and ease of living."

"You view the humans as superior?"

"In some ways."

Thallon's eyes narrowed with doubt. "So you agree with them? They lay siege to our lands and slaughter our people, yet you live among them? Train them?"

Reiman raised a hand to quiet him. "Please. You underestimate me, young scholar. I am not on the side of the humans. I'm on the side of coexistence. Their leaders have indoctrinated the masses. Turned them against us. Made them see anyone not of *pure human blood* as demonic or unclean." He paused with intent. "I train Nerana so that she can put an end to their reign."

"You want us to coexist? After all the blood we have sacrificed? All of the children they've slain in honor of their precious *divines*?"

"You may be a scholar, Thallon, but do not confuse your knowledge of books and ancient teachings with wisdom and understanding. The world holds far more complexity than the stories we're told by those who've only seen one side of war."

Thallon fell silent as they approached the village gates. The murmur of foreign voices erased the tranquil hush of the scalding wasteland as the group stepped through the arched entryway of I'vasaar.

Villagers walked by in a hurry, carrying on their morning chores. As the group wandered further, the locals took notice of their unkempt appearances. Blood, dirt, rips, and stains littered their clothes and skin. Many y'lenae gasped at the strangers, who looked more like struggling wanderers than capable warriors. The days of journeying saw them without proper hygiene or healing.

A silence fell over the wakening village, and crowds slowly formed along the streets, watching as the group headed toward the center of town. Vaxros guards broke through the curious onlookers. Weapons in hand, they blocked the street.

"Why does this *nesiat* bring *grot'meget**here?" the scarless vaxros said. He was smaller than the others, with not a wrinkle or crease marking his smooth face.

"I am Y'ven of atulg'shelarr," he growled, "and I have been absolved of my shame."

The guard's humorous smirk trembled before he erupted with laughter. The others joined in. Their thunderous voices blasted through the canyon. Y'ven tightened his fists as he glared. Dru's tinkering voice sounded through their laughter, and she shook her fist at the insolent guards.

"Please," Aélla stepped forward. With her hand on Y'ven's shoulder, he exhaled a deep breath. The creases between his brows softened, and his anger released. "Tell them we need a place to stay."

Y'ven reluctantly explained, and with a loud hock in his throat, the young guard spat at his feet. The others rumbled with laughter.

"There is no room for traitors or outsiders here. Leave. Before we cut you down where you stand."

---

* As mentioned previously, nesiat is a term used to describe the lost or soulless, while grot'meget is a derogatory slang meant for anyone not born of the desert.

A female guard peered through the group. Her eyes fell to Thallon, and her gaze narrowed. With a snarl, she pushed her companions aside and marched toward the evae, who quickly revealed the shield hidden in the bar on his arm.

"You…!" she hissed, slashing her axe at his head. "You were meant to die in Mors'groval!"

"Stop this!" Aélla shouted. "We do not need to fight!"

Thallon ducked aside and gripped his ribs in agony as he drew the crossbow from his back. As the guard lunged forward, Thallon released a bolt into her arm. She staggered back. Blood slid down her muscular arm and dripped from her fingers. With a snarl, she ripped the bolt from her skin and tossed it to the ground.

Blood splashed across Thallon's face, but he stood stiff and strong behind his shield. His eyes narrowed with anger as he watched the vaxros seethe. The guard exhaled a vicious growl while lifting her axe and charging forward.

Thallon raised his shield and prepared for her attack. Her thunderous steps vibrated the ground as she moved closer. She plunged her axe downward, and Thallon spun aside to bring himself out from beneath the deadly strike.

She stumbled forward as her axe dragged downward in the place he once knelt. Thallon stepped behind and plunged the edge of his shield into her spine.

With a violent hiss, the guard fell to her knees. She flung a handful of dirt into Thallon's eyes, and he covered his face in agony. The guard leapt to her feet and struck at the evae. As her axe swiped at his neck, she was frozen in place. The sharp edge of her blade was just a hair's breadth from his skin.

She wheezed and gagged, her eyes darting around in search of the force that detained her.

The vaxros lifted their weapons to the outsiders, who had already drawn their swords in Thallon's defense. Watching the female with bewilderment and surprise, they gazed at each other, before turning to Neer.

Her face was red with fury. Veins swelled in her neck and forehead as she held the vaxros in place. Curled fingers tightened as she reached toward the guard, who whimpered louder as her bones began to crunch.

Aélla's eyes widened in horror. Before she could speak, Reiman stepped to Neer's side. He placed his hands on her shoulders and looked into her eyes.

"Stop this," Reiman demanded. "She is disarmed."

The muscles of her jaw tensed, and her lip twitched. She glanced at Thallon, who backed away with red, swollen eyes. As she slowly released her grip, the vaxros fell to the ground with a hard thud. She gasped and wheezed as she lay, unmoving.

Two guards rushed to her aid, while the others held their weapons to the strangers. "Take them to *mors'groval*," an older guard with a thick, long beard said. "Let the *shadosalaan** feast on their bones."

"Wait!" Aélla cried as two guards tore her away from Thallon. The scholar fought against the much larger vaxros, but they restrained him. Y'ven stood with his chest puffed as the younger guard stepped closer.

"*Leuik!*" The raspy voice of a y'lenae native reigned over the chaos.

Silence fell over the street, and a man wearing colorful robes of animal hide stepped forward. He wore a wide headband holding two large backward-facing horns above his ears. His rope-bound staff was adorned with feathers and rocks.

Deep wrinkles creased his face as he spoke to the guards, who were stiff with anger. The y'lenae man pointed at each of the outsiders.

---

* As mentioned previously, Mors'groval is a wasteland meant to punish those who have caused disgrace or strife.
Shadsosalaan translates to creatures of darkness.

The guards were hesitant and glanced at one another. Aélla was pushed away as her captor sneered. His companions reluctantly followed before gruffly stomping through the crowds.

The group was silent as the y'lenae man looked at each of them with hesitance and curiosity. His aged voice was laced with power and confidence as he spoke in his native language.

Y'ven listened intently, before translating to the others. He spoke his native tongue to better explain. "This is Aldír° Nälevarta'e. He is the leader of I'vasaar and protector of the temple."

Aélla smiled with a graceful bow. "It is nice to meet you, Aldír Nälevarta'e. We have come to seek refuge and enter tre'lan Aenwyn."

As Y'ven spoke, the Aldír's face twisted with disgust. He pointed a stubby, callused finger to the eastern side of the city. "You may find refuge at the Elessan inn. They accept all travelers who survive the journey this far into *Atria'Erquiseaan*."

"Into what?" Thallon asked.

"Ashes of the damned," Y'ven explained. "Aragoth." The group was perplexed by this title.

Before they could ask, the y'lenae continued, and they were made speechless beneath his harrowing gaze as he gravely warned, "Under no circumstance are you permitted into the halls of the temple."

° Spoken in the language of the y'lenae, Aldír refers to a chieftain or leader.

While the y'lenae and vaxros do not speak the language of the other, they are able to communicate by understanding key words and phrases

CHAPTER FORTY-TWO

PURPOSE OF ILL INTENT

"Magic is the purest form of energy and those born of its power shall set us free."

— Tenet of the Broken Order Brotherhood

BEAUTIFUL MUSIC STRUMMED THROUGH THE air as a harpist played a calming melody in the corner of the inn. The large, open room held long tables and benches of stone. Tall windows gave warmth and light to the spacious tavern, where cheap ale and tough bread were the meal of choice for its many patrons.

Neer bit into her bread and tore off a small piece. The tasteless, overbaked dough was hard to chew and left her mouth dry. She sipped her mead and turned to Aélla as she said, "We must find a way into the temple."

"Look at you, breaking the rules," Thallon stated with a sly smile. "I figured you would get us foot soldiers here to do your dirty work." He bit into his bread and cast her a daring, playful look.

Unamused by his teasing, she stared at him as if his words were spoken in a language she didn't quite understand. Glancing to the others, she continued, "We have to gather the element of rock. It's possible for me to teleport inside, but that would cause chaos with the locals."

"So, we rile up some y'lenae," Thallon stated with a shrug. "It's better than not getting the element at all."

Aélla sighed and ran her fingers through her hair. She leaned forward and closed her eyes.

Neer averted her gaze when several patrons brushed against her back as they walked through the crowded room. She wrapped her hands around her mug and stared at the sweet drink. The taste of honey filled her palette as she finished her mead and then wiped her mouth with her dirty sleeve.

With a sigh, she crossed her arms. "We need a room," she griped. "And a bath."

Reiman leaned forward with his hands together. "You always underestimate me, dear child." He glanced at her with the glimmer of a smile. "We have accommodations in the upper wings. After we rest, we'll find our way into the temple."

They finished their drinks and followed Reiman upstairs. Past several doorways and down a long hall, they entered their room. Sunlight filtered into the narrow windows, keeping the room warm and comfortable. A large canopy bed sat along the left-side wall. Silk sheets and fur blankets were layered atop a thick featherbed.

Three smaller beds furnished with the same elegant sheets were across the room. Along the back wall was a small hearth with several fresh-cut logs resting within the fireplace. A silver serving dish and teapot with golden trim sat upon a round table with two chairs.

While the others made their way to the bathhouse downstairs, Neer stepped across the room. Staring out the window, she overlooked the city. Wide cobble streets wove through the city, breaking the homes into small, clustered sections. Those closest to the outer gates were meant for warriors and guards. Smithies and armorers crafted their goods for their soldiers in the neighboring clusters.

Merchants made up the next several sections, selling trinkets, clothing, and normal wares. Cooks, taverns, inns, and other craftsmen had shops all throughout the city. Between each section were civilian homes, and each section seemed not to permit anyone of a different race. The y'lenae and vaxros residents remained in their respective areas of sunlight and shadow. As the sun waned and the shadows drifted, so, too, did the crowds, though they were never permitted within the homestead areas of their opposing race.

Occasionally, a few villagers would slip into the wrong section, but the others seemed to pay them no mind. It was as if they didn't exist at all.

Neer watched them with curiosity, never before seeing such a city of such racial interaction. As far as she knew, all throughout Laeroth, every race segregated themselves from the others. Dreleds were the only people she knew of who could coexist with everyone.

Everyone, that is, except the humans, who claimed the peaceful shapeshifters to be the blood of Nizotl and banished them from Laeroth decades ago. She was glad that Gil had found his way to the Brotherhood and settled in Llyne with the others.

Observing the crowds, she noticed several people kneeling in the streets. They wore rags that were filthy with dirt and scrubbed the streets with wooden scrub brushes. Y'lenae villagers would step around them with a sneer or purposefully dirty up the street as they walked by.

"What are they doing?" she asked as Reiman came to her side. He peered out the window and surveyed the streets.

"They're cleaning," he remarked with a hidden smile.

She huffed with a playful, scolding glare. Returning her gaze to the window, she said, "I think they're slaves."

"It's possible. I'vasaar seems to be built on a system of hierarchy, much like any advanced civilization." He stepped to the table and removed his cloak. The filthy garment was carefully smoothed before being folded over the back of the chair. He leaned against it and turned to Neer. The cheerfulness of his eyes vanished when their eyes met. "It's the way of the world, Nerana," he warned. "I know you have pity for these people—we *all* do—but you mustn't—"

"*I* was a slave. For three years, my life was torture. We can't allow this. We have the power to—"

"To what? Destroy the city? Gather more enemies?" He exhaled a deep sigh. The chair scrubbed against the floor as he pulled it back and took his seat. With a glance to Neer, he motioned to the empty chair across the table.

She stole another glimpse of the slaves before reluctantly coming to his side. Sitting with her arms crossed, she gave her father a pressing look—one you'd find on a mother beckoning her mischievous child for an explanation.

To her surprise, her father smiled. He leaned back and slowly tapped his fingers against the table. "You've always been headstrong," he said. "Always willing to do whatever it took to help those in need."

She turned away, and her lips pursed together. "Kindness is a weakness," she stated. "I should've been wiser. Then, maybe so many people wouldn't have had to die." She paused. "Why didn't you teach me patience or understanding?"

He chuckled, and the disdain grew heavier in her eyes. "You severely underestimate your will, child. Even our most seasoned warriors couldn't tame your spirit." He paused as he recalled the memories. "Truth be told, when you first arrived at our gates, I wanted to confine that troubadour to the dungeons for bringing such a sickly, frail child into our midst. I told Gilbrich and the others that this wasn't a place for you, and that you'd be in much greater harm in our company." His smile became one of pride and reflection as he glanced at Neer. "Gilbrich told me that he had spoken to Loryk, and the boy—foolish as he was—wasn't an imbecile. He'd never have brought you to us had he believed you weren't worthy."

"He saved me," she said with reflection.

"That he did," Reiman agreed. "Do you remember the first thing you said when we were to send you to the orphanages in Styyr? It was the reason I allowed you to join our movement."

350

She thought for a moment, before silently shaking her head.

"You said, 'If you're this afraid of a little girl, then you're just as cowardly as the Order.'"

She scoffed with a laugh. "*That* made you reconsider my acceptance?"

"It wasn't *what* you said, but how you said it. There was fire in your eyes. You weren't afraid of the Order. You loathed them. *Hated* them. There you were, a frail skeleton of a child, staring up at five of the fiercest warriors known to man, yet you were unafraid. You felt challenged by our wit and strength.

"I saw something in you that I hadn't seen in anyone else, and I knew that this Brotherhood wouldn't break you. It was quite the opposite. *You* would strengthen *us*."

"So, I'm just a tool to use against the Order? That's all I am to you?"

"Don't start feeling sorry for yourself." With a mischievous grin, he teased, "If we could find another sorcerer, we'd trade you out in a minute."

Looking into his eyes, she was comforted by his smile, and a rush of peace overcame her. Neer was brought back to a time before the desert and loss, back when she and Reiman would sit at home, telling stories and talking all night.

For a moment, she was home, and the familiarity was a comfort she wouldn't waste. Staring into his eyes, her scrunched smile diluted the playful glare she cast at him. A vibrant smile brightened his face, and he boasted with laughter. Neer followed, and the room sang with their breathless chuckling.

They sat for an hour more, speaking of old memories and sharing stories over steaming mugs of tea. Their smiles never faded as they shifted from one topic to the next.

"Gods," she said with a deep exhale. "Feels like years since I've smiled."

He grinned. "Yes. Time surely has had its way with us, hasn't it?"

"I'll say. I'm hardly twenty-four, yet I feel damn near a hundred."

"Try *being* damn near one-hundred," he remarked with a laugh.

Neer shook her head with a smirk. Tracing the edge of her mug, she was quiet. Stumbling from one thought to the next, she finally asked, "Why did you leave the forest?"

He choked down his drink and remarked in evaesh, clearly caught off guard by her question. Speaking his common language was something he seldom did, mostly out of haste or by accident. Neer understood his surprise. This wasn't a topic he ever saw fit to engage. Even as a child, she would ask of his time in Nyn'Dira, or why he became the leader of a human rebellion, and his answer was always the same. *It is what fate arranged.*

This explanation no longer satisfied her, and now that they sat alone, sipping tea and surviving forbidden lands, she wanted to know. "Why did you leave?"

He lifted his chin in the way he always did in condemnation. She stared into his eyes, unafraid of his power. They were equals now. She couldn't be reprimanded like a child, and he knew it.

Turning aside, he broke their long gaze. "I suppose the time has come for you to understand why I allied myself with the humans. Or better more, why I defected from my own kind." He straightened in his seat and turned to her. His fingers clasped together, and he leaned closer, getting comfortable. "I was you," he explained, and she was puzzled. "Cast aside by my people for things beyond my control. I devoted my life to the cause — to fighting for what I felt was right and just — but my leaders were unrelenting in their persecution."

"What did you do?"

He looked into her eyes for a moment longer. "I was born during a time of great injustice. Sons were banished or murdered for the crimes of their fathers." She was quiet as he turned away. "I didn't choose to leave my people behind…They forced me to go. It wasn't until I came upon a human farm that I realized your people aren't as monstrous or twisted as we had believed.

"These farmers took me in, gave me work and a bed to lay in. I learned about your Divines and the Order of Saro and quickly discerned that our people weren't so different. We all fought for the misguided belief that the enemy is unworthy.

"I spent many years in your human lands, learning all that I could about your history and culture. Never in our time have the evae or humans come together to find the truth. But I did. Just one man could see that all faults lay within the apex of your civilization. The reason for all misunderstanding and segregation hailed from the High Priest."

"I'm sure the evae aren't as prized as you make them out to be."

"Certainly not. We are none without faults. There may never be peace between us. I cannot guarantee the outcome of our purpose, I can only drive it forward and hope that the consequences are worth the effort."

They backed away when the door creaked open. Neer hadn't realized how tense they had become as their conversation fell into heavier matters. Leaning back into her chair, she watched the others slowly filter into the room.

Aélla smiled and came to the table. "We have discussed the matter of the temple," she explained, "and we believe it would be best to find a middle ground with Aldír Nälevarta'e, the leader of this great city. If we can get him on our side then—"

"Hang on," Neer interrupted with her hand in the air. "Why are we banished from the temple in the first place? You're First Blood, right? Isn't it your right to enter the chambers of your ancestors?"

"It isn't that simple. The y'lenae use this temple, and the vaxros protect it. If we enter without consent it could lead to

353

another conflict. We could be killed, or worse, create war between our people."

"The klaet'il are slaughtering entire villages, and you're worried about a war over a temple? A temple we need to gain entry to in order to finish this damned quest!"

"Nerana," Reiman lightly scolded as her temper flared. She leaned back with a huff, and he turned to Aélla, furthering the conversation. "What do you suggest, Master Drimil?"

Aélla leaned forward onto the table. Her head fell, and her eyes closed. "We should offer our services in some way. Maybe spend time with the priests of the temple. Let them know that we aren't here with irreverence. If we can do this and gain their trust, then—"

Neer scoffed with a sour smile. "I understand you have to keep good and do what's right, but sometimes that isn't the best. These people could have us work like slaves for months and still regard us as enemies. How long do you plan to do this? What if we never gain their trust?"

"Well, I—"

"There is a war in the forest right now. Your people are dying. Avelloch could be dying. We don't have time to waste on gaining the trust of those who would rather see us kissing their feet than stepping into that temple." She stood and stepped closer. "We're sorcerers, Aélla. We have the power to make these people do what we want, either by fear or magic. We can get into that temple."

"I will not threaten these people into submission. Not over something as sacred and meaningful as their faith. We will find another way."

Neer glared. She wouldn't spend her time scrubbing the ground these people walked on. "Faith is a lie," Neer said with a hiss. "A delusion meant to keep the feeble-minded in line. If they allowed strangers into their *sacred* temple, the entire system would crumble. It would no longer be meant for the worthy if they allowed filthy, deranged, *wild* humans and evae into their doors." She paused with fury. "Nothing is going to change their minds. We can either play nice and allow the forest to burn, or we can do what needs to be done."

Aélla's jaw tensed as she glared. Everyone was silent, glancing between them. The orange glow of a fading sun caused the redness of their faces to brighten, giving them a fiercer, angrier glow.

Thallon carefully approached them. He flipped through a leather notebook and pressed his finger to a page littered with evaesh writing. "Sorry to interrupt, but I may have some relevant information that could help you navigate the temple."

While Neer held her furious gaze, Aélla softened her expression with a slow exhale. Closing her eyes, she composed herself and then focused on Thallon, waiting for him to explain.

He turned the notebook to her and slid his finger across the page. "I spoke with a local in the bathhouse. She was a priestess of the temple. It is a fascinating place. They worship Aenwyn and allow anyone in the upper ring of the city to enter and exit as they please."

"How does this help?" Aélla asked, her voice still wavering with affliction. Her eyes veered across the room, where Neer now stood by the window, overlooking the city and the slaves scrubbing the cobbles.

"The temple is located in the securest part of the city," Thallon explained. "The doors are never locked, but the temple is empty at night." Their eyes met. "If you or Neer were to teleport inside, gather the element, and return by morning, no one would be the wiser."

Aélla kindly grabbed the notebook and read through the scribbled notes. "We don't know where to look for the realm. If there are guards then—"

"It's a temple," he said with a chuckle. "There are no guards. And I know of this place. I've read about it in my studies. They say if you gift Aenwyn with your blood, the temple will open, and you may enter the realm."

The book closed with a loud slap as she passed it back to the scholar. With her hand on her forehead, she paced the room. "I cannot use my magic in such a way," she said. "To purposefully cause chaos or disorder would disrupt the balance."

"I'll do it." Neer said, peeling her gaze from the window and turning to the others. "I'll enter the temple and get the element."

"You mustn't use your magic for ill intent either," Aélla explained.

Neer scoffed with a slight laugh. "If ill intent keeps me alive, then it's what I'll have to do. Sometimes, the world forces us to make hard decisions."

"You always have a choice, Nerana. The path you take is yours to decide and no one else's."

Neer snatched the magical staff from its place against the wall and peered at the glowing crystals. Two of four were filled with swirling magical energy. They had been in the desert for months yet were only halfway through their journey.

"I'm doing this," she said, before turning to the others. "Do any of you disagree?"

No one spoke, though Aélla's hardened eyes were enough to express her concern. She never argued further, and with the silent approval from the others, Neer resolved to enter the temple at night and take the energy before sunrise.

While she gathered her things, Thallon collected a small sampling of Aélla's blood into a vial. He passed it to Neer and explained, "Most of these enchantments are unlocked through First Blood. Take this, in case you need it."

"Thanks." She placed the vial into her satchel and then turned to the others. Holding the staff, she gave them each a stiff nod, and with a final gaze to Aélla, who still had a disapproving look, she vanished from the room.

CHAPTER FORTY-THREE

ROCK
Nerana

"Beneath your soles lies the dust of the ancients, forgotten and withered by time. Naught but their energy remains."

– Fyet'muskar; tome of the elements

THE TEMPLE STOOD TALL AND PROUD atop a towering hillside. Footsteps pattered lightly against the aged stone steps as worshippers and the devout quietly left the sacred chambers.

They each wore robes of evergreen with four cords of white, orange, brown, and green tied at the waist. Y'lenae priests of the temple were the last to exit. Their white silk robes carried not a speck of discoloration or stain. Crowns of woven vines and twigs were placed atop their smoothly shaven heads.

Neer hid within a small pocket of trees and grass at the base of the stairs. She peered through the leaves, watching the last of the priests walk from the temple and make their way down the quiet streets.

She waited until the moons had risen and gifted the world with their soft, ambient glow, allowing her to better hide deep within the shadows.

Stepping from the brush, she approached the stairs. Hundreds of wide steps led to an open doorway at the center of the walls etched with beautiful, calligraphic designs. Enormous columns of cracked stone withstood the weight of the thick gabled roof.

Still weak from the jump that took her to the base of the temple, she mustered what energy she could and transported herself to the top of the stairs.

The rift was loud, tearing through the empty air. A bright rip formed from where she fell. The rippling magic rumbled like a roaring fire before collapsing in on itself and disappearing.

She rolled across the stone with a deep gasp as air escaped her lungs. Crawling forward, she coughed and wheezed with exhaustion. She rested on her knees and gazed up at the beautiful stone walls and ancient pillars surrounding the entryway.

Thick double doors were left open for anyone in the upper ring to enter and exit as they pleased. With a glance to the city below, she was relieved to find not a soul wandering the quiet streets as night blanketed the land with its cold embrace.

Firelight illuminated from each window, casting flickering light that danced throughout the streets in waves of orange. She could see far into the desert, past the walls of I'vasaar and across the ridges to the jungle bordering the western horizon.

Winds drifted through the air and set a deep chill in her bones. She crossed her arms and returned her attention to the temple as the soft glimmer of firelight grew within the doorway.

Clutching the hilt of her sword, she stood and walked carefully through the shadows. She peered into the temple to be sure it was empty and slipped inside. The air was warm and heavy with the sting of magic. Energy softly pricked her chest, beckoning her forward into a large open chamber.

The elongated hall was made entirely of beige marble stone. Not a crack or crevice marked the beautiful, polished walls and flooring. Pillars of sandstone lined the walls and bore the weight of a beautifully rounded arch ceiling.

Statues of different men and women in various poses rested between each of the pillars. In their hands were the stone-carved depictions of floating rocks, swirling water, raging fire, and empty air cupped in their palms like a ball.

Neer glanced through the room for what felt like the hundredth time before carefully approaching the statues. They were taller than vaxros, with traits that gave them both evaesh and human features. Their layered robes were long and covered their feet.

In the back center of the room, turned with her head facing up to the sky, was Numera, or as the evae called her, *Aenwyn*. She stood alone with her arms open wide and eyes closed. A skylight in the tall ceiling allowed moonlight to cast down upon her face.

Neer stepped to the statue and gently ran her fingers over the smooth stone. Staring at the magic staff, she laid it gently against the statue and then retrieved the vial of blood from her pack. She knelt before the Divine and closed her eyes. "Please let this work," she said before uncorking the vial and dripping the blood onto the stone.

The room was silent as she waited, watching the statue she had hoped would glow or shift. Seconds passed, but the glow never came. Not a movement in the wind or creak of the stone lifted the heavy silence.

She stared at the ground and wondered what to do. Thallon mentioned that gifting Aenwyn with your blood would allow you entry…Maybe she needed Neer's blood.

Neer removed her dagger from its sheath on her belt and placed the sharp edge of the blade into her palm. With a deep breath, she closed her eyes and pressed the blade to her skin.

As she prepared to slice her palm, a faint shuffling came from behind. Broken of her confidence, she turned quickly to the intruder. Staring into the darkness, she noticed the shimmer of pulsing blue light emitting from a nearby hall. She studied it for a moment, perplexed at the sudden appearance of light in the once dark corridors.

She turned back to grab the staff, and her heart sank when she realized it was gone. Panicked, she searched the empty room, never finding a trace of the weapon or person who stole it.

With another glance to her surroundings, her gaze set to the empty hall. She approached the doorway pressed against the wall before peering into the narrow passage. Sandstone walls were illuminated with a row of blue gemstones. Each gem glowed brighter than the last, pulsing like a wave moving deeper into the hall.

Neer stepped carefully into the corridor, keeping her dagger close to her chest. Her boots pressed softly against the polished floors as she stayed close to the wall.

Moving deeper into the long, lonesome hall, she spotted an empty doorway at its end.

She turned back with her weapon drawn at the sound of distant footsteps echoing from behind. They moved down the narrow hall, never becoming louder as they tapped in a constant, steady rhythm.

She waited, fingers tingling and chest still burning from her weakened magic, when suddenly, there was silence. Not a sound came from the hall, nor a shadow or intruder. Her fingers ached as she clutched her weapon.

Following the flow of the gemstones, she came to the doorway. The weight of magic was crushing. Every breath was a struggle as her energy was twisted and compressed.

She clutched her chest and peered through the doorway. Inside were glowing gems creating beautiful patterns that encircled Aélla's staff that hovered in the center of the room.

Neer stepped forward and was met with the rush of weightlessness from the absence of flooring. She leapt back and pressed against the wall. Carefully reaching forward, she attempted to transport the staff into her grasp, but the magic never burned or strengthened in her chest, and she realized she was absent of its power.

This was the realm of elements. The blood had worked. She looked around, searching for a way to retrieve the staff, but there was none. Whatever test she was given, she knew the answer would be found within the stone.

Sheathing her sword, she placed her hands to the walls and focused on her energy. Her magic grew heavy, converging with the deep, rumbling vibrations of the ancient walls. She could feel the life of the world moving through her. The spirit of Erolith whispered and spoke of tranquility and forgiveness, honor and peace.

Her limbs grew tired as she felt the force of stone compressing her soul. As her magic strengthened, cracks split across the walls. The fractures sent shockwaves through her. The pain was intense. Her body trembled and strength waned. But she couldn't stop. This was the only way.

With a scream, she forced her magic to be stronger, and the temple shifted and shook. Dust rained from the ceiling, and wide fissures split the solid stone. Every sharp rift sent pain through her. The density of her magic lifted for a moment, only to fall heavier as the temple pressed its weight against her.

Slowly, a stone platform slid out from beneath the doorway and extended into the empty room. It moved outward toward the staff, creating a narrow bridge. Neer could feel the rock and stone sliding into place as it shifted deep beneath her feet.

The chasm echoed and shook as the ceiling started to collapse. Large slabs of marble stone crashed to the ground from the main hall. Its vibration creaked against her stiff and tired bones.

With a pained cry, she backed away, and the weight of her magic was lifted. Tired and aching, she fell back and knelt to the ground. Breathing heavily, she fought to catch her breath as her throat burned, and her chest ached.

Her eyes shifted back to the room with the staff as the blue glowing stones slowly lost their luster. One by one, they darkened, trailing back to the entry. Once the lights had diminished, blue stones appeared along the edges of the narrow bridge.

Neer turned back, searching for another way out, but the corridor that once led to the main hall had been sealed with fallen rocks. Glancing to the bridge, she held her breath to repress her fear and stepped across.

The stone crumbled and cracked as she moved toward the staff. Approaching its end, she reached out to grab the weapon, but her hand moved through the empty air as the staff evaporated into mist.

A deep rumbling shook the temple. Loud grinding echoes came from all around as the walls shifted and creaked. She turned to run, but found the bridge led to darkness. The doorway had disappeared, and she was trapped, standing on a floating ledge, surrounded by endless darkness.

The air grew cold as she stared into the void. Her breathing was loud against the silence. Chills traveled up her arms and stood her hair on end.

She gasped as the ledge shifted and crumbled into dust beneath her feet, and she hurdled into the abyss. Cold winds became warm the further she fell, and light illuminated far below, growing brighter as she came nearer. It reflected against a deep pool lying at the base of a cave.

Neer held her breath and then crashed into the water. Coming to the surface, she looked upward to find the ceiling she fell from was solid and covered in stalactites. She looked around in a panic, wondering where she had wound up. Her eyes fell to flowing streams of light moving through the water, and she followed their path, which led her to a large open chamber covered in pulsing blue gems.

They illuminated along the walls just as they had in the temple. Several paths of gemstones came together around a pile of crumbled stone. The large pieces of debris were smoothly carved on their outer edges, revealing the fallen structure to be a statue.

Pulling herself onto the rocky shore, she stumbled over mossy rocks and sharp stone fragments. Searching through the fallen rocks, she noticed the glowing crystals of Aélla's staff buried within the crumbled sculpture.

Closing her eyes, she placed her hands to the large debris and entangled her magic with the stone. Beneath the surface of loose rocks and debris, she felt something solid. It wasn't part of the statue. It had been buried, barricaded and concealed. Harnessing the rough, strong energy, she crushed the debris lying beneath her palms.

Magic sliced through its surface and crumbled it to dust, but it was unbearably heavy. Every breath was a deep draw, burning her throat and putting an ache in her muscles.

As the crumbled stone became a thick pile of dust, Neer released her hold and fell back. Closing her eyes, she paused to rest. When her eyes fell upon the staff, she quickly gathered it into her hands. Examining the crystals, she found one to be missing.

Clouds of grey puffed into the air as she dug for the crystal. She choked on the haze and continued searching, until her fingers touched against a smooth, shaped stone.

Neer carefully cleared the dirt to find the face of a large statue staring up at her. The beautiful woman had closed eyes and a soft smile, relaxed appearance, and Neer realized it was a statue of Numera. She touched Numera's cheek, wondering if this was all an illusion, or if fate had intervened. Neer was gifted the prophecy of this journey by a woman she believed to be the Numera, and now she stood at her crumbled and broken statue in the midst of a magical realm.

"What's happening?" Neer asked. "Why have you led me here?"

"*Miórën, nek'valör…*"

A voice echoed through the chamber. She recognized it from long ago, during her time in Mange, when this very goddess approached her beneath a crumbled and dying Tree.

"A sorceress walks in our midst. *Vákalá.* Trembling. Fearful." The woman's voice echoed through Neer's mind. It overlapped with the voices of all those she had lost.

The sound of Loryk singing his most famed song, *Vaeda,* played over the whisper of her mother's voice. Reiman's angered sigh and his fatherly reprimand as she failed once again at her youthful training. Klaud's apology as he stole the arun in the cave. Avelloch's harsh voice as he told her to *trust no one.* Her childhood friends' laughter, and the haunting screams of those who were cut down with her parents.

She clutched her ears, trying to rid herself of the haunting noises. But they continued, splitting her mind into fragments of rage, confusion, regret, and denial. She begged for the woman to stop. For the visions and illusions of this cave to cease. But the realm was unforgiving, and the prophecy continued. The eyes of the statue began to glow, and the voices of the others grew louder.

The light brightened and consumed the cave with whiteness, and then suddenly, there was silence. Neer closed her eyes. She couldn't feel. Her body was weightless. Nothing existed but the prophecy as it echoed softly before disappearing completely.

"Stay close to the light, or all shall end."

CHAPTER FORTY-FOUR

DISOBEY

"We watch from above the ants who build and destroy. For centuries they march, searching endlessly for a purpose they'll never come to find."

– Words of the Triandal

NEER CLUTCHED THE STAFF AND held her eyes shut. Echoes of the soft voice replayed in her mind as the light faded, and the world fell dark and cold. Magic weighed her chest with a deep pull of sorrow and strength. The air was heavy and warm. Smooth stone rested beneath her knees. Slowly, she opened her eyes and stared up at the statue of Numera.

She turned sharply to search her surroundings. Deep cracks crawled across the marble walls and polished floors of the temple of I'vasaar. Moonlight filtered into the chamber through the large open doorway. The world was quiet, and she sat alone, wondering what had happened and how she had returned to Aragoth.

Her gaze shifted to the staff still clutched in her aching hands. She lifted it closer to inspect a brown glowing crystal. Three of the four swirled with magic, and she was anxious to retrieve the fourth. Anxious to get home and save the others from the war to come.

The thought of war shifted her thoughts to Avelloch, and in a panic, she reached for his sword on her side. She sighed with relief, glad to find it tucked safely into the scabbard on her belt.

Soft chimes of pattering footsteps echoed into the chamber, and shadows appeared at the entrance of the temple. Too exhausted to stand, she remained in her place as Aldír Nälevarta'e came into view. He walked alongside two vaxros warriors wearing colorful robes with white scapulars. Four cords with colors representing the four elements were tied at each of their waists.

While one carried a steel spear, the other held a small blow dart. Neer sat taller and reached for her sword as their shadow engulfed her in darkness. A dart was swiftly released in her direction and sank into her neck. She screamed as the sharp sting of electricity erupting through her, and her body became stiff and rigid. She collapsed to the ground, trembling with convulsions.

As the current slowly dwindled, she was lifted from the ground and tossed over a warrior's shoulder like a sack of waste. Aélla's staff lay on the temple floor as she was carried outside. The second vaxros lifted it from the ground and inspected the glimmering crystals. He secured it onto his back before following the others down the hundreds of ancient temple steps.

The night air was cold as they marched her through the upper city. Villagers crowded the main square where Nälevarta'e instructed the vaxros guards to drop Neer on the street. She winced and groaned as she was thrown against the cobbles.

Chaos disrupted the tranquility of night. The villagers hissed and spat at her, raised their torches and tossed excrement and rotten food as she lay motionless, too weak to fight.

Aldír Nälevarta'e raised his arms to quiet the raging crowds. He turned to Neer with condemning eyes and then lifted Aélla's staff into the air. The villagers gasped and wailed. Some fell to their knees sobbing, while others began shouting with rage.

Neer covered her face as more filth smacked against her skin. The taste of blood pricked her tongue when a rock cut deep into her lip. She winced as a guard grabbed her by the hair and pulled her forward onto all fours. Still on her knees, she faced the dirt, forced to crane her neck as the second guard held his axe high above his head.

The aldír spoke to the angry crowd while the guards waited. Neer closed her eyes. She couldn't teleport while being held, not without taking this guard with her and risking both of their lives. Her magic was too weak to transport without injury.

The harrowing thoughts of death were put to ease as the crowd split and Aélla pushed her way through with Y'ven. She glanced at Neer, and her eyes widened in horror. The guards placed their spears to Aélla as she stepped to Neer. Her lip twitched, and she looked at the men twice her size. "What are you doing?" she demanded. "Why is she your captive?"

Y'ven translated between Aélla and the aldír. "She has disobeyed a direct order," the aldír demanded. "The temple is in peril. This cannot go without punishment!"

The aldír glared as he awaited her response. Aélla stepped closer, taking thoughtful strides as she bridged the gap between them. Their anger never faltered.

Never once did she show a sign of weakness or fear as they stood close together. Fury lingered in her eyes. "You have disregarded the sanctity of my pilgrimage," she said. "You have broken the treaty which allows me passage to each of the realms. And now you threaten my ally with death."

The aldír's voice cut like glass as he spoke in harsh phrases. Y'ven stammered for a moment, unable to infer what exactly the aldír had said.

With her fury came impatience, and Aélla placed her hand on the aldír's forehead. In the same motion, she lifted her arm to the vaxros charging from behind. A blast of energy pushed them back and allowed her the time to focus on the magic she entwisted with their leader.

Energy fizzled through them, becoming warm and sting-ing. As it faded, she removed her hand, and glared hatefully into his eyes. "Now you speak to *me*," she demanded in his native language.

Behind the aldír's glare was confusion and anger. "What have you done?" he asked curtly. "You've cursed me! You savage evae are all blinded by rage and power!" He trembled before calling out for his guards. "Place her with the other! I want both of their heads on spikes!"

As the guards stepped closer, Aélla lifted her hand in their direction behind her. Her eyes remained on the aldír as the vaxros began to choke and wheeze. They clawed at their throats, unable to take full breaths.

The leader transcended from anger to panic as he glanced between the guards and the woman stealing their lives.

"Why have you refused our passage?" Aélla asked. "Why do you threaten Nerana?"

Thallon stepped through the quiet, fearful crowd. He gasped and took half a step forward. "Aélla…" His words were careful and timid as he attempted to calm her. "Just take it easy, all right? You can't do this."

"Tell me," she demanded of the leader. Her fingers curled into a half fist, and the vaxros fell to their knees. She paid no mind to Thallon. Her gaze was set to the aldír.

Taking half a step back, the leader trembled with rage and uncertainty. "It is sacrilege to enter the realm! We all felt the tremors as she broke the barrier between this plane and the next! The temple will fade to ruins! It's been defiled and dis-graced!" He paused. "Magical blood will doom us all!"

"Magical blood created this temple!"

"We have survived in this arid wasteland because of our devotion to Aenwyn! We sacrifice at her altar, and she gifts us with life and a way of survival! To desecrate her gifts by entering her sacred realm is an outrage! She will seek punish-ment for this! The temple has already begun to crack and wane!" He pointed at Neer. "This heretic must seek pen-ance!" The village cheered and called for her head.

"The realms are meant to be entered," Aélla said with a voice cold as ice. "There is no retribution for following the path laid out by those far wiser and greater than you or I will ever be."

"Look at the world, Master Drimil! Magic has destroyed it all! There is no hope left in the blood of sorcerers! It all be-longs to the Great Overseers! The sun-bloods and ancients have made this known! The great realms are meant for our *protection*—not our intrusion!"

Aélla glanced at the crowd as they shouted in agreement. They were fools, deluded by their own twisted faith. Neer was right in her judgement. He'd have never allowed them into the temple or realm, and nor would they allow Neer to leave with her life.

But neither would Aélla allow them to take it.

Closing her eyes, she released her grip on the vaxros, and they fell forward, hacking while they caught their breath. She lifted her eyes to the aldír, and he took a timid step back.

The staff disappeared from his grip and came instantly into her hand. She looked down to the leader with the same condemnation he gave Neer moments before. "There will be no bloodshed," she said. "You will release her, and we will leave this city unharmed."

As she stepped to Neer and reached for her hand, the aldír nodded silently to his guards. Their axes lifted high into the air, ready to strike down their intruders, when a violent screech came from the sky.

Everyone turned upward as black shadows raced over-head. Fires erupted from the west, sending ash and smoke into the cold night air. Screams and panicked cries overlapped as they grew louder, converging into an influx of shrieks and cries echoing through the city.

Footsteps rumbled the ground as stampedes drove past. Aélla grabbed Neer, and with the help of Reiman, they pulled her away from the chaos overtaking the streets.

Warriors with axes and war hammers pushed through their much smaller neighbors, heading west, toward the apex of the chaos.

Shrieks sounded from the sky as the shadows moved overhead, and the spine-chilling sounds vibrated through the cold air as klaet'il attacked from above.

CHAPTER FORTY-FIVE

FALLEN LIGHT

LOUD, ANGRY SHRIEKS CAME FROM above. Shadows stalked the village as two dozen glynfir with klaet'il riders on their backs invaded the skies. The streets trembled as people raced to their homes, searching for safety.

Klaet'il warriors shouted battle cries before another explosion rocked the city. Neer watched them from below as they roamed the skies. Her knuckles cracked as she gripped her sword tightly. She glanced at Reiman who stood beside her, leering at the intruders that struck upon their unsuspecting victims.

Flames soared through the night sky like a collection of shooting stars as the klaet'il rained fiery arrows from above. Neer inhaled a deep breath and expelled a powerful blast from her palms. Her magic ripped through the air, snapping through the arrows.

The glynfir reared and screamed when Neer's shockwave pushed them off course.

Reiman pulled her aside while Aélla shielded them with a barrier. Unlit arrows were released in their direction, and Aélla winced each time her magic was struck. White cracks fragmented her invisible barrier like spiderwebs, growing thicker with every impact.

Screams filled the air, and villagers lay bleeding, trampled in the stampede.

Neer stumbled aside as an explosion rumbled the air. The buildings shook, and the ground quaked. A cloud of black smoke rose from the east before the dark mist evaporated into the dark sky.

As Aélla's barrier shattered, she fell to her knees with a gasp.

"Move!" Neer shouted, grabbing Aélla and teleporting back.

They landed several yards away and rolled across the ashen cobbles of a narrow alley. Bricks fell from the walls, and smoke rose from the place they once stood. Neer crawled to her feet, searching for Reiman.

Another explosion caused more bricks and dust to crumble from the buildings. Neer lifted her arms to shield herself from the falling debris and peered through the haze of ash and smoke.

"Reiman!" she called, before choking on the fog.

Arrows fell from above, striking close to her position. The shadowy figure of a glynfir flew above the alley, and she ducked into the shadows, watching as arrows struck against the cobbles and snapped in half.

Breathing heavily, she pushed herself into view and stood below the glynfir as it hovered above. The klaet'il rider spoke viciously to Aélla, who stood with the magic staff in hand. Her armor and cloak were singed and torn. Ash and blood crawled across her face and arms. A deep scowl twisted her face with a depth of fury Neer had never seen. She was frightening, and the klaet'il above seemed to enjoy the challenge.

Neer waited, watching as Aélla glared up to the man taunting her. The glynfir's long wings beat in a steady rhythm, hovering in place.

With a snarl, Aélla lifted the staff toward the glynfir, and the crystals, along with her eyes, brightened with light. Winds swirled around her, creating a shallow vortex that strengthened as she inhaled a deep breath.

Neer leapt back when Aélla thrust the staff toward the klaet'il. The wind tunnel followed, and the glynfir screeched, kicking as it fought against the winds. The klaet'il rider growled and struggled to stay atop his mount.

Holding steady, Aélla followed as the animal fought to escape. Its wings beat as it swiped its long neck from left to right, trying desperately to keep itself steady. The rider's bow fell from his grip and spun through the air before crashing against a building. His voice was demanding as he shouted at the animal.

Focused on the glynfir, whose rider was struggling to stay upon the saddle, Neer didn't notice when another klaet'il warrior spotted her in the crowd. The female warrior pulled back an arrow and released it toward the unsuspecting human.

The arrow darted through the sky, moving quickly toward Neer's spine. As it came closer, she was thrown aside and shadowed by a shield. Lost for breath from the impact, her eyes met with Thallon's as he curled around her with his shield in the air. He tensed as the arrow struck against its steel face and cracked.

"You all right?" Thallon asked.

With a subtle nod, she straightened and then turned to Aélla when the magic slowly dwindled from her staff. The glynfir unleashed a menacing shriek and flew away as his rider plummeted to the ground.

Neer stepped to the edge of the alley as the hordes pushed through the streets. Thallon pulled her back and lifted his shield as four vaxros soldiers hurried past, though he didn't need to. She was far enough from their stampede to not be injured. Neer pulled herself from his arms and watched as the vaxros pushed through the y'lenae, heading to taller homes.

Climbing to the flat roofs, they positioned themselves along the edges of the walls and heaved their spears into the air.

A glynfir screeched when it was struck deep in the chest, and its wings flailed as it hurtled to the ground. Its rider fell from the saddle, crashing hard against the cobbles with a bone-shattering smack. His skull opened on impact, spewing blood and brain into the street.

High above, a klaet'il man pulled the reins of his flyer hard to the left, and the glynfir spun with a quick twist to dodge several arrows. As it leveled out, its warrior heaved a dark orb at the roof.

As the vaxros tossed their spears into the air, the orb struck at their feet. Thick glass shattered, and black smoke shrouded them in a foggy haze.

Trapped within the mist, the warriors began to choke. Their spears dropped to the ground as they collapsed to their knees. Gargled breaths obstructed their lungs. Fingernails broke, and flesh was torn from their necks as they clawed at their throats. Their eyes reddened as blood dripped from their noses, lips, and ears.

"Neer! Aélla," Thallon urged. "We have to go!"

They ran from the alley as dozens of klaet'il flew overhead. Panicked villagers packed the streets as arrows and spears filled the skies. Another explosion of black smoke erupted from a watchtower to the north.

"I see Y'ven!" Thallon exclaimed.

Pushing through the crowds, they stood by their companion. He heaved a spear, and his weapon tore through the leathered wing of a glynfir. The creature screeched and fell off rhythm, nearly bucking its rider from their saddle. Dru cast fire in its direction and set the stirrups ablaze.

An ear-shattering screech vibrated the air as another glynfir landed on the black-hazed roof. The fog cleared, and they could see that not a soul was left standing. The vaxros warriors' bodies were leaning over the edges of the roof as they had tried to escape the poison. They lay unblinking and immobile, blood still dripping from their bodies and cascading down the edges of the home.

The glynfir's talons clawed deep into the back of a warrior leaning over the wall. Sharp teeth were exposed as the glynfir reared its head, sending another vicious scream into the air. It lifted the warrior like a doll and flung him into the streets. His large body crushed several fleeing residents, landing with a bone-crunching thud. The klaet'il sat on the saddle and watched the people below. A black orb in hand, he held a sinister smile as they scrambled.

The twisted grin slid further up his face, and the orb was hurled overhead to the street. His menacing eyes watched as it fell further, getting closer to the stampede of terrified villagers.

It disappeared beneath the sea of nameless faces, and the man's smile slowly began to fade. Neer watched him with fury, apporting the orb into her grasp and throwing it back at the warrior. The glass orb shattered, striking the wall just beneath the glynfir's talons.

The flyer drew back with a shriek as black smoke quickly surrounded them. Its large wings beat as it flew off, spreading the poisonous cloud through the air. The shadow of a vaxros warrior, gasping on obstructed breaths, became visible through the fresh smog as he attempted to sneak up behind the klaet'il on the rooftop.

As another black orb fell from the sky, Neer pushed it away with a pulse of energy. It flung high into the air and came back down in another part of the city. People screamed as black smoke rose above the buildings.

Several more were tossed in her direction, and she was lost, struggling over what to do and how to survive without killing others. As the orbs fell closer, she started to panic.

Her eyes darted through the village and then landed upon a figure perched atop a roof. He sat on a large glynfir, its leathered skin was black as slate with bright red warpaint staining its face and wings. The man mounted onto the saddle watched the massacre below, devoid of expression or pride. His dark eyes were just as empty as she remembered, and the sudden recognition of his bleak, emotionless gaze stole her breath.

He was the Nasir.

"Nerana!"

She turned as Reiman called out to her and then tackled her aside. Pulling her close, he hovered over her, shielding her from the impact of the orb. She closed her eyes, and glass exploded mid-air. Reiman was tense, only for a moment, before releasing his hold and turning upward toward the eruption.

Neer followed his gaze and stared in shock as dark mist surrounded a barrier protecting them. Standing within the small dome were Thallon, Y'ven, and Dru, along with several vaxros warriors and two terrified y'lenae. Aélla sank to her knees in the center of the barrier. Her arms were outstretched to the sky as she struggled to maintain the shield.

She wailed when several orbs were shattered around her magic, thickening the black smog around them. Drenched in sweat, she forced herself to retain the barrier as it began to crack and discolor along the bottom edges.

Reiman stood with Y'ven across the dome, and they peered through the rising mist, enraged as the busy street, once full of innocent civilians, was now quiet. Dead bodies lay in droves. Blood spilled from every orifice, creating deep rivers of crimson, soaking through into the cobbles.

Neer stepped closer to overlook the destruction, when she realized something odd. "They're all vaxros," she stated.

Everyone glanced at each other before peering into the streets. The y'lenae must've escaped in the dense fog, as the fresh bodies oozing with blood were all vaxros victims.

Y'ven growled and tightened his grip on his battle axe. The others recoiled as he unleashed a hellish scream, tearing through the air and vibrating loudly within the confined space.

Dru ducked within Neer's hair and watched his rage unleash.

The calm mist swirled when the klaet'il surrounded the barrier. Sharp talons sank deep into the flesh of the deceased as the glynfir landed atop the bodies. A red flyer, with a left eye that had been cut from lid to lid, leaving it white and unable to see, perched on the street nearby.

Neer stood taller, recognizing the woman from their imprisonment in the vaxros camps long ago. Her glowing green eyes were evidence of the magical energy burning inside her, waiting to be released. Chills ran down Neer's spine as she imagined fighting such a fierce and powerful warrior.

Thallon glared at the woman. "Ithronél," he hissed.

Blood squished beneath her boots as she approached the barrier. Aélla breathed heavily, watching the klaet'il through falling, tired eyes. Her arms shook and body trembled with exhaustion and pain.

Ithronél's thin lips pulled into a sinister grin. She took two measured steps back, staring at Aélla. Her green eyes glistened as she lifted her arms and thrust them forward. The fires burning in the streets followed her movement and spun together into a raging vortex of heat and flames.

Neer leapt forward and expelled her magic to fortify the barrier. She screamed in pain as the fires crashed against the invisible dome. Smoke and flames tore through the air in every direction as Ithronél continued with her assault.

Neer sank to her knees. Burning pain gripped her nerves, and her energy was scorched. Sweat soaked through her clothes and slid down her face. Her lips curled to expose her gritted teeth as she held onto her energy, not allowing it to fade.

She closed her eyes, pushing through the agony as strong fires pummeled against the barrier and sprayed through the city. As her magic weakened, she leaned forward, gasping for breath.

Aélla rose to her feet while Neer struggled to maintain the thinning barrier. The weight of Ithronél's energy was crushing, and she depleted herself to block its strength.

Aélla held her magic staff and lifted her arms outward into a wide circle, before meeting them together at her chest. Turning to Neer, she met her gaze and gave a confident nod.

Falling weaker as the energy burned through her veins, Neer exhaled a fearful breath and let go of her magic.

A wave of scorching heat moved past as the barrier disappeared, and Aélla stumbled back while lifting her staff toward the flames. Wisping tendrils of heat became shallower as they met the weapon. Veins swelled and muscles tensed in Aélla's neck. Her boots slid back, pushed by the weight of Ithronél's magic.

A coolness filled the air when the heat and flames suddenly vanished. Through deep breaths and a chilling growl, Aélla stepped forward. Her deadly eyes set upon Ithronél, and with a furious scream, she thrust the staff forward, expelling the energy back toward its caster.

Hot magic erupted from her staff, and waves of furious heat moved through the scorched streets.

Ithronél leapt into an alley while her glynfir soared into the sky. Its tail caught the heat of Aélla's fire and rage. The pummel of flames slowly vanished as her magic depleted. Smoke and embers settled over the ashen city where bodies of the weak and deceased lay scorched and blackened. Buildings and homes were left half standing in the wake of such destruction.

Aélla sank to her knees and caught her breath. Redness covered her skin, and sweat dripped from her temples. She closed her eyes and knelt atop the ashes.

Boots crunched over piles of bodies as the klaet'il raced through the streets. Neer grabbed her sword and stood with her back to Reiman, watching as the raging warriors came forward.

The first klaet'il approached Neer and swiped at her face. She leaned aside to evade the hit and clipped his shoulder. He struck again at her head, but with a swipe upward, her sword plunged into his gut. Entrails and blood fell like a waterfall from his abdomen. She tore her blade from his body and kicked him aside.

Neer lifted her sword as another warrior lunged forward. He raised his weapon before coming to a sudden stop when a blade ripped through his chest. Reiman withdrew his weapon and ducked beneath a blade as it swiped at him from behind. Moving with perfect precision and grace, Reiman danced around the klaet'il. Sparks ignited as their blades slid together.

The warrior gasped in sudden agony as their dance ended. Reiman stared into his eyes with his dagger sunk deep into his gut.

Blood sprayed as the weapon was snatched from his flesh, and Reiman turned swiftly around, plunging his dagger, blade to hilt, into the face of a klaet'il approaching from behind. Neer watched in amazement as he flowed through the warriors like water, anticipating their movements and attacks before they ever made them.

He kicked the warrior back and slashed his sword, which he held in his right hand, to the left, forcing the next warrior back.

Neer returned to his side to protect him from behind. She eyed the fight as klaet'il ripped through the streets. Blood and entrails painted the city in a shade of dark crimson, filling the air with red mist.

As the pressure of his stance shifted, Neer ducked beneath the heave of his sword. He struck down a klaet'il warrior to her left, creating a split that opened their stomach. With a hard kick, Reiman pushed the klaet'il back and resumed his offensive posture with Neer at his back.

Nearly two dozen klaet'il surrounded the group. Their flyers were perched atop the roofs, watching with hungry eyes as their riders attacked from below.

Neer's eyes averted to Thallon as he fell to his knees with a loud cry when his shoulder was slashed.

The klaet'il warrior standing above him lifted her sword, and he swiped the edge of his shield into her leg. Her shin cracked before she fell to her knees. With a hard push, he smashed against her face with his steel shield.

She fell back, blood spilling from her broken nose, and he crawled over her. The wound on his arm tore as he lifted the shield above her face, and the klaet'il slipped a hidden dagger from the holster on her side.

As her blade moved closer to his ribs, Neer apported the weapon into her grasp. The klaet'il's empty fist smacked against Thallon's side, and his shield sank into her skull. Blood sprayed across his face as he shouted with anger.

Y'ven stood with three vaxros warriors, fighting the klaet'il. Dru hovered above him, sending waves of heat and flame that set the klaet'il ablaze. A glynfir shrieked, and at the command of its mounted rider, dove from the roof toward the faeth.

Dru continued with her assault, focusing heavily on another klaet'il dodging each of her attempts. Y'ven sank his axe into the skull of an evae and turned to the glynfir ready to devour Dru.

With a growl, Y'ven snatched her from the air and swung his axe upward, slashing into the beast beneath its jaw. The jolt caused the glynfir to flip backward. Its large talons scratched the air as it fought desperately to steady itself.

Its thick wings smashed into two klaet'il on the street and knocked them back. The vaxros warriors, who had huddled beneath Aélla's barrier, were quick to attack while the evae were prone and defenseless. Their weapons smashed against the chests and skulls of the klaet'il, before they, too, were attacked from behind.

Neer turned back and slashed her weapon at two charging klaet'il. Her side was slit as the edge of a sword drew across her skin. With a pained grunt, she plunged her weapon into the chest of her attacker while his companion aimed at Reiman.

As Reiman swung for his head, the klaet'il ducked and jabbed his sword upward toward Reiman's groin. Before the weapon could slice into his skin, Neer reached out and stole his sword with her magic and then sank it between his ribs. His bones crunched as she twisted the blade.

Aélla stood across the street, spinning her wooden staff as she danced around two klaet'il fighters. They hissed and smiled as she evaded their attacks. With a quick swipe, her staff cracked against the skull of the warrior to her right. He stumbled aside in a daze, blood dripping from the incision above his ear.

She turned to defend against the man to her left, when his blade pressed against her throat. Her angry eyes set upon his, and his lips pulled into a sinister smile.

"You cannot kill me," the klaet'il remarked. He spoke a variation of evaesh that was slightly different from her own but was one she understood. "It is not your way." Her glare deepened, and he chuckled. "We kill this village. We slaughter these people…Yet you fight with a staff." His maniacal laughter echoed above the sounds of clashing steel. "This is why the world is better without you. This is why we are *all* better without you." He pressed the blade firmer against her neck, and she stiffened, never fading from her anger or eye contact. "You are *weak*. Your brother was *weak*. Your father —
"

His words were silenced when she lifted her hands and thrust him back with a powerful blast of energy. Stone crumbled beneath his body as he smashed into a wall. His brain spilled from the split in his skull like hot porridge.

Her lip twitched, and a tear fell from her eye. Tight fists were held at her sides as she stared at the man she killed.

A dark shadow overcame the street as the black glynfir swooped down from the rooftop. The creature landed on top of the bodies, and the Nasir leapt from the saddle, bolstering with confidence. He marched over the scattered corpses without a glance to the chaos around him. Faces and bones were crushed beneath his weight, and his long black cloak dragged over their burnt, ashen bodies. The sharp blue of his sunken eyes bore into Aélla's as he approached her and stood with deadly affliction. The mark across his temple was prominent against his remarkably pale skin.

"Why are you doing this?" Aélla asked, another tear slid down her cheek, betraying her feigned confidence. Her voice was drowned by the clashing of steel and cries of the fallen.

Neer plunged her sword into the chest of a klaet'il warrior and then caught a glimpse of the Nasir as he stood before Aélla. A black crystal was held behind his back as he looked into her tear-filled eyes. It wasn't like the black orbs that poisoned the village. It was something else. Neer spied it for a moment longer, when it started to glow.

As she reached out to apport the crystal, Ithronél slashed into her forearm. She withdrew with a scream, and the klaet'il warrior lunged at her chest. Reiman pulled Neer back while Y'ven swung his battle axe at Ithronél.

The klaet'il nimbly evaded his attack with a quick flip backward. Landing atop the bodies, she glanced at the Nasir with a smile. Everyone turned as he clutched Aélla's arm, and they disappeared into a cloud of smoke.

CHAPTER FORTY-SIX

TEARS OF NUMERA
Nerana

THE DARK MIST EVAPORATED INTO the air. A soft breeze passed with the scent of blood and smoke. Neer turned sharply to Ithronél as the klaet'il called for her glynfir. The large, one-eyed beast soared through the sky, prompting the others to take flight. Shadows darkened the sky where the winged beasts soared above in wide circles.

Neer charged forward, blood splattering beneath her boots as she approached the klaet'il with her sword drawn. The glynfir landed between them, striking its jaws in her direction. She vanished as its teeth snapped and then appeared behind Ithronél.

The klaet'il turned and lifted her weapon to block Neer's attack. Their steel clashed, and Neer glared hatefully while Ithronél stood with a confident smirk. With a hand hidden behind her back, Ithronél twisted her fingers and wrist.

Neer's glare faltered when her blood became hot. Beads of sweat formed along her brow, and boiling agony contracted her limbs, shriveling her organs with scorching heat. She stumbled back as steam seeped through her pores. The blood oozing from the slash on her arm bubbled like water in a hot cauldron, and she unleashed a deafening shriek. Pain blazed through her like a raging fire.

The one-eyed glynfir stomped its feet as Reiman and Y'ven darted closer. Its large wings created a dark barrier, blocking the street. Klaet'il shouted as they charged the vaxros and evae, their weapons colliding against iron and steel as Y'ven and Reiman fought against the horde.

Thallon slipped between the shadows and ducked into an alley. Darting through an empty home, he climbed up to the roof and looked down over the chaos below. Three vaxros warriors fought against six klaet'il to the west, while his allies stood together in their battle closer to Neer.

He loaded a bolt into his crossbow and held it steady. "Come on…," he begged, staring down the sights. With a watchful eye, he waited for the glynfir to lower its wing and reveal Ithronél, standing behind it. Seconds passed, and the glynfir was motionless in its place. Thallon pulled the trigger, and the bolt released with a faint click.

Thallon grimaced when the glynfir shrieked and lifted its wings as the bolt plunged into its arm. Dark blue blood spilled from its injury, and it screeched and stomped with fury. Neer collapsed to the ground, unmoving, as Ithronél released her hold when her flyer stumbled back and pushed her aside.

Thallon released another bolt that grazed Ithronél's shoulder. She staggered and touched the shallow incision, then clutched her hand into a hard fist. Her eyes moved to the east where Thallon stood atop the roof. He released another bolt, and with a quick swipe of her blade, she knocked it off course.

Glaring at the man that attacked her, she released a menacing growl and lifted her palm in his direction, sending smoke and ash spinning through the air in a vortex to pummel the rooftop. Thallon stumbled back, fighting against the weak current of the winds, and ducked behind the edge of the roof.

Neer curled on top of the ground, gasping for breath. The burning in her veins had reduced to a low simmering heat. Her muscles were rigid and hard to move, and she reached shakily for her sword, just out of reach.

Ithronél stepped aside, and the winds ceased. With a disgusted glare to Neer, she climbed onto the saddle of her glynfir, and with a final glance to the city, she took flight. Thallon released several bolts at the quick moving glynfir, each of them gliding past a mere hair's breadth from its leathered hide.

Y'ven pulled Dru and Reiman aside as the remaining glynfir swooped down from the sky. The klaet'il cheered and shouted, leaping onto their mounts and trailing behind Ithronél.

As they departed into the sky, the city was quiet with ashes and ghosts. Blood coursed through the streets, like rivers of crimson, staining the cobbles and splashing over soot-covered bodies.

Heavy footsteps sounded over Thallon's panting breaths as he raced from the home and chased after the disappearing klaet'il. He stood in the street and released several bolts. As each of them soared through the sky, far from the warriors for which they were aimed, he dropped his arms and unleashed a deep, furious scream. His face was red, and veins swelled in his neck.

"You bastards!" he shouted. "What have you done!"

Y'ven stood with Reiman and a lone vaxros warrior in the midst of ash and smoke. Their eyes were heavy with grief and exhaustion, and their bodies were painted with different shades of blood.

A soft cry came from the rubble, and Reiman lifted his gaze to Neer. The color washed from his face as he ran to her side. Ash swirled in a grey cloud at his knees as he knelt and carefully pulled her into his arms. Her skin was blistered and shriveled with internal burns. She trembled and shook from the pain.

"You did well," he said. "Just rest. You did well."

A tear dripped from her eye as she met his gaze. The hot liquid was cold against her skin, sliding through the filth along her cheek. "I'm…sorry…" she said. "I…f-failed."

"You will not die here," he said. "I will not allow it."

Her heavy, half-opened eyes peered to the right where a bright glow hovered nearby, and she smiled as Dru came to her side. The faeth withheld heavy tears, touching Neer's cheek. Footsteps shuffled as Thallon broke through the crowd gathered around Neer. His eyes widened with sadness and rage, and with a vicious snarl, he turned away and exhaled a quick, angry breath. He wiped his face to repress his emotions.

Glancing through the wreckage, his eyes paused on the temple towering over the smoldering streets. He stepped closer in deep thought and said, "I think we can save her."

Reiman stated, "Now is no time for anecdotes or —"

"The temple!" Thallon remarked. "It's said to be a place of great healing. The waters of Aenwyn can restore any ailments. It can cure her."

Reiman agreed. Turning to Y'ven, he said, "Can you carry her to the temple? Thallon and I will escort you. If we're to come into trouble, you carry on. We'll stay behind and fight."

With a nod, Y'ven carefully pulled Neer into his arms and carried her though the streets. The vaxros warrior who fought alongside them marched ahead and blocked their path. Y'ven growled with fury. Blood drained from the slash across his forehead, giving him a fiercer, more intimidating appearance.

"Worry about your people," Y'ven remarked, "and I will worry about mine."

The warrior slowly lost his glare. With a glance to the others, who stood ready to fight, he stepped aside and allowed them to pass.

Y'ven and the others ascended the temple stairs, which were cracked and uneven from Neer's time in the realm. Y'ven peered into the dark entry before stepping inside.

Thallon gripped his aching chest as he led them down a hall to the left. They passed by several doorways and open corridors before coming to a large room with a glowing pool. The water's reflection brightened the room, glistening against the cracked stone walls and ceiling. An altar constructed of stone sat at the far end of the long pool. Its curved top dripped with water, slowly filling a deep bowl made into its base.

The water rippled as Y'ven entered the pool. Black mist formed around him as he stepped further into the depths. The water rose to his waist, and he submerged Neer, leaving just her face and ears above the surface. Black mist overtook the pool, and her burns slowly healed.

He held her in place, watching as the blisters dissolved and her skin returned to its natural color. She opened her dreary eyes and then gave Y'ven a subtle nod, holding her breath as he dipped her beneath the surface. The pain that had stricken her was lifted, and the energy of the water embraced her with warmth. Her injuries faded to mist, seeping through her pores, further darkening the mystical waters.

As the pool faded to black, the room darkened. Y'ven lifted her from the water, and she inhaled a deep breath. The fresh cuts and matted blood covering her skin and armor had washed away.

"Thank you," she whispered.

Y'ven gave a stiff nod as her eyes slowly closed, and she collapsed in his arms. He carried her to the edge of the pool and laid her on the floor.

"Is she all right?" Thallon asked.

"Yes," Reiman said before Y'ven had the chance. "The waters healed her wounds, but her mind is weary. She needs to rest."

Thallon sat against the wall and removed his boots. He shook the ash from his hair before staring at his blood-soaked hands. "*Kila*," he remarked. "What are we going to do? We can't let them take her."

Reiman got comfortable next to him and exhaled with exhaustion. "He's sure to have Aélla obtain the last element so that Ithronél can enter the realm and gain the full strength of her power."

Thallon scoffed. "That's all that we need. Ithronél is the most powerful drimil I've ever seen. If she unlocks her full potential, there will be no stopping her." He paused with worry. "If he kills Aélla, there is no stopping *him*."

"We have another sorceress. If Aélla doesn't make it, Nerana can take her place."

His face twisted with anger and remorse. "You can't just replace her! She's First Blood! And we can't trust a lanathess to take on the responsibilities of Drimil'Rothar!"

"Nerana is a sorceress with powers unmatched. If given the chance, she'd make the wise decisions."

"Aélla will make it! She can defeat the Nasir. This isn't the first time he's tried to kill her."

"Yes, I've heard about his attempt at cursing her."

Thallon nodded. "She'll make it. She's stronger than you think."

A smile tugged the edge of Reiman's lip. "That she is."

Their conversation came to an end when Y'ven approached. With his arms crossed, he asked, "What is the plan?"

Reiman straightened, and with great authority, he said, "The plan, brother, is to wait. We will rest here for the evening, heal, and come morning, we'll see our way to Elandorr.°"

Thallon argued, "Elandorr is far. Past Sandir and Zaos! We'll never make there before the klaet'il."

"It's unwise to underestimate me, scholar. There is always a plan." He collected a black crystal from his pack and tossed it to Thallon. "We'll arrive before sunset, and when the klaet'il gather, we'll be waiting."

° The temple that holds the final realm of elemental power. Its sealed doors are only to be opened by the energy secured within the elemental staff, the rástalfür.

CHAPTER FORTY-SEVEN

FORGIVENESS
Aélla

A DARK RIFT SHOOK THE silence as magic tore through the air. Aélla fell from its height and landed on the ground. Her long hair collected dust as she sat on her knees, coughing and wheezing.

The rippling magic crackled before collapsing in on itself and disappearing.

Crawling forward, she clutched the magic staff lying in the dirt ahead. Three glowing crystals illuminated with magic. With a groan, she sat straighter and viewed her surroundings. Dirt and rocks stretched as far as she could see to the south. Beautiful aurora hovered in the sky above, and she was glad the Nasir hadn't taken her back to the forest, which was where she had expected them to go.

Leaves rustled from behind when a slight breeze carried through the air. She turned around to find herself at the edge of the jungle. Water dripped from large leaves, and mist blanketed the understory.

The slow, steady pace of footsteps approached from behind, and she realized she wasn't alone. Kneeling with her head down, she waited for him to speak, to do anything, but there was silence. Cold, intentional silence.

She lifted her head to view the silhouette of a man behind her. His face was hidden beneath the shadow of his cowl. Not that she needed to see it. She knew who stood before her, hovering like a wraith in the night.

"Why did you bring me here?" she asked, a slight tremble in her voice. "Why are you doing this?"

He stood without a word spoken. She wasn't sure if he had a voice at all. Glancing around, she realized they were alone. He hadn't commanded the others to meet here after her capture.

Crawling to her feet, she stood before him and stared up into the darkness of his hood. She remembered his face from long ago, before it lost its color and life. Before he became the monster standing before her. She remembered it fondly and with great pain. "Why are you doing this?" she demanded. "Answer me!"

Not a sound came from the man before her.

Her face was red, and tears swelled in her eyes. "I'm here because of you!" she screamed. "You did this to me! You forced me on this path!" His silence chipped away at her sanity. It created chaos deep inside, chaos she fought daily to contain, and she could feel herself cracking. The darkness that lived inside her, as it lived inside everyone, grew stronger. It consumed her. *"Speak to me!"*

A pulse of energy erupted from deep inside and sent a shockwave tearing through the trees, stripping them of their leaves. Shallow cracks formed along the ground and traveled away from her like thin spiderwebs. The Nasir was unmoved by her magic. His cloak waved in the harsh wind, and his hood was swept back across his shoulders.

His ashen skin glowed beneath the moonlight. Dark eyes held no emotion or luster. They were as cold and dark as death itself. She breathed heavily, looking into the eyes of the man she once knew. He was different. Something inside him had been twisted and changed.

She turned away and closed her eyes. A slight huff caused her shoulders to fall. "I know what you are," she said, her voice heavy with guilt and regret, "and I know why."

A tear fell from her eye, and she quickly wiped it away. With a sniff, she straightened and turned to the jungle. The dense trees and heavy green reminded her of Nyn'Dira, of her home. She was stricken with sorrow, longing to be back.

"You want me to enter the realm so that you can take the staff and have Ithronél gain the power in Elandorr, don't you?" She paused without turning in his direction. "I fight to keep everyone safe. To restore the balance that you've disrupted. To bring honor back to our people and begin anew."

Clutching the staff, she gazed to the crystals. One element was all that remained. She could enter the jungle and be one step closer to ending her journey, a journey she never wanted to begin. A journey that would see her to the Realm of Light and bring balance back to a world of unrest.

"I just don't understand," she said, "why you have to kill me. Why you *want* the cycle to remain. For naik'avel to consume and destroy."

He was quiet. Not a hint of a reaction or emotion passed his eyes.

"If I do this, there is no turning back," she said. "Our paths are set, and you will always be my enemy." Her eyes shifted to the ground, and she was consumed in sorrow. "I always wondered why you made the horrible choices you did. Why you betrayed everyone you loved and disappeared…but now, after all I've done and seen, I understand why you felt compelled to do the things that you did. Why you chose death and murder over forgiveness and strength." She turned to meet his gaze and was saddened to find the same cold, emotionless exterior he always displayed. "But I can't allow you to be my downfall. The hatred that I feel for you consumes me, and I know that I have to let go."

She stepped closer and gently touched his face. A spark of life glinted in his eyes, and it filled her with regret.

"I can never forgive you," she said. Her eyes burned with tears and her throat tightened as she withheld her agony. "But I will always love you."

Staring into his eyes, she took a deep breath and lunged her dagger at his chest. Before the blade met his skin, he grabbed her wrist with his right hand and then clutched her throat with his left. She gasped as he squeezed her neck, stealing her of breath. Scratching his arm and pushing against his face, she fought to be released.

The hot swirl of energy burning through her had faded in his presence. She was devoid of its power and unable to fight. The absence of her strength left her weak and depleted.

Her lungs burned and arms grew tired as his grip remained on her neck. Scratches from her nails left red lines of pain across his cheeks and brow. Staring into her eyes, he released a monstrous growl and then heaved her into the jungle.

CHAPTER FORTY-EIGHT

AFFLICTION
Aélla

LEAVES TORE AND SPRAYED WATER through the misty air as Aélla was thrown into the jungle, landing hard atop the ground. She rolled across thick grass and twisted vines.

Her chest was empty of the heaviness and warmth that came with her magic. Instead, it was calm and light. Every raindrop pattering against the leaves and collecting on the ground rippled through her.

She collected the magic staff that was thrown in after her, and then stood and walked further into the lonesome, dangerous trees, knowing the only escape would be in finding the element. Every step sank slightly into the soil. Vines splashed her with water as she sliced through the thick vegetation with her dagger. As she stepped away, the plants she tore through slowly formed back together.

A stream babbled nearby, illuminating blue light as it splashed against rocks. She sank to her knees by the water's edge and sipped from the wide creek. The water was refreshing against her parched tongue. With a sigh, she drank several handfuls before dousing her sunburnt skin.

She closed her eyes with a soft exhale. The scent of rain and grass reminded of her home, and though Nyn'Dira wasn't as wet or overgrown as the jungle, she was comforted all the same.

The slow pattering of rain created a soft chime as it drenched the trees and grass. She listened to its song, when the offbeat rustling of grass twitched her ears. Her eyes opened, the serenity lost, and she peered at her surroundings.

The crunch of wet grass came closer, and she turned around. Her dark blue eyes moved from left to right, and she scanned the empty jungle, until a man whispered from the east, and she was frozen by the familiar voice.

"You shouldn't be here," he said.

Holding her breath, she stared wide-eyed at the trees. Not a breeze or shuffle broke through the harrowing silence as she waited.

"Klaud?" her voice was silent, and she looked through the jungle, hoping it wasn't true.

Footsteps pattered from the east, and she chased after him. She cut frantically through thick vines, pushing away dense branches as she trailed behind his steps. Water dripped into her eyes as a heavy rainstorm swept through the swaying trees, growing stronger with her every step.

The heavy pulse of rain drumming against the leaves was broken by echoing voices. Their soft whispers carried through the wind, and they gripped and clawed at her mind.

Pain swelled in her chest as the soft crescendo of whispering voices grew louder with her every step. While carving through a thicket of rail-thin vines and leaves as big as her hand, she was stricken with intense agony. Her dagger splashed against the soil as she stumbled forward, clutching her chest.

The influx of agony swelled, and the voices hailed over the sounds of the wind and rain, suffocating her with their cries of pain and regret. Lost for breath, she collapsed to her knees. The anguish of a thousand souls burned inside her.

Covering her ears, she struggled to quell the noises tearing her mind. But she was absent of the magic. Only the gentle vibrations and fluidity of the rain and water flowed through her.

She could feel the disturbances in the moisture and puddles. Shadows stalked the undergrowth, their pounding footsteps moving through her like a thrashing wave.

Collecting her wooden staff, she whipped her head from north to south, searching for the hordes sweeping around her. Through a narrow break in the trees, she caught a quick flash of several figures running past her position. Water dripped across her face and arms as she pulled back the curtain of leaves to clear her view.

She was surprised to find the shadows were people racing through the trees. Bright symbols of red and blue were painted across their dark skin in sharp patterns that matched the markings on their spears and blow darts. Feathers and sticks were twisted into their long, tangled hair, and their clothing was nothing more than short loin cloths covering the waistlines of both men and women.

While several people fled further into the trees, many crouched into the bushes with their weapons aimed at the shadow creeping across the sky. The overcast glow of sunlight was shrouded in darkness, and a wave of black stretched above the treetops.

Spears were thrown as the people screamed. A screeching, world-shaking roar penetrated the air, sounding from the sky, both menacing and beautiful. A collection of grating soprano and bass rang sharply through the air.

At the sound of its voracious call, a wave of heat engulfed the jungle, and the ground quaked. A pillar of fire was unleashed from the sky. Trees buckled and snapped beneath the weight of its fury, creating clouds that hazed the air.

Desperate screams were silenced as the heat ripped through the trees. Aélla curled into her arms as the fires surged around her, yet not a wisp of heat or flame touched her skin.

As the pillar of flame and smoke moved further through the trees, the shadow followed, and the world was doused in rainfall. The sky was made clear, and the world faded to ash as the fires devoured all in its path. Scorched and blackened bodies lay beneath piles of grey as the fires raged.

"*Aélla!*"

She turned around in the direction of Klaud's voice, and the world was instantly silent. The fires vanished. The dense trees standing tall and proud were nothing more than thick piles of ash at her feet.

The world was a dark and quiet tomb where ghosts would never sleep. Their whispers flowed softly through the air like a gentle, dying wind. Their pain no longer gripped her, but she could feel it tugging at her soul, pulling her further from the destruction and toward a faint glow looming in the distance.

Ash swirled upward from her feet as she stepped through the remains of a once strong and beautiful forest. She moved closer to the horizon, and the long branches and thick trunk of a Tree appeared like dark lines within the pale glow.

She focused hard on her magic, hoping to find a shred of energy to transport her closer to the Tree. But the light sting of her energy never came. She was without her magic, only capable of producing the energy bestowed by the realm.

Breaking through the haze of grey, she stepped into the glow and came to a large clearing of grass and sunlight. She turned around to find the jungle alive and flourishing. Not a speck of ash or floating ember was left by the devastation it had endured.

Returning her attention to the glade, she found no tree or glowing apparition standing in the meadow. Instead, there was a deep intentional trench snaked with vines and overgrown grass.

Suddenly, the voices returned.

They overtook her thoughts, shrieking and pulling from every direction. With a scream, she fell to her knees, unable to break from their hold. Her lungs were tight and body was rigid from the agony subduing her. She could feel their lives slipping away and heard every last breath and pleading cry.

A subtle draw pulled her closer to the pit, and she crawled over thick grass and colorful flowers before coming to its edge. And the world became deafeningly silent as the voices ceased.

Timid breaths shook from her throat as she peered down to those who summoned her. Her eyes were wide with terror and sorrow, staring down at the thousands of skeletons piled together in a mass grave. Grass and vines wove through the broken cartilage, tethering them forever to the dirt.

"Kill..."

"Forgive..."

"Sacrifice..."

Their voices overlapped as they whispered with the wind. Leaves rustled, and grass swayed in the slight breeze, filling the desolate forest with life and sound.

"Kill!" The voices grew louder, shrieking with pain and anger. *"Kill...!"*

A shadow rose from behind, slowly shrouding Aélla with its darkness. She turned quickly to view the intruder behind and her color drained.

Ithronél slashed her weapon forward.

CHAPTER FORTY-NINE

WATER
Aélla

THE BLADE STRUCK CLOSE, AND Aélla ducked beneath its hit, feeling the sword swipe a hair's breadth from her scalp. She lunged her staff forward and struck against Ithronél's abdomen. The klaet'il staggered back with a heave and lifted her arms into a wide circle.

Droplets of water followed her movement, lifting from the grass and hovering in the air along with the rain. The mist suspended in the air surrounding her. Glaring into Aélla's eyes, Ithronél's face twisted into a hateful snarl, and she thrust her arms forward. The trapped moisture swirled into a raging vortex, moving quickly toward Aélla.

Her staff dropped to the ground, and she lifted her hands toward the attack. Winds swept past as the vortex moved closer, drenching the grass and trees, tearing through the air. Aélla braced herself, and the sudden crash of water collided with her palms.

Waves of heat and pain coursed through her as she fought to ward off Ithronél's magic.

As Aélla's strength waned, her arms pushed back toward her chest. Veins swelled in her neck, and her face was flushed. She forced herself to stand against the power afflicting her. Stricken with pain by every splash and droplet, she wove her magic into Ithronél's, wincing as every pulse and wave tore through her.

Slithering like an angry eel, the energy was difficult to contain. She pushed harder, mustering every ounce of strength. Gathering their energies, she took hold of the force assailing her. Her teeth clenched as she gripped the magic binding her, absorbing its strength and rage.

Standing taller, she pushed against the vortex with stiff arms. The energy swirled within her, and she unleashed a violent scream before thrusting it back toward its caster.

Winds swept through the jungle, stripping the trees and uprooting grass. She pushed harder against Ithronél's attack as the crash of waves caused by their colliding energy moved further against the vortex. It traveled toward the klaet'il, and Ithronél slid back across the grass, struggling against its strength.

A flash of heat tore through Aélla's chest as she took hold of the energy constricting her. She unleashed it in a final wave, and an eruption of water crashed against Ithronél, who was flung back into the dirt. Landing hard on her back, she wheezed and choked for breath.

Aélla dropped her hands, and the heavy vortex fell from the air, battering the ground with a deep splash.

Her legs trembled with weakness, and she stepped forward, then collapsed to her knees. Mud soaked through her robes as she knelt to the ground, clutching her raw, aching chest. Her tired eyes lifted to Ithronél, who rolled to her stomach before crawling to her knees.

Lines of red dripped blood across her cheeks and forehead, while grass and mud clung to her armor and limbs. Her shoulders broadened with every heaved breath, and she reclaimed her strength before pushing herself to her feet.

"*Kill me*, Drimil," Ithronél said. "Show me the true power of your blood! Unleash the darkness festering inside you and be consumed with greatness!"

Aélla lowered her gaze into an intense glare. Rising to stand, her intensity never wavered. She breathed deeply with confidence as the energy of the realm filled her with its power.

"Why do you hide behind your title?" Ithronél said with a sneer. She stepped closer, yet Aélla never moved. "Drimil are the pinnacle of existence. You hold the strength of our ancestors, yet you refuse to strike down the ones who wish to see you dead." Standing before her, peering into Aélla's glaring eyes, she said, "Your family deserves every bit of tragedy they've endured."

Aélla's hand curled into a shaky fist as rage consumed her. Mist gathered from the ground, withering the grass and draining it of life.

Ithronél smirked with a twisted smile. "You will die, just as weak and pathetic as your mother."

Aélla tightened her fist, and her eyes darkened. Anguish and fury filled her with madness. The mist thickened into a deep fog, swirling around them and becoming colder. Ice formed within the vortex, slicing their skin with trails of red.

She thought of everything she had lost and the suffering brought to those she loved. The anger consumed her, rising like a fire blazing within, unleashing the misery she was forced to withhold. Misery that was caused by those who were unforgiving and inexorable in their beliefs.

Ithronél was silent. Her deadly eyes locked with Aélla's, and a smile crept across her face. She wanted this, to release the darkness and power Aélla fought to contain, the very power that would shift fate and turn the tide of all existence.

The darkness was gripping, taking hold of her thoughts and tearing her soul to shreds. She *wanted* to be angry, to unveil her wrath and exact justice on those who sought the world harm, and it terrified her.

Her teeth clenched and lip twitched as she fought to suppress the fury radiating deep inside. It grew stronger, and her anger deepened. She was unable to stop it, unwilling to let go.

A tear fell from her eye and lifted from her cheek. She turned to the sky and allowed the crashing motion of the energy to flow through her, entangling with her rage and unrest, darkened by her fears and failures. Twisting her energy through the water soaking the land and giving life to the trees, she took hold of the vines weaving through the grass and wrapped them slowly around Ithronél's ankles. They climbed up her shin and to her thighs, slipping beneath her fingers as she fought to free herself.

Unable to escape as they coiled to her waist, Ithronél became immobile and tethered to the ground. Vines twisted between her fingers and bound her wrists to her sides. As Ithronél fought, the struggle sent waves through Aélla, weakening her resolve. Closing her fists, the vines tightened, and Ithronél was compressed by its strength.

Aélla stepped closer and stared at the woman she captured.

The voices of the dead, lying in the pit behind, cried out, beckoning her to kill. Overlapping as they demanded her to make a choice.

Kill her...!
Forgive...!
Make the choice...!
The world is watching...!

Aélla held stronger to her magic, and Ithronél fought against it. The calm, freeing energy grew hot, crashing through her, coursing with fire and pain.

Her fury wavered at the sound of her mother's voice. It reigned over the others, weaving softly through the patterns of echoing screams as it faded.

"Aes'prínehn fortaal nuala…"
We are what we choose to be.

The calm voice replayed in her mind, embracing her with familiarity and warmth. Slowly, the mist polluting the air evaporated. Rain drizzled from the sky, and Aélla's hard fists loosened. Her fingers ached as she released the energy stealing life from the grass, consuming her with madness.

Staring into Ithronél's furious gaze, Aélla dropped her hands to her sides. The vines encasing her dropped to her feet.

Tears welled in Aélla's eyes, and she took a measured step back. "I won't kill you," she said. "That isn't my destiny. It isn't who I will be."

Ithronél hunched forward and took several deep breaths. She glanced up at Aélla and slowly turned away. Cracks crawled across her neck and cheeks, arms and waist. The dark fissures were reminiscent of fractured stone, bleeding with dust. Aélla watched in horror as the strong klaet'il warrior faded into a pile of ash.

Aélla stood motionless, watching as the ashes faded away in the rain, wondering if this was true. Only one person could enter the realm at a time. If Ithronél had entered the jungle, they'd have never crossed paths. The realm would've taken them to different places.

Her shoulders slumped, and she exhaled a deep, relieved sigh. This was all a test. A way to measure her strength and resolve. She feared what might have happened had she chosen to follow through with her pain and ended Ithronél's life.

The thoughts eluded her as winds swept from behind, bringing warm energy blazing with a flash of light. Aélla covered her eyes and turned around, watching the brightness fade into the soft luminance of a Tree appearing above the pit. Its branches were wide and covered with glowing flowers.

She stepped closer, allowing the subtle tug of warm energy to pull her forward. Sunlight peeked through the clouds and caressed her damp skin, filling her with its comforting embrace.

Roots and vines twisted beneath her feet like serpents, moving closer toward the Tree, before twisting together at the trunk and solidifying into a tall pillar. Unblinking, Aélla stepped to it and placed her hands upon vines and roots.

A flash of energy strengthened her power, converging with the realm. The intensity was sudden, like a strike of lightning, sending tendrils of scorching heat throughout her veins.

With a gasp, she opened her eyes. The Tree was glowing brightly, never fading in its luminance. Its energy shimmered in the air like a protective dome, yet the vines and grass surrounding it had withered to ash.

Stepping back, she tripped over the roots and fell to the ground. Nestled beside her, twisted within the slithering roots, was the magic staff. Three crystals glowed brightly, while the fourth remained dormant and empty. Just one more element, and she could enter the final realm and then return home.

She tugged and pulled against the weapon until it broke from the roots encasing it. Shifting her gaze to the pillar, she noticed a shallow impression near its top. Doubt crept through her mind, and she feared what might come once she collected the last element.

Aélla turned around and gazed upon the rainforest, saddened to know she would never revisit. Fate was unforgiving in the path it laid for her. Standing taller, she inhaled a deep breath and gave a respectful bow to the lost home of the ancients.

She turned to face the pillar, plucked the crystal from its place on the staff, and held it over the impression. Gulping down her fear, she carefully placed it into the groove. Light sparkled against its smooth edges, and the rain and moisture swirled into a slow-moving vortex.

The water funneled into the stone, and it glowed with blue light. As the winds faded into a light breeze, the vortex became narrower before being absorbed into the stone.

The crystal was hot with energy when she collected it from the pillar and set it back into its place on the staff. The weapon quivered as all four stones glowed brightly. A deep rumble of churning rock shifted the ground, and cracks slid across its surface. Tendrils of brown light rose from the soil like heavy mist, and strong winds were followed by a sudden rainstorm falling from the dark sky. A pungent scent of sulfur masked the air when waves of red heat brightened the deep cracks splitting the ground.

Aélla covered her face as the four energies collided, causing the world to tremor and shake. A strong current of wind and rain thrust her aside. The ground rippled like waves, causing her to roll aside. Smoke rose from the fractures, and scorching heat brightened the surface, spewing lava into the air.

The boiling magma fell like rain and landed in droplets, singing and scorching the dirt.

Aélla crawled to her knees and pressed her palms to the ground. The convolution of such power and rage twisted through her like grinding stone. She screamed, fighting against the constant tremors and wind, but her magic wasn't strong enough to control the chaos around her.

Winds and rain pummeled her aside as the ground crumbled. She rolled across its uneven surface. The world split, pulling grass and vines into darkness. Aélla's heart stopped as the surface fractured into dust beneath her, and she fell weightlessly beneath the ground.

Heavy winds swept past as she tumbled through the empty air. Fighting against the currents, she slowly brought her hands together. Energy sparked inside her, and she gripped and clawed at the wind, ignoring the agony that pulled her soul. The wind slithered through her fingers. Clutching hard to its energy, she swept her arms outward and forced the wind up into a soft draft, lessening her fall.

With the winds beneath her receding, she drifted slowly onto cold, wet stone. She crawled on her knees and inhaled several deep, pained breaths. Beads of sweat formed along her brow as she heaved with exhaustion.

Turning her gaze upward to view her surroundings, she noticed a faint speck of light above revealing the depth she'd fallen. Her eyes shifted to the walls surrounding her, and hundreds of ancient runes began to glow. Too afraid to move, afraid of what might happen should she touch one of the magical apparitions, she sat perfectly still, but as a faint glow appeared beneath her knees she scurried backward.

It was a large rune, glowing brighter than the rest, sitting alone on the stone floor. Voices whispered through her mind, becoming louder as they spoke. Their noises overlapped as they screamed and begged for help. Clawing her mind and gripping her soul, she was crushed by their anguish and fear.

Her heart pounded loudly in her ears, masking the voices that called from within. She turned quickly from left to right when footsteps scraped across the ground. Peering through the dark cave, she was frozen by the sight of hundreds of glowing orbs appearing gradually in the distance.

They were the eyes of centry, fiendish ghouls that haunted the caves of Anaemiril. She couldn't fight them off alone. Not without the use of her full magic, which had yet to return. Her fear mounted as angry snarls and hisses echoed through the chamber.

Her eyes darted between the large rune and the racing footsteps, and she struggled over which path to take. The rune glowed against her eyes as she studied its design, hesitant to touch it and release the magic inside, while the growling and hungry snarls of the centry grew louder. Their fingernails scratched against the stone with an ear-shattering ring, and the ground trembled as the sea of white eyes grew closer.

With another glance to the light above, and to the runes surrounding her, she knew she had no choice. Should she fight these creatures, it wouldn't lead to her escape. There was one way out, and with a deep breath, she gazed upon the rune and touched its surface.

CHAPTER FIFTY

THE FORBIDDEN REALMS
Nerana

THE WARMTH OF FIRELIGHT RADIATED against the cold night air while flames born of alchemy burned atop the desert floor. Long shadows cast behind those who sat around its heat, like the spokes of a wagon wheel fading into darkness. The soft glow brightened the long and forlorn faces of Neer and her companions as they waited out the night in silence.

After the events of I'vasaar, where Neer had been healed of her wounds and allowed to rest, Reiman collected a transporting stone from his pack and brought them all to the steps of Elandorr. The enormous sandstone temple sat just behind them, reflecting with moonlight that brightened the cracked and eroded bricks of the ancient courtyard.

The gentle rhythm of stone sliding against steel chimed through the air as Reiman sharpened his sword. Thallon sat to his left, scrawling into his journal, while Y'ven engaged in a quiet conversation with Dru. Unable to be healed by the temple's pool, his right arm was wrapped in thick bandages and held close to his chest in a tight sling.

Neer sat next to him, raking her fingers through her hair. It had been hours since anyone spoke, and the silence was becoming insufferable. Each second ticking by was another flash of worry and anger. Aélla still hadn't returned, and Neer couldn't escape the troubling thoughts of her fate.

"What if she doesn't come back?" she asked, her voice a bit too loud and harsh.

Reiman straightened and looked into her eyes. "If she doesn't return, the Nasir or Ithronél surely will, and they'll do so with the staff."

Neer scoffed with a sour expression. "I'm not entering that place until Aélla gets here. This is *her* journey."

"It's *both* of your journeys. You seek the same path with different ends. Don't forget why you're here. What *your* purpose is. Stopping the High Priest and liberating your country will bring forth a new era of coexistence we haven't seen in centuries. You are paving the way for a new future, Nerana."

She turned away with a huff. "It's too late. The High Priest is already invading the forest. The evae will *never* forgive them of this. There *will* be war. A great one. Even if he's dead."

"That isn't true. If we act now, my people will see that a human—a natural born magic user—rose up against her own leaders for our freedom. There is still a chance for redemption and peace."

Embers sprayed into the air when logs settled, bringing their conversation to an end. Neer's boots scraped against the dust as she stood and gave herself space from the others. Standing in the darkness, beneath the glow of moonlight, she clutched the woven trinket Avelloch gifted her. It was a symbol of comfort, meant to bring peace to those who are lost.

Her thumb absently stroked the edge of the trinket as she stared into the desert, waiting anxiously for Aélla to arrive. She recalled the terrors inflicted upon her by the Order when she was taken as a child, how they brutalized and branded her. The Nasir was ruthless and calculating, and if Neer understood anything, it was that those who are in power sought to stay in power, no matter how disastrous the consequences might be.

The soft tread of footsteps pattering across the dirt came from behind, lifting her of her thoughts. She stared up at the sky as Thallon stood next to her.

He placed his hands into his pockets and followed her gaze. "You all right?" he asked.

She shrugged. "I just hope we can find her."

"The Nasir can't stop her. She'll wind up where she needs to be."

"And if she doesn't?" Their eyes met, and she was frustrated to find the same confident, knowing smile he always held. It wasn't confidence of arrogance but of wit. Thallon was smart, and he knew it. Neer, on the other hand, was still to be convinced. He was intelligent, there was no doubt, but he wasn't all-knowing. She broke from his gaze and stepped to the pedestal that once held a small Tree.

The eroded stone was cold beneath her palms, and she leaned against it, reluctant to admit a terrible, dangerous secret. Shaking her head to ease the pressure of her thoughts, she explained, "There is a serum that can block our magic. The Order has it…and the Nasir could too."

Thallon exhaled a deep breath. With crossed arms, he leaned back against the pedestal and faced Neer. "The Nasir has his tricks, just as your *Order* has them. But a great warrior does not falter beneath the fear of their enemies. You *conquer* them. I'm telling you, lanathess, Aélla will be all right. I have known her my entire life."

Their gaze lingered for a moment as she considered his words, still unsure of their verity, but choosing to believe them. Hope was too fragile a thing to lose in a time of such despair. Turning away, she lowered her head and closed her eyes.

"So, what now?" she asked, mostly to herself, though she hoped someone else could give her the answer. "Am I to enter this place and gain the full strength of elemental energy? Is this truly my path?"

Her tension eased when Thallon placed a hand on her shoulder and said, "That's up to *you* to decide."

With a sympathetic grin, he quietly stepped back to the others. As he took his place by the flames, Neer shifted her gaze to the temple and considered the possibility of Aélla's prolonged disappearance, or death. The thought struck her with pain.

Entering the realm was foretold by Numera herself. Neer was *meant* to enter and gain the strength of the realm. But now, standing in the face of her destiny, she was unsure. Completing this quest without Aélla felt broken, unclean. This was *their* destination, and they would see it through together.

Clutching the trinket tightly in her fist, she turned back to the others, ready to tell them of her decision. Ready to let them know she wouldn't continue without first finding Aélla, when suddenly, magic ripped through the air with the sound of igniting flames.

The others leapt to their feet, while Neer turned toward the noise with her sword drawn. Her heart thudded hard in her chest, silencing the world with its heavy thumps, rising to her ears and throat. Rippling magic radiated from a dark tear hovering over the base of the temple steps.

Another sound like rumbling fire was released from the magic, and a figure emerged from the darkness, stumbling forward on their feet. Moonlight shone against Aélla's shadow, and Neer exhaled a deep, relieved breath. The rift disappeared, and Thallon and Y'ven rushed to Aélla's side. Her wavy hair dripped with water and hung to her lower back in its weight.

"What happened?" Thallon asked while touching a cut along her face. "Are you all right?"

"Where is the Nasir?" Reiman questioned as he approached.

Aélla glanced around hurriedly and then gazed upon the temple behind. "It brought me here…" she said, her eyes wide with shock and confusion. Clutching the staff, she stepped carefully to the enormous temple. Her eyes veered to the left of the large double doors where a now glowing rune sat upon the wall. "We still have a chance."

"What are you saying?" Thallon asked.

She gripped her forehead and closed her eyes. "I believe the Nasir forced me into the jungle so that he could take the staff when I returned to the desert and then allow Ithronél to enter the realm. But there was no reason for him to believe it would bring me here." She glanced at the sky, then back to the temple. "We must hurry, before they come."

As Neer came to her side, Aélla's jaw dropped, and with quiet gasp, she pulled Neer into a tight embrace. "I'm glad you're okay," she said.

Neer stood frozen, surprised by her affection. She hugged her back before they stepped away. "Speak for yourself," Neer said.

"It's all right," Aélla stated. "The Nasir has tried to kill me before, and I'm certain he'll try it again."

Neer eyed her suspiciously. She knew of one other whom the Nasir wanted dead.

"Maybe third time will be the charm?" Thallon said with a playful shove to Aélla's shoulder, and she chuckled at his teasing.

Her eyes peered at the glowing crystals on her staff, and sorrow overtook her fleeting smile. She touched each of the shards, carefully admiring their beauty and power. "I suppose this is it," she said. "We can enter the temple."

"Why do we have to enter a temple if we've already gotten the elements?" Neer asked. "Shouldn't our energies be strengthened enough?"

"Elandorr holds the last piece of tre'lan Aenwyn. Inside will be different than the others. We'll be gifted with the full strength of our energy."

Neer sighed. "I don't think I can take another realm. These visions and nightmares are maddening."

"I don't believe we'll have to face anything like that here. Whatever test the realm gives us, this is the final one. We can do this, Nerana." With a kind smile, she reached for her hand and asked, "Are you ready?"

Fear mounted in Neer's chest, making it hard to breathe. She glanced at the glowing rune etched into the temple wall. It was too late to turn back now. Once she entered, she would return stronger than before. More powerful in her magic and energy. She would be one step closer to defeating the High Priest.

Turning to Aélla, she clutched her hand, and together they walked up the stairs. The others stayed behind, watching as they ascended to the large door.

The dull green glow of the rune softly illuminated their skin as they stood before it. The tug of its energy drew them closer to its warmth, beckoning them to relinquish the energy of the staff and enter the forbidden and final realm. Aélla lifted the staff to the rune, and the crystals glowed brighter.

Magic swirled within them with fire, water, rock, and air. The light shimmer of energy grew outward from the staff, and it trembled, growing red with heat. Aélla released her hold on the weapon, and it hovered in place.

Tendrils of brown, orange, white, and blue energy swirled upward from the crystals. They wove together as the magic drew closer to the rune, absorbing into its surface.

The vortex swirled faster as the magic within the staff dimmed, and the relic glowed with shimmering light. As the staff was depleted of its energy it fell to the ground, no longer burning or trembling, the crystals clear and empty.

Neer and Aélla stumbled back as the temple creaked and shook. Dust rained from the pillars and ceiling, and the heavy stone door shifted open. Taking half a step back, Neer studied the darkness within the narrow crack of the doorway. Aélla drew a deep breath, and with a reassuring smile to Neer, she stepped closer to the door and slipped inside.

Cold air escaped the temple as Neer peered into the darkness and wrapped her fingers instinctively around the hilt of her sword. She removed the weapon from its sheath and carefully stepped inside.

"Aélla?" she called, stepping into a dark, empty void. Her voice was silent, never echoing or resounding from beyond the reaches of her ears.

She was alone, just as Thallon said she would be. Only one person may enter the realm as it brings you to a different plane.

Neer crossed her arms and shivered. Beneath her step was the familiar etch of stone. Reaching into the darkness, her fingers grazed against something hard and damp. She recoiled with a quiet gasp. Her body trembled and breaths were loud as she was consumed with fear. Closing her eyes, she gulped down her emotions and forcefully reached her hand outward toward what she had touched.

As her fingertips connected with the surface, she fought the urge to withdraw and felt roughness of a stone wall beneath her palm. She exhaled several deep breaths. To the right, she felt the same stone and realized she was standing in a hall.

"What do I do?" she asked herself. "Where do I go?"

Consumed with panic, she took a moment to recenter. Slow, deep breaths helped to calm her nerves and gave her a sense of peace. She could do this, with her magic.

Kneeling to the ground, she pressed her palms to the stone flooring. The crushing energy of rock compressed her, and she fought against its weight, following the flow of energy that passed through the walls.

Down the tunnel, she felt the emptiness of a large room. Weaving through the walls, there was a shift in the energy at the back of the room. It was a weakness in the structure that muddled her energy.

Unable to decipher the anomaly along the wall, she released her grip on the energy twisting inside her. The stones creaked when she removed her hands from the ground.

Rising to her feet, she slid her hand along the wall and stepped carefully into the room. The air was lighter as she stepped through a doorway and into the large room. Keeping along the wall, she walked along its edge and came to the back where the energy felt twisted and uncertain.

But the stone was as solid here as it was throughout the room, so she felt around, searching for anything that could have led to such a disruption in her energy—a crack, or mark, or rune, but there was none.

Feeling helpless, and without guidance, she placed her hands to the surface, and a flash of heat struck her with pain. She released a deep groan and pushed further into the wall, not daring to let go. Sharp pain cut through her as she converged her energy with the walls. Slowly, it began to shift beneath her touch.

A light grinding filled the silence, and the stone buckled and creaked beneath the weight of her magic. A hidden door slid back just half an inch. She pushed harder and ignored the agony, her desperation outweighing her desire for relief.

Slowly, the door opened, and light filtered through the darkness. With a grunt, she shoved it just enough to shimmy through and then stepped out of the dark, cold room.

Grass crunched beneath her feet, and sunlight and fresh air warmed her skin. She lifted her arm to block the heavy light burning her eyes. Blinking away the pain and blurriness of her vision, she lowered her arm and gazed upon the beautiful meadow where she stood.

A light breeze rustled the leaves of a large Tree, creating a soothing chime that swept through the grasses. Blue sky and grass rested along the horizon in every direction. Another breeze pressed her forward, and the calming tug of energy drew her toward the Tree.

Neer followed the pull, stepping across the meadow, following the roots twisting through the soil. They overlapped as they came to the trunk, and a deep pool of water rested in the roots woven to contain the moisture. The clear water shimmered with magic, and as she leaned forward to scoop it into her hands, a voice came from behind.

She turned quickly and was shocked to see the young girl she met in Ravinshire months ago. Her frizzy red hair was pulled back, and a deep blood stain coated her blue dress where the priest's sword had struck her chest.

She was the innkeeper's daughter from Ravinshire. The one Neer had hoped to save but ultimately cost her everything. The girl looked back at Neer without expression.

"Enid…" Neer said, still seeing herself in the eyes of the young girl who wanted so much more from life. Neer climbed carefully from the roots, and when Enid spoke, she came to a sudden stop.

"You must sacrifice," Enid said. "Just as I 'ave. Just as we all 'ave."

Neer shook her head. "I don't understand. What do you mean? What should I —"

"Give up somethin' that you love. Somethin' worth more than gold. Toss it into the pond. Only then can you leave."

Her voice echoed softly with the wind as her body began to fade. Neer ran forward, desperate to catch her and keep her from vanishing. As she reached for Enid and wrapped her arms around her tiny frame, the girl vanished, and Neer fell through the empty air. She landed on her knees and stared at the dirt. Pain and regret coursed through her as the weight of her actions tore at her soul.

Tears glistened in her eyes, and as she turned back to where Enid had been there was nothing but empty air. She was gone, never to return. Her life cut too short because of the actions of the Priest…because of Neer's decision to end his life and destroy a village of innocent bystanders.

Her chest grew heavy with sorrow and grief. She sputtered through a tight throat and quickly wiped her tears.

The winds increased, beckoning her to the pond. A gentle hum played through the air as the leaves broke from their branches and soared through the sky.

She had to leave this place. There wasn't time for pity or guilt. Her tears wouldn't bring Enid back to life. They wouldn't resurrect the people she lost. Only strength and war would avenge them. She wouldn't allow herself to fall victim to sorrow.

Neer wiped her face, exhaled a deep breath, and shook away the pain festering inside. Pushing it aside, she forced herself to the water and stared into the pool, struggling over what to give.

"Something that I love…worth more than gold…"

Her eyes slowly moved to the hilt of Avelloch's sword, and she pulled it from its sheath. It had been with her since Nha-mashel, protecting her in his absence. The thought of parting with it filled her with emptiness and sorrow, as if she was sac-rificing her loyalty or any hope of his return.

The glowing veins reflected in the water as she held the sword over its depths. Her hands trembled as she prepared to drop it into the water, when a thought suddenly occurred, and sickness overtook the void plaguing her. Leaning back, she fought through her tears as she pulled Loryk's note from her boot.

Trembling hands unfolded the letter that she memorized long ago. Every elongated "S" and "H" were as familiar as an old friend. The thought of parting with it left her irreparably broken and lost. Tears fell from her eyes as she stared at the parchment, whose enchantments truly had withstood the test of time, and she hoped that wherever the notebook wound up, its enchantments, too, had kept it preserved and safe.

She glanced between the items, knowing each could be used as a sacrifice. Her eyes fell to the rare and enchanted sword. It would be foolish to lose such a weapon in the fight to come. She knew she would need its strength and power to see her to the end, but destroying the last thoughts and words of her closest friend…her brother…was too much to bear.

Her heart ached. She understood which path to take, which path would lead her to the road of redemption and free-dom. But it came at a terrible cost. The cost of her devotion and family. The cost of her friendship and love.

Setting the sword aside, she gripped the letter. Leaning over the water, she closed her eyes and fought through the tightness in her throat. "I'm sorry…," she cried. Her tears landed upon the page and rolled gently down its edges, never soaking through or ruining the ink. "I'm sorry I couldn't save you. I'm sorry that I caused you to die." She clenched her teeth as more tears fell. Her breathing trembled, and she fought to speak, to say her last words before they were gone forever. "You deserved far better. But I'll see you again…in another life…"

The hole in her chest grew larger as she prepared to release the note. Her face twisted with agony and tears as she sobbed. "Thank you for loving me," she whimpered. "I'll never forget you."

With a painful cry, she dropped the note. The water glowed as the parchment sank further and then disappeared.

She curled into the roots, consumed with grief. The loss she felt was reminiscent of his death in Nhamashel. A deep, empty weight tore a hole in her chest where belonging and comfort used to be. She couldn't accept her new reality without him, yet she had to, and it was crushing.

Lost in her sorrow, she didn't notice the winds swirl around her, becoming stronger as they swept through the air. Grass was pulled from the ground, and rocks were lifted to join in the cyclone.

Neer rose to her knees as the winds whipped through her hair. Her tears lifted from her eyes to join with the water from the pond as it swirled with the wind. Fires burned and streamed from the sun, creating tendrils of heat spiraling in the vortex.

It circled around, moving closer in a thin cyclone that reached out and touched her chest. A flash of heat and electricity flashed through her as their energies converged. With a gasp, her back straightened and her eyes lifted to the sky as she was stricken by a surge of energy.

She was stolen of breath, the vortex swirling angrily, absorbing into her body. Their magics twisted together, creating heat and pain that moved through her like hard, crushing waves. Her white glowing eyes became grey.

A tear fell from her eye as the last of the magic spun into her chest, and she breathed in the power of its strength.

CHAPTER FIFTY-ONE

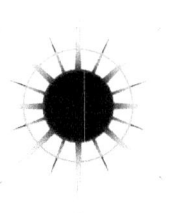

LETTING GO
Nerana

"When I'm gone... just remember my songs. They're all about you, y'know?"

– Loryk to Nerana

DUST SWIRLED ALONG THE FRAYED edges of Reiman's cloak as it drifted softly in the breeze. Standing alone at the base of the temple stairs, he gazed upon the sky, searching for a shift in the darkness that would alert him of the klaet'il's arrival. Watching the stars, waiting for a glimmer or shadow to sweep past in the form of a scout, he was silent. Calm. Undisturbed by the potential of another ruthless battle. In all his years, he had never come to know a more callous or unpredictable leader as the Nasir, and he knew that patience would be their greatest strength.

Patience and acuity.

He was broken from his thoughts when a deep rumble shook the ground. Light illuminated within the temple, shining brightly through its weathered cracks and windows.

"What's happening?" Thallon asked, stepping to Reiman's side. It had only been minutes since Neer and Aélla had entered the realm. Surely, they couldn't be through its trials.

Y'ven followed with Dru on his shoulder as a thin stream of light traveled from the door and slithered down the stairs. The sound of grating stone filled the silence as the door slid open and the light grew brighter. Reiman stepped closer, and through narrowed eyes, he watched a shadow emerge from the luminance. His breath caught in his throat as he waited, watching the figure step through the doorway.

Her long, wavy hair was bright against the light shining from behind, and Reiman turned away with a rush of disappointment. Thallon and Y'ven made their way quickly to Aélla's side as she stood alone by the doorway.

"Are you all right?" Thallon asked, touching her shoulder.

Aélla gripped her forehead. "I am okay. Where is Nerana?"

"She hasn't returned. You've been gone for just a few minutes. Did something happen? Did you harness the energy?"

"Time moves differently in the realms," she said. "You know that."

"Did you get it?" he pressed.

She nodded in response, and he exhaled a sigh of relief.

"Great," he said. "So, what did you have to do? Do you feel stronger?"

Y'ven grumbled. "Too many questions. Allow her rest."

Aélla smiled. "Thank you, Y'ven, but it's fine. The realm was peaceful. I was sitting on a dock overlooking a lake. It was beautiful and quiet. I meditated, and the water circled around me. Then, the world changed, and I knelt atop a rocky mountain, then a field with a large, bright sun in the sky, and then I was in a forest with the wind. The elements circled around me until I had contained them all."

Thallon said, "I wonder what Neer is going through. Everyone's experience is different, you know? The realm tailors itself to each sorcerer."

Aélla's eyes fell away. As a soft breeze drifted by, she closed her eyes, now able to hear the whisper of the wind and feel the calmness of its energy. The stone quivered, and a gentle vibration traveled through her like ripples over the crest of calm waters, growing shallower as they moved past. She turned to its door, alerting the others of Neer's approach as she stepped through the light.

Reiman came up the stairs while the others circled around. Her eyes and face were red from tears, and her clothes were saturated with water, leaves, and dirt.

"What happened to you?" Thallon asked.

Reiman kindly pushed him aside and looked into Neer's eyes. He removed a blade of grass stuck to her cheek and then exhaled a deep breath. "Are you all right?" he asked.

She nodded before turning away. "Yeah."

Thallon asked, "Did it work? Have you harnessed the full power of the elements?"

With a shaky breath, Neer lifted her hands. She, too, felt the calmness of the wind and the strength of the stone beneath her feet. Focusing on the magic twisting inside, she created a spark of flame that flashed orange light across her face. As the heat grew, it ignited with a spark into a ball of fire.

Thallon's eyes grew wide with excitement. The flickering glow of firelight danced across his face, and he leaned closer to inspect the flames. "Magnificent…Even Ithronél cannot produce flames. She can only manipulate the energy around her."

Neer swiped her hand and curled her fingers into a loose fist, extinguishing the heat into a light grey mist. "I suppose the realms are more useful than we thought."

"I'll say."

Aélla stepped closer, and Neer lifted her eyes to view the evae. There was comfort in their shared experience. She knew Aélla would understand the heavy price that came with inheriting this power. "What did you give?" Neer asked. "What did you have to sacrifice?"

Aélla's brows pulled together in confusion. "Sacrifice?"

"Yes," Neer's voice was raw with pain. "I had to sacrifice something important to me."

Aélla's eyes widened, and her jaw dropped. She glanced at the others before turning back to Neer. "I'm sorry…" She closed her eyes. "If that's what the realm created for you, then it's what you needed the most."

With hard eyes and repressed anguish, Neer stepped away from the others to be alone. She reached instinctively for the note in her boot and was quickly reminded it was no longer there.

Aélla stood nearby and watched her with regret and sorrow. Heavy boots thudded against the stone, and her attention averted to Y'ven as he stepped to her side. They stood together in silence, overlooking the courtyard. From atop the temple stairs they could see far into the dark and quiet desert.

His gruff voice chiseled through the silence as he said in his common language, "It was an honor to fight by your side, Master Drimil."

She turned to him with tear-filled eyes. "You aren't coming with us?"

"I am sun-blood. Aragoth is my home. I will stay and fight with the Brotherhood." He paused. "Thanks to you, I am no longer nesiat."

Her lip quivered as she forced a smiled. "You were never nesiat, Master Y'ven." His glowing eyes met with hers in a proud gaze. "The honor was mine."

He leaned forward with a respectful bow, and she wrapped her arms around him tightly. Slowly, his arm moved to her back, and they shared a light hug. They backed away and Aélla wiped her eyes before turning to Dru, who had large tears sliding down her fiery cheeks.

Aélla pulled her close. "I'll miss you most of all, Druindarvenia. Take care of your warrior."

As they said their goodbyes, Thallon paced in front of the sealed doorway, scribbling hastily in his notebook as he updated his journal to include all he had learned about the realms, particularly Neer's experience and survival. Only once had he learned of a human who possessed magical abilities, and he was fascinated to be in the presence of another.

His boots scraped against the stone as he walked back and forth, lost in his thoughts. With a finger to his lip, he studied the markings and then slapped the notebook shut. He glanced at the others and thought of their reasons for being in the desert, which reminded him of his own.

Digging into his pocket, he collected the ring and unwrapped it from the black cloth he used to secure it. The polished black steel was wrapped with pulsing white veins. He ran a finger along its surface, wondering of its power and why the Eirean had risked war to have him retrieve it.

As he admired the dangerous, forbidden artifact, whispers seeped into his mind. They were both a comfort and terror, speaking as softly as the wind in an ancient, forgotten language. Darkness clouded his vision, and his eyes crossed as the growing pull of energy consumed him.

"Thallon?" Aélla called, and he was jolted from his trance.

With a gasp, he wrapped the ring back into its cloth, and said, "We need to leave. The Eirean are waiting. They—"

His words fell silent when a bolt ripped through his flesh and he crashed into the wall, wailing. Blood spilled from the wound in his shoulder.

Reiman was the first to his side. He overturned his bag and emptied its contents, searching through vials and ointments. Aélla dropped to Thallon's side and pressed her hands to his shoulder where the bolt was still lodged deep into his flesh.

"Drimil," Reiman warned without glancing in her direction. "Conserve your energy. He will survive."

She hesitated as her eyes met with Thallon's. He breathed through clenched teeth, and his body trembled in pain before he groaned a vulgar curse in evaesh.

Reiman uncorked a round jar of thick orange paste and then turned to the scholar. He gently clutched the shaft of the bolt, and Thallon screamed. "Hold him steady," Reiman demanded.

"I can heal him!" Aélla argued.

"They're here." Reiman grimly warned. "Protect us with a barrier. Do not sacrifice your energy where it isn't needed!"

She glanced at them, conflicted over what to do. Y'ven brushed Aélla aside and placed a hand on Thallon's uninjured shoulder. Reiman gripped the shaft of the bolt, and with a quick tug, he withdrew it from his skin. Thallon unleashed another scream as Reiman smeared travaran across his wound, where bright orange veins had started to form.

"Drimil!" Reiman growled. "Now!"

Aélla flinched and turned quickly to the courtyard. Shimmering magic rippled from her palms as she created a translucent barrier. The half dome was enough to protect them without keeping them fully enclosed. As the magic solidified and became transparent, her eyes shifted to a shadow creeping through the darkness below. He was as large as a vaxros with a severed metal arm that glimmered in the moonlight.

"Nerana!" Aélla called, and Neer left Thallon's side to stand beside her. "How did he find us?"

Neer turned to the hunter who stalked forward, and hatred fueled her with rage, setting fire to the energy growing within her. She knew he had been following her since her arrival to the desert, but after their last encounter she had hoped he would have lost her trail.

Thorne lifted the crossbow, and Neer snatched her sword from its sheath, then teleported behind him. As instantly as she landed, Thorne swiped his arm back and collided his elbow with her nose.

She staggered aside with tears welling in her eyes and blood dripping down her face. He turned and released the bolt in her direction, and she vanished again. Coming up behind him, she swiped at his side, ducked beneath the swing of his fist, and then plunged her sword into his gut. Blood spilled down his side when she yanked her sword from his flesh. With a hellish growl, he swung his fist, and she leapt aside to evade his hit.

Neer stood strong and watched as he gripped his deep, bleeding injuries. Hunched over in agony, Thorne's shoulders rose and fell with every hard breath. She waited for him to fall, to succumb to his wounds and collapse to the ground, but he never did. Instead, he stood taller, broadened his shoulders, and with a look of pure rage, he charged.

She leapt aside and flipped across the ground. Coming to her feet, she turned back with her sword drawn. He wouldn't die. It wasn't possible. His injuries were too severe to allow him to continue fighting with such prowess and strength.

Something was keeping him alive.

The blood drained from her face as she came to a harrowing realization. Staring at the hunter, she understood his power, as she had heard of it many years ago during her study of forbidden rituals and curses.

He wasn't surviving because of his strength…he was surviving because he was cursed.

Blood Magic, as it was called, bound two souls together, allowing them to survive the most unfeasible of odds. Those tied together could only perish at the hands of the other, or by a direct assault that destroyed their brain.

Her lip twitched with a heavy snarl. She lowered her chin and set her heavy glare on Thorne. Lifting her arms in his direction, she slipped her magic around his skull and squeezed.

He staggered aside and grasped his head. Neer clenched her teeth with a growl and fought harder. Her magic pressed against the hardness of bones but couldn't penetrate through. The energy beneath his flesh was hot, much hotter than bone would naturally be.

It felt *metallic*.

Her arms shook as she clutched her magic tighter, clenching her hands into tight fists. With a raw cry, she released her grip, unable to bend or seep through the metal plating encasing his skull and crush his brain.

He straightened as the weight of her energy was lifted and then marched forward. Neer closed her eyes and melded her energy with the rock beneath their feet. And then she waited.

His footsteps pounded through her with every crushing impact. As he stalked past the pedestal that once held the Tree, she curled her hands into tight fists and pulled his feet beneath the ground. He fell aside to catch himself on the pedestal, and she enclosed his hand within the stone.

High above, a loud shriek came from the skies, and Neer ducked as the shadow of glynfir swooped overhead, snapping its jaws in her direction. Turning back, she lifted her arm and chased after the quick moving glynfir with a wild, hard-to-control tunnel of flames produced from her palm.

As the glynfir slipped into the darkness, moving farther than her reach, she withdrew her hand, and the flames ceased. She leaned forward to catch her breath as her chest burned with weakness.

She peered to the sky when several menacing screeches echoed from above. They came from every direction, descending upon the temple. Neer stepped back and lifted her sword as a dozen shadows raced through the sky.

She turned as a glynfir shrieked from the east, and then a hard gust of wind flung her aside. Ithronél swooped down from the west, and Neer dropped her sword as she rolled across the ground before smashing into a rock. The hard impact shook her lungs and stole her of breath.

Ithronél spun with a wide kick, pulling a large boulder from the ground. As it barreled toward Neer, drawing closer with incredible speed, it erupted into dust. The thick cloud caught in Neer's throat as it drifted through the air. She lifted her eyes to the temple and realized it was Aélla who had disintegrated the boulder. She stood with her arms stretched toward Neer.

Ithronél lifted her hand in Neer's direction, preparing to strike her with magic, when Reiman leapt from behind and struck his sword at her back. Ithronél turned and kicked his stomach. As her boot pressed against his abdomen, she thrust her arms forward with a strong wind current.

Before the winds could disrupt his stance, Reiman swiftly spun aside and sliced deep into her left palm. The winds ceased, and she stumbled back with a horrid, agonized scream. Blood dripped from her hand in large droplets, and she clutched her wrist, wailing.

As he lifted his sword to strike through her skull, a glynfir swooped down from above.

"Reiman!" Neer shouted.

His glaring expression never faded as he turned to the glynfir and sliced down its middle. Black, tarry blood spilled from its body, and it fell lifelessly to the ground. Innards plunged from its carcass in a steaming puddle of black.

The sky was alive with the sound of overlapping screams as the remaining glynfir dove to the ground with their riders. They swooped over the battlefield and klaet'il warriors leapt from their mounts.

Two male warriors charged at Reiman as he swung at Ithronél. A warrior, with dark facial markings and a chipped tooth, stared hatefully into Reiman's eyes as their weapons collided with a loud clash. Reiman pushed him back and spun aside, ducking beneath the swing of the second, much smaller, warrior. Reiman kicked the smaller man back and with a wide swing of his sword, he sliced through both of their throats.

They gagged and choked before collapsing to their knees. Blood drained from their necks and saturated their armor.

Reiman shifted his eyes through the fight, searching for Neer. She stood behind him and ducked beneath the swing of a klaet'il warrior as he swiped at her neck. Her eyes were tired, and her lips parted as she breathed with short, heavy breaths.

Reiman raced across the courtyard and plunged his sword through the back of Neer's adversary. Kicking the klaet'il away, he came to Neer's side. "Find your strength," Reiman warned. "This isn't over yet."

She nodded and wiped the blood from her forehead with the back of her sleeve. Her eyes darted to a klaet'il who charged closer. With a deep breath, she pushed him back with a blast of energy. Her chest burned as her magic weakened, and she leaned forward with a tired gasp.

Neer swiped to the right as a warrior approached and struck for her side. His blade drew across her shoulder, and she yelped as hot blood spilled down her arm. The warrior struck at her a second time, and Reiman caught his sword with his blade before kicking him away.

Standing with Reiman in the courtyard, Neer eyed the klaet'il, hissing and snarling like angry vipers. Her gaze broke from the menacing warriors as the shadow of a large glynfir soared overhead and landed by the temple stairs. She was stiff with fury and fear as the Nasir leapt from his flyer and climbed the ancient steps. He walked with confidence and poise, as if nothing could touch or harm him.

As if he was invincible.

Neer was pulled back into the fight as a klaet'il struck at her side.

Atop the temple stairs, Y'ven raised his axe and swiped across the chest of a female warrior. Blood gushed like a waterfall from the deep wound, and she fell to the ground, unmoving. He then turned and struck at another klaet'il charging from behind. The nimble evae flowed like water beneath his movements, diving and flipping. With his right arm secured at his chest, Y'ven was weaker than usual, and it made him furious. He stomped forward with a thunderous growl and lunged his weapon at the quick-moving evae.

Dru hovered above like an ember, casting small flames that set fire to the klaet'il loosing arrows from the sky. The faeth turned to Y'ven as he roared, and her aura dimmed at the sight of a dagger sinking into his stomach.

In a rage, Y'ven grabbed the evae by the throat and lifted him from the ground. The klaet'il scratched and clawed against Y'ven's thick hand. His nails ripped and bled as he fought to free himself from the unbreakable hold.

Marching to a pillar along the temple's edge, Y'ven smashed the klaet'il against the stone. Three times, he slammed his body, the blood behind his head becoming thicker as his skull cracked.

When the klaet'il fell limp he was dropped to the ground. Y'ven took several deep, pained breaths. With a growl, he gripped the hilt of the dagger still lodged in his stomach and pulled it from his body.

He stumbled into the wall, clutching his abdomen. Blood poured from his flesh like a spilled glass of ale. As he sank to the floor, Dru was at his side, pushing flames into his deep injury. He leaned against the wall with tightened fists and closed eyes.

Aélla stepped closer, prepared to heal him further, when slow footsteps pattered from behind. She turned with her arms raised, and the fierceness of her eyes cracked. Her shoulders fell and lips slightly parted as she faced the Nasir.

He stood close, towering over her like a wraith. His eyes were heavy with an odd mixture of rage and calmness. He was confident and unafraid.

Aélla took a measured step back, and the Nasir followed with his eyes. His feet never shuffled. He remained in his place, watching without a word as she faltered beneath his power.

His eyes were empty, devoid of warmth or life, as hollow as the night is dark, with an expression matching his callousness and strength. With a slow blink, his gaze shifted aside to Thallon, who had fallen ill to the poison-laced bolt and lay unconscious at Aélla's feet.

Aélla lifted her hands and coiled her energy through the Nasir's spine, keeping him frozen in place. But the strength of her magic was disrupted and hollow. She clutched harder, grasping for any shred of energy she could connect to and keep him from moving, but there was none. Her magic was absent in his presence, and he stepped forward, untethered and unharmed by the energy she fought to constrain him with.

As he inched closer, she created a barrier around herself and Thallon and was baffled by its immediate creation. She glanced around in confusion before setting her eyes to the Nasir and was filled with sudden dread. It wasn't her energy that had been weakened, but rather something *inside* him that was blocking it.

He couldn't be touched by magic.

Several klaet'il circled the barrier as the Nasir approached her. He stared emotionless into her eyes and then stepped through the barrier as if it weren't there at all. She watched him with fear and uncertainty as he knelt beside Thallon. Her eyes darted to the klaet'il approaching, and she knew that releasing the barrier would lead to their attack.

"Please! Stop this!" she cried as the Nasir pried open Thallon's fist.

He carefully took the black ring from Thallon's grasp, his eyes wide with wonderment and surprise. The glowing cracks glimmered as he turned it aside, inspecting its authenticity.

With a deep, rumbling snarl, the Nasir stood and pressed his boot against Thallon's throat. The scholar choked as the leader pushed harder against his neck. The same lifeless, cold expression painted on the Nasir's face as he stared at the man whose life he was draining.

"No…!" Aélla cried. She inhaled a deep breath, clutched at the energy swelling deep inside, and released it outward in a shockwave that flung the klaet'il warriors back. They smashed into the walls and were thrown over the edge of the temple, sent falling to their deaths from its height.

Desperate to save Thallon, Aélla swiped a dagger from a fallen klaet'il and lunged at the Nasir. He was motionless as she sank her blade deep into his back. With a sharp gasp, she backed away, guilted and ashamed of what she'd done. Her tear-filled eyes were set on the man standing before her, blood draining down his back.

He turned to her and released his boot from Thallon's throat. Aélla grabbed the wooden staff from her back, prepared to fight, when suddenly she was thrown aside as Ithronél came forward and struck her with a gust of wind.

Aélla was flung through the air and crashed into the wall. Lying on the ground, her body ached with broken bones and bleeding cuts.

In the courtyard, Neer fought alongside Reiman. As her sword plunged into the chest of the man striking at her arm, her eyes flashed to the temple where Aélla lay motionless on the ground.

Reiman cut his gaze to the temple and swiped at the woman attacking him before kicking the man slashing at Neer. "Take the others and flee!" he warned while dodging another attack. "Before it's too late!"

"I can't leave you!"

"Go! I'll survive!" His weapon crashed against the sword of the female warrior. He spun to dodge her attack and kicked her side. She stumbled back with a furious snarl. "*Now!*"

Neer pushed through her indecision and obeyed. Too weak to rely on her magic, she raced over the bodies of the fallen warriors and ran past the Nasir as he strode down the steps of the temple. Coming to Ithronél's side, Neer lunged with her sword.

Ithronél turned back, collected the smoldering fires burning atop the fallen warriors, and sent a weak vortex of flames in Neer's direction. Neer rolled aside to dodge the attack and rushed forward. She dipped beneath Ithronél's sword and sliced deep into her side.

As Ithronél staggered back, Neer dropped her sword to the ground and struck her in the face with her fist. Blood spilled from her nose and busted lip. With a vicious scream, Neer struck her again. Ithronél staggered aside, her face blossoming with purple bruises. Neer quickly gripped the back of her head and smashed it against the stone wall. Blood dripped from Ithronél's forehead, and she collapsed to the ground, unmoving.

Aélla whimpered nearby, struggling to lift herself from the ground. Neer ran to her side and helped her stand.

"Come on," Neer said. "We have to go!"

With Aélla's arm around her shoulders, they stepped toward Thallon, and Aélla released a sudden gasp that halted their movement. Neer glanced at her and was stricken by the fear in her wide eyes and colorless face. Following her gaze, Neer turned hesitantly to the courtyard, and watched as the Nasir approached Thorne.

The hunter released furious shouts, fighting against his restraints. Dried blood left long streaks slithering down his face and neck. The Nasir stepped to him and then touched his face. Thorne shook his palm away and swung his severed iron arm.

The Nasir casually stepped back, ignoring the furious roars of the man before him. He lifted the ring and admired its power before extending his hand and slipping it onto his middle finger.

"No…!" Aélla gasped before a shockwave blasted through the courtyard.

Neer and Aélla were thrown back as the blast erupted through the air. Smacking hard against the stone, Neer's vision flashed with darkness. She gripped her head and crawled forward. Blood and entrails squished and slopped beneath her hand, and she shook herself of the haze clouding her vision.

In the distance, she watched as the Nasir stepped closer to Thorne. Shaking her head to clear her mind, though it remained less than clear, she grabbed her sword and stumbled to the steps.

Thorne fought against the Nasir as he extended his fingers and slowly placed the ring to Thorne's forehead. When the black steel touched his skin, Thorne released a monstrous, vibrating scream. While the others remained unaffected, Neer fell to knees and clutched her ears. His inhuman voice chiseled through her, etching away as it clawed deep into her mind.

Pushing through the agony, she peered at Thorne. His skin melted from his body like wax on a candle. Holes burned through his flesh, and he released another metallic, mind-shattering scream. Bones cracked loudly as he twitched and contorted with unnatural movement.

Smoke rose from his body like a slow mist as he grew taller with leathered black skin. The Nasir backed away, watching without expression as the hunter mutated before his eyes.

Neer sat motionless on the steps, forgetting where she was or had been as a vicious four-legged creature stood in Thorne's place. With a deep, rumbling screech, the rock restraining Thorne's arm and legs crumbled as the creature tore away from its prison. The powerful beast turned to the sky and roared with fury. Its large jaws were made of torn flesh and bones. Skin dark as night and smooth as satin wrapped the fragmented antlers and spikes protruding from its back.

Neer had heard of these creatures before. It was a *gaelthral*, a vicious and terrifying creature of darkness. Her eyes flashed to Reiman. He knelt to the east of the courtyard where he had been flung and clutched a black transporting stone.

He was safe.

He had an escape.

The Nasir turned his gaze to Neer, and with a slight nod in her direction, the gaelthral that was Thorne charged. Stunned, she fell back and stumbled up the stairs, racing to the others.

Falling to Y'ven's side, she called for Aélla. The temple quaked as the gaelthral moved closer. Its thick claws scratched deep into the steps, leaving thick scratches etched into the ancient stone.

"Where do we go?" Neer screamed as Aélla quickly pulled Thallon into her arms. "Aélla!" she called.

Her dark blue eyes were timid and afraid. "Go to the forest! Find my brother…" She wrapped around Thallon's chest as the gaelthral pounded forward. "Find Avelloch."

Neer sat in disbelief. Avelloch's sister was Azae'l…the First Blood woman cursed by the Nasir that he and Klaud were meant to save.

The one the world couldn't survive without.

Her eyes widened at the realization. Questions filled her mind, mixing with the panic and dread as the clawed steps of the gaelthral swiped closer. Before she could speak, white magic enveloped Aélla and Thallon, and they disappeared.

The creature slid across the platform and came to the top of the stairs. Turning to Neer, it unleashed a hellish roar and lunged forward.

Neer wrapped tight around Y'ven's chest, feeling the warmth of his blood soak into her skin as she focused heavily on her magic, hoping to find herself at the edge of the forest.

"Dru…!" she screamed as magic burned through her. The trembling scratches grew louder as the gaelthral raced over dead bodies, tearing their skin and filling the air with thick red mist.

Dru launched to Neer's side and hid within her hair. As the magic radiated from deep within, Neer released a pained, fearful scream. The creature lunged forward and swiped its razor-sharp claws through the empty air as they vanished from the desert.

EPILOGUE

ARRIVAL
Nyn'Dira

"Never venture into the land of the elves, for the forest is teeming with darkness and monsters who prey of the souls of the pure."

– Human Warning against Nyn'Dira

RAIN PATTERED AGAINST THE THICK canopy of the forest, a land teeming with mystery and danger. The large droplets of fresh water dripped endlessly from the thicket of leaves hanging tall on limbs that scattered the sky with the colors of green.

Beneath the slow-moving clouds was the soft glow of a setting sun. As it peeked beyond the grey shrouding its light, golden beams were cast through the trees, dispersing, and they traveled closer to the misty understory.

The thick paw of a direwolf splashed into the mud as it raced quickly through the grasses. Sapphire eyes gleamed beneath the sunlight. Its head lifted and ears perked at the sound of snapping twigs as voices hard with authority seeped through the quiet trees.

A man stepped beside the beast, scanning the trees with narrowed eyes. His dark armor bore several tattered and frayed holes from blades and burns. A tight scarf and cowl kept his face hidden as he crept through the shadows of dusk.

Moving silently, the man and wolf followed the noises. Not a track or trail was left behind as they swept through the forest, drawing nearer to the settlement of Amália. The small stead was tucked deep within the trees along the foothills of the Whispering Mountains. Home to less than thirty residents, it was a place not drawn on many maps.

Up the hill, ash soon replaced the rain and filled the air with a dense, unbreathable fog. Clouds of darkness rolled through the trees, and smoke billowed into the air, shrouding the remains of a once bright sunset. It was a sight he'd seen too often, and one that shrouded his eyes with hatred and darkness.

Standing atop the hill, he stared down at the settlement where sixteen wooden cabins made of birch and pine were scattered throughout the trees in no discernable pattern. Not a trail or road connected the homes to one another or the settlement to any outlying village, the closest of which was half a day's walk.

Smoke rose in a plume of black from each of the burning homes. Fires cast out the darkness created by the blanket of smog hazing the treetops. Bodies lay blackened and unmoving in the grass, while men, *humans*, stalked their remains. Not an evaesh soul spoke or breathed as the invaders trampled over their lifeless corpses.

They were fat men, six in total, with large waists and thick red beards. They held clumsily to their shoddy iron weapons and stood with the hunched backs of laborers, not soldiers. Thin leather armor was stretched and split at the seams. The evaesh man was glad of this, as only the most seasoned of human fighters stood any chance against evaesh warriors, and these men would be challenged against a child with a sparring sword.

The evaesh man tilted his head aside as a gruff voice sprayed over the sound of cracking flames and burning wood. He spoke a language the evae couldn't understand, and it infuriated him. His voice, as well as the others, were the sound of madness.

He glanced down to the direwolf, who held the same infuriated gaze, and then returned his attention to the village. Polished, unchipped steel slid from its sheath as he collected his sword. The creaking sound of leather whispered beneath the shouting as he tightened his grip on the hilt and charged.

A sawing growl erupted from the direwolf as it followed its companion, surpassing him in speed with powerful strides.

Two men turned sharply to the wolf that approached and shakily lifted their swords and axes. Loud whimpers escaped their throats when the beast leapt from the shadows, tackling them to the ground. The tearing of flesh was stifled by shrieks of anger and fear.

Two men fled into the forest, leaving their dying comrades behind. The evae hurled his dagger toward the man on the right. His blade sank deep into the man's back and he collapsed to the ground with a sharp gasp. As his companioned turned to give him aid, he glanced at the evae approaching from the haze. Stumbling back, the human tripped over his feet and fled quickly into the forest.

The evae averted his attention from the fleeing man to the others who lifted their axes toward the direwolf. With a low growl, the evae raced closer, mud splashing beneath his boots as he quickly filled the space between them.

As the first man swiped downward at the wolf's spine, the evae slashed his sword between his ribs. Blood sprayed through the air in a red mist, and he fell to the ground screaming.

Turning to the final man, the evae stood tall and strong. Beneath the heavy shadow of darkness, he became nearly invisible. Only the faint purple glow of the veins pulsing across his sword alerted the human of his position.

The human, with wiry red hair and a cracked iron sword, raised his hands in surrender, though his heavy scowl never lifted from the wrinkles around his eyes. He collected an item from a pocket on his breast, and the evae stiffened.

Raising his hands in defeat, the human peered into his eyes and held a wanted poster in his thick, callused fist. He spoke to the evae who couldn't understand.

"*Child…!*" the man said. "*We jus' want the girl.*"

The evae's shoulders rose and fell with every hard breath as he clutched his weapon. A low growl came from the direwolf as it turned from its victims. Licking the blood from its snout, it sank lower to the ground and exposed its teeth beneath a vicious snarl.

Deep wrinkles faded along the human's wide brown eyes, and they filled with terror. He stumbled back, glancing between the shadow and wolf. Soft whimpers came from his throat as the wolf crept forward.

The evae stepped away, allowing the wolf to take care of the human while he searched for survivors. But he knew there would be none. The humans were thorough in their pursuits, attacking small settlements or homes during vulnerable hours, such as dusk when families are gathering for supper or in the dead of night while they were asleep.

A home collapsed, sending embers and smoke high into the air, and the direwolf lunged at the man, biting deep into his throat. The evae stepped to the body of the escaping man and yanked his dagger from his back. His eyes scanned the forest, searching for the other. He wouldn't make it far. They never did. And the trail would be easy enough to follow.

His thoughts were broken as the pattering of paws thumped against the grass. He turned to the wolf as it came to his side and lifted its blood-spattered face in his direction. The evae's eyes narrowed, and he collected the parchment the direwolf carried with his teeth.

Unrolling the blood-soaked note, he stepped closer to the blazing fires, peering at the odd symbols and detailed portrait drawn onto the page. Struggling to see through the fading ink and blood, he took pause as the familiar face became visible. Sadness glazed his eyes as he timidly touched her portrait, and with a pained grunt he crumbled the warning poster into his fist.

A raven soared through the sky before landing upon a limb nearby. Its loud caw broke through the evae's thoughts, and he lifted his eyes to gaze at the familiar animal. Altvára cawed once again before swiftly taking flight.

The fires brightened when the evae tossed the poster into the flames and then marched hastily into the forest.

"Find her," he said to the wolf at his side. *"She's here."*

The story continues…

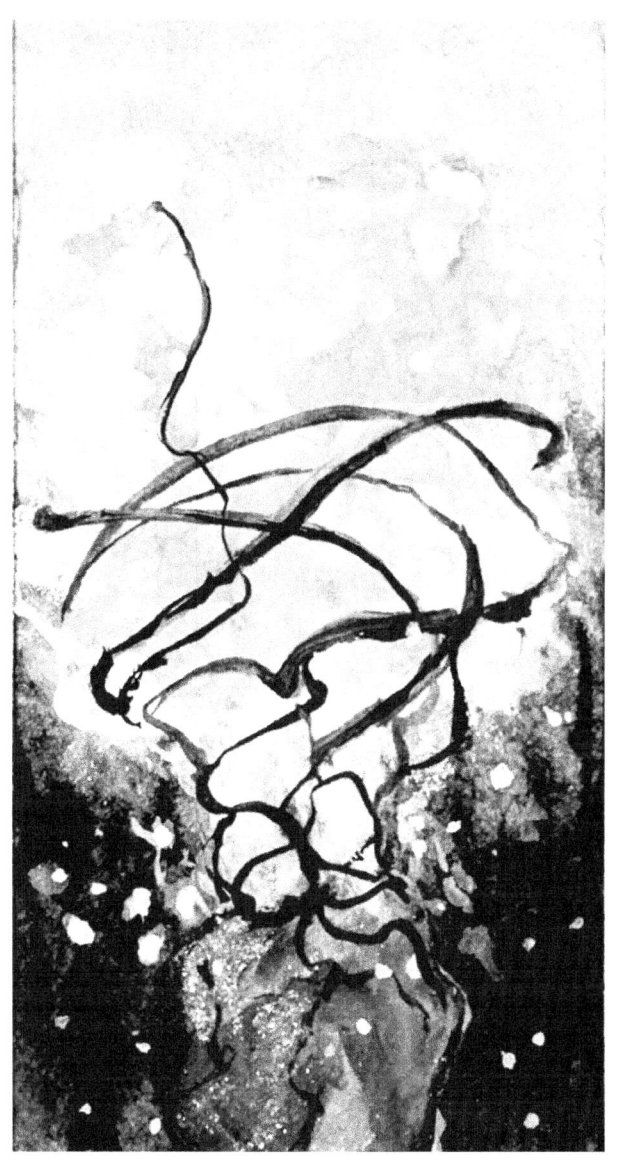

Watercolor art by Olive G.

EXCITED FOR MORE?

The Banished, a side-story following Avelloch and Klaud during the events of *The Forbidden Realms*, is available on Amazon.

Shadows of Nyn'Dira, the third installment of the *Fallen Light* series, is expected to release in late 2023.

As many of you know, self-publishing can be *very* hard! I do *everything* on my own, and while I have some help along the way, the most successful authors are those who have a loyal fanbase and lots of reviews on GoodReads and Amazon!

If you would, please take a moment to leave a review or rating.
It helps more than you know.

Sign up for the email newsletter and be the first to know about special projects, new releases, events, and giveaways!

Be sure to follow H.C. Newell on
Facebook and Instagram!

hcnewell.com

About the Author

H.C. Newell is a Nashville based #1 best-selling epic fantasy author. She started writing screenplays as a child, and that passion for creating stories grew into a love of fiction. In 2014 she started her novel series, and quickly realized that the adventures and lore of an epic fantasy world was her calling. It was then that she devoted all her time, passion, and love into creating the world and characters of *Fallen Light*.

When not writing, H.C. enjoys hiking, photography, playing video games, and spending time with her niece and nephews.

For more information about H.C. Newell
and the *Fallen Light* series, please visit:
www.hcnewell.com

Acknowledgements

I would like to say a special thank you to each person listed below, for encouraging me, believing in me, and allowing me to bother you non-stop about my story.

You have truly made my dreams come true.

To my husband, for supporting my passion and allowing the characters of my imagination to pull me away from reality time and time again.

To Rasha Deirani, Michelle Robichaud, Lora Wilson, Steph Heads, and Amalia Tselemegkou, for all of the hard work and incredible feedback you have given to help make this book as perfect and entertaining as possible.

To my cousins Nikki and Sage, for all of your endless support and politeness when I know you want me to STFU!

To my friends, Keith and Cristian, for being a major help in brainstorming and creating this world.

To my followers and friends who support this series and encourage me to keep going… *thank you.*

Glossary

This glossary is meant to be read <u>after</u> completion of the novel. It contains all characters, references, and places visited throughout the novel.

Aélla Líadrinel........ First Blood sorceress

Aenwyn.............. See *Numera*

Aeshan................Continent northeast of Laeroth; home of the humans

Altvára............... Raven companion of Aélla

Alveryan Steel........ Strong Ahn'Clave material that can hold enchantments

Al'yavan.............. Vaxros warrior pact

Ahn'Clave........... Ancient race of evae that disappeared centuries ago; previous inhabitants of Anaemiril

Anaemiril........... Ancient cave system that spans the reaches of Laeroth

Aragoth.............. Desert region of Laeroth; home to the vaxros and y'lenae

Atülg'Shelarr......... Childhood tribe and home of Y'ven

Avia.................. Steam powered airship

Binderis.............. Vaxros term meaning *settlement*

Broken Order

Brotherhood......... An organization meant to dismantle the Order of Saro; also known as *The Brotherhood*

Child of Skye......... Label used by the Order of Saro in regard to Vaeda Vindagraav

Creatures of
Darkness............. Manifestations of dark energy from the deceased

Draak................. Vax term for ancient and powerful dragons

Dreled............... Triantrophy halflings

Dren'seol............. Evaesh animal companions

Drimil............... Evaesh term meaning *magic user*

Drimil'Rothar........ Evaesh term meaning *Mage of Light*

Druindarvenia........ Fire faeth; companion of Y'ven

Order of Saro......... Religious faction that oversees the human led territories of Laeroth; also known as *The Order*

Priest Ealdir........... Priest of the Kirena; resident of Ravinshire

Rástalfür .... Elemental staff that is use as a key to open the gates of tre'len Aenwyn

Reiman Leithor........ Founder of the Broken Order Brotherhood; adoptive father to Nerana

Rhyl.................... Evaesh forest clan

Shadosalaan........... See *creatures of darkness*

Shadow Blades....... Human mercenary group

Shelarr................. Vaxros term meaning *tribe*

Sin'Lohai............... Evaesh and vaxros treaty of peace

Steam and Stable Inn. A steam powered Inn located in Aragoth

Sun-Blood............. A vaxros term for those who gain energy and strength from the sun

Tiaaven............... Small evaesh wreath meant to at tract peace

Thallon Galadúr...... Evaesh scholar; companion to Aélla and Nerana

Thorne............... A notorious bounty hunter with the Shadow Blades

Tree.................. Human term for *Ko'ehlaeu'at*

Tre'lan............... Evaesh term for *magical realm*

Tre'lan Aenwyn...... Evaesh term for the *Realm of Elements*

Ürok.................. Vax term meaning *human*

Vaxros................ Race of large, muscular, red-skinned Warriors; native to Aragoth

Vaeda Vindagraav... Birth name of Nerana

Vitru................. Vaxros dual to the death

Y'lenae............... Evaesh race; natives to Aragoth

Printed in Great Britain
by Amazon

38953648R00270